the further adventures of

SHERLOCK HOLMES

THE WEB WEAVER

the further adventures of

SHERLOCK HOLMES

THE WEB WEAVER

SAM SICILIANO

TITAN BOOKS

THE FURTHER ADVENTURES OF SHERLOCK HOLMES
THE WEB WEAVER
Print edition ISBN: 9780857686985
E-book edition ISBN: 9780857686992

Published by
Titan Books
A division of Titan Publishing Group Ltd
144 Southwark St
London
SE1 0UP

First edition: January 2012
10 9 8 7 6 5 4 3 2 1

Visit our website: **www.titanbooks.com**

What did you think of this book? We love to hear from our
readers. Please email us at: readerfeedback@titanemail.com,
or write to us at the above address. To receive advance information,
news, competitions, and exclusive Titan offers online, please register
as a member by clicking the 'sign up' button on our website:
www.titanbooks.com

A CIP catalogue record for this title is available from the British Library.

Printed in the USA.

To my wife, Mary, for many years of love, companionship and support. I can't imagine that time without you. None of my novels would have been the same, if they even existed—especially this one.

Preface

Dear Reader,

As I mentioned in the preface to an earlier book, the death of my cousin Sherlock Holmes released me from a vow of silence; thus I could relate his exploits at the Paris Opera in what I felt was his most bizarre case. As I also noted in my earlier preface, I offered my writings as a corrective to John Watson's distorted portrayal of Holmes. Watson and I were never on good terms, nor (his writings to the contrary) was he Holmes' eternal bosom companion.

I was involved in other interesting adventures with Holmes, but the case I am about to present offers unique insight into my cousin's character. Because of its intimate and personal nature, I debated long and hard before taking pen to paper. I am not one who believes celebrated people, dead or alive, lose all right to privacy.

However, my wife Michelle at last persuaded me that the story should be told and that we two were the only persons who might tell it fairly and completely. She could not bear that my cousin should be remembered as an unflinching misogynist—and a cold-blooded one at that. The passionate side of his nature was not restricted to music, and a certain woman was much more important to him than any other. Watson to the contrary, Irene Adler was most definitely not "*the* woman."

My wife Michelle and I have both passed our eightieth year, and we decided it would be tempting the Reaper to delay any longer. Although the events described herein occurred nearly fifty years ago, they are still fresh in our minds. Both Michelle and I also kept extensive journals. Since our involvement was often separate—I frequently accompanied Holmes, while Michelle was with the woman in question—we decided to divide our tale. Thus you will find that Michelle narrates certain chapters, while I narrate others.

There is one other matter I must briefly touch on. Nothing like the story you are about to read could ever have appeared in print during the time it took place, early in the 1890s. It would have been considered outrageous and immoral. Although the queen's long reign was nearing its end, "Victorianism" was in full flower. If writers dealt with prostitution, adultery, or divorce, it was only in the most hackneyed and conventional terms. All too many people—including many physicians—took their cue from the celebrated Dr. Acton and honestly thought that women had no sexual feelings, men were by nature lustful brutes, and the marriage act was a necessary evil for the propagation of the species.

Although the current generation always seems to think it has invented sin (especially sins of a sexual nature), one need only visit the cinema with its scantily clad females and suggestive dialogue to see that something has changed in the last fifty years. As an old man, I should bemoan the passing of the good old days and the good old morality, but I do not. Michelle and I saw, first-hand, too much misery caused by sheer ignorance of basic human biology and emotions.

Certainly by modern standards, there is nothing salacious or indecent in my narrative. It is, in one sense, a rather simple story with tragic overtones. God is my witness that I would never deliberately discredit my cousin or injure his reputation. If anything, my narrative should show, once and for all, that Sherlock Holmes was not a mere automaton or collection of eccentricities, but a man whose heart was, in every way, the equal of his brain.

Dr. Henry Vernier
London, 1940

One

On a cool rainy afternoon in early October I decided to pay a visit to my cousin Sherlock Holmes. Having just visited an ailing patient who lived near 221B Baker Street, I was dressed most formally in a black frock coat and top hat, my medical bag held in my left hand, my umbrella in my right hand.

The long-suffering Mrs. Hudson smiled when she saw me. "Good day, Dr. Vernier. Please come in. Mr. Holmes has never been... tidy, but brace yourself."

The thick, sweet odor of pipe tobacco filled the room, and the disorder was monumental, even worse than usual. Some problem must be under consideration. Stacks of newspapers and books covered nearly every surface, volumes large and small. Holmes himself sat on the sofa, pipe in hand, his gray eyes frowning down at the massive tome upon his lap. He wore his favorite dressing gown, an ancient one of faded purple wool.

"One moment only, Henry, and then I shall attend you."

I nodded, then gave Mrs. Hudson a sympathetic smile as she took my hat and coat. A coal fire was going, and I stretched out my hands to warm them. I glanced at Holmes' desk, stepped closer, and noticed that the newspaper was a notorious scandal sheet.

My eyes caught the merest suggestion of movement. Oddly enough, one end of the desk had been left clear, and a fly was buzzing faintly and trying to move across a triangular-shaped, opaque surface, which I soon discovered was a web. A spider appeared and ran down from the corner of the web and seized the fly, which buzzed more loudly and tried, in vain, to escape.

"Good Lord," I murmured, taking a step back. I did not much care for insects and spiders. I wondered if it would be permissible to roll up one of the newspapers... "Sherlock, Mrs. Hudson has been remiss in her duties—there is a filthy spider on your desk."

"Do not disturb her."

"Mrs. Hudson?"

"No. The spider."

"The spider? But surely...?"

Holmes slammed his book shut loudly. "Very well, Henry. You have my attention." He stood and walked over to the desk. He seemed paler and thinner than the last time I had seen him. He withdrew a magnifying class from a niche in the desk and bent to peer at the spider. The frantic buzzing of the fly had begun to subside. "She has him nearly bound. Would you care to have a look?"

"No, thank you. I do not much care for spiders."

"That is unfortunate. They are remarkable creatures."

"Perhaps. How long has that one been there?"

Holmes drew in on his pipe and rubbed thoughtfully at his chin with the fingertips of his left hand. "Almost a year."

"*Almost a year?*"

A smile pulled at his lips. "You seem to doubt your hearing today. It has been a battle royal. Mrs. Hudson has most definitely *not* been remiss in her duties. She takes this innocent creature here to be the very symbol of the encroaching filth that God put women such as her on this earth to destroy. Our war, too, has lasted over a year. At first she asked me daily if she could not remove the vermin. Despite my instructions, I think she would have killed the spider long ago had I not threatened to seek other lodgings should she do so. I have told her that other spiders are fair game to her broom or dust mop, all save this one." My perplexed expression made him laugh. "Come, Henry—have you never had a pet?"

"You know we have Victoria." Victoria was our cat whom Michelle had most irreverently named.

"Then consider this small carnivore my pet. She is a prime specimen of *tegenaria civilis*, the common British house spider. She is a lady of great courage and determination, as well she must be to survive the undeserved hatred and abomination of the female of our species."

"Not only the female!"

"As a physician, you should know that the fly is the great enemy of mankind. The fly is the carrier of infection and disease. The spider is our ally. Do have a look at her."

Unenthusiastically I took the glass. The spider seemed immense, small hairs coverings its legs, spots covering its back. The fly was half smothered in silk, yet it still shook periodically, and I heard a faint buzz.

"Disgusting." I set down the glass and turned away from the desk, hoping to steer us away from the spider.

Holmes smiled briefly. "I had no idea you were so fond of flies."

"I am not fond of flies!"

This made him laugh. "Come, let us sit down. You need not watch her devour her prey." I sat in one of the armchairs near the fire, while Holmes took the other and crossed his legs. "You look the very model of a prosperous physician today, Henry. And how is Michelle?"

"Now there you have the prosperous physician. Luckily avarice is stronger in my disposition than male pride. Her practice is thriving, and she makes far more money than I. Several women of the upper class have discovered that they prefer a woman physician, and she has become quite the rage. She will soon have to begin turning away patients. Only last week she snared Lady Connely. Old Thurswell must be furious. He has preached against women doctors for years. To have his wealthiest patient snatched away by a female half his age... It is rather delightful."

Holmes laughed. "Come, Henry, you make her sound like my friend *tegenaria civilis* with her fly. I am glad to hear you are both prospering. What of her work with the less fortunate?"

"She would turn away Lady Connely first. She has made a vow that for each rich patient she takes on, she will have a poor one in the balance. We both still work at the clinic weekly."

"I wish all physicians shared your charitable sentiments."

"And you, Sherlock—what is all this? It does seem a bit... messier than..." A gesture with my hand took in the books and papers scattered about.

"I have been working on a puzzle, a very curious one." He sat back in the chair and exhaled a cloud of smoke. "Tell me, Henry, did you ever read Watson's story, *The Final Problem*?"

"Given your attitude toward his stories, I have always scrupulously avoided them. Is that not the one, however, where you die at the end?"

Holmes was amused. "Yes. At the Reichenbach Falls. And have you heard of Moriarty, Professor Moriarty?"

"No, I have not."

"He is my arch-enemy, the Napoleon of crime, Watson has me calling him."

"Does this Moriarty have any basis in reality?"

Holmes set down his pipe and leaned forward, his eyes suddenly bright. "Ah, that is the question—that is the puzzle. Even a week or two ago I would have told you he was a complete fiction. I would have been adamant. Watson's stories to the contrary, most crimes and criminals are stupid. Only very rarely does a man of first-rate intelligence turn to crime. Most often we have only drunken ruffians or groups of them who bash in someone's head, snatch a purse, or rob a bank. The true criminal genius is rare, and the notion of an evil mastermind behind the crime in London is a silly one. Watson has me comparing Moriarty to a huge spider at the center of an evil web sensing every motion, every criminal movement, in this great metropolis. Of course, I would never have come up with such an obviously preposterous metaphor."

"Why preposterous?"

Holmes shook his head. "You know nothing about spiders either. Only a female spider can spin a web; only *she* sits waiting for her prey—and not necessarily at the center. If Moriarty were a woman, the metaphor might have made sense, but for a man, it is a foolish one."

"Perhaps poetic license…"

· "I do not take poetic license with the natural world! If Watson wished to make such an inane metaphor, he should have had it coming from his own mouth." His face had grown quite red. "Pardon me. My irritation with Watson is only too ready to come to the surface. People are always comparing men to savage creatures such as wolves or spiders, but in reality, man is the only animal capable of true evil. There is no malice in the wolf or spider. I watched my spider devour her mate."

"*What?*"

"Yes, she is one of the varieties which frequently consumes the male. The male is much smaller than the female. The female *tegenaria* will devour other spiders of either sex or even her own children after a certain age. It is curious how the roles of the sexes are reversed with spiders and humans. But I digress. I was telling you about Moriarty and the foolishness of the notion of a mastermind behind much of the crime in London."

"Yes."

"Unfortunately, I am no longer convinced it is so foolish an idea."

His smile vanished, and as I stared into his gray eyes, I felt a kind of chill about the heart. "Good Lord," I whispered.

"I am not certain, Henry. Perhaps I am wrong—I hope I am wrong." He tried to draw on his pipe, but it had gone out. "Blast it." He set down the pipe, stood, and walked to the large bow window overlooking Baker Street. "The past several months I have had a growing sense of… uneasiness. I thought at first it was only nerves, but now I think I had begun to sense a pattern, a shape—a web, if you will." He glanced over at his desk. "Forgive me, *tegenaria*. Something is happening, I believe, but still it eludes me. It began only as an intuition, but I have been pondering the problem, reading over the papers for the past several months, checking certain leads, certain odd crimes. There may indeed be a Moriarty. It is ironic." He laughed.

"What is?"

"If it were not for Watson's preposterous creation, I might never have hit upon the idea. Two weeks ago I asked myself, what if there were a Moriarty? Only then did I begin to sense the pattern. So far I have no idea what kind of person he may be. If this pattern is real, then a major intellect, a truly imposing mind, is behind it. The design is intricate and very subtle. He is the opponent for whom I have always longed."

I frowned. "How could you long for such a monster?"

"Have you never wanted to slay a dragon?"

"No, I can't say that I have."

Holmes leaned upon the windowsill, staring down at the street below. "Now what have we here? A visitor, if I am not mistaken. He would have given the cabby's poor horse a workout. A little under eighteen stone, I would say. His clothes proclaim him a gentleman, but he has the physique of a boxer or stevedore. Ah, yes! He is at the door. I am tired of musing over insubstantial cobwebs, and it has been frightfully dull of late. Perhaps he has an interesting case for me."

"I suppose I had better be going."

"Not at all, Henry. You can play the part of Watson. Most of my clients expect to find him at my side. Besides, it is too early for supper. From what you told me of Michelle, she is probably engaged for the rest of the afternoon."

"Yes, it is her day at the clinic. Very well, I shall stay. Medicine has also been rather dull of late. Let us hope your visitor has some interesting tale to relate."

Holmes took off his dressing gown while he walked to his bedroom, and he returned wearing a frock coat, just as Mrs. Hudson appeared at the door: "Mr. Holmes, there is…"

"Yes, Mrs. Hudson, I know. You may send in Tiny."

She rolled her brilliant blue eyes and withdrew.

Despite Holmes' description, I was not prepared for the bulk of the man who entered, his head barely clearing the doorframe. He wore formal dress, the ubiquitous black frock coat, waistcoat with gold watch chain showing, and striped trousers, the toes of his boots shiny, but all in all, he did not appear at home in his grand apparel. He had a slightly frumpled look, his tie askew, an errant lock of hair almost standing up.

At one time, he must have been a superb physical specimen, but now, nearing forty, he had the look of a man in transition toward corpulence. His shoulders were still broad, but his waist was thick, his neck too fleshy and full under the square chin. All the same, at a good six and a half feet tall, with an eighteen-inch neck, fingers thick as sausages, and a weight nearer three-hundred than two-hundred pounds, he was an imposing figure. His hair and mustache were light brown, his eyes blue, his skin fair with a tendency toward redness. His gaze shifted from me, to my medical bag, to my cousin.

"Mr. Sherlock Holmes?"

"Yes. I am he. What may I do for you, Mr.–?"

"Wheelwright, Donald Wheelwright." His immense paw briefly swallowed Holmes' long, delicate fingers.

"This is my cousin, Mr. Wheelwright. As you noted, he is a physician."

Wheelwright's hand now swallowed mine. It felt sweaty, big, very strong, and I noticed the reddish-brown hair on the back. "Dr. Watson," Wheelwright said softly.

I raised my eyebrows. Holmes' gray eyes had a wicked gleam, and he turned Wheelwright aside before I could apprise him of my true identity. A very faint, floral scent touched my nostrils. I glanced at my hand and sniffed cautiously. Lavender?

"Now then, Mr. Wheelwright, do be seated and tell me how I can be of service."

Wheelwright sat warily, and the chair was dwarfed with him in it. He gave a sigh, and his mouth stiffened. "I– This is a black business, Mr. Holmes. I usually like to keep my affairs private, but… My safety and my wife's safety are at risk, and the police don't seem to be of much use. I didn't quite know where to turn, but I was told you were the very best for this type of deviltry. I'm not superstitious, mind you, but all the same…"

"Who has threatened you, Mr. Wheelwright?"

His eyes showed a sudden coldness. "Who told you I had been threatened?"

"You did, albeit in a roundabout manner."

He nodded. "I see. Well, there have been letters, and… See here, did you ever hear about the business with the gypsy at Lord Harrington's ball?"

Holmes' fingers tapped at his leg, and he frowned. "Was that nearly two years ago?"

"Yes, that's right. Two years in January it will be. You know about it then?"

"Only vaguely. Something about a gypsy curse, was it not? I saw a brief article in one of the papers. Tell me about it, Mr. Wheelwright."

Wheelwright sighed and shifted restlessly in the chair, which creaked ominously. "She was– There was this old hag. She appeared during the dancing. This was the Paupers' Ball, and we were all in costume. She told us we should be ashamed–as if having money was a fault–and then she said how wicked we were. She had a piercing voice that got a grip on you, and at first no one was quite sure whether she was part of the entertainment. She came down the stairs and cursed everyone and wished the most terrible things on us all. And then…" His mouth stiffened, his brow furrowed, and he shook his head. "It was not wise. My wife tried to talk to her. The gypsy began to shriek at her. Finally, Harrington's servants seized the gypsy and threw her out. The party was spoilt, though."

Holmes gave a sharp staccato laugh. "Yes, I'll wager it was. What did the gypsy look like?"

"Like a gypsy."

Holmes forced a smile. "And what does a gypsy look like? What did this particular gypsy look like?"

"An old hag, as I said, in a bright dress–red, I believe. She had a hooked nose and bad teeth. Oh, and she wore big round golden earrings. What an old witch."

"But her voice was piercing rather than feeble?"

"Oh, yes. Everyone in the hall could hear her."

"And your wife confronted her?"

He gave his head a shake. "She was across the room from me, or I'd have stopped her. You don't try to reason with a lunatic."

"And what did Mrs. Wheelwright say to the gypsy?"

"She told her that our being dressed up meant no… disrespect, and that only the Almighty could punish, and she even…" He drew in his breath. "She asked the old hag to pray with her for God's mercy."

"And the gypsy did not take kindly to these suggestions?"

"No, she was still cursing my wife as they dragged her off."

"What exactly was the nature of these curses?"

Wheelwright's tongue appeared briefly at the corner of his mouth. "That she and all she knew would have bad luck, and… die in torment, and…" His face lost some of its earlier ruddy color. "And that she—my wife—would be… barren."

Holmes took his elbows off his knees and sat back. "And by barren did she mean childless?"

Wheelwright nodded slowly. "Yes."

Holmes tapped at his knee with his fingertips. "I do not wish to appear insensitive, Mr. Wheelwright, but it must be asked. Do you and your wife have any children?"

Wheelwright's eyes narrowed, a brief hint of ice showing in their blue depths. "No. My wife… she is… But it was not the blasted gypsy!" His neck grew redder. "We already knew, long, long before the ball… I said I'm not superstitious, and I'm not."

Holmes nodded thoughtfully. "How long have you been married, sir?"

"Nearly eight years." Wheelwright seemed to grudge each word.

"I see. So the gypsy cursed your wife in particular and everyone else at the party. How very dramatic. The newspaper article comes back to me now. The curse involved general ruin, misery and misfortune, lingering illness, and early death, I believe. A crowd of London's high society mesmerized by a vengeful gypsy who appears out of nowhere at the ball. Somewhat like Poe's 'Red Death.'"

"What's this red death? I don't recall her saying anything about any red death."

"I was alluding to the story by Edgar Allan Poe."

"Who's he?"

"An American writer of some note. But we digress, Mr. Wheelwright. Something more immediate than the ball has brought you to see me."

"That's right, Mr. Holmes." His big hands formed fists. "Some strange things have happened to several of the people who were at the ball. Harrington himself cut his own throat. It's enough to make a man nervous. And then... then there was this note..."

Holmes placed his hands upon his knees. "Note? Let me see it, please."

"It's... it's not very... nice."

"I must see it."

Wheelwright sighed, then reached into the inside pocket of his frock coat. Holmes opened the brown, folded paper, read it, then handed it to me. The writing was a reddish-brown color resembling dried blood:

By now you know my curse was a true one. Your womb is all ashes and bitterness, and you will have no fruit. Perhaps I shall send the Master himself to claim you. You may burn every light in your home as brightly as can be, but it will not save you from Him. Let your foolish God try to protect you now! Watch out for the black dog, the crow and the spider, for they be my allies. Know that nothing you can do will possibly save you. No man, no power, on earth can help the pair of you. You are doomed. You shall soon meet me and the Master in Hell.

A.

I shook my head. "What deranged creature can have written this?"

Holmes took the paper and held it up to the light. "It, too, is very dramatic, and this appears to be real blood. The aged parchment is a nice touch. I can see why this might unsettle you and your wife, Mr. Wheelwright. Did it come in the post?"

"No. My wife found it one morning."

"Where exactly?"

"In the library."

"And how did your wife react to this hateful note?"

Wheelwright hesitated, then shrugged. "She's not the hysterical sort, but she doesn't much care for it."

Holmes' smile was close to a grimace. "Of course not." He sat back in his chair and regarded Mr. Wheelwright through half-closed eyes. The big man shifted about in the chair uncomfortably. It was small for him.

"So you have been married nearly eight years?"

Wheelwright nodded. "That's right."

Holmes' eyes were fixed on him. "And I suppose you are... fond of your wife." I could not be sure, but I thought I heard irony in my cousin's voice.

"Fond enough. See here, Mr. Holmes, I didn't come here to have you ask questions about me and my wife. I want this gypsy business resolved, but leave me and my wife out of it."

"That may hardly be possible given that you both seem to be at the center of the affair."

"All the same, I won't tolerate questions about my personal affairs. Violet—my wife—is my business and my business alone."

"Yes, yes, Mr. Wheelwright. You do understand that I will have to extensively question her and your household staff."

I sat up abruptly. "Excuse me." Wheelwright gave me a look, which suggested he had forgotten I was in the room. "Your wife is Violet Wheelwright?"

He nodded.

"We have not met before, but my wife is her physician—and her friend, as well. In fact, they are engaged in some charitable actions together today, if I am not mistaken."

Wheelwright frowned slightly. "The lady doctor is your wife? But she has some French-sounding surname, not Watson."

"I must clear up a misapprehension, sir. I am not Dr. Watson." Holmes, I could see, was amused. "I am Dr. Henry Vernier. My wife is Dr. Michelle Doudet. She uses both our names: Doudet Vernier."

"Ah yes, I forgot to mention Henry's name, did I not? Now then, when may I question your household, Mr. Wheelwright?"

"Soon, Mr. Holmes." He withdrew an ornate golden watch from his waistcoat pocket and opened it. "I'm afraid I must leave. I have other business. I shall send word." He stood up and glanced about the room, obviously displeased with its untidiness.

Holmes also stood. "There is the matter of my fee."

"I shall pay whatever you wish. Will five hundred pounds be enough of an advance?"

I was impressed, but Holmes nodded politely. "That will do nicely."

"I have my checkbook. If you have a pen…" He started for the desk.

"You need not pay me now, Mr. Wheelwright. I only…"

Wheelwright had almost reached the desk when he suddenly turned and dashed back behind the chair, moving remarkably quickly for so large a man. His blue eyes were wild, his face very pale. He raised his hand and pointed his thick forefinger at the desk. "*Kill it!*"

I took a hesitant step toward him. "Are you well, sir?"

"Kill it. Take one of those papers and kill it!" His hand began to shake as he lowered it.

Puzzled, I gazed at Holmes.

"I am sorry to have alarmed you, Mr. Wheelwright. I shall dispose of the spider. You can send me a check later. I believe you said you had an engagement?"

Wheelwright kept his eyes fixed on the desk. "Yes, I do. You... you will be hearing from me, Mr. Holmes. You should... *clean your desk.*" He strode to the door, glanced behind him at the desk to make certain the spider was not pursuing him, then swiftly closed the door.

I shook my head and returned to my chair. "Your spider will cost you a client one of these days."

Holmes also sat. "Elephants do not truly fear mice, but the relation in size is about the same with our Mr. Wheelwright and *tegenaria.* Perhaps I shall have to try to move her, if only for her own protection. Luckily he was too fearful to attempt to kill her himself. So, Henry, Michelle and Mrs. Wheelwright are friends, are they? And what is the lady like?"

"Not like her husband. She is of medium stature and slightly built, a brunette, a vivacious, amusing lady who is also quite beautiful. I would never have suspected such a husband."

"What of her intellect?"

"She seems most intelligent. And Michelle is not generally fond of stupid women."

Holmes gave a sharp laugh. "No." He sighed and sat back in his chair. "I feared as much, but it does not surprise me."

"Whatever are you saying?"

"It is regrettable she is married to such a man."

"Come now, he may not have an impressive brain, but I am sure he is fond of her and a responsible husband."

"No—no—*no.*" Holmes rose up in exasperation, then sat again. "Your responsible husband has just lolled away the afternoon with his mistress."

I stared in disbelief. "What on earth are you talking about?"

"Henry, I begin to think you are as hopeless as Watson. Was it not obvious where Mr. Wheelwright had just been?"

"No."

"Did you notice his dress?"

"He did seem... frumpled."

"Exactly! One of his waistcoat buttons was unfastened, his tie was crooked, a button on his left boot undone, and his hair ruffled. Can you not surmise why?"

"Why?"

"Because he had been lying in bed with his mistress until the last minute. He then dressed in great haste and came to see us in his disordered state."

I shook my head. "Perhaps he is just sloppy."

"Did you notice the quality of his clothes and his watch? He is a rich man of business, and he would not make it through the day in so slovenly a state. To begin with, no valet of minimal competence would let his master out the door looking that way. Even if the man's servants were incompetent, his colleagues would have discreetly mentioned that he might straighten his tie or button his waistcoat. He also smelled faintly of cheap perfume."

I put my hand on my head. "I did smell something! Perhaps... perhaps he was with his wife."

"Could you not tell from his manner that things are amiss between them? Besides, married people do not indulge themselves in the afternoon. That time of day is reserved for expensive harlots and their clientele."

"Balderdash! That is simply not true."

Holmes' smile vanished, and he stared thoughtfully at me. "Is it not?"

"Well, I cannot speak for all respectable married couples, but... no, I think not."

Holmes looked away, then scratched briefly at his chin. "I must defer to you on this, but you said his wife is with Michelle. Besides, I doubt his wife would use such foul perfume, not if she has any taste at all."

I sighed wearily. I had only met Violet Wheelwright a few times, but I had liked her. Wheelwright, on the other hand... And if he were an adulterer, too... "I cannot believe it."

"Henry, you should know how common such behavior is."

"It may be common, but it is *wrong*. Blast it all, Violet is so pretty! Why would he trifle with a prostitute when he is married to a woman such as her?"

"Is that not also obvious? Because he is a dullard, Henry—a blockhead. Her beauty does not matter. He wants someone equally obtuse who will flutter her eyelids and tell him how handsome and clever he is. I doubt his wife would do that."

I shook my head. "No."

"Wheelwright seems a familiar name... Of course—Wheelwright's Potted Meats! I'll wager he's that Wheelwright's son and heir. The old man has a reputation for being shrewd and ruthless. I cannot picture the son maintaining the family empire. Perhaps there is an elder brother."

"They are rich. Michelle commented on it, and Violet has been only too willing to purchase medicine, food, and clothing for the poor. You have put me in an awkward position, Sherlock."

"In what way?"

"I do not like to keep secrets from Michelle, and what you have deduced about Mr. Wheelwright concerns her good friend. Should I tell Michelle, she may be similarly perplexed, but knowing her, she will want to tell Mrs. Wheelwright about her husband's infidelity. Who knows what misery may then ensue?"

"Oh, nonsense." Holmes crossed his legs, took his pipe, and began to cram tobacco into the bowl. "If Mrs. Wheelwright is anywhere near as intelligent as you claim, she already knows about her husband's infidelity. In my experience, the wife usually knows about the mistress, and so long as the husband is discreet, not particularly abusive, and continues to make his income readily available, she does not much care."

"What a horribly cynical viewpoint."

"Marriage is the institution created for cynics, but do not blame me for your dilemma. Mr. Wheelwright is the guilty party. If he makes a habit of leaving his afternoon rendezvous in such disorder, then others must have remarked upon the fact. By the way, had you heard anything of this gypsy curse?"

"Not a word. That note was certainly vile. What do you make of it?"

Holmes drew in on the pipe. "Probably some discontented servant, nothing more. The whole business is far too melodramatic to be genuine. It reeks of artifice, of histrionics."

"But what about the gypsy at the ball?"

"The author of the note probably has no relation to the gypsy, but that affair also seems suspicious. An old gypsy cursing all of well-to-do London is simply too dramatic, too sensational. I always suspect reports of anything even faintly supernatural, and this is very dubious. I shall be interested in meeting Mrs. Wheelwright and hearing her version of the events. Wheelwright certainly has no flair for storytelling."

"I think she will please you. She is remarkably beautiful, but her wit and liveliness are what captivate one."

Holmes laughed. "You make her sound a very paragon. I suppose I must guard my heart, for she is, after all, a married woman." His irony had a weary edge.

I sighed but said nothing. I could think of no rejoinder.

"Do not tell Michelle, Henry. I would not have her worried as well. Perhaps in this case, I should have kept my deductions to myself."

He rose, glanced out the window, then walked to his desk and examined the spider with his glass. "Her meal is half gone. My poor *tegenaria*, you had another close call. Luckily the massive Mr.

Wheelwright was too cowardly to strike you. Come, Henry, cheer up. Would Michelle spare you this evening? I am tired and have not dined out in a while. A good piece of beef at Simpson's would be the very thing. Given Mr. Wheelwright's promised check, I can afford to be generous and feed an industrious physician."

I forced a smile. "Oh, very well. Michelle may be late herself since she is with Mrs. Wheelwright."

"Good. It is settled then. Wheelwright, gypsy curses, and my mysterious Moriarty and his web will be forgotten for the rest of the evening."

"You must tell me more about Moriarty."

"In due time I shall, but not tonight—tonight, British roast beef shall rule supreme, and only topics conducive to good digestion will be discussed."

Two

As usual, by late Wednesday afternoon, I was weary in body and soul. In the morning Violet, her footman Collins, and I had walked about and visited the patients who were too ill to come to the clinic. I was fairly well known as the lady doctor, but Collins provided security in so rough a neighborhood. A big, tall, strapping fellow with a ready smile, he was known to be good with his fists.

We trudged up many dark narrow flights of stairs which stunk of human waste and visited the cold, dimly lit rooms where entire families dwelt, squalor and misery their perpetual companions. The weather had recently changed, the golden warmth of early fall giving way to the foul yellow fog and drizzle which were harbingers of winter. I dreaded the change because I knew what would happen to so many of my patients. With the bell of my stethoscope pressed against their chests, I could hear the consumption devouring their lungs. Suggesting a change of climate, wintering over in Italy or Spain, would have been a cruel mockery to those who could afford neither adequate nutrition nor shelter. Many would not live to see another summer.

At the clinic, in the afternoon, the parade of human suffering continued. I saw many children and infants with runny noses, coughs and fevers. If they were lucky, it was only a head cold or the first croup of the season. The weather had also aggravated the rheumatism of the elderly.

One woman about my age (just past thirty) had the most beautiful chestnut hair. She also had a dreadful black eye and a split lip. "It hurts when I breathe," she said. I had her disrobe to the waist so I could examine her. Her skin was very pale, truly almost white, her frame slender. The outline of the humerus showed through her skin, and the shape of each curving rib was clearly defined. Her fingers were long and thin, the bones prominent—an artist's hands—but red and rough from toil. She was frail and beautiful; somehow she reminded me of a painting of Saint Sebastian stuck full of arrows. From her sagging breasts and slightly swayed back, I could tell that she had borne children, and the proof—a small pale girl with the same chestnut hair—waited beyond the screen.

On her left side was a fist-sized bruise, its bluish-purple contrasting with her fair skin. I drew in my breath. Behind me Violet muttered, "Dear God." The woman's face grew even paler.

I tried to probe gently, but soon tears streaked her cheeks. However, she made no sound. Half naked, she seemed so weak and vulnerable that it was hard to understand how any man could have hurt her so.

"I'm afraid you have some broken ribs, my dear." I taped them up carefully and told her to come back to see me in two weeks time.

While she finished dressing, I turned to Violet. She had gone to the window, and now stood with her back to me, staring out at the street below. The pale nape of her neck showed under the long black hair that had been carefully wound about and pinned up.

"How are you?"

She said nothing.

"Violet?" I put my hand on her arm and felt, briefly, her muscles trembling violently, but then she slipped away and turned to face me. Her brown eyes had an odd glint–fear or rage, I could not tell which. She held her head very stiffly, but high and proud. She had the longest, most slender neck of any woman I knew. Her nose was also long and thin–aquiline–the nose of an aristocrat.

"I am perfectly well, Michelle."

"You do not appear perfectly well."

Her eyes shifted toward the woman with the chestnut hair who was just leaving. "I suppose you see many such cases."

"Far too many."

She drew in her breath and clenched her fists; I could see her will asserting itself and bringing her under its control. "I wish I could send Collins to visit the drunken brute."

"That would do little good. You would only provide me with yet another patient, and the waiting room is already overflowing. Besides, such women are often fiercely protective of their husbands. She may even love him."

"Love? You dare to speak of love, when..." She drew herself up even straighter and now the rage made her eyes shine. "Oh, if I were only..." She seized her lower lip between her teeth. "Forgive me, Michelle. You have work to do."

I smiled. "You have done quite well. This is, after all, your second full day out with me. Most of my friends cannot even last through a single morning."

That was at about three o'clock, and I saw the last patient around half past five. Unfortunately, it was the type of case which never fails to upset me. The woman was barely twenty, her baby just six months old. The infant seemed half dead, his eyes glazed over, his limbs long and spindly; he resembled some plant raised in darkness, the long stems a desperate attempt to grow its way out of the dark and into the light.

"How many drops have you been giving this child?" My voice shook and I tried to regain my composure.

The girl's eyes regarded me warily. "Drops?"

"Drops. What is it—laudanum?"

"I wouldn't give 'im no laud'num or whatever. It's only cordial."

I sat back wearily on my desk. I did not believe in corsets, stays, bustles, and voluminous clothing, so it was fairly easy for me to do so. My head had begun to ache, and I kneaded my forehead briefly with my palm. "Godfrey's Cordial, I suppose?"

The girl still regarded me warily, and with reason—a sudden urge came over me to slap her. She nodded reluctantly.

"I don't suppose you know what an opiate is? No, of course not. Godfrey's is only a weaker version of laudanum. If you keep doing this to your child... You might as well poison him outright and be done with it."

Her eyes filled with tears, and she put her fist over her mouth. "Poison 'im?"

My anger drained away, leaving me both tired and sad. "I don't mean to be cruel, but Godfrey's is very bad for babies."

"I 'ave to get my sewin' work finished, and 'e just won't keep quiet otherwise."

I handed her a handkerchief. "Blow your nose, dear, and don't cry. It will do no one any good." She complied loudly. "Have you no relative or friend who could help care for the child during the day?"

She shook her head. "No one, ma'am."

I sighed, then clenched my teeth. Violet seized my arm. "You look so weary." She took her purse and turned sternly to the girl. "You must work, I suppose, so that you and your child can live?"

The girl nodded again. "Yes, ma'am."

"If you did not have to work, would you promise not to give the baby Godfrey's Cordial?"

She thrust her jaw forward. "But I 'ave to work."

Violet took a gold sovereign from her purse. "Not necessarily. This should get you by for a while, and if the baby is better I will give you another, then another." The girl stared in amazement at the coin. "Will you promise me?"

The girl again put her fist over her mouth, then nodded.

"Take it, then."

The girl clenched her fist about the coin, then clamped her hand over her chest. She stared at Violet in disbelief as if an angel had suddenly appeared before her.

"Bring him here in a month, and if he is better, you will have another coin. The doctor will see to it."

The girl nodded wildly. "Yes, ma'am." She put the coin in her tiny purse, then took the baby, who had hardly moved.

"Wait," I said. "You must stop the Godfrey's only gradually."

I gave her instructions on how to taper off the dose and had her repeat them. She stammered them out, then curtsied first to me, then Violet. "Thank you, ma'am. Bless you for savin' me and my babe."

Violet would not seem to look at her. "Remember your promise."

"Oh, I will, ma'am—I swear." She turned, slid aside the cloth curtain of the screen, and departed.

I sat down on my desk once more. "I too thank you, Violet. I have often thought... If only I could hand out fistfuls of money, more of my patients would live. I don't know what to do with such cases. They make me so... *angry.* Angry at everyone—the stupid girls, their wretched employers, our proud, self-righteous countrymen... Pardon me, I know it is late for the soapbox. Why do you not sit down for a moment? I think we are actually finished for the day."

Violet stared longingly at the chair. "Perhaps I shall, but only for a moment. My corset is so tightly laced I fear I cannot both breath and sit simultaneously."

"I warned you to wear your stays loose."

"But then I would need a new wardrobe because none of my dresses would fit. Alas, Dame Fashion is a stern mistress. We of the gentler sex must keep ourselves ever beautiful, must we not?"

She said it so gravely, that I gave her an incredulous stare. She began to laugh in earnest. "The look you gave me! Oh, now I shall never be able to sit."

I also began to laugh. Our laughter had a certain frayed, lunatic edge to it. We had passed a very long day together.

The curtain opened, and a hesitant face appeared. Blonde curls showed under the volunteer nurse's cap, as well as rosy cheeks and blue eyes. The face radiated youth, health and eagerness, a combination all my poor patients lacked.

"Dr. Doudet Vernier?"

"Yes, Jenny?"

"Is everything… well?"

"Oh, yes. Violet and I were only… We are fine. Are we finished?"

"Yes, Doctor."

"Good." I stood up and set my stethoscope on the desk.

Jenny was watching me carefully, the hint of a frown showing on her broad, smooth forehead. Her father was a well-to-do merchant who sold fine china and silverware, a proud man who had not forgotten his humble origins and who did not aspire to social snobbery. His wife was a bit insipid for my taste, but Jenny was both intelligent and good-hearted. I had met her at a party six months ago and casually discussed the clinic with her. Next week and every week since, she had come to the clinic on my day there. We had talked about women and the medical profession on several occasions. Jenny was very shy, but I had tried to encourage her to consider becoming a physician. She was to be married in a few months, and I hoped her husband would not be the type to lock his wife up in the castle tower. Obviously she wanted to ask me something.

"What is it, Jenny?"

She stared at me gravely, licked her lips, but said nothing.

"Come, my dear, what is it? You can tell me."

"It is something… of a personal nature, Dr. Doudet Vernier."

"Yes?"

She gazed past me at Violet who was taking off the white apron which all the nurses and volunteers wore. Violet raised only her right eyebrow—a feat I had always envied. "I shall tell Collins to have the carriage brought round."

"I shall not be long, I think." I gave Jenny a questioning look.

She shook her head. "No, Dr. Doudet Vernier."

Violet closed the curtain behind her, and I sat wearily on the wooden chair by the examining table. "Jenny, we have known each other long enough and our ages are near enough that you could call me Michelle. Dr. Doudet Vernier seems too formidable coming from you."

Her eyes widened. "Oh, I couldn't do that!"

"Whatever you are comfortable with. Now, what do you wish to talk about?"

She licked her lips again, and then spoke so softly her voice was quiet as a whisper. "I am to be married soon I think you know." She stopped speaking. Her naturally rosy complexion grew even redder, a slow flushing spreading from about her ears.

"Yes, I know."

"Well, I only… I wondered… I…" Her jaw seemed to lock, and she turned away abruptly. "I think I must leave."

Comprehension dawned—I had seen these symptoms before; I knew both the cause and the cure. "Wait." I smiled, stood, and seized her wrist. Her face was positively scarlet. "Has your mother told you nothing, then?"

"Only…" She shook her head. "Nothing."

Not only insipid, but thoughtless. I drew in my breath. For better or worse, I was long past false modesty. "And you want to know what makes a man and woman, husband and wife?"

"Yes." Embarrassed she might be, but her sense of relief was palpable.

"I shall tell you, and you certainly should know before you are married."

"Oh, I think so, too,"

I hesitated for a moment. The biology was straightforward enough, but that was never all there was to it. "What is your young man's name, Jenny?"

"Henry."

I laughed. "What a dreadful name!" She immediately appeared stricken. "Oh, forgive me—that is my husband's name. Teasing is a habit with me. And are you fond of him?" She nodded gravely. "Your father gave you some say in this matter?"

"He did."

"And is Henry agreeable to look at?"

She gave a quick nod.

"More than agreeable?" Now she smiled, and her smile told me a great deal. "And do you think he cares for you?" Again she nodded. "And does he respect you?"

"I believe he does."

"Then I think everything will go well." I sighed, praying it would be so. So many things could go wrong. If the man were rough and insistent, the wedding night could be disastrous. I caught a glimpse of impatience in Jenny's eyes, and I laughed. "Forgive me, Jenny. I shan't be evasive. Let me explain." And so I did, briefly and directly, as I watched Jenny closely. When I finished she stood staring at the window.

"How very odd. My mother only said… Is it not… something of an ordeal?"

I could not restrain a laugh. "Oh no, my dear. No, no. Perhaps at first it might be somewhat painful, but if you love one another and are patient with one another… It is most definitely not an ordeal–never let anyone persuade you of that, although many will try. A famous doctor has written that most women have no sexual desires whatsoever. That is utter nonsense. Some may have such feelings killed off by cruelty, indifference, or sickness, but when everything is right–when a man and woman truly love one another and consummate that love–it is the closest we ever come to heaven on this poor earth."

Jenny's cheeks were flushed, and now my own face felt hot. "Pardon me for being so blunt, but…" Jenny seized my big hand in hers. "Oh, thank you, Michelle–thank you!" She smiled at me. I laughed, and put my arm about her.

Someone brushed against the curtain, and it slid open. Violet had seized the cloth with both hands, her slender frame swaying. Her face was ashen, her mouth half open, her eyes wild.

Suddenly her legs gave way, and down she went, pulling the curtain with her as she fell. Jenny cried out. I went to Violet's side at once. Her face was absolutely white, her lips almost blue, and she felt icy to the touch. Perhaps it was a seizure, but there was no muscle tension or spasm. She gasped for air and groped for my hand.

"I cannot… breathe."

"Is she all right?" Jenny murmured.

"Get me some water," I asked Jenny.

"Oh God," Violet sobbed.

I rolled her over and started to unfasten her dress. I have large fingers, nothing dainty about them and, growing impatient with the endless row of hooks, I seized both sides of the dress and tore it open. When I saw the knot on her corset, I said a very vulgar word.

"Will she die?" Jenny asked.

"No. Not today. Hand me the scalpel from the table, would you? Careful now–it's sharp." I took the blade, cut through the knot, and then began to loosen the laces. "No wonder you can't breathe. Oh, Violet, I thought you knew better." I sat her up and took the glass from Jenny. "Have a drink."

She took a big swallow, then drew in a deep breath. "Oh, thank you." Her color had begun to return. She took her lip between her teeth, glanced at me, then away. "Oh, I feel such a fool, such a silly fool."

She started to get up, but I grasped her shoulders. "Do not try to stand, not quite yet. Take a few more deep breaths. Does anything hurt?"

"I am fine, Michelle. You were quite right about loose clothing. My stays were far too tight. I could feel the whalebone and steel cutting into my flesh. Perhaps I shall throw out all my corsets."

"Whalebone is truly the bane of womankind," I said. Violet smiled, and I heard Jenny suppress a laugh. "Let me help you up. Are you certain you…?"

"I am well, Michelle. I only feel as if I were a very idiot."

Jenny helped me get Violet to her feet. "Sit on the table for a minute," I said. "I want to check your heart and your lungs."

"Michelle–honestly, I am perfectly well."

"I insist." My voice had assumed its resolute physician's tone. "Slip out of the sleeves of your dress." I warmed the bell of my stethoscope with my hand and put it on her sternum. "Take a deep breath."

I listened carefully, then took her wrist between my thumb and finger and checked her pulse.

Violet held her head high, her lips pursed in a half-mocking smile. "Tell me the truth, Doctor—will I live? Be honest with me. How long do I have?"

I closed my watch and put it away. "Everything appears normal. Provided you do not squash all your insides to mush with a corset, you should live to a ripe old age."

Violet smiled and slipped her long white arm back into the blue silk sleeve of her dress.

I turned to Jenny. "Thank you for your help. We must continue our conversation another time. There are some things you should know which will make it easier for you."

The rosy flush returned immediately. "Thank you again, Dr. Doudet Vernier."

"I am flattered you are willing to confide in me, my dear. We women must help one another. And now I really hope my medical duties are finished for the day."

Violet's smile had faded away. She looked pale, her eyes curiously vacant. She slipped down off the table. "Can you fasten me up? And do my stays—but loosely."

I frowned. "I'm afraid I have made a mess of things, but I did not want you to suffocate." Since I had cut off most of the laces, I had to unthread the top part so I would have something to tie. "And half the hooks on your dress are gone. I don't know how we shall get you decent again."

Jenny said, "I know there are some safety pins."

"Oh, do get them." I shook my head. "I think you would actually have more room in the dress without the corset."

"I stand before you a convert. Remove it, Michelle."

I pulled out the laces, then with some effort, slipped her corset out of the dress and folded up the hard, nasty thing. Jenny returned, and she held the dress together while I pinned it. When I had finished, I stepped back and nodded at Jenny. "Not half bad."

"I wouldn't try to bend over," Jenny said, most seriously. But then a laugh slipped out.

"I shall be wearing a coat over the dress, so decency will be maintained," said Violet. "Collins and the coachman must have given me up for lost. Please, let us go. Jenny, we shall give you a ride home."

"Oh, I can take a cab."

"No, no. You and Michelle have saved me from a hideous death. A ride home is the least I owe you. Come, gracious ladies, fellow angels of mercy—I am spent."

I am worldly enough that the vulgar meaning of "spend" flashed through my mind. I gazed curiously at Violet, but she was unaware of the innuendo.

The old man who mopped the floors tipped his hat to us, his smile revealing several missing teeth. Next to him was the young constable who watched over the clinic. "Night, ladies," they both said.

"Good night, Mr. Platt, Constable Owens," I replied.

Outside it was drizzly, the air cold and heavy. The brick buildings across the street from the clinic were drab and dingy, the advertisements soiled or defamed, and the men on the street all wore dark shabby jackets and caps. Even the cobblestones seemed soiled. Violet's carriage, a luxurious four-wheeler with the footman and driver up top, had recently been painted blue, green, and gold. It was magnificently out of place, and I was happy to see it. I was always glad to leave the clinic, and tonight I was exceptionally weary.

Collins jumped down, opened the door and pulled down the steps. His grin revealed a gap between his two upper front teeth. He was formally dressed, but was spared the wig, the eighteenth-century jacket, and buckle shoes, which some of the pretentious wealthy insisted upon.

"Sorry for the delay, Collins," Violet said. "We were detained."

I let Jenny go first, then followed. Collins, as I had noticed before, enjoyed viewing the backsides of ladies while assisting them into the carriage, but I did not begrudge him this simple pleasure.

Violet leaned out the window. "Tell Blaylock we shall be taking Miss Ludlow home first. Reynolds Street, I believe."

The carriage swayed as Collins climbed back up, then we heard the crack of the whip and the clop of the horse's hooves on the cobblestones. I sighed and sank back into the cushioned seats. I knew from experience that the carriage was very comfortable, its springs providing a gentle ride, and I briefly wished that I were alone so I could take a nap. It was a busy time of day; outside we heard other carriages and the cry of voices.

"So you have been a volunteer nurse for some six months," Violet said to Jenny. "I admire your stamina. The work is difficult."

"It must be done," Jenny said. She was seated beside me, and I reached over and gave her hand a squeeze.

Violet smiled. "Ah, but most people are content to leave the work to others. And do you dream of being a physician like Michelle some day?"

I stared curiously at Jenny. Although it had taken considerable effort, I had avoided asking her that question. She was staring down at her hands: they held her gloves and were white, her fingers long and shapely. Most men would have claimed she was far too lovely to be "wasted" as a doctor.

"Perhaps. I do not know if I have the skills or the aptitude."

I smiled and gave her hand another squeeze. "You would do very well."

Violet had slouched back in the corner of the seat, and she regarded us through languid eyes. "And have you discussed this matter with your fiancé?"

"Yes. He does not... forbid it."

Violet's mouth formed the familiar mocking smile. "How gracious of him." The irony went over Jenny's head.

Violet continued to question her. She had visited the London

Women's College of Medicine, and quite wisely, had sent her skeptical father to talk with Dr. Elizabeth Garrett Anderson, Britain's first qualified woman doctor.

While they talked, I closed my eyes. Visions of my patients drifted briefly through my head, all those wasted, diseased bodies and pale faces, those eyes full of suffering, but the gentle swaying of the carriage and the sound of the horses' hooves was soothing. I drifted, I floated. When the carriage came to a stop I jerked my eyes open and sat up abruptly.

"Thank you for taking me home," Jenny said.

Violet nodded. "You are quite welcome."

"Good evening, Jenny," I said.

She hesitated an instant, and then smiled at me. "Good evening, Michelle."

Collins opened the carriage door and helped her out. We waited briefly while he saw her to the door.

Violet put her fingertips over her mouth and yawned politely. "Would you care to dine with me, Michelle? Donald is off at some wretched business meeting."

"I hate to abandon Henry."

"Oh, he will do quite well without you for one evening. We shall go to Simpson's and fortify ourselves after our busy day with some rare and bloody roast beef, hearty British fare. It is just the thing for languishing females."

"Simpson's?" My eyes widened. "Just the two of us?"

"Yes. Actually I wish we were men and could go to a pub and drink strong dark stout and eat chips and thick sandwiches on black bread with horseradish, but that would not be ladylike. More to the point, we would not be admitted. So what say you to Simpson's?"

"Very well, but I prefer my roast beef well done."

"So be it." She thrust her head out the window. "Collins, Dr. Doudet

Vernier and I shall be dining at Simpson's."

The horses resumed their clopping. Violet sat back and watched me through half-closed eyes. "Jenny is a sweet girl, and you have obviously made a conquest. She worships the ground you tread upon. The poor child—one can only imagine all the insipid nonsense she has had to endure, tales and poesy of romantic love and marital bliss... Have you been married long, Michelle?"

"No. It will be two years next spring. I was well past five and twenty, that age of confirmed spinsterhood. My medical education took so long, and I had not thought men worth the trouble until I met Henry. All the same, ours was not a conventional courtship."

She smiled. "Why am I not surprised? Yes, Jenny is lucky to have met you. Tell me, though..." She bit briefly at her lip, a certain wariness showing in her eyes. "I could not help but overhear some of what you told her at the clinic."

I frowned in puzzlement.

"Her question of a personal nature which she never quite managed to ask."

"Oh, that." I shrugged.

Violet continued to watch me warily. She seemed to be willing me to speak, but I said nothing. "I suppose..." she began. "So you really do find it... pleasurable?"

I was so tired it took me a while to comprehend. I laughed. "Yes!"

Her mouth twisted into a smile, but her dark eyes had a blank look. "I suppose I should not be surprised, although most of my acquaintances—those who will discuss the subject in the first place—find it tolerable at best."

I frowned slightly. "And you?"

She drew in her breath, her lips stiffening. Her gaze shifted out the window.

"Forgive me, Violet—what a presumptuous question on my part! I don't know…"

"No, no—we are friends, are we not? Let's just say… I doubt I am the first to find my husband… uninspiring. Boorish, even."

My lips parted. "Oh." I had only met Donald Wheelwright twice. I had not much cared for him, but I had assumed Violet must… Since I was a woman and a physician, some of my female patients had revealed that they could not bear their husbands' touch. Their disgust always saddened me. To think that what was for me one of life's great joys, for them was only bitterness. My head had begun to ache again, and I closed my eyes.

Violet sighed. She seized my wrist. "You are too good-hearted. We will not discuss anything more of a serious nature. Men, especially, are to be a forbidden topic!"

My laughter sounded hollow. "Oh, very well."

By then we were riding along the Strand, one of London's busiest streets. Various carriages, four-wheelers and hansoms, packed the way, and men and women crowded the pavements. We drove past many theaters, some of the marquees all lit up with new electric lights. The traffic stopped briefly before a building front plastered with signs: haircuts within for four shillings, shaves for two; and in bright, capital letters:

Violet raised a gloved finger and pointed. "*I* would not touch it," she muttered, "let alone eat it."

At last we came to our destination. Above the ornate facade of the first floor were metal letters a good three feet tall, SIMPSON'S, and alongside, only slightly smaller, TAVERN & DIVAN. The carriage door swung open and Collins helped us down. A blustery wet wind wound its way through the people and carriages, knocking a hat or bonnet astray here and there.

"Give us two hours, Collins. I am sure you and Blaylock would like to take some refreshments yourself."

Collins grin blossomed as he tipped his top hat. "Yes, ma'am!"

Simpson's was warm inside and brightly lit. Violet walked past some waiting people to an oaken counter. Although her height was only about five foot two or three inches, a half-foot shorter than I, she seemed to *feel* tall. The authoritative man behind the counter had an enormous mustache and a completely hairless head, its dome glowing under the lights.

"Good evening, Oswald. We are ravenous. Can you seat us soon?"

"Certainly, Mrs. Wheelwright. And Mr. Wheelwright?"

"He should be along shortly, if he is not detained."

Fetched by Oswald's nod, a waiter in a black suit appeared. "Give them a table on the second floor," Oswald said.

Violet gave him a radiant smile, which breached his stern exterior. "Thank you very much."

I frowned. "I thought you said Donald had a meeting to attend."

Violet smiled halfway up the stairs. "He does."

The dining room upstairs was quieter, but no less spacious and inviting. Chandeliers with gas-lit globes hung from the ceiling; spotless linen, sparkling silver, and glasses were at every table. The quiet murmur of voices and utensils in action was pleasant after the noisy street.

The waiter gestured at a table. "May I take your coats, ladies?"

It was quite warm, and I nodded.

"Certainly," Violet said, turning her back to the waiter.

I stiffened, then suddenly lunged for Violet's coat, seizing the lapels even as the waiter tried to slip it off. "No!" I exclaimed. Violet looked as if she doubted my sanity. I mouthed the words "your dress!"

She tipped her head back. "Ah." She turned away from the waiter who was staring at us. "I am rather cold, after all, but my friend has a robust constitution. You may take her coat."

"Oh, I shall wear mine, too."

"Do not be foolish, Michelle."

The waiter approached hesitantly, waiting to see if I would again change my mind, then helped me out of my coat. He seated first Violet, then me, and set a menu before each of us. "I'll be back in a moment ladies."

"We know what we want," Violet said, glancing at me. I nodded.

"Very well, ladies." He took out a small notepad.

Violet pushed the menu aside. "I shall have the large roast beef special, rare."

The waiter's forehead creased. "The large, madam?"

"Yes. I have a tapeworm and must eat for two." She said this so seriously I could not repress a laugh. I covered my mouth.

"And you, madam?"

"The regular roast beef, well done—preferably an end piece."

"And I would like a pint of the house stout," Violet said.

Usually I drink claret with roast beef, but I said, resolutely, "And I shall have the same."

The waiter's forehead wrinkled again. He opened his mouth, closed it, then nodded and fled. Another laugh slipped from my mouth. An elderly couple at the table next to ours regarded us warily.

Violet placed one hand graciously over the other. "Why, Michelle, whatever is the matter?"

"I had no idea dining at Simpson's with you would be such an adventure!"

Violet smiled, and took a sip from her water glass. "I must confess to feeling rather silly. Donald is always so stuffy when we dine out. While the cat's away, as they say."

"You seem to have recovered from your faint. You gave me something of a scare."

Violet's smile withered. "Oh, that. I was such an idiot. I do not approve of fainting."

"I am glad you feel better." I took a bite of a bread roll. "Oh, I am starving."

Our waiter reappeared, set two large glasses of stout on the white tablecloth, and again fled. Violet took a hearty swallow, while I sipped. The liquid was almost black. "It is very... substantial," I said.

Violet took another swallow. "I like stout. My father and I used to drink beer together."

"Your father?"

"Yes. We used to drink beer together because Oxford dons and their daughters are not supposed to drink beer." She took a roll from the basket. "Thank you for coming with me." Again she smiled, but then, as she looked about, the corners of her mouth fell. "I fear we are not to banish men this evening after all."

"What do you mean?"

"I mean your husband was sitting at a table in the far corner of the room, and now he and another man who somewhat resembles a human ferret are headed our way."

I turned and saw Henry approaching, Sherlock Holmes behind him. Henry seemed amused, and I wondered how long he had been watching us. Sherlock appeared thinner than I recalled, his gray eyes curiously wary, his mouth stiff.

I smiled at Henry and briefly took his hand. "Here I was, thinking you were at home starving to death or eating cold and greasy mutton."

"Sherlock invited me to dine with him. We have just finished and were enjoying the amusing spectacle of the two of you being seated. You seem to be having a splendid time. Perhaps we should be leaving—we don't wish to intrude upon your meal."

Holmes nodded brusquely. "Yes, this is obviously meant to be a festive evening, one reserved for the female of the species."

Violet was surprised. She stared up at them, reflected for a moment, and then smiled. "Oh, do sit down for a moment." She laughed. "I am not an utter churl. I shall give you five minutes or so, and then you will be banished."

I put my hand on Henry's arm. "You know my husband, Henry. This is his cousin, Sherlock Holmes."

Violet dropped her roll, and her nostrils flared. "*The* Sherlock Holmes?"

Obviously pleased, Holmes bowed from the waist. "The same."

"This is my friend, Mrs. Violet Wheelwright."

Holmes nodded, his eyes fixed on her. His nostrils also flared. He pulled the chair out, sat, and crossed his legs.

Violet tore a small piece from her roll. "I have followed all your exploits with great interest, Mr. Holmes."

"Indeed? Then I must warn you that Watson's narratives are mostly fiction."

"Oh, I am glad to hear it. I feared we were in for some tedious deduction."

Holmes' dark eyebrows rose. "Tedious deduction?"

"I must confess I find all the deductions less than convincing. No doubt that is the fictional part to which you refer."

Holmes' eyes narrowed. "That is the only part he has right."

"Oh dear, then I suppose we are in for some deducing. You will no doubt know where Michelle and I have been, on account of the unusual mud on my skirt."

Holmes' mouth twitched briefly into a smile. "You are skeptical of the art of deduction?"

Violet put another piece of bread in her mouth and chewed thoughtfully. "Moderately skeptical."

Henry toyed with the end of his mustache. "Have a care, Violet. You are hurling down the gauntlet."

Holmes shook his head gravely. "No, no, good taste forbids."

Violet gave him a quizzical look. "Good taste?"

"It would be indelicate to refer to your dress being so awkwardly damaged or the state of your undergarments."

Violet dropped her knife; it clattered loudly on the plate.

"And I am sure a woman such as you would not like to be reminded of any feminine weaknesses." Her eyes widened, then her mouth opened. "Such as fainting."

Violet stood up, knocking over her chair. She pointed a finger at me. "You told him!"

"I swear I did not! We have been together all day, Violet. Whatever is the matter with you?"

She sighed, then realized everyone in the immediate vicinity was staring at her. She shook her head, picked up her chair, and sat down. "Do forgive me. This is the second display of feminine weakness today, Mr. Holmes. I hope the stories were correct in that you will now explain how you arrived at your remarkable conclusions."

Holmes nodded. "Gladly, madam. You are wearing your coat although it is warm in here. Moreover, earlier I noticed Michelle leap to prevent the waiter from removing your coat. Also, your dress and your collar are not properly aligned. I suspect a tear or breach in the back which has been pinned together."

Violet nodded. "Oh, very good. And the feminine weakness?"

"I had to ask myself how a woman such as yourself might have damaged her dress. Henry told me you were with Michelle at the medical clinic. You would have been subjected to unpleasant sights and smells—wounds, lacerations and sores. Perhaps the sight of blood became too much for you, and you swooned. Knowing Michelle's views on female dress, she would have tried to loosen your garments—it would be easy to tear a dress in the process."

I clapped my hands. "Bravo, Sherlock."

Violet's mouth formed the mocking smile. "And the disarray of my undergarments?"

Holmes reddened about the ears. His face could not be called handsome. His nose was too large, his features too sharp, his hair too black and oily. All the same, I was so fond of him that I liked his face: it had great character and showed his every mood. His gray eyes were particularly large and expressive.

"As I said earlier, modesty forbids."

Henry laughed. "When her coat is open, even an undiscerning oaf such as I can tell whether or not a woman is wearing a corset."

"Henry!" I exclaimed.

"A corset distorts the female shape," he said. "It and the bustle make women resemble primitive fertility symbols. At least the bustle has fallen out of fashion."

Violet shook her head, and finished the last of her roll. "Fairly beaten, Mr. Holmes. The first round goes to you, but next time I shall be better prepared."

The waiter appeared and set down our plates before us. The smell of the beef set my mouth watering, and I quickly took a spoonful of the potatoes.

Holmes eyed the slab of red meat on Violet's plate. "I see you are in earnest, madam. You must be in training. Already you have begun to fortify yourself. The Simpson's large is a truly prodigious cut."

He withdrew his watch from his vest pocket. "I fear we have exceeded our allotted five minutes. We should leave the ladies to dine in peace."

Violet sawed at one end of the meat, cutting it into small, neat strips. "You may stay a while longer if you will promise to make no further deductions about me."

"You have my promise, Mrs. Wheelwright."

"And some of the details were not correct. It was *not* the sight of blood which made me faint."

"No?" Holmes leaned forward. "What then?"

Violet's brown eyes glanced my way. "Weariness," she said sharply. "And a corset laced far too tightly."

I swallowed a mouthful of beef. "I can vouch for her, Sherlock. She watched me stitch up several wounds without flinching."

Holmes' lips pursed briefly, and his fingers tapped at the tablecloth. "A detail only, as you said."

Violet raised her eyes and swept them briefly from face to face. She dabbed at her mouth with the napkin. "No, it was not blood, as you may well deduce from this bleeding slab of bovine tissue before me."

An explosive laugh slipped from Sherlock's lips. Violet, although at first taken aback, seemed pleased by his response.

"Violet," I said, "your comment is too perceptive for someone who has spent time in the anatomy lab."

Violet finished chewing another piece. "I am sorry, Michelle. Anyway, it was not blood which made me faint. I have been under something of a strain of late." She bit her lip and glanced at Holmes, who had not taken his eyes off her.

"Have you, Mrs. Wheelwright?"

"Yes, Mr. Holmes. And are you as chivalrous in real life as in the narratives?"

Holmes' upper lip twisted back. "'Chivalrous?'"

"Under your misogynous front beats a heart of gold."

Holmes' mouth twitched. He sighed. "It is at moments such as this that I most despise Watson's efforts. You have me at a disadvantage, madam. Although we have only been acquainted a quarter of an hour, you assume you know my character because of some foolish words you have read. I would ask—I would beg of you—to reserve your judgment until you know me better."

He stared at her so gravely that her smile faded away. "Perhaps I have done you an injustice, Mr. Holmes, although you must admit that your deductions were decidedly in keeping with Dr. Watson's portrayal."

"Granted, madam, but you must admit that you invited—no, you positively begged for—a certain comeuppance."

Violet laughed, then set down her fork and clapped her hands. "Bravo, Mr. Holmes. We are fairly matched. I shall try to know you better, especially since you are related to my good friend."

While they had been talking I had finished my roast beef. With a contented sigh I pushed my plate back. "Take care, Sherlock. Be wary of dining with her at Simpson's. You may discover more adventures than you thought possible."

Violet's mouth formed an ironic smile. "At any rate, Mr. Holmes, I am glad you are not dead. *The Final Problem* gave many of your admirers a scare. I have often wondered about Professor Moriarty."

"Moriarty is another fiction, madam. Regretfully, he does not exist."

"Regretfully, Mr. Holmes?"

"There are so few truly first-rate criminal brains. An arch-foe of Moriarty's caliber would be welcome; battling him would surely be the high point of my career."

Violet laughed. "A pity. I shall pray that some day you find yourself a Moriarty. Are you certain he does not exist?"

Holmes hesitated a moment. "Yes, madam."

I frowned. "Surely you would not wish such a monster upon London, Sherlock. There are enough problems as it is."

"Boring and insoluble problems, Michelle—a Moriarty I could handle. Besides, all of London enjoys a good crime, the bloodier the better."

"What a dreadful thing to say!" I said.

Henry turned to his cousin. "Sherlock, perhaps we should allow the ladies to at least eat their desserts in peace."

Holmes nodded. "Yes. We have intruded long enough."

"You need not run off on my account," Violet said.

Both men stood. They each wore long black frock coats. Sherlock was slighter than Henry, but both were just over six feet tall. Holmes gazed down at Violet. "It has been a pleasure, Mrs. Wheelwright."

"It has, Mr. Holmes. In the future I hope to provide less fertile ground for deduction. I do trust we shall meet again."

Holmes' smile was brief and harsh. "Oh, we shall, madam."

Henry appeared rather grim. He touched my shoulder and said, "Do not be too late."

I put my hand over his. "I shall not."

Violet and I watched them leave. Violet put a piece of meat in her mouth and chewed slowly.

"My comment about bloody tissue was unwise. I may never eat roast beef again."

I laughed. "Now that the men are gone, you need not finish."

"Donald always orders the large portion. I have always wondered if I could eat so much. I have learned that I can, but it seems a hollow triumph. Well, hardly hollow, since I am completely stuffed. I fear I must forgo dessert."

"Not I. They have a very good cream cake."

Violet resolutely swallowed the last bite and pushed the plate back several inches. "You never told me you were related by marriage to Sherlock Holmes, Michelle. He is not so handsome as Mr. Sidney Paget draws him, but he has a most interesting face. He certainly startled me with his deductions."

"You seemed rather upset, my dear. What is this strain you spoke of?"

Violet gazed at me, and I could sense the wheels, the small gears, turning inside. "I shall tell you another time. This is still our night out. We must not spoil it with seriousness."

"I hope the men did not ruin it for you. I have had a wonderful time." I reached over and grasped her hand with my big fingers, which were reddened from carbolic acid.

"I, too, Michelle. You are very good company. We must see each other more often. Too many of my acquaintances are vapid and ineffectual, wearisome to be around."

"Oh, I know exactly what you mean."

The waiter came, and I ordered dessert. We lingered afterwards talking until I realized that it was nearly half past eight. Violet insisted on driving me home. My house near Paddington Station was not far. In the carriage I began to yawn, and she complained, jokingly, that it was contagious.

Climbing the stairs to the second floor was an effort. Henry was waiting for me in the sitting room. We embraced, and he initiated a kiss, which made me briefly forget my fatigue.

"Oh, Henry, a day around women makes me appreciate you all the more. I enjoy the company of my sex, but I could not live with them day after day."

He ran his fingertips along my cheek. "I feel the same about men."

"Oh, my feet hurt."

He kissed me again. "Do sit down."

I lay on the sofa. He sat at the far end and began undoing the buttons on my right boot.

"The clinic was a madhouse today," I said. "These were supposed to be sensible shoes, but they are still not comfortable. You and Sherlock were oddly grim before you left the restaurant."

Henry slipped off my boot and began to massage my instep. Only one lamp was lit, but a big piece of coal glowed in the fireplace. His eyes stared at the fire, his mouth taut beneath the thick mustache.

"Do not stop," I said.

"What?"

"Massaging my foot."

"Oh." His fingers worked at my foot through the thick stocking. "Donald Wheelwright came to see Sherlock today." He told me about the visit: the gypsy curse, the note and Mr. Wheelwright's reaction to the spider.

When he finished I murmured, "How horrible."

We were both silent. I tried to make sense of what he had told me, but it made my head hurt. "Henry, I do not think that Violet… She may not much care for Donald."

"From what little I saw of him, I can see why."

"I cannot understand how she could have married such a man. Someone like Sherlock would be perfect for her."

Henry smiled. "She made quite an impression on him, despite himself."

"I could see that. I wonder how Donald feels about Violet." Henry gazed again at the fire, and his mouth seemed to slump. "What is wrong?" I asked.

He hesitated. "I... I do not like the whole business."

"Nor do I, but Violet is my friend. She may need my help."

"And knowing you, you will give it to her."

I took his free hand. "Would you have it otherwise?"

He let go of my foot, turned my hand, and kissed my palm. "No."

Weary as I was, I felt a flicker of longing in my throat. I remembered Violet in the carriage, the muted loathing in her voice, and I squeezed his hand. "Oh, Henry, I do love you so."

He stared at me. "Let's go upstairs." Our bedroom was on the third floor.

"I am so tired you will need to carry me."

"I shall if you wish."

"If I weighed as much as Violet, I would let you try, but I do not wish to treat you for an injured back. If you will provide an arm to lean on, that will suffice."

We stood. He slipped his arm about my waist. I picked up my boots with one hand, put the other on his shoulder, and we started for the stairway.

Three

එ

The following Monday a telegram from Holmes arrived early in the morning:

I shall be visiting the Wheelwright home this afternoon to question the household. If your practice is anemic and you wish to join me, be at Baker Street by one.

When I showed the note to Michelle, her eyes lit up. "Oh, Henry, you must go! I shall cover for you."

"There will be little to cover, but more to the point, why should I go at all? This is hardly my affair."

"But Violet is my friend. We must do all we can to help her."

"Perhaps you should go then."

She laughed. "Sherlock did not invite me. Besides I have several patients coming."

"No anemia for you."

She took my arm and kissed my cheek. "You are a very good doctor,

Henry. In time you will obtain the appreciation you deserve."

I shrugged, hardly so convinced of either of her assertions. "Perhaps. Visiting the Wheelwright home should be interesting, and Sherlock needs someone to look after him. Violet may have actually charmed him."

The hansom stopped before 221 Baker Street, just before one. The cabby, who was as thin and worn looking as his horse, took his fare and tipped his hat. The rain of the past few days had abated, but the sun seemed feeble, only a muted yellow through the clouds.

Holmes had company. The stranger's mustache was neatly trimmed, but the reddish hair about his ears was thick and curly, its abundance contrasting with his balding pate. His complexion was ruddy, and his blue eyes regarded me warily. He was impeccably dressed, black silk highlighting the lapels of his frock coat, a diamond pin in his cravat.

"Lord Harrington, this is my cousin, Dr. Henry Vernier."

Harrington shook my hand, then pulled on his gloves. "Please give this matter your consideration, Mr. Holmes. I do not wish my brother's reputation—" he glanced briefly at me— "to remain sullied."

"I shall do what I can. We shall continue our conversation another time. As I said, I have other business this afternoon."

"Very well, sir." He put on his top hat, took his walking stick in his right hand, and marched out the door.

"Have a seat, Henry," Holmes said. "A carriage from the Wheelwrights should be arriving shortly. Lord Harrington had an interesting story."

"I thought Lord Harrington had killed himself."

"And so he did. Joseph Harrington left no heir, so his brother Michael, whom you just met, is now Lord Harrington. He is skeptical of the official version of his brother's death, as well he might be. Men rarely kill themselves in that manner."

"What manner?"

"By cutting one's throat with a razor."

I felt a stir low in my belly and repressed a shudder. "I have never heard of such a case."

"Although rare, it does happen. Lord Harrington also told me his brother was notoriously long-winded, yet the scrawled note only said, 'I cannot go on.'"

"Wasn't Harrington supposed to have remade his fortune after squandering much of his inheritance?" I asked. "Some mysterious investments."

"Yes. His brother did not go into the detail, but that is true. He suspects foul play, and he has revealed an enticing detail the police did not discover. His brother had a female visitor the afternoon he died."

"Why were the police not told?"

"Most of the servants had been given the afternoon off, and the elderly butler who had let her in feared a scandal. Lord Harrington is convinced she murdered his brother. He chooses to overlook the more obvious explanation."

"You mean…?"

Holmes nodded, then rose and walked impatiently to the bow window. "Lady Harrington was out of town visiting her sister. I know you told me the afternoon is not reserved for fine gentlemen and harlots, but it does seem a preferred time."

"But why would Harrington have killed himself?"

"How should I know!" Holmes exclaimed. "Perhaps it was self-loathing." He put his fingertips against his forehead, and his voice quieted. "It all grows so… wearisome. The man had everything–wealth, a title, good breeding, education–and yet he could rise no higher than… a mere animal. Is man's nature truly so base?"

I shook my head. "No. Perhaps you are also thinking of Donald Wheelwright."

Holmes turned to me, angry. "Perhaps I am."

"All men are not like him or Harrington."

Holmes glanced out the window. "The carriage is here, Henry, a fancy four-wheeler. We travel in style today." He reached for his top hat and stick.

During the ride we were both rather pensive. I knew I could never forgive myself if I were unfaithful to Michelle. I might still have longings toward other women, but it was one thing to have such longings, another to act upon them. All the same, despite the great facade of moral rectitude, Holmes was right—adultery was all too common amongst upper-class men.

"Have you discovered anything yet about the Wheelwright case?" I asked.

"Only that which is of general knowledge. Violet Montague married Donald Wheelwright eight years ago this November. She was twenty-two years of age, he some six years older. She was the daughter of a widowed Oxford don, Alexander Montague, an eminent naturalist whose specialty was entomology. He had died, unexpectedly, a year before the marriage at the peak of his career. His obituary in *The Times* mentioned his intellectual brilliance, his eccentric charm and his musical abilities."

I nodded. "That explains much of Violet's character."

"Donald Wheelwright is the son of *the* Donald Wheelwright, founder of Wheelwright's Potted Meats. The elder Wheelwright was born a virtual pauper. He destroyed most of his competitors in the early seventies, and by 1882 he obtained an exclusive contract to supply the British Navy with canned meats. He is now one of the wealthiest men in England, and Donald junior is his only son and heir. He has a daughter, Julia, who is married to a marquess."

I pulled at the end of my mustache. "I am surprised Donald was spared a similar fate."

"That was considered. Donald was seen with a duke's daughter, but then he married Violet quite suddenly. The papers mentioned an extended honeymoon on the continent, but it was cut short when Violet fell ill in Venice."

"The old man could not have approved. He must have been furious."

Holmes nodded. "No doubt—although he appears to have been reconciled with his son and daughter-in-law. The couple has dwelt in the same townhouse for six years, and five years ago the Wheelwrights, father and son, purchased an enormous country estate in Norfolk near Sandringham. They have sunk a small fortune into refurbishing the dilapidated manor house."

I smiled. "Country squires."

"Exactly. Young Wheelwright is second in command at the potted meat business, but the old man rules with a hand of iron. His son keeps brief office hours and is, as we know, often free in the afternoon. He does not seem particularly interested in the family business, nor does he seem particularly competent. The old man is tight with his money, while the younger seems to take his wealth for granted. All in all, the shrewdness and driving passion so central to the father are absent in the son."

"That is often the case."

"Mrs. Wheelwright is widely known for her many charitable activities and for her charm and her abilities as a hostess. Largely because of her, the Wheelwrights are a part of London's best society. She is known to have one of the best cooks in town."

"Ah," I said, "you fail to mention her other obvious appeal. Besides charm and having a good cook, there is her great beauty."

Holmes hesitated for a moment. "I am aware of that."

We had reached a neighborhood of imposing homes and little traffic. These were the townhouses of the wealthy, not country estates, but they were still mansions compared to the three-story home in which

Michelle and I dwelt. Here lived not only the families of the owners, but a multitude of maids, footmen, gardeners, coachmen and cooks. The Wheelwright dwelling was the largest on the street. Green ivy covered its red brick, the paint about the doors and windows a sparkling white.

A footman let us in, and the butler, traditional head of all the servants, soon appeared and introduced himself. Although the lines at the outer corners of his eyes proclaimed him to be in his late thirties, his shiny black hair had no hint of gray. A blue-gray shadow covered the lower half of his face, a dimple marked the center of his chin, and I wondered if he had to shave more than once a day. He wore a black morning coat, a wing collar, and black-and-gray striped trousers, all his apparel radiating cleanliness and order.

Holmes nodded. "I am Sherlock Holmes, and this is my cousin Dr. Henry Vernier. Mrs. Wheelwright is expecting us."

The butler's gaze remained fixed on him. "May I say, Mr. Holmes, as one of your admirers, that we are most honored to have you under our roof. Certainly if anyone can untangle these unfortunate events, it is you." He made a fluid gesture with his right arm toward the elderly manservant who had appeared behind him. "You may leave your hats and stick."

We did so, and followed the butler past a staircase with an elaborately carved oaken banister, and down a hallway to the library. Violet closed a book and rose to greet us. She looked rather better than she had last Wednesday evening. Her cheeks had a pink flush, and her eyes glowed. She wore a mauve dress that emphasized her tiny waist and slim figure.

I had reflected before that she appeared to have Italian or Spanish blood. Her lips were full and naturally red; her hair pure black; her nose slender, but pronounced; her eyes an unusually dark brown. Her skin, however, was very fair. Her bearing was regal, and she was one of the most beautiful women I had ever seen. Little wonder Holmes found her beguiling. All the same, she was a bit thin for my taste. Michelle could never be considered fat, but I preferred her more substantial bounty, her abundance of curves.

"Ah, you have met Lovejoy—he and his wife are the true masters of our house. Without them, chaos would reign." Violet raised her arms and swept around in a circle, her skirts flaring outward. "See, Mr. Holmes—no pins today. The sweet disorder in the dress is remedied. A logical mind such as yours must abhor all such disorder."

Holmes had reddened slightly, but he recovered immediately. "Had you ever seen my chambers you would know better."

Violet laughed, and gave me a nod. "Good day, Henry. It is wonderful to see you."

"You are looking well," I replied. "So you have recovered from your adventures at the clinic and at Simpson's?"

"I must confess to sleeping some ten hours on Wednesday night."

"I asked Henry to accompany me," Holmes said. "You can, of course, rely utterly upon his discretion."

"Oh, certainly." Her face momentarily lost some of its animation. "For a moment I had managed to forget that your visit was not purely social. Shall we discuss this business here or in the sitting room? I confess a fondness for the library."

Holmes gazed at the wall opposite the windows. The bookshelves went all the way to the ceiling, some twelve feet, and they were packed with books. The room had a southern exposure, and the light from the tall windows flooded a massive oak table and its matching chairs. "You like books," Holmes said. It was a statement, not a question.

"I do. They have been my solace my entire life."

"Indeed?" With a fingertip he opened a thick book that lay upon the table. "*Middlemarch.* Ah. And do you—like Dorothea or Saint Theresa—seek some great cause?"

Violet's smile grew bitter. "Perhaps. But I know better: there are no great causes. Please sit down. These chairs are more comfortable than those at the table." She gestured at some plush armchairs.

Holmes sat, but leaned forward restlessly. "Did your husband tell you about his visit to Baker Street?"

She stiffened, her chin rising. The impression I had was that of a cloud passing across the sun, effacing its brilliance. "He did."

Holmes had crossed his legs, and his foot began to bob. "Please tell me in your own words about the events at the Paupers' Ball."

Violet shook her head. "I was a fool. I should have kept quiet. For once Donald was right, but I felt someone must say something. I was speaking with Lady Harrington. She was dressed as a scullery maid, while I was in the guise of a flower girl. The gypsy first appeared at the balcony above the hall, and naturally we assumed she was one of us. I remember thinking that she was remarkably good in her role. However, it soon became clear that she was not acting."

"In what way did it become clear?"

Violet thought for a second. "Her hatred, Mr. Holmes. No one could feign such hatred. 'Curse you,' she cried. 'God curse you all! May you all be struck down, may you suffer even as those you pretend to be. May God make you all honest paupers! May you die poor and miserable!'"

"Do you recall her appearance?"

"Yes. She was close to my height, about five foot three, but with a stoop. Her hair was pure white, her skin dark brown and lined. She had a beak of a nose with a mole at the end and the blackest eyes I have ever seen. Her teeth were discolored, and one or two were missing. She wore gold hoop earrings, a soiled red dress, a black handkerchief tied over her hair, and a heavy black shawl. She had several gaudy rings of gold and silver on her fingers. Oh, and she walked with a slight limp."

Holmes nodded. "Very good, Mrs. Wheelwright. You have an eye for detail. And what was the reaction of the spectators to the gypsy?"

"Shocked silence. She had a piercing voice, Mr. Holmes. Age might have withered her, but that voice carried to every corner of the room." She frowned. "I have asked myself many times why I spoke to her, but I cannot explain it even to myself. Perhaps I was offended at her treatment of Lady Harrington, our hostess, a long-suffering woman. Perhaps I wanted to show how... how clever I was. Oh, I don't know why I behaved so foolishly."

"It must have taken courage," I said.

Violet gave me a mocking smile, a characteristic expression. "Some might argue it was rather stupidity."

Holmes foot began to bob again. "What exactly did you say?"

"I tried to calm the woman. I told her God must be weary of being asked for vengeance, that she might rather request He soften our hearts and give us compassion. Finally, I suggested we pray together. She was outraged. She turned all her fury on me. She..." Violet's voice suddenly shook, and she covered her face with her hand. Her fingers were long, her hand slender and delicate.

Holmes uncrossed his legs and sat upright in his chair. "Mrs. Wheelwright, we need not continue if..."

She removed her hand, and sighed. "Her curses mostly involved botanical metaphors—withering up, being struck barren and without fruit—that kind of thing."

Holmes removed the folded parchment note from his coat pocket. "As in this note?"

Violet nodded. The fingers of Holmes' left hand tapped idly on the chair's arm.

"An unpleasant business. And how...? I suppose this encounter has left you shaken?"

She shrugged. "Mr. Holmes, I shall not raise doubts in your mind by protesting too often; let me merely say once and for all, that I am not superstitious. No one enjoys the spectacle of a depraved and hysterical old woman, especially when one becomes her principal target. All the same, I do not lie awake at night fearing malevolent gypsies and the weight of the curse about to fall upon me."

Holmes' smile was mirthless. "Many people find that their resolution deserts them in the early hours of the morning."

Violet squared her shoulders. "I am not such a person, Mr. Holmes. All the same, no one wants to be hated." Her dark eyes glistened. "You are too polite to inquire, but I am not capable of having children. This became clear long before the old gypsy's ravings."

I frowned. "Have you discussed this with Michelle?"

She hesitated. "Only briefly. Several years ago Dr. Dawson recommended me to Dr. Cabot." Her mocking smile returned. "Donald insisted we pursue the matter with the best physicians in London. The quest was fruitless." Her mouth twisted at the irony of the final word.

"Nevertheless, you should not give up hope."

"I would... I would... like to have a child..." Her voice had an odd timbre, and her eyes appeared almost feverish.

I stared closely at my cousin. As a physician I had discussed such matters with my patients, but he was clearly uncomfortable. "The information is pertinent, Mrs. Wheelwright," he said. "However, you need elaborate no further. From what you have said, I assume this is a matter of regret to your husband."

"Oh, yes. And to my father-in-law. They would like to have an heir, ideally a male—a son. To carry on the dynasty of potted meat pharaohs." She said this last with sudden venom. A single tear slipped from her left eye and trickled down her cheek. Angrily she wiped at it with her fingertips, then drew in her breath and closed her eyes.

I turned to Holmes. "Perhaps we should continue with this interview at another time."

He gave a brief nod, but Violet shook her head. "Not at all. Please forgive me. I should not have... I am perfectly well."

"This interview need not last much longer," Holmes said. "The incident at the ball occurred nearly a year and a half ago. When did you find this note?" He raised the piece of parchment.

"Almost two weeks ago, Mr. Holmes. I came into the library at around eleven in the morning. It was on my desk there." She pointed to the corner. Above the desk's surface were pigeonholes, papers stuffed into many of the holes, while books and envelopes were stacked neatly to the side. "I do not think that the content bothered me so much as finding such a thing in my own home."

My hands tightened on the chair arms. "I imagine so. Rather like discovering a large spider in one's bed."

Violet only shrugged. Holmes briefly raised his black eyebrows. "Spiders do not disturb you?"

"Do not all proper, God-fearing British women despise spiders?" Her ironic smile faded away. "No, I do not care for them."

Holmes nodded, then stood up abruptly and went to the desk. "This is an impressive piece of furniture, Mrs. Wheelwright. Ah, all the pigeonholes are labeled: grocer, greengrocer, milliner, haberdasher, tailor, cobbler, and so on. I take it you manage the household accounts?"

"I do, Mr. Holmes. With Mr. and Mrs. Lovejoy's assistance."

"That must be no small task for a household of this size. How many servants do you employ?"

"Thirty-three here in town."

My jaw dropped slightly. Michelle and I employed a woman to do the cleaning and the cooking, and it was difficult to imagine two people requiring so many servants. Of course, there would be the cook and her two or three helpers, a variety of maids, footmen, gardeners to care for the grounds, men to maintain the horses and carriages, and so on. I simply would not want such a mob under the same roof with Michelle and me!

Holmes returned to his chair but did not sit. "You found the note in the morning two weeks ago. When had you last been in the library before then?"

"The afternoon before."

"Would your husband or anyone else have used the library in the interval?"

Violet's mocking smile returned. "No. He prefers billiards or his club to books. My maid Gertrude tidied the room at about nine, but no one else would have come in here."

"You said you were not superstitious, Mrs. Wheelwright. Therefore one other person obviously came in here. As the room was left unattended for over twelve hours, almost anyone might have crept in and left this foul thing." He raised the paper in emphasis. "Who do you think might have left it, Mrs. Wheelwright?"

She drew in her breath, squaring her shoulders. "I honestly do not know. Logically, I suppose it must have been one of the servants, and yet, I know them all, and I cannot think that any of them would have done it."

"You know them all?"

"Yes. I interview all the servants before they are hired, and I make it my business to know them. I want them to feel welcome in my home."

Holmes was genuinely astonished. He opened his mouth, then reconsidered and closed it. Finally, he said, "When was the last time you hired a new servant?"

Violet's brow wrinkled briefly. "I think it has been nearly two years."

Again Holmes could not hide his astonishment. I had heard several of my wealthier patients complain about getting and keeping decent help. To have had no turnover in such a large staff in two years was remarkable.

"What exactly did you do when you found the note?"

"I showed it to Mrs. Lovejoy. She could not imagine where it came from. No, that is the wrong way to put it—she believes the note is the devil's handiwork. And I showed it to Donald that evening when he came home."

"He seems to think the gypsy curse has been effective, that several of the partygoers have been struck down."

Violet laughed. "I know. It is so reassuring to blame our misfortunes on malevolent spirits rather than blind chance or our own failings."

"You do not believe that the gypsy curse had anything to do with Lord Harrington's death?"

She shook her head. "No. To me he always seemed a trifle… peculiar. His wife had much to bear. Age, sickness, and death always take their toll. The crowd at the ball was so large that misfortune would naturally have struck many of the participants."

Holmes nodded thoughtfully. "So one might think."

Violet raised only her right eyebrow. "You seem skeptical, Mr. Holmes."

"I always am, so early in a case. One must not leap to conclusions. Is there anything else you wish to tell me, Mrs. Wheelwright? No? In that case, I shall want to talk separately to Mr. and Mrs. Lovejoy."

"Very well, Mr. Holmes." She stood and adjusted the skirts of her dress.

"Thank you for your assistance, madam."

She gave him a glorious smile. "The pleasure was mine."

Holmes' gaze lingered on her as she left the room. His guard was down, and his admiration for her was apparent. I thought of making some jest, but I knew it would anger him. And who could blame him?

She was a beautiful and desirable woman. Some men might be put off by the power of her intellect, but certainly to Holmes it made her all the more appealing. Were I in his shoes, I would have cursed the divorce laws for compelling such a woman to remain with a man who was so poor a match for her.

Holmes stood up, again walked over to the desk, and peered at the pigeonholes. "Mrs. Wheelwright is obviously not fearful of doing her sums. Ah, do come in, Mrs. Lovejoy. Please be seated."

Mrs. Lovejoy was a rather austere-looking woman of about the same height and build as Violet, perhaps a bit older, but with none of her employer's beauty or animation. She parted her black hair down the middle, leaving exposed a white furrow, and her skin was very pale. Her eyes were large, brown and rather vacant, her face narrow, almost gaunt, with prominent cheekbones. She wore a black muslin dress, a plain cut, with a multitude of tiny black buttons down the front. All in all, she recalled a dour Puritan of Cromwell's time. She sat down and regarded Holmes warily.

"And how long have you been in Mrs. Wheelwright's service, madam?"

"About six years, sir." She was very soft spoken.

"And what kind of mistress is she?"

"The very best there is, sir."

"And Mr. Wheelwright, what kind of master is he?"

She blinked twice. Her eyelids were almost translucent; the skin between her dark brows and her lashes a faint blue. "The master is... a fair man."

"Indeed?" Holmes sat back against the tabletop. "And what do you make of the business with the gypsy curse and the note Mrs. Wheelwright found?"

"The devil's work, sir—the devil himself."

A smile pulled briefly at Holmes' lips. "Do you know why the devil would have singled out your mistress?"

"Because of her goodness. She cares for all us servants and sets an example for all the cruel and stingy mistresses and masters, and she works to help the poor."

"And does your mistress have any enemies? Besides the devil?"

"No, sir."

"Has she dismissed anyone for bad conduct in the last year or two?"

"No, sir."

"Has she reprimanded anyone publicly or lost her temper at any of the staff?"

Mrs. Lovejoy shook her head. "Certainly not."

Holmes nodded. "I see. We are dealing with an angel."

Mrs. Lovejoy's eyes rolled upward. "You do understand, sir. She is a veritable angel."

"No doubt. An angel of the Lord."

Mrs. Lovejoy's eyes opened wide. "She is not! She is only…" She cut off her words, her face reddening. "I mean to say… she is… she is the angel… of this *house*. Our good angel of the house." Her voice grew soft again.

As puzzled as I, Holmes stared at her closely. "And do you honestly believe in angels and devils, Mrs. Lovejoy?"

"Yes, sir."

"And what does the devil look like?"

"He has horns and a tail."

"Does he have a mustache and a goatee?"

She stared angrily at him. "It does not do to mock the Evil One."

"And have you thought much about the nature of evil, Mrs. Lovejoy?"

"What?"

"Of what does evil consist? Come—you must have reflected upon the matter."

She hesitated, then the words burst forth. "It is those with power abusing the helpless, the less fortunate—it is men who beat and humiliate women, men who lie and brutalize and…" She cut off, suddenly.

Holmes stared at her. "Ah." Her cheeks had turned red. "It is the drunken laborer who comes home and beats his wife," he said.

"That is a good example."

"It is the manufacturer who employs men and women for long hours of toil under deplorable conditions, pays them a pittance, ruins their health, then dismisses them."

"Yes." She nodded. "Yes, that is exactly it."

He was still watching her. "It is the rich man who dallies with a lady of ill repute until her looks are gone and then casts her adrift."

Mrs. Lovejoy hesitated only an instant; her eyes had caught fire. "*Yes.*"

"I see. And what do you think should be done about such evil?"

Mrs. Lovejoy's eyes showed a wild animation that I would not have expected from such a person. "I would make them…" Her voice rang out, suddenly loud and strong. She closed her eyes, and the muscles in her slender throat rippled as she swallowed. When she spoke her voice was again earthbound. "I pray, Mr. Holmes, every day, that such evils may be averted."

"And do you think the Deity hears your prayers?"

She nodded solemnly. "Oh, yes. Someday He will come again, and London will become the New Jerusalem. All will be transformed."

"Tell me, Mrs. Lovejoy, is there any evil of the variety you describe in this household?"

She stared at him, warily. "I have already said the mistress is an angel."

"And your master?"

A hint of anger showed in her brown eyes, but vanished almost immediately. "I am only a servant, sir. It is not my business to say."

Holmes sat down in a chair and stared closely at Mrs. Lovejoy. She demurely lowered her eyes. Holmes set the fingertips of one hand against those of the other. "Madam, which church do you attend?"

Her head jerked upright. "What?"

"I asked which church you attend?"

"I... Why—why is it your business to ask such a question?"

I was surprised by her haughtiness, but Holmes only smiled.

A flush spread across her cheeks. "Forgive my... impudence, sir. One must... must struggle always against Pride. That was Lucifer's great sin, which cast him from Heaven. I pray every day for all the sinners, but in this great evil city, this den of wickedness, I have had a hard time finding a worthy church. I meet occasionally with a few goodly women of like mind; we meet to do God's work, to... to pray together and..."

Holmes was puzzled. "A congregation of women?"

"No, no—not at all—an informal prayer group only, and there is a church I occasionally attend, a church on... Hampstead Street. The minister there is... tolerable."

"Ah, yes," Holmes nodded. "I know that church well. Is that not the Reverend Dunbar's church—Obadiah Dunbar?"

She moistened her lips with her tongue, hesitating. "I... believe so, although..."

"Yes, yes, a large hardy fellow with a white mustache who laughs a great deal and..." Sherlock said.

Mrs. Lovejoy closed her eyes and promptly fell out of her chair. I was at her side at once. I turned her over, but her eyes were closed. I glanced up at Holmes, but he seemed completely undisturbed. She moaned, and fluttered her eyelids. "What...?" she murmured.

I massaged her small, cold hand. "Do not try to get up yet, Mrs. Lovejoy."

"What am I doing on the floor?"

"You fainted."

"Oh." She put her hand on her forehead. "My head feels so very odd."

I turned to Holmes. "You had better find someone to help her."

"My interview was nearly finished." He strode toward the library door, opened it and stepped into the hall.

"Have you felt ill in the last day or two, Mrs. Lovejoy?"

"A bit dizzy in the morning, sir, and I do have something of a queasy stomach."

I put my hand on her forehead. Her brown eyes stared at me from under half-closed lids. Again I noticed how translucent the skin over her eyes appeared, the faint blue veins showing through. "You do not seem to have a fever. Have you eaten much today?"

"No, sir. With the queasiness I thought…"

Holmes and Lovejoy appeared at the door. Violet swept past them, the copious garments under her skirts rustling as she walked. "How is she?"

"She needs to eat something," I said, "and then lie quietly." Lovejoy knelt beside me. We helped her up into the chair.

Violet shook her head. "She has been working far too hard. I told her she might delay this interview, but she insisted."

Mrs. Lovejoy took a deep breath. "I feel better. Pardon my foolishness."

Lovejoy held her arm tightly. "You must take better care of yourself, dearest."

She smiled weakly and let Violet and Lovejoy lead her to the door. Holmes brushed aside his frock coat and slipped his hand into his trouser pocket. "I should like to speak with Mr. Lovejoy now, if he has the time."

"Certainly, Mr. Holmes."

"I shall take good care of Abigail," Violet said.

Violet paused as she and Mrs. Lovejoy reached the doorway. With her back to us, Violet said, "Jonathan, may I have a brief word with you? There are... some chores."

Lovejoy glanced at Holmes and me. "Pardon me, gentlemen. I shall be with you in an instant." He returned almost at once. "Now then, Mr. Holmes, how may I assist you?"

"Do sit down, Mr. Lovejoy." We all sat. Holmes crossed his legs. "We were discussing church when your wife swooned."

Lovejoy shrugged. "I would know nothing about that, sir. My wife does the churchgoing for us both. I believe in the Deity, but I cannot abide having some sanctimonious man in a black gown preach at me."

"Your wife seems to have a religious bent."

"She does, sir. She is always praying for everyone and trying to save us from the devil's snares." Lovejoy seemed faintly amused.

"I would presume your wife attends church every Sunday?"

"Ah, you might well think that, but she does not. She has rather strict requirements for a congregation and preacher; she has found no church that truly satisfies her."

Holmes' gray eyes watched the butler closely. "That does seem odd."

"She is very opinionated, sir, very opinionated indeed, but a good woman and a good wife, despite all her talk of the devil."

"She did mention a church she attends occasionally."

Lovejoy nodded. "On Hampstead Street, I believe."

"Is not that the Reverend Obadiah Dunbar's church?"

Lovejoy smiled. He had very good teeth, white and straight. "As I indicated, Mr. Holmes, you are asking the wrong man. I have not set foot in a church for many a year. Are you a frequent churchgoer yourself?"

"I am not."

Lovejoy gave a brief laugh. "Then we understand one another."

"We digress, Mr. Lovejoy. What can you tell me about this ugly business with the note?"

Lovejoy's smile vanished. "Not much, I fear."

"How long have you been employed by the Wheelwrights, Mr. Lovejoy?"

"My wife and I have been with them for about six years. Before that we were with the Stamps of Liverpool, the small household of an elderly couple. After their deaths—which followed closely upon one another—we came to London."

"Who employed you?"

"Mrs. Wheelwright. She is a very capable wife, Mr. Holmes. There are those ladies who have neither the ability nor the inclination to manage a large household. Mrs. Wheelwright, to the contrary, involves herself in every detail. Not a meal is cooked, not a room furnished, not a maid hired, not a bill paid, without her consideration. She is a brilliant woman, sir, kind-hearted and charming as well."

Holmes nodded. "So I have seen. And what of your master?"

Lovejoy's enthusiasm was checked midair and seemed to spiral slowly downward. "Well, sir, Mr. Wheelwright is an honest, decent man. Frankly, I do not deal with him so often as with the mistress. He has his personal valet and does not much concern himself with the running of his household."

"He lets his wife manage it for him."

Lovejoy nodded. "Exactly, sir. She is very good at it, and after all, it is a wife's duty."

"Does Mrs. Wheelwright have any enemies?" Holmes asked. "Or is there anyone on your staff who might harbor some minor resentment against her?"

"No."

"Your wife appeared equally certain."

"There is no question of it. No one in London pays better wages—you would be surprised how stingy some of the illustrious wealthy can be."

Holmes shook his head. "No, I would not."

"Moreover, she treats everyone from me and Mrs. Lovejoy to the lowest scullery maid with equal respect. I have never had an unkind word from her. She has no enemies under this roof."

"What of Mr. Wheelwright? Does he have enemies?"

Lovejoy hesitated. "Perhaps."

"Who in the house dislikes him?"

"'Dislike' is perhaps too strong, sir. There have been misunderstandings on occasion. Normally Mr. Wheelwright is a quiet sort of man. He is not easily roused, but beware of him when he is. He is quite particular about certain things."

"Such as?"

"The time of day at which meals are served. That his shoes are brushed and set where he can find them. Nothing makes him angrier than being unable to find something. Mrs. Wheelwright once gave away some worn clothes, which included a favorite jacket. There was… an unpleasant scene. His valet, old Osborne, is always threatening to quit."

"Why?"

"He says he does not like the way the master treats him, but I think he actually fears him. Poor Osborne is barely five feet tall, and well, you have seen the master. He rarely strikes anyone, but…"

"Whom exactly has he struck?"

Lovejoy raised his black eyebrows, his eyes suddenly mournful. "I am sorry, sir, but I can say no more. I may have already been indiscreet."

"Very well, Mr. Lovejoy, we shall not pursue these domestic matters. Do you know of any enemies outside the house?"

"There I am on unfamiliar ground. You must ask Mr. Wheelwright himself. I gather he is not so... unpopular as his father, but I am only speculating."

"Yes," Holmes said. "I have heard how the elderly Wheelwright crushed his rivals. I have also heard some curious speculation about the content of his products."

Lovejoy said nothing but gave a very slight, reluctant nod.

"Thank you, Mr. Lovejoy. I shall be returning another day to speak with the staff."

"I shall have the carriage brought round, sir. I hope I have been of assistance."

He stood. His was a very imposing presence in his black morning coat, his posture, diction, and bearing perfect. Butlers were sometimes portrayed as buffoons on stage, but theirs was a position of great responsibility. Capable and intelligent, Lovejoy was more of a gentleman than many gentlemen.

I stood up and stretched my arms. Holmes went to the bookshelves. He pulled out a volume, and soon his upper lip wrinkled in disdain.

"What is it?" I asked.

"*The Adventures of Sherlock Holmes.*"

I could not help but laugh.

"Mrs. Wheelwright has diverse tastes: natural histories, entomology, biology and geology; Jules Verne's romances, Watson, Dickens, and Eliot. Ah, what have we here!" From one of the shelves hidden below the table, he pulled out a violin, the wood a lustrous reddish brown. He examined it minutely. "I do believe—yes, it is a Guarneri!—a Guarneri del Gesù. It is not inferior to my Stradivarius. I must try it."

He tuned the instrument, plucking at the strings and adjusting them. Finally, he pulled a large handkerchief from his pocket, and tucked that and the violin under his chin. Standing very straight, he held the bow loosely at the end of his long outstretched arm; he closed his eyes, raised the bow in a single fluid gesture and brought it down across a string, playing a long sustained note. "Oh yes, a very warm tone, exquisite." The fingers of his left hand danced about as he played some scales. "Beautiful, absolutely beautiful." Eyes still closed, he launched into a piece.

The melody began plainly enough, but quickly grew more complicated. When a contrapuntal line was introduced, I decided Bach was probably the composer. Holmes' playing emphasized the music's majesty and dignity, but the instrument's tone added warmth. Rather awestruck, I listened from my chair without stirring.

After the final note had died away I heard a tremulous voice: "Oh, bravo, Mr. Holmes—*bravo*."

Holmes lowered the violin, his handkerchief falling to the floor. "Forgive me for not consulting with you first, Mrs. Wheelwright, but I could not resist such an instrument."

Violet stood by the doorway, her dark eyes blazing and face flushed. She wiped at her eyes with her long fingers, and laughed. "Emotion is such a foolish, senseless thing. Most of the world can listen to music without being much affected, but it moves me so much. I said books were my solace, but music is another, one which warms my blood as mere words never can." She laughed again. "I am pleased that Dr. Watson did not invent your musical inclination, but he does not do you justice. Do you really own a Stradivarius?"

Holmes nodded, his eyes fixed on her. "I do."

"I envy you."

He raised the violin by its neck. "It is no better than this instrument. I take it this is yours?"

"Yes. My father left it to me."

"And do you play, Mrs. Wheelwright?"

She had gradually approached us and stopped about a yard from Holmes. She gave a slight nod. They stared intently at each other.

"Was that Bach's music?" I asked.

"It was the Allemande from his Partita Number One," Violet said.

Holmes handed her the violin, then stooped to pick up the handkerchief and gave it to her as well. She stepped back, tucked the violin under her chin and played a few notes. "You have a good ear—it is well tuned." She drew in her breath through her nostrils, her rosy lips clamped together, and began to play.

I have no great ear, but I could tell this was more Bach. The melody went much faster and teemed with notes. It must have been fiendishly difficult. Although the music was very formal, very dignified, its passion was striking; she gave it such pathos, such yearning. My eyes shifted to my cousin. He was absolutely transfixed. I had seen him absorbed before, but never with such fire in his eyes, such color on his cheek. When she finished at last, he drew in a great breath, opened his mouth, then turned and went to an armchair, virtually collapsing. Mrs. Wheelwright watched him. She too was flushed.

"That was also Bach, was it not?" I asked.

Violet nodded. "Yes, from the same partita." She set down the violin and bow, and held the handkerchief out to Holmes. He raised his head, then took it.

"Brilliant, Mrs. Wheelwright. Your playing is extraordinary."

"Thank you, Mr. Holmes."

"It was quite remarkable," I said.

She smiled at me. "Thank you, Henry."

Holmes ran his hand across his forehead and back over his oily black hair, then stood. "I think we have intruded upon your household long enough."

"I have something for you both." She went to her desk, then selected two envelopes from a stack, and handed one to each of us. "I am giving a small dinner party a week from today, frightfully formal,

I fear, but you are both invited—and Michelle, of course. Perhaps you can liven things up. My cook is truly formidable, so I can promise you a memorable meal."

I glanced down at the invitation. "How very kind of you."

"Not at all. Michelle is especially dear to me, and I have been intending to have you as our guests for some time."

"We shall be happy to attend."

She smiled again. "I am glad. And you, Mr. Holmes? It is next Monday. I do hope you can come."

He stood and thrust the invitation into his coat pocket. He was nearly a foot taller than Violet. "I shall." They were staring at each other, again.

"Oh, good." She laughed. "This will also give you the opportunity to investigate our friends and relations. You can decide who is in league with the old gypsy."

Holmes gave a snort of laughter. "No doubt."

She led us back downstairs. She and I chatted, but despite some glances from her, Holmes remained unusually quiet. We tipped our hats, said good day, and stepped outside. The yellow glow of the sun was gone, only gray showing in the sky.

"She is an exceptional woman," I said.

"Yes." Holmes was still clutching his handkerchief.

"By the way, I meant to ask you earlier—who is that minister you mentioned, the Reverend Obadiah something?"

Holmes took a deep breath, which seemed to clear his head. He smiled. "The Reverend Obadiah Dunbar is my own invention. He does not exist."

Four

After we reached Baker Street, I told Holmes I would be happy to accompany him again on an afternoon, because my practice was not particularly demanding at that time. Thus, two days later, I received a telegram inviting me to meet with royalty and high society.

I had some difficulty getting away and arrived late, shortly after one. No royal barouche was present at Baker Street, only an antiquated carriage whose scowling driver possessed a huge black mustache. The horses, however, were regal, massive creatures whose dark brown and black coats had a glossy sheen; they were cleaner and better cared for than many London children.

Their apparent owner sat before the fire in the chair of honor, and both he and Sherlock rose to greet me. What an extraordinary costume! His frock coat was double breasted and of a brilliant maroon velvet, a style which had been fashionable decades ago. However, the big shiny silver buttons, which matched his belt and shoe buckles, must be recent additions. His waistcoat was purple silk, his trousers gray wool. He had deep brown, leathery skin, and a fine network of cracks about his eyes and mouth. His mustache and the long hair spilling onto his shoulders were white, but his eyebrows remained a stark black. His eyes themselves were dark brown, large, and curiously intense.

"This is my cousin, Dr. Henry Vernier," Sherlock said. "Henry, this is the king of the gypsies." A faint smile played about Holmes' lips, but his eyes remained serious.

"A pleasure to meet your majesty," I said.

The monarch had a grip like a steel trap, but a brief glint of irony showed in his dark eyes. He held a foul-smelling cigar between two fingers of his left hand.

"I am sorry to be late," I said.

Holmes opened his desk drawer and took out a wooden box. "His majesty has only recently arrived." He raised the lid, and I could smell the tobacco. "Would you care for one of mine?"

The gypsy flicked his wrist lightly, tossing the remnant of his cigar into the fireplace. "Ah, yes. Good of you to remember." He stuck the long cigar in his mouth, then withdrew a clasp knife from his pocket and opened it. Light glistened upon the long shiny blade. He lopped off the end of the cigar, threw the fragment into the fireplace, and let Holmes light the cigar. Soon he gave a contented sigh, releasing a cloud of fragrant smoke. Sherlock used a more gentlemanly cutter on his own cigar.

"This is truly wonderful, Mr. Holmes." He glanced at me. "Your cousin is not only my friend, but a friend to the gypsies. He has saved my son from rotting in an English jail."

Holmes crossed his legs and exhaled. "He was most unjustly accused."

"Still, I am in your debt forever. What can I do for you? Your note did not say."

Holmes took the thick cigar between thumb and forefinger. "Did you hear of the gypsy woman appearing at the Paupers' Ball a year and a half ago?"

The gypsy said nothing, but his eyes changed rather subtly. Until then he had appeared an exotic, even faintly comical figure, but now I saw something dangerous in his countenance. Certainly that clasp knife was not used only for cutting cigars. He muttered something in Romany, the gypsy language, which was obviously a curse, then nodded.

"What can you tell me about her?"

"I can tell you she was almost certainly one of the *gorgiki*."

"Who are the *gorgiki*?" I asked.

Holmes glanced at me. "The term is a generic one for non-gypsies. So your majesty does not believe she was a gypsy?"

The gypsy shrugged. "Who can be sure of anything in this life? All I know is the business has a bad smell. We gypsies do not go looking for trouble, not like this woman did. Also, no one can tell me who she is, not even the gypsies who saw her."

I frowned. "There were gypsies at the ball?"

The king gave me a stern look but said nothing. Holmes shook his head. "That does not interest us. So you made inquiries as to her identity?"

"Yes. There are not so many old gypsy women in London, not true gypsies, and especially not sorceresses. No one can tell me who she is. Also, her English is too good. I hear she has no accent and bellows like a bull."

"Do you have any idea who might wish to do your people harm?" Sherlock asked.

The gypsy laughed, hard and sharp. "All of the *gorgiki* seem to wish us ill. We are not saints, but we are accused of every crime, every unpleasantness. Forgive me, my friend. I do not include you and your cousin amongst our enemies, and in all honesty, I do not think I would include this woman at the ball. She meant no harm to gypsies. She was only acting a part."

Holmes picked up a small brass vase and knocked his cigar ash into it. "My thoughts exactly. And I suppose an old gypsy woman would not have written this?" Holmes took the parchment note from his pocket and unfolded it.

The king glanced at the note, then laughed in earnest, a roaring sound. "You joke with me, Mr. Holmes. I do not know of any old gypsy women who can write English."

Holmes gave a nod. "I thought not."

"Read me the note, my friend."

The gypsy listened, cigar between his lips. The smile faded from his mouth, his eyes growing cold. "Truly a bad business. It has the stench of evil—probably a witch or sorceress, but not one of my people. Wishing barrenness upon a woman is very bad. A gypsy would hesitate before unleashing such a curse, and we do not drag our women into our quarrels."

"It is signed only with the letter A. Do you know what that letter might stand for?"

The gypsy shook his head.

"What you have told me only confirms my conclusions, but I wished to be certain. I knew that you must know if any gypsy had truly been involved."

"I ask of you one favor, my friend. Should you find this person, and she is not a gypsy—as we both suspect—will you make this known? Every time there is such a story, your proper Englishman and your police feel they must go out and kick the nearest gypsy."

Sherlock knocked off more ash into the vase. "If it is at all possible, I shall make certain the newspapers print the true facts."

We chatted for a while, the conversation turning to less serious matters, while Mrs. Hudson served tea. Finally, the king rose and said it was time to leave. Glancing at me, he asked if I were an equestrian, and he was clearly disappointed when I told him I was not.

"Should you ever wish to buy a horse, see me first." He made it sound more a command than a request, and I assured him I would do so.

From the bow window, we watched the aged carriage and its magnificent horses depart. "He seems a pleasant enough man," I said.

Sherlock gave a sharp laugh. "So long as you number him among your friends. He makes a most fearsome enemy. Little happens anywhere in the London underworld that he does not know about."

"His eyes had… an unusual glint."

"How old would you take him to be?" Sherlock asked.

"His late fifties."

"He is nearly eighty, but woe to any youthful fool who should wish to fight him! His first wife bore him several sons before expiring, one of whom was driving the carriage, and his new wife is expecting a child, no doubt another son." Holmes took his top hat and stick. "The weather is exceptional. Let us walk for a while."

"Where are we going? High society, I presume."

He smiled. "Oh yes."

We started down the street. The gloomy weather of the past few days had lifted, winter retreating before a returning autumn. Great coats and mackintoshes had been left at home. The golden sun was low in the sky and lit up the bronze leaves of an oak tree across the way.

"Do you recall Lord Harrington visiting me on Monday? Yesterday, I went to the home of his deceased brother, the former Lord Harrington, and spoke with his coachman and an elderly butler. I convinced them at last to give me the name and address of the woman he was seeing. I assured them I would not involve the police or allow their master's good name to be impugned. They seemed genuinely fond of him. The coachman had often seen the woman greet his master at her door, and that particular day, the butler admitted her into the house. An hour later, he found Lord Harrington in a pool of blood, and the lady had fled. He was not surprised, because his master had been acting oddly and had even bid him farewell earlier that day. Harrington was a big strong man, and neither the coachman nor the butler thought the small woman could have possibly murdered him in such a violent way. Hence their silence with the police."

"So we go to question the lady. And her address? She must dwell in one of the more respectable houses of accommodation." Sherlock took a piece of paper from his pocket. I stared at the writing for a few seconds. "Good Lord—there must be some mistake."

"There is no mistake."

"But one must be well-off and above reproach to live on that street."

Holmes smiled again. "Obviously only the first is true."

We soon hailed a hansom and took a brief ride through the sunny streets. There were wealthier neighborhoods than our destination, but none more respectable; it was a favorite of retired officers, rising young bankers, and solicitors. We went to the main entrance of the house in question, and Holmes rapped with the door knocker.

"Contradict nothing I say," he said. "I want our quarry to believe we are prospective clients."

I gave him a suitably dumbfounded look. The door swung open. In the musty shadow stood an enormous woman dressed in gray. Her colorless, soiled hair was parted exactly down the middle, and she had a greasy curl before each ear. Her chin and mouth floated upon a great moon of flesh, which bloated forth from a lace collar. Two grayish-brown eyes, like flecks of mud, stared from under half-closed lids, and two rosy spots on either cheek, obviously rouge, clashed with the rest of her complexion. The pink of her tongue flickered across her lower lip, and she smiled at us, an expression which made me want to turn and run.

"Good day, gentlemen. What might I do for you?"

Holmes held his hat in his hands, long fingers clutching at the brim. "We wish to see Miss Flora Morris."

The woman's chin bobbed in its sea of flesh. "Ah, yes—my niece, Flora. And what business would you gentlemen have with her?"

"A friend recommended her to us, madam. He said her acquaintance might prove a fruitful one." Holmes winked at her and attempted to leer.

The woman gave a great *hah!* of a laugh. "Fruitful, yes—that's very good."

"I can assure you that it will be a very profitable meeting, if you take my meaning." He gave his pocket a pat.

The woman laughed again. "I'm sure!" She glanced about somewhat warily. "Do come in, gentlemen. No use standing about in the street."

We stepped inside, and she closed the heavy oak door behind us, shutting out the warm sun and the autumnal breeze. The parlor had an odd odor; dark maroon curtains hung on either side of the tall windows, the blinds pulled almost to the sills, leaving it dim and chill. I shuddered as I glanced about. The furniture was massive and solid; ornate lace doilies were pinned to the arms of the overstuffed chairs and sofa. The carpet was thick and appeared new, a pattern of somber reds and purples.

"I am Mrs. Morris. I can take you to Flora. However..." She glanced at me, her eyes briefly conducting an appraisal. "I have another niece, Louise, who will be back shortly."

"We both wish to meet Flora," Sherlock said.

Mrs. Morris scratched at her chin. "It will cost you extra."

"The expense is not a problem."

I opened my mouth to speak, but Holmes dug his fingers into my arm and smiled grotesquely. "My friend is very shy."

Mrs. Morris smiled again. "We shall remedy that."

She turned and started for the stairs. She must have weighed well over two hundred and fifty pounds, but she wore a bustle, the worst possible fashion for such a figure. The gray dress was fully cut, not tight, an expensive-looking fabric—and there were yards of it. Her upper arms were as big around as a stevedore's, though not so hard, and the girth at her waist reminded me of a young oak growing before the house. We followed her up the stairs. My cheeks felt warm as I reflected upon the few brief words between her and my cousin.

"Exactly how many nieces do you have, Mrs. Morris?" Sherlock asked.

"Just the two, and very good girls they are. They do me proud." We went down the hallway, and she wrapped at a door. "Flora! Flora! Visitors, dear."

The door swung open. The girl inside was so different from Mrs. Morris that any lingering doubts that they might actually be related vanished at once. She was a slight little thing, frail, blonde, and very pale. She was not truly beautiful, but she had a pleasant enough face: large blue eyes, a narrow mouth with almost colorless lips, and a small, slightly turned-up nose. She smiled at us, revealing a pair of dimples, but she seemed weary. Her blue silk dress was well cut with the puffy upper sleeves coming into fashion. It emphasized her tiny waist.

"These gentlemen said a friend had recommended your acquaintance."

Flora's chest swelled as she inhaled. I could not hear any whistling, but she appeared almost consumptive. "Do come in, gentlemen."

Mrs. Morris folded her arms as we walked by. "I'll be close by if you need anything. And I shall want fifty pounds." She spoke in such a way that she sounded both accommodating and threatening.

Flora closed the door. She was a good six inches shorter than her supposed aunt. We were in a large sitting room, the furniture, carpet, drapes, and decorations all of the highest quality. "Do sit down, gentlemen."

She herself sat in a wicker chair near the window, the light quite flattering. She wore gloves, but she pulled them off. Her hands were small and slender, and I could see the blue veins under the skin. Her smile had vanished, but she attempted to resurrect it.

"A friend gave you my name? I hope he was pleased." Something about her articulation was a bit strained; her "H"s were overemphasized.

Holmes had sat at one end of the velvet sofa. Even the furniture seemed suggestive. "I presume so, Miss Morris."

She ran the fingertips of one hand across the palm of the other; the skin of her palm had a rosy orange flush. Despite the smile fixed on her lips, her blue eyes seemed detached, curiously vacant. I could almost see her thoughts losing focus and drifting, but then she willed herself back into the room, again becoming conscious of our presence.

"We do our best to please. Would you gentlemen care to go out somewhere for supper, or would you prefer...?" The sudden awkwardness did not fit with her profession, but she was so very young—at most a year or two past twenty—that she could not have been thus employed for long.

"We would prefer a brief chat," Holmes said. "Perhaps you would like to know the name of the person who told us about you?"

"Surely." Again there was something oddly vacant about her smile.

"Lord Joseph Harrington."

If this was a test, it produced the desired effect. She sat bolt upright, and every last vestige of color drained from her already pale face. One hand rose, covered her mouth.

"I see the name is familiar to you."

She let her hand drop. "What is this?"

"We are friends of the late Lord Harrington, Miss Morris, and we wish to put some questions to you."

She said nothing, but her terror was palpable, showing most of all in her eyes. "I didn't do nothing."

Holmes peered at her. "Did you not, Miss Morris?"

Her hand slipped down to her chest, her fingers splayed out across her bosom. "I swear to God I didn't."

"So you did not kill him?"

I would not have thought she could be more frightened, but her mouth opened wide, revealing discolored teeth. She tried to speak, but nothing came out. She shook her head wildly. "No—*no!*" Abruptly her eyes seemed to go liquid, and tears trickled down her cheeks.

I glanced at Holmes, then at her. "Calm yourself, Miss Morris. If you are truly innocent, you have nothing to fear from us."

Holmes' gray eyes were fixed on her, and his visage seemed monstrous, gargoyle-like, with that beak of a nose, sharp chin, and probing stare. "That is true. If she is innocent." The irony in his voice was cutting.

Her hands shook, but she still seemed unable to speak.

"For God's sake, Sherlock—you will make her ill."

Suddenly, she leaped to her feet. "Auntie!" she screamed. "Auntie!" I wanted to cover my ears, her voice was so loud.

The door swung open at once, and the old woman appeared. All pretense of amiability was gone, and she resembled a vicious cur, her face red with anger. Behind her stood a tall man whose visage was completely at odds with his dress. He wore the formal garb of a butler, but he had the face of a pugilist, worn and aged. His nose was twisted and had been broken more than once; he had a great scar over one eye.

I too had leaped to my feet, but Holmes remained seated. He opened his coat, withdrew a revolver, cocked it, and leveled the barrel at Mrs. Morris. "I mean your niece no harm, madam, but I will speak with her."

The old harpy glared at him. She was, luckily for us, a good ten feet away, or I think she would have rushed him. The revolver did not seem to frighten her, but the gigantic butler appeared subdued. He backed up slightly into the doorframe.

"Give me ten minutes with your niece, and then I shall leave. We need to ask her a few questions about Lord Harrington."

The name, which had so frightened Miss Morris, seemed to enrage the old woman even further. Her great chest swelled, and her face grew so red I thought she might burst a vessel in her brain. "You get out of here!"

"Ten minutes, Mrs. Morris."

"*Out!*" she bellowed.

Holmes reached into his pocket with his left hand and threw several gold coins at her, which I recognized as sovereigns. "Ten minutes, my good woman. I would prefer paying you to shooting you."

I could not believe he would actually shoot the old dragon, but if he had any doubts, you could not see them in his face. The old woman snatched up the coins while the pugilist butler stepped sideways, out of the line of fire.

"Ten minutes," she hissed at us, then stepped backwards and out of the room.

"Close the door, Henry, and then pour yourself and Miss Morris some brandy. You both look ill."

Miss Morris collapsed into the chair. Her hands trembled. "Oh God," she murmured.

"Lock it," Holmes said.

There was a key in the latch, and I turned it. I would not have expected a lock, but given the nature of Miss Morris's business, it was not surprising. A crystal decanter sat on the dark cherry-wood sideboard upon a lacy covering. My own hands were somewhat shaky, but I poured some brandy into two glasses and took a healthy swallow from one. The burning impact of the drink was a shock, but it steadied me. I took another swallow, then walked over and offered the other glass to Flora Morris. She was frightfully pale and obviously badly frightened. She gave her head a wild shake.

"Drink it," Holmes commanded.

She took the glass, swallowed some, and began to cough.

"Have another swallow," I said, "but more slowly."

Her blue eyes gazed up at me, her lips parted slightly. I could not bear to see such fear. I put one hand on her shoulder. "We shall not harm you."

"*If* you cooperate with us, Miss Morris. Where is the note?"

She held the glass with both hands clutched against her, and I could see it quiver, the liquid sloshing slightly. "Note?" She was genuinely confused.

"Lord Harrington's suicide note."

"I–I don't know nothing about no note."

Holmes gave a sigh. "If you will give me the note and tell me what happened, we shall leave you in peace. Otherwise I fear we must take you directly to the police."

She stood quickly, the brandy tumbling onto her dress, the glass rolling onto the floor. "No! Not that! Please, sir..."

Holmes had thrust the revolver back into his coat pocket. He extended his right hand, palm up. "The note, then. We do not want to alarm your aunt unnecessarily."

She swayed briefly, and I seized her shoulders with both hands. I was accustomed to Michelle, and by contrast, there seemed almost nothing to this girl. I doubt she weighed more than eighty pounds. Perhaps she was consumptive. "Sherlock!" I exclaimed. "Be merciful–she is only a child."

"She is no child, and she was hardly merciful to Lord Harrington. Now get me that note."

She drew in her breath, and I released her. Her eyes still glistened with tears. "Thank you," she mumbled. She walked over to a bureau, opened the bottom drawer, dug around a bit, and then withdrew a folded piece of paper. She handed it to Sherlock.

"Please sit down," he said.

She collapsed into the chair and began to weep in earnest. Sherlock opened the note. I stood behind him where I could read it. The writing was very small and filled the entire page.

My dear Harriet,

When you read this, I shall be no more. Forgive me, my dearest, but my life has become such an agony that I can no longer bear it. This seems the only way out, the only honorable refuge after so dishonoring you, myself, and my friends.

Should anyone approach you after my death with stories about my baseness, know that in my heart of hearts, I have loved you and you alone. I have been weak; I have been heir to the sins of the flesh that so beset Adam's descendants; but you have always been my inspiration, a beacon of light and virtue shining through in all this wretched darkness. Words cannot convey the disgust I feel toward myself for my actions. I cannot explain why a man with a wife such as you would fall into the mire. The weakness is mine and mine alone. Do not blame yourself, my darling. I bear sole responsibility. Had I been stronger, had I not erred at an early age, perhaps I could have resisted the devil, but I could never forbear wicked pleasures. Now I pay the price for my worldly sins. If only I had followed my angel, none of this would ever have happened. No one else ever meant anything to me. Always remember, my dearest wife, that you and you alone were the one true love of my life.

As for my friends, I hope they too can forgive me, for I fear I have let loose a devil amongst them. This demon took advantage of my weaknesses. He made me a fortune, knowing full well he meant to reclaim it, and he introduced me to the harlot who would ensure my downfall. I cannot be certain, but I believe he is planning the general ruin of others. Denounce _____ my dearest. The children of Israel are known for their rapaciousness, but no Jew exults so in the destruction of their victims. It is all money with them. Not so with this ghoul, this vampire: he most desires blood, not money. Warn the others to have a care. He and that gypsy must truly be infernal agents. I can fight them and my own weak nature no longer. I pray that some day the Almighty and you, my dearest, will forgive me.

With all my love,
Joseph

I shook my head. "The poor, tortured devil."

Holmes had finished reading before I had. His lips twisted. "His brother was correct about his being long-winded. Little wonder he could not accept a note which said merely, 'I cannot go on.'"

I shook my head. "Have you no heart at all?"

"I have heart enough, but my brain grows weary with human stupidity. All these professions of love—what good are they coming from a dead man? If he loved his wife so much, why did he not live? These pathetic, trite scrawlings are small consolation indeed." He turned to the girl weeping on the chair. "We are nearly finished, Miss Morris, but you must honestly answer a few questions first. You had decided to blackmail him, had you not?"

She raised her head. Her eyes were red, and her nose was running. She sniffled and wiped at her face with her sleeve. "It wasn't my idea! They told me to do it. How was I to know 'e'd kill himself?" Her hysteria had weakened her studied articulation.

"Who are 'they'? Your aunt?"

She nodded eagerly. "Yes, and her friends. The Angels."

Holmes frowned slightly, his gray eyes suddenly hot. "Angels? Of the Lord?"

She nodded again. "I didn't want to do it. He was always a nice enough sort. Peculiar if you take my meaning, but harmless. Half the time he didn't want to do nothing but stare at me. They said we could retire on the money, and so we shall."

"How much did you ask for?"

She licked her lips. "Five thousand pounds."

"Good Lord!" I exclaimed. "And he gave it to you?"

She nodded, then her mouth twitched, and she sobbed once. "Why'd he have to do it right when I was there? *Why?* I didn't mean no harm. He gave me the five thousand, then called me devil and 'ore. He had a razor, and I thought for sure he'd murder me, but he opened up 'is own throat instead. Oh God, there was so much blood! And he was choking terrible and..." She covered her face with her hands and wept loudly.

Holmes ran his long fingers up his forehead and through his oily black hair. "Yes, it is all perfectly clear. You came to collect the money, and perhaps to threaten him and ask for more." She shook her head wildly. "Regardless, he knew you and auntie would never let go once you had your talons in him. He paid you off, then cut his own throat. You may have been upset, but you retained enough presence of mind to take this note, then scrawl 'I cannot go on' upon a piece of his stationery. Afterwards you fled the house."

She nodded. "Yes."

"Very well, Miss Morris. One last thing. You must tell me whose name has been scratched out on the note."

She raised her face. Her eyes were all puffy, and she looked even younger than twenty. She was genuinely surprised. "Scratched out?"

Holmes stood up and approached the chair. She scrunched down. He thrust a finger at the paper. "Here."

"But I didn't do that. It was Auntie. She said we might sell the note later."

"What was the name?"

"I don't remember."

Holmes gave a great sigh, folded the note and put it in an inner pocket of his jacket. "I honestly do not want to turn you over to the police."

This brought on a renewed outburst; she covered her face again, sobs shaking her slight frame.

"Sherlock, do not bully her. She is already frightened half to death."

He glared angrily at me. "I must have the name. Compose yourself, Miss Morris."

"I cannot remember! Oh God, I would tell you if I could!"

I shook my head at Holmes. "You have her so upset she can hardly think." I walked over and put my hand on her shoulder. "Now then, Miss Morris, please calm yourself–*please*. We are going soon, and we will not harm you. Think, though, can you not recall the name? Please try."

She gazed up at me, and I felt an inner pang. Perhaps I am a weakling, but I cannot bear to see a woman suffer. "I... I cannot remember it. Auntie will be very angry with me if..."

"She need not know. Please try to remember."

She stared at me; she did seem calmer. "Turnford?" she murmured. "Turn? Or something like it. Stuh..."

Blows rained upon the door, and she clutched at my arm, wincing in terror. "Do not let them take me!"

"Open this door!" The old woman's immense lungs made her voice boom, and I recalled the wolf in the fairy story who could blow down doors. "Your ten minutes is up!"

Holmes sighed and withdrew his revolver. Miss Morris squeezed my arm more fiercely. "Do not murder me!"

"He will not hurt you."

Another blow made the door shudder in its hinges. "Open, I say!"

"One minute, madam," Holmes shouted. "Turn the key, Henry, and then retreat as quickly as you can."

I glanced down at the girl, then slipped my hand inside my coat and pulled out one of my cards. "You need to get away from that old monster. My wife and I can give you refuge. By now you must know that you have chosen wrongly."

She nodded. "Oh, yes."

I gave her the card, and then gently pried her hand loose from my arm. "You are very young. It is not yet too late."

She gave her head a shake, too moved to speak.

Another crash came, louder still. "Open, by God, or we'll break it down!"

I went to the door, turned the key, and withdrew hastily.

Holmes had the revolver aimed at the door. "Turn the knob, madam."

The door burst open, revealing the old woman and the pugilist butler. He shrank back at the sight of the revolver, but she strode into the room.

"That is far enough, madam."

"You'd shoot a harmless old woman?"

"Not a very apt description, madam. We shall leave now, but I warn you I need the name you crossed out of Lord Harrington's suicide note. I shall be back for it."

"Never set foot in this house again!"

"I prefer not to, just as I prefer not to involve the police. They might not look kindly on the activities of you, your nieces, and your angelic accomplices."

The old woman clenched her fists. Perhaps they were mostly flesh, but they had quite a span. Holmes' words had infuriated her all the more. "You dare not!"

"I want that name. Think upon what I said. Now stand aside, and you, sir, either come in here where I can keep an eye on you or get away while you can."

The pugilist eagerly followed the latter suggestion; we could hear his footfalls as he went down the hallway, then down the stairs. Glowering at us, the old woman stood aside as Holmes and I circled about her. She gave us a final look of utter hatred, which chilled me, then went to the girl. "Don't let them make you cry, dear. They can't hurt us."

"Oh, Auntie!" Miss Morris stood and practically fell into the old woman's arms; they engulfed her, those sausage-like fingers digging into the blue silk of her dress.

Something seemed to catch in my throat; I had never felt such repulsion. I wished Holmes would shoot the old creature and close those dreadful, evil eyes once and for all.

"Come, Henry."

Holmes put his hand on my arm, but I wrenched free of him.

"Henry." He took my arm again, and I glared at him. His lips formed a bleak smile, but his eyes were pained. "Come on. We have both had quite enough of this."

I took a great breath of air and realized my heart was beating rapidly. "Yes. Let us go."

Holmes kept the revolver out, but there was no sign of the butler. The parlor was still dim and musty. Once we were outside, I could not seem to get enough air—the light was so bright, and everything seemed so clean. I stopped, took another step and realized my legs were not functioning so well.

Holmes' hand closed again about my arm. "Easy, Henry."

"I…" The pavement seemed to tilt, the trees across the street suddenly wavering.

"Keep walking. You will feel better soon."

It was good advice. A short way down the street, I felt nearly normal.

I remembered the old woman's face as she glared at us, the girl in the blue dress swallowed up in her arms. "That filthy pig," I muttered.

Holmes gave a curt nod. "She was an odious creature."

"That poor girl."

"You are too chivalrous, Henry. She is old enough to know what she is doing. Taking Harrington's suicide note and leaving a substitute showed remarkable self-possession."

"But if that thing has her under her power…"

"Their association was no doubt voluntary, and it has proven profitable to them both."

I stopped abruptly. "Do not talk that way! *Do not!*"

Holmes' lips twitched. "Very well, Henry."

We walked for a long while. I merely followed Sherlock, but gradually the furor that had seized me abated. I felt exhausted and very much wanted to go home to Michelle. The beauty of the day was quite lost on me.

My cousin spoke at last. "I am sorry, Henry. I am accustomed to such people, but I should have spared you. I knew we were likely to encounter such a reception."

"It… I have never seen anyone like that old woman."

"She was an unusually vile specimen of her kind."

We continued to walk. An omnibus went by, and I reflected on all the respectable people it seemed to contain. Men in bowler hats and well-dressed women sat on the upper level, taking in the sunshine. "I should have never come," I said almost to myself.

"I am glad you did. I…" Holmes lowered his eyes. "Perhaps I have grown too hard, too cynical. I wish… virtue were more common in females. Youth and innocence, the general views to the contrary, do not always go hand in hand. Anyway, your gentler methods succeeded where I failed."

"What are you talking about?"

"We have the hint of a name. Turnford, or perhaps 'Stuh' something. Stuford?"

"Why on earth would the old monster care enough about the name to cross it out?"

"Perhaps because she and these Angels have some connection with Mr. Turnford."

"Who are these damned Angels?"

Holmes laughed. "'Damned Angels' is a bit of an oxymoron, unless they are of the fallen variety. I do not know who they are, but I shall find out. They are allies of Mrs. Morris and Flora. Turnford must have introduced Harrington to the girl. The note says as much. Harrington also thought Turnford was behind the blackmail."

"But why?"

"Turnford wanted his money back—and he did not want his name blackened by Harrington. Now Harrington is conveniently out of the picture. Turnford can continue with his business, and Mrs. Morris has a great deal of money."

My head began to throb. "Preying off mens' weaknesses—I wish you had shot the hag! Such a creature does not deserve to live!"

"Calm yourself, Henry. Life and death have little to do with deserving. I shall have to go back there tomorrow and try to get the name from her."

"You would not dare."

He gave a sharp laugh, his gray eyes suddenly dangerous. "You know me better. I shall not be cowed by her or that pathetic ex-pugilist."

"I shall have to come with you."

Holmes stopped abruptly. "I think not."

"I cannot let you face them alone."

"We shall see. I know of a tavern close at hand, and a pint of bitter is most definitely in order."

"I wonder if the girl will get away from her. I hope she takes my invitation to heart. If only Michelle could speak with her…"

Holmes gave a short, sharp laugh. "Do not expect her at your door, Henry. I would like to be proven wrong, but it is most unlikely."

We returned to the house the next day, but repeated rapping on the oak door brought no response. An old man with white sidewhiskers, sitting on his front door step next door, beckoned us over. He told us that Mrs. Morris and her two nieces had left early that morning, taking several large trunks, and he did not know when they might be back.

"A nice enough woman. Always had a smile for everyone. And the girls were certainly beauties. I'll miss them."

Holmes smiled at him but said nothing. I was immensely relieved. I had slept poorly, and the old woman had lurked in my dreams, gray and terrible, while Flora's tearful face stared up at me in mute appeal.

Five

Violet's invitation to dinner had given me an excuse to buy a new dress, but I was troubled by thoughts of my poor patients at the clinic. I set aside an equal sum to distribute there.

The dress did suit me, although it was somewhat risqué. My shoulders and part of my bosom were left bare. The silk fabric was of medium weight, a beautiful shade of green, with no wretched train dragging about on the ground. Our maid Harriet helped me do up my hair, then I put on pearl earrings and a gold necklace, both gifts from Henry. Glancing in the mirror, I was pleased with everything except my hands. They were large and red—fashion and carbolic acid were clearly incompatible. Luckily, gloves were to be worn with my dress, and once I had put them on and tugged their ends up past my elbows, I could pretend to be one of the idle rich.

When I came down Henry was seated in his favorite armchair. The top of him was white—waistcoat, dress shirt, and bow tie; the bottom was black—trousers and patent leather shoes. His black tailcoat was thrown across a nearby chair. He looked very handsome, his brown hair and mustache slightly shaggy. (I hated the shorn Prussian style.)

He glanced up at me. "Good Lord," he murmured. "And who can this be?" He stood, walked over and kissed my throat, then my mouth, his arms encircling me, the starchy sleeves rustling slightly. A little later I pushed him gently aside and tried to catch my breath. His warm hand lingered on my bare shoulder. "I do believe it is Michelle."

"You make me dizzy," I said.

"I might well accuse you of the same crime. If you dress this way, you must expect to be so accosted. Perhaps we should send the Wheelwrights a note that you are feeling ill, and then we might spend the evening at home."

"Oh, no. After all this effort at appearing beautiful, I must be seen."

"And I must suffer every brute at this party ogling my wife!" He shook his head mournfully. "At least I shall have the satisfaction of knowing that the most beautiful woman there will be leaving with me at the end of the evening."

I kissed him lightly on the mouth. "You are a dear." He drew me closer. "No, Henry, you must not get me all hot and bothered." Dimly, we heard a knock at the door. "That must be Sherlock," I said.

Henry released me. "Bad timing on his part."

Footsteps sounded on the stairs, and then Harriet and Holmes came into the sitting room. His black overcoat was unbuttoned. He also wore a dress shirt, waistcoat, and bow tie, his top hat in hand. He appeared very tall, the coat almost like a black cape. With his beaked nose and piercing eyes, he reminded me of some dark bird of prey. Henry helped him off with his great coat, then handed it, the hat and stick to Harriet.

Holmes pulled off his gloves and glanced briefly at me. "Michelle, you look… quite remarkable." He turned and stood before the fire, rubbing his hands.

"Thank you," I said.

Henry withdrew his watch. "The Wheelwrights' carriage will be here shortly."

"It was kind of Violet to insist on sending a carriage," I said. "Sherlock, have you discovered anything further about this mysterious affair with her and the gypsy?"

He turned to us, one hand clasping the other wrist behind his back. "My lack of progress is annoying. Mrs. Wheelwright seems to have no enemies whatsoever, and if someone were angry at Wheelwright, a likelier possibility, why would that person not torment him directly? Especially since he does not much care for his wife."

I sighed. "Oh, Sherlock, are you certain of that?"

He glanced at Henry, then at me. "Yes."

"Are you two sharing some confidence?"

Holmes shook his head. "No." But I saw reluctance in Henry's eyes.

From below came a rapping at the door. Henry stood. "That must be the carriage. I'll get your coat, Michelle."

"I shall wear the black velvet cloak and a shawl."

Henry kissed me on the back of the neck while Sherlock was turned away, then set the cloak over my shoulders. "You are a dreadful pest," I whispered affectionately.

The men put on their black overcoats and took their top hats, and we all trooped downstairs. The evening was a blustery one, the wind cool and heavy with moisture. The clouds had swept in late that afternoon, and I was afraid that our fair sunny weather was gone for that year. The carriage was the one Violet and I had used, and Henry remarked on the smooth ride.

Holmes sat across from us gazing out the window. As we passed a gaslight, his face was lit up, then covered again in shadow. He was staring at me.

"Michelle, I do not wish you to betray any confidence, but can you tell me anything about Mrs. Wheelwright that might assist my efforts on her behalf?"

"You put me in an awkward position, Sherlock. She is both my patient and my friend."

"Anything you tell me will go no further. Need I remind you that she has been threatened and that her life may be in danger?"

I frowned. Sherlock surely had her best interests at heart, but certain suspicions—if that were not too strong a word—I would keep to myself. I had noticed some oddities, which I could not explain even to myself.

"Her general health is good, but she is highly strung. She has almost too much energy. Unlike some of our colleagues, I do not believe in rest and idleness as a treatment for nervous women, but she rushes about constantly. As a result she often has difficulty sleeping. At one time she relied on laudanum, but she assures me that she now takes it only as a last resort. I have told her it is best to rise and read a book or walk about the house, and that seems to have helped her. She suffers from occasional dyspepsia, again I believe because of her frantic activities. She sometimes becomes weary and depressed, but even when her spirits are at their lowest, she keeps up a brave front."

Henry laughed softly. "Insomnia and an excess of energy. Oddly familiar."

Holmes was silent for a moment. "And her childlessness?"

"There are no obvious anatomical problems, but that is often the case with infertility. She was also examined a few years ago by a specialist."

Holmes watched me. "It seems a matter of regret to her."

I bit at my lip. "I... am not so sure." Violet had shown almost no squeamishness during her two days at the clinic: lacerations, wounds, sores, pus, and blood made no impression. But childbirth... A woman had barely made it to the clinic and given birth immediately. Jenny remained at my side, but Violet had simply vanished for those few brief frantic moments.

Holmes gazed out the window. "No instinct is stronger in women than the maternal one."

I opened my mouth, but then closed it. I had learned not to contradict men when they made such overblown generalizations, as it was usually futile. Sherlock had so little real experience with women—how was he to know any better? All the same, in his work he must have met some women in whom greed, ambition, or hatred were stronger than a maternal instinct. Henry gave my hand a gentle squeeze, his way of commending my restraint.

The carriage stopped before the Wheelwrights' house, and Collins opened the door for us, the familiar gap-toothed grin on his face. Inside stood the butler, Lovejoy, his hair and his dress impeccably black. He bowed deeply while other servants took our coats. "Good evening, Doctors. Welcome, Mr. Holmes. It is a pleasure to see you again."

We stepped inside, the great hall already filled with people. Donald Wheelwright stood at one side of the room towering over the two older men next to him. Looking about, I found Violet on the opposite side of the room speaking with someone I recognized—Dr. Matthew Dyson—my predecessor as her physician and a good friend. She saw me, put one hand on Dyson's shoulder, and swept toward us.

She was radiant and absolutely beautiful. Her gown was a pale lavender silk, a darker purple lace forming a pattern, which began at her bosom and flowed down the front of the dress. (She favored the color which was her name.) About her long slender neck she wore a necklace of gold and diamonds; small diamond earrings glittered on each ear. The pallor of her skin and the subdued hue of her dress contrasted with her black hair and dark eyes. Her shoulders were far narrower than mine, the muscles firm, the lines of her throat and arms long and clean.

I glanced to either side of me. Henry's eyes were fixed on her, while Holmes appeared faintly intoxicated.

"Michelle, you look lovely!" she exclaimed.

"Not half so lovely as you."

"Nonsense! I'm sure Henry feels otherwise, as will most of the others here."

Henry put his hand on my waist. "I tried to persuade her to remain at home with me this evening."

The smile on Violet's face did not waver, but confusion showed briefly in her eyes. "How selfish of you! I am glad you decided to share her." Violet turned to Holmes, who had not taken his eyes off her. "It is good to see you, Mr. Holmes. I am glad you could come." He nodded but said nothing. Violet put her lip between her teeth, and glanced about. "You must have some champagne or sherry. Both are available."

A certain awkwardness had crept into her voice, and it surprised me. "Your dress is beautiful, my dear," I said, "and those diamonds!"

She shrugged her bare shoulders. "I think a simple gold chain like yours is more flattering, but Donald insists the family jewels be flaunted."

"Good Lord," Holmes murmured. "Now there is a veritable fortune."

We all turned and saw a sour-looking woman of middle age who wore an incredible necklace. Three of the diamonds were at least an inch across; red rubies and green emeralds surrounded them.

Violet let a ripple of laughter slip from her lips. "Yes, tonight Mrs. Herbert's jewels eclipse all others. I fear the Wheelwright diamonds can hardly compete."

"However, the situation is exactly opposite with regards to the wearers themselves," Holmes said.

Holmes did not look at Violet as he said this, and it took her a second to catch his meaning. She caught at her lip again with her teeth and smiled. "Thank you for the compliment, Mr. Holmes."

"It is no compliment, madam, only the simple truth."

Dr. Dyson approached us with his wife. "I am happy to see, Dr. Doudet Vernier," he began, "that you are taking good care of Mrs. Wheelwright. She appears fit enough. You also appear quite spectacular yourself. If our compatriots who still believe women have no business in medicine could see you now, you might charm them, Circe-like, into changing their minds. Of course, they are already swine." While he spoke he maintained the gravest composure.

I seized his arm. "You are a rogue, but a charming one."

His wife shook her head. She appeared slightly younger than he, just shy of sixty, but she had pure white hair. Her expression was as good-humored as his. "Pay him no attention. He's always pestering someone."

"Michelle, do you remember my wife, Margaret?"

"Of course," I lied. "And you know Henry. And this is his cousin Sherlock Holmes."

Dyson's bushy gray eyebrows dived inward. "Good Lord—the consulting detective?"

Holmes' mouth twitched into a brief smile. "None other."

Mrs. Dyson's eyes had grown very large. "I thought you were dead, Mr. Holmes."

"A rumor only."

Violet laughed. "Thank goodness! I shall not try to introduce you to everyone, but I fear I must at least present you to Donald's parents. Would you excuse us briefly, Dr. Dyson?"

She started through the crowd, stopped briefly before a servant with a tray, and handed each of us a glass. "You must be properly fortified before meeting father Wheelwright."

I took a quick sip. The champagne was cold, bubbly, and delicious.

Ahead of us was Donald Wheelwright, that head with the neatly trimmed brown hair and mustache, the thick neck and wary eyes, rising above all others. He wore the same black evening dress—white shirt and tie—as the other men, but the coat was enormous. I had only met him once or twice, always in passing, and somehow his sheer size had never struck me so forcibly as now. I had not seen him since Violet revealed her physical indifference toward him, and I wondered suddenly what he might be like if he were truly angry. Violet was so small and slight. Given his size and his strength, he might do whatever he wished with her. Despite the glitter of jewels and the extravagant chandeliers overhead, I felt a momentary chill. There was something about his eyes... I took a big swallow of champagne.

"What is it?" Henry whispered, his hand on my waist.

I slipped an arm about him. "Nothing. I'm only a little dizzy." He stared at me, his eyes full of concern, and I thought again how much I loved him. We might occasionally quarrel, but never in all the time I had known him had I been afraid of him. He had always been so very gentle. I realized Violet was speaking.

"I believe you have all met my husband, Donald?"

I raised my head and nodded. You are being foolish, I told myself. Do not make him into a monster. Perhaps he is fond of Violet.

"And these are his parents, Mr. Donald Wheelwright, Senior and Mrs. Jane Wheelwright. This is Dr. Henry Vernier, his wife Dr. Michelle Doudet Vernier, and this is Mr. Sherlock Holmes."

Old Wheelwright and his wife seemed shrunken alongside their son—hard to believe they could have conceived such a giant! His father was not even six feet tall, his wife a good foot shorter. The old man stooped slightly and was quite lean. The pink skin of his scalp showed between the thin strands of white hair; a few bristly hairs jutted forth from his large nostrils; and his blue eyes showed a hint of long-simmering anger.

His coat appeared slightly wilted, and his white shirt had a faint yellow tint. His short, stout, matronly wife in her black dress reminded me of Queen Victoria, but in the brown eyes of her broad, somber face I saw the first resemblance to the son. Their eyes showed the same wariness.

Old Wheelwright managed a ferocious smile, his watery eyes fixed on my bosom. I wished I had my shawl to cover myself. "You're the lady doctor my daughter-in-law is always talking about, eh? I'm not sure I approve of lady doctors." Somehow he made "daughter-in-law" sound insulting.

I was annoyed and said the first thing that came to mind. "I'm not sure I approve of gentleman meat barons."

He scowled at this, while his wife's jaw slackened and dropped, then he laughed. "You don't, do you? I like a woman with spirit, Doctor…" He glanced at Violet. "What was the name again?"

"Doudet Vernier," I said.

"Why two names, tell me that?"

"Since my husband is also a physician, it becomes confusing otherwise. Hence, he is Dr. Vernier, I am Dr. Doudet Vernier."

"I suppose there's some sense in that." His eyes drifted briefly downward as he again ogled my bosom. What a foul old man, I thought. "And this is the great Sherlock Holmes?"

Holmes stared coolly at him. "You may keep your superlatives in reserve. Few men of fame live up to their reputations, I find."

Wheelwright's brow furrowed. "My son has told me what he is paying you. I hope you are worth the price."

"Father…" Donald Wheelwright began, but a sharp glance from the old man cut him off.

Violet kept her smile, but her cheeks reddened.

Holmes also colored slightly, his gray eyes icy. "'Treat every man to his just deserts, and who shall escape whipping?' The phrase may not be exact, but Hamlet said something similar."

The old man gave a gruff laugh. "They do say you are the best, Mr. Holmes, and I am glad to have you working for us in this unfortunate business." It was not quite an apology, but it was the best we might expect.

Holmes nodded brusquely, then turned to Mrs. Wheelwright. "And you, madam, what are your thoughts on this unfortunate business?"

She seemed dumbfounded that she had actually been addressed. "People should not go asking for trouble," she said, "especially since the powers of the devil are strong."

Her husband's lip curled; he laughed sharply. "The virtuous need not fear the devil! I don't believe in curses. The Lord knows, I've been cursed often enough, and yet here I am."

Violet stepped between Henry and me and took our arms. "I must introduce them to some other people, then speak with Mrs. Lovejoy and the cook. Dinner will be served shortly."

The elder Wheelwrights nodded. Henry stared intently at them, and then downed his champagne in a single swallow. "It is always a pleasure meeting one of the pillars of British nutrition. The picture on the tins does not do you justice." He said this so gravely that only Sherlock and I would have known he was joking. The old man appeared puzzled, really seeing Henry for the first time.

"Come, my dear." I drew him away. I could see that Violet was amused. "You will have us thrown out of the party," I whispered.

"I do not much care. I like staring at a pretty woman as much as any man, but there is such a thing as discretion. Oh well, the poor fellow was sorely tempted."

I smiled, but whispered, "Hush."

Violet waited until we were well out of earshot, and then said, "I hope you will forgive my father-in-law's rudeness. He believes that his wealth gives him the right to treat the rest of humanity as his inferiors. Let me introduce you to the Herberts—you can have a better look at the necklace, Mr. Holmes—and then I really must see how dinner is coming along."

Mr. George Herbert was a portly man whose joviality clashed with his wife Emily's sour countenance. Given that he was Mr. Herbert, not Lord Herbert, he must have made his fortune in trade, his wife's necklace the beacon of his success. Herbert grinned as he was introduced, then offered Holmes his plump ruddy hand. Emily Herbert tried to smile, but the rest of her face would not go along.

Violet gave my arm a squeeze, bade us goodbye and turned to leave. Her dress left half her spine and both clavicles exposed, her long slender neck shown to good advantage. I noticed Holmes staring past me at her bare back.

"Well, Mr. Holmes," George Herbert said, "I have followed your career with some interest, and it is a great honor to meet you."

Reluctantly, Holmes turned his gaze upon Herbert. "I am pleased to hear it, sir."

"I have even read your pamphlet on various tobaccos."

"Indeed? You surprise me."

"Of course, I'm partial to hats and coats—they are the key to a man's character. You've heard the business about the eyes being the windows to the soul? Nonsense. I believe it to be the coat. A shoddy tight-fitting coat means a narrow parsimonious soul. A spaciously cut, ample coat is the sign of a generous, expansive nature. Whenever I meet a man, I always take his measure by the coat upon his back."

"How, then, do you judge the fair sex?" Henry asked.

Herbert's smile faded, and he shook his head. "There you have me, sir. I'm afraid the fair sex is something of a mystery. Wouldn't you agree, Mr. Holmes?"

"Yes."

I turned to Mrs. Herbert whose smile was at odds with her

strained, disapproving eyes. "And what do you think of your husband's theories?"

She shrugged her formidable shoulders. "They keep him occupied."

My laughter put some warmth in her smile. She wore a pink dress that did not at all suit her, a gaudy ostentatious thing which clashed with her reserved manner. Surely it was more a clue to her husband's nature than her own.

Holmes was staring at the necklace with the three enormous diamonds–it was difficult to ignore. "Tell me, Mr. Herbert, that necklace–did it not belong to the Duke of Denver? I recognize it by reputation."

Herbert nodded. "Very good, Mr. Holmes. I purchased it from the duke himself some five years ago. His misfortunes were my gain."

Sherlock stared coolly at the man's self-satisfied countenance. "Perhaps, sir." He hesitated. "I have often thought such spectacular jewelry to be more trouble than it is worth."

Mrs. Herbert's eyes abruptly caught fire. "Exactly, sir. *Exactly.*" We all stared at her, surprised by her sudden vehemence. "I have often tried to tell him so."

Herbert gave an embarrassed smile. "My wife, oddly enough, has never cared for the necklace. Why do you say it is more trouble than it is worth, Mr. Holmes?"

"There are literally thieves everywhere, Mr. Herbert. This is tantalizing bait."

"But if one is careful... I assure you the necklace is kept locked in the best safe money can buy, absolutely unbreakable, and whenever my wife wears it–only a few times a year–our stout footman, a very trustworthy fellow, accompanies us everywhere."

Holmes smiled grimly. "That safe only gives you false confidence. As I often tell my clients, such jewelry is best kept locked in a bank vault and treated like bars of gold bullion. Its ornamental value causes one to take foolish risks. One would not blithely wear several thousand pounds in notes strung about one's neck."

Mrs. Herbert gave a ferocious nod. "I am never comfortable in it—*never.*"

Mr. Herbert's face reddened, some of his joviality evaporating. "Surely you exaggerate, Mr. Holmes? Such a thing of beauty should be seen! There must be precautions one might take. What would you advise?"

"Keep a written record of each time you have the necklace out of the safe, never take your eyes off it for even an instant, and have it appraised annually."

"What on earth for? I do not plan to sell it."

"Have it appraised to make sure it is what you think it is—a clever thief could substitute a worthless fake, and the theft might go unnoticed for years."

The color slowly drained from Herbert's face. His wife seized his arm. "George, are you well?"

He took a big swallow of sherry. "Such a thing could not happen." He managed a smile. "We are too careful."

Holmes shrugged. "I recall a case involving a large emerald which had been in the family for years. When the owner went to sell it, he discovered he had only a fake. The theft may not have even been during his lifetime."

Herbert took another glass of sherry from a passing servant. "Well, at least I had it appraised at the time of purchase. The theft must have happened in the past five years." He gave a hearty laugh, but his wife was not amused.

"I think you should take Mr. Holmes' advice and lock the wretched thing up."

"No, no, Emily. You look far too charming for me to be willing to shut it up."

She gave a weary sigh, but for the first time something like affection showed in her face. "Oh, George, you are hopeless."

"After all, my dear, I got it for you."

"So you always say."

From somewhere above us came a booming crash. Holmes whirled about. Lovejoy stood on the balcony above us holding a pair of cymbals, his demeanor magisterial. Beside him stood Violet.

"Dinner is about to be served. Do come upstairs and be seated." She stepped back, and Lovejoy crashed the cymbals again. A muted laugh swept through the gathering.

"Lord, those things gave me a start," Henry said.

Holmes nodded. Mrs. Herbert said, "She does something different every time. In August it was trumpets."

We started for the stairway. I took Henry's arm. Mr. Herbert gazed about warily, worried now that some jewel thief lurked nearby.

Dr. Dyson and his wife Margaret waited for us. He stroked thoughtfully at his white, gray and brown beard, his fingers lost in its depths. Margaret held his other arm loosely with her gloved hands.

"Michelle," he said, "you do have a prosperous look. Of course we know why, do we not, Henry? Her practice is thriving because she has stolen all our patients—batted those charming blue eyes—brained them and hoisted them away in her bag."

"Matthew!" his wife exclaimed. "What a dreadful accusation! You wretched men certainly deserve the worst. How you love to prod and poke at us poor creatures! Say what you will, women are gentler."

Another woman spoke to Margaret, and she turned away. I slipped my hand about Matthew's arm. "You know, of course," he said, "that I was only jesting. I'm happy to see you succeed. Pioneers like you have shown your opponents' fears to be mere prejudice."

I laughed, but I was moved. "Oh, Matthew, you are such a dear. Not only do you ridicule accusations of patient-snatching, but you actually refer people like Violet to me. You are the most good-hearted soul I know."

Dyson flushed slightly, but I could see he was pleased. "I knew Violet would do better with you. She is a charming lady, and like you, she laughs at my jests, only..." We were halfway up the stairs.

"Only...?"

"Something was troubling her, I could tell, but she would never confide in me. Of course, I was only her doctor, not her minister, but I felt I was missing some vital information."

I thought about Violet's distaste for Donald. "We all have our troubles," I murmured.

Dyson laughed gruffly. "Too true, but this did not seem the usual thing." His voice dropped almost to a whisper. "Not the usual marital disharmony. Not childlessness either."

My amazement must have shown, and he laughed. "We stodgy old men are not all blind, Dr. Doudet Vernier. At my age, you have seen certain... patterns repeat themselves so often that you have an instinct for them. I am rarely surprised anymore, but, with Violet I... Oh, pardon me, Mr. Holmes. I should watch where I am going."

Holmes had been farther ahead with the Herberts, but he was suddenly just before us, and Matthew had nearly walked into him. I knew at once that he must have been listening.

"Not at all, Dr. Dyson. The fault is mine."

The large double doors were open, and as I stepped into the dining room I gave an involuntary gasp. It was like an enchanted palace. The light came from enormous candelabras of ornate silver, two and even three feet high, with white tapers each a foot long. The candelabrum at the center of the long table held ten candles, the flames at a level taller than a man. The warm yellow-orange light glittered and sparkled off countless surfaces of glass, crystal, and silver. The damask tablecloth had a subtle, white-on-white pattern, and each place setting had four sterling silver forks, four spoons, four knives, and four glasses, all resplendent. The napkins were neatly folded and stood like elfin crowns. Crystal vases and pale white china bowls held exotic flowers—lilies, orchids, roses—or luminescent yellow-green moss or darker green ivy. In the corners of the room were ferns, huge potted things, which belonged in some prehistoric jungle. The guests cast flickering shadows against the dark wood and floral wallpaper.

Violet appeared at my side and took my arm, the diamonds at her throat catching the candlelight. "I have been selfish," she whispered. "I put you and Henry near me." Her skin had a warm glow of its own.

"Oh, it is all so beautiful," I murmured.

Violet released me before my chair, which Henry politely pulled out for me. At my place were the menu and a folded card with my name on it. Ravenous, I felt ready to devour all five courses on the menu—soup (turtle), fish (poached salmon), meat (beef Wellington or stuffed quail), sweet (chocolate cake), and dessert.

Henry shook his head. "The tablecloth looks clean enough to operate upon. A pity we must spoil such splendor by actually eating here."

The man beside me, a clergyman who recalled a mournful raven, gave us a disapproving stare. The two elderly Wheelwrights had the place of honor at the head of the table, and to their left were this elderly clergyman in black and his equally thin, dour wife. Donald stood to the right of his father, surveying the room and his guests, his face placid, his eyes uneasy. Soon everyone at the table except Donald and the minister were seated, but hovering nearby were Lovejoy and the footmen in formal attire.

"Reverend Killington will say the benediction," Donald said loudly. His voice had a nervous edge. He sat, and we all bowed our heads.

"Father in heaven, we thank thee for thy bountiful gifts which we are about to receive, and we pray that in these troubled and iniquitous times our hearts may remain pure and unsullied. When the dreadful judgment day comes and thou strikest down the wicked and sendest them into the fire, we pray thou wilt have mercy on our poor souls. We ask this in the name of thy son, Christ our Lord."

The Reverend Killington had a piercing tenor voice worthy of an Old Testament prophet. As I was seated next to him, I was relieved when he finished. I raised my eyes and across the table saw Violet's mocking smile. Briefly she raised her right eyebrow.

Everyone joined in the "amen."

"Thank you, Reverend Killington," Donald said.

Smiling fiercely, the elderly Wheelwright nodded. "The Reverend knows how to pray."

"It is my profession." The Reverend Killington sat absolutely upright—as if his spine had no curve to it. His face was thin, his hair mostly gone on top, but he had black bushy eyebrows and brown eyes which glowed like two hot coals.

Violet introduced us to the Reverend and his wife. The room, meanwhile, had filled with maids in black dresses and white aprons who served soup from tureens on carts. The soup was green and smelled odd.

Henry shook salt and pepper on his, and then took the first spoonful with great relish. "I have not had turtle soup in a long time."

I forced a smile. I did not care for turtle soup, but I knew I must eat some. The Reverend Killington had an odd look in his fiery eyes. He certainly did not approve of woman physicians, and he probably also thought my dress was a deliberate provocation, my flesh offered up as a temptation.

"So you are a doctor, madam?"

I knew at once from the accusatory tone that I had guessed right. I nodded and tried to smile. From the brief downward shift of his eyes,

I saw that my other guess was also correct. He was less obvious than Donald's father, but dinner would be an ordeal if I had to spend it with the two old men leering at my bosom between mouthfuls.

Violet must have read my thoughts—certainly she was likely to share my fate since her lavender dress revealed both shoulders and the curve of her breasts. "She is a very good doctor, Reverend, and a stout-hearted one." A faint hint of truculence was in her voice. "I am sure she has seen sights which would make your hair stand on end, but she is a great comfort to the sick. I can vouch for it."

Killington's long nose pointed toward her. "What exactly do you mean?"

"I have worked with her at the clinic for the poor."

"Violet..." I began.

"Oh, how can you bear it!" exclaimed Mrs. Killington, going even paler. "I do so hate sickness. It makes me positively ill."

"It is God's work," Violet said. "Does the Bible not bid us care for the sick and dying?"

Donald Wheelwright said nothing, but his bland face somehow radiated disapproval.

The Reverend Killington reddened. "You presume too much, Mrs. Wheelwright. I do not believe the Almighty meant the weaker sex to be subjected to bloody sights and death. That stern conflict is reserved for men. Women should remain at home and provide their husband and their children with the shining example of their virtue."

"This soup really is delicious." Henry smiled at Violet. "My compliments to the cook. I do not much care for bloody sights and death myself, and I have never been able to figure out why Michelle should be so much less squeamish than I. Truly the ways of the Lord are mysterious. Why would He give such a strong stomach to a mere woman?"

Killington seemed too surprised to speak. Violet laughed and said,

"Would you care for more soup?"

"Yes, but I think I shall just take Michelle's. She is too polite to tell you that she does not care for turtle soup. She had a pet turtle as a child who was quite dear to her."

I laughed and put my hand over his. "It is true. Françoise *la tortue.*"

"And what of you, Mr. Holmes?" Violet said. "You are very quiet."

"The soup demands my concentration, madam. It is very good."

"And do you also disapprove of women doctors?"

He glanced at me, then said gravely, "I dare not."

Henry nearly choked on his soup. "A wise answer, Sherlock."

"I suppose," the Reverend Killington said to me, "that you also believe in the vote for women?"

I sighed wearily. The two older women looked shocked.

Violet raised her right eyebrow again. "Oh, she could not!"

"Oh, no," I said. "Of course not."

Henry began to cough and had to help himself to a glass of water. The maids took our soup bowls and passed out plates with pink fillets of salmon.

"I am relieved to hear it. Such an inversion of the natural order would mean the ruin of the British Empire, its total collapse."

"I wonder if the good weather we have had will return." Under his breath Henry whispered, "Only an hour or two to go."

"How many glasses of champagne did you drink?" I whispered back.

"Oh, I do hope so!" exclaimed Mrs. Killington. "Jane, dear," she said to Mrs. Wheelwright, "we must go out for a carriage ride should the good weather return."

"The devil is close at hand," Killington muttered. "This great metropolis is little better than Sodom or Gomorrah, harlots everywhere. We invite the wrath of the Almighty, his avenging angels, we beg for it." His eyes fell on Donald Wheelwright. "Do you not agree?"

"These are… uncertain times."

Violet turned to Sherlock. "Have you seen the new production of *Il Trovatore* at Covent Garden, Mr. Holmes?"

"No, but I am going later this week."

"How fortuitous. Donald and I shall also be attending. I hoped you might tell me whether it was worthwhile."

"The cast is first-rate, and the productions have been very strong this season, both musically and dramatically. *Lohengrin* was sublime."

Killington nearly dropped his fork. "Wagner!" he said, stabbing at his salmon. "The profligate whose music glorifies lust."

"I thought so, too," Violet said, "but you surprise me. I believe one must have a fundamentally romantic nature to appreciate Wagner."

Holmes shrugged. "I would not know about that. The music is beautiful."

"But what could be more romantic than a white knight riding on a giant swan to rescue a maiden in distress?"

Holmes smiled. "It is a curious mount."

"Familiars of the devil," Killington muttered.

The maids began to circulate again, gathering up the fish plates. A girl appeared behind the older Wheelwrights and set a large plate before each of them. The meat baron had a slab of rare beef Wellington, while his wife's appeared practically burned. Beside the beef was a mound of mashed potato, yellow melted butter floating on top.

Holmes and Violet were discussing leitmotifs in the music dramas of Richard Wagner, much to the amazement of the Herberts and another couple across from Henry. Donald and his father were talking, or rather the old man was speaking about, the day's business. Jane Wheelwright and Mrs. Killington listened to the Reverend denounce the poor for bringing their afflictions upon themselves. Henry occasionally joined in the musical conversation, although I had often heard him say it was not humanly possible to stay awake during an entire Wagnerian opera.

I accepted a plate of beef Willington rather than the stuffed quail. The buttery potatoes did look delicious, but courtesy dictated that I wait. Jane Wheelwright seemed to feel the same temptation. Her face was directed toward the Reverend Killington, but it was obvious where her thoughts were focused. She had not eaten any salmon. The short plump fingers of her right hand toyed with the beautiful sterling silver spoon. She glanced at her husband, then at the Reverend and his wife, and quickly took a spoonful of potato. Confusion showed momentarily in her brown eyes, then fear.

"Aghh!" she cried, mashed potato dribbling from her mouth. "*Aghh!*"

"Jane—what on earth…?" began her husband.

She spit out as much of the potatoes as she could. "Poison!" she cried. "Poison!" Her chair fell back as she stood and pointed one finger at the mashed potatoes. "They are bad! Oh, that taste—get me something! Do something!"

Violet, Donald, Henry, Sherlock, and I all stood at once, while all conversation in the dining room came to a halt. I could see the sudden fear on all of the faces about us.

Holmes stepped around to Mrs. Wheelwright's side. "Calm yourself, madam."

"He is right," I said. "Do sit down."

She gazed up at me, and I could feel her shoulder trembling under my hand. "They taste so awful—it burns. Oh, I am sure I shall die—poison, it must be poison!"

"No one would poison you, my dear. Please sit down."

Holmes had picked up the plate; he placed it under his large nose and sniffed vigorously. His brow wrinkled. He set the plate down, then took a bit of potato on his long forefinger and touched it to his tongue.

"Have a care, Sherlock!" Henry said.

"It is poison!" Mrs. Wheelwright wailed. "Poison…"

"Hush," I whispered. "You must not frighten everyone."

Holmes took a larger taste and chewed thoughtfully. In a loud clear voice, he said, "It is not poison, but only soap. I would not recommend the potatoes, but I guarantee no one will die from eating them."

Relieved laughter greeted the pronouncement. Everyone began talking at once.

"Soap?" Violet's voice was incredulous. "Soap?"

Holmes' mouth formed an ironic smile. "With cayenne pepper mixed in, not paprika."

"Oh, Lord," Violet whispered. Her mouth contorted into an odd smile, and a laugh slipped from her lips.

"How can you laugh?" Donald Wheelwright's voice was soft, but his anger was all the more pronounced.

"Oh, do sit down," Violet said. "As Mr. Holmes said, no one will die from eating these potatoes. I shall have extra rolls served. The poor cook will be mortified. How shall I ever break it to her?"

"Break it to her?" Wheelwright's hands made fists a good six inches across. "Dismiss her at once!"

"She is not responsible. She would never do such a thing, and she will feel far worse about this than you."

"Let me accompany you, madam," Holmes said. "I want to have a look in the kitchen before anything is touched."

"Ah." Violet nodded. "The Case of the Peppered Potatoes. If anyone can get to the bottom of this mystery, it is you, Mr. Holmes. Come, the game is afoot!"

Her husband stared at her as if she had gone quite mad, but Holmes began to laugh, gently at first, then with rare gusto. Violet started for the kitchen, and he followed, still laughing.

"It was not poison?" moaned Mrs. Wheelwright.

"It was soap, Jane," her husband said.

"Soap? But it burned."

"The cayenne pepper," I said. "Sit down and eat something. It will make you feel better. I am sure you are hungry."

"I couldn't eat a thing. This awful taste. It won't go away."

"Have a drink of wine. It will help wash away the taste."

"I don't usually drink wine," she said. I took a glass of claret, then helped her drink it. "It is very strong." She took another sip, then sighed. "I do feel better."

"Have some meat now."

She glanced at the potatoes and shuddered. "Get them away—please get them away!" I took her plate, used a knife to push all her potatoes onto my own plate, then sat hers back before her. "Thank you, Doctor."

With a sigh I sat down, put my napkin on my lap, then cut off a big piece of meat and began to chew.

Killington scowled down at the mashed potatoes. "This is the devil's work for certain."

I let my knife drop and turned to him. "Do be quiet!"

I must have been the first woman to ever speak that way to him; his astonishment was complete.

"Eat your meat, Jeremy," his wife said.

"Please pass the rolls," I said to Donald Wheelwright. Everyone else had begun to eat, but he still sat staring dumbly about, his eyes wrathful. I would not want to be the person who had put soap in the potatoes if Wheelwright ever discovered his or her identity. He handed me the basket, and I took a roll.

"The beef is excellent," Henry said to Donald, "very tender."

Wheelwright nodded but said nothing. Eventually he composed himself and began to eat. Although the main course was off to a shaky start, the food and wine soon restored everyone's spirits. Even Mrs.

Wheelwright appeared better after she had consumed her burned meat and several rolls. Only the Reverend Killington was reluctant to eat, no doubt because he believed the meal came from the devil's kitchen.

Holmes and Violet soon returned.

"Well, Mr. Holmes—" old Wheelwright gazed up from his half-consumed rare beef— "have you found the perpetrators?"

"I have not."

"A bar of soap is missing," Violet said. "Somehow it must have fallen into the hot potatoes. I am certain it was an accident."

Her husband's face darkened, and Holmes appeared skeptical. Old Wheelwright gazed at him sharply.

"You do not believe it was an accident, Mr. Holmes?"

"I do not. One accident might be a possibility, but that would not explain the cayenne pepper."

Old Wheelwright gave a snort of laughter. "Probably some sly devil's idea of a joke."

His wife's eyes widened in horror. "A joke—*a joke!*"

The old man turned to his son. "By the way, I've done some checking on that Steerford fellow. Can't find out anything bad about him, but I wouldn't give him a penny."

Mr. Herbert was talking with Henry, but he suddenly turned toward the Wheelwrights, his interest all too obvious.

Wheelwright raised a bony finger and tapped the side of his nose. "I trust my nose, and it tells me things don't smell right."

"But Steerford comes highly recommended, and he seems a decent enough chap," Herbert said. The two Wheelwrights stared silently at him, their disapproval evident. Although they were not physically alike, something in their gaze—in the expression itself—was uncannily similar. Herbert reddened slightly. "Begging your pardon, that is—if I might intrude."

Violet smiled at him. "Such conversation is reserved for that time after the ladies depart. Finance and tobacco go well together, but monetary matters should never be mixed with food. Indigestion is sure to result."

Herbert laughed, his stout body quavering. "Your point is well-taken."

I had finished eating, and the serving girl asked if she might take my plate. I nodded. Herbert was telling Henry about some business difficulties. I pretended to listen, but the Reverend Killington was difficult to ignore. He was explaining to Violet and the two elderly ladies that the decline in British civilization was caused by women turning from the old ways and their proper sphere. Violet showed the patience of a saint, but I had to fight to keep my temper. The Reverend obviously meant me to hear—he wished to provoke me—but I would not give him the satisfaction.

Holmes had dissected his quail with all the skill of a surgeon—only tiny bones remained. Now he seemed to be listening to several conversations at once, probably in the hope of discovering something significant. He was like some predatory creature waiting silently and patiently.

At last Killington turned directly to him. "Do you not agree, Mr. Holmes? Does not this outrageous behavior of these contemporary females disturb you? Wherever will it all end?"

Holmes gave a slight shrug. "Such matters are hardly my concern. Nor do they much interest me."

Violet's mouth formed the familiar mocking smile, but her dark eyes were not so detached. "You are lucky, Mr. Holmes. We ladies are rarely allowed the luxury of disinterest."

Killington's eyes widened in disbelief. "The public morality does not interest you, sir?"

"Frankly, Reverend, it does not."

Killington, all too briefly, seemed at a loss for words.

After the plates had been carried away, Lovejoy entered pushing a cart bearing an enormous chocolate cake covered with small flaming candles. Several *ah*s were heard. I was speaking with Violet, who had not seen the cake. "Whose birthday is it?" I asked.

"Birthday?" She set down her water glass, touched her lips with her napkin, and looked over her shoulder. "Oh, no." She shook her head. "I am not to be spared, after all." She turned to her husband. "Have I you to blame for this?"

He said nothing, but a faint smile played about his lips. Perhaps he has some feeling for her after all, I reflected.

Donald moved his chair aside, and two of the maids set the cake on its silver tray before Violet. I had never seen such a large cake; it was nearly two feet wide.

Mrs. Lovejoy stood smiling nervously behind her mistress, her pale face contrasting with her black dress. "Begging your pardon," she said timorously. "Excuse me, ladies and gentlemen." The room grew silent. "Today is a special day, our beloved mistress's thirtieth birthday, and this seemed too good an opportunity to miss. She insisted there be no fuss, but it was not difficult to convince her to have her favorite dessert served—cook's special devil's food, six-layer chocolate cake."

"Devil's food," Killington muttered darkly.

"We hope you will all join us in a birthday song."

Everyone sang. Violet rolled her eyes upward and sat silently, the mocking smile pulling at her lips. When we finished, there was applause. "Blow out the candles, ma'am," said Mrs. Lovejoy.

Violet looked at Henry and me. "Given Pasteur and Dr. Lister's theories, I doubt our house physicians will approve of my spreading microbes, but I swear I am in good health." Everyone laughed, and she blew the candles out.

"Well done!" Herbert said, and there was yet more applause.

Mrs. Lovejoy took a plate and a silver knife. "The first piece is for you."

"Let me get it. Besides, that way I can make sure it is large enough." This statement drew more laughter.

Violet sat almost directly across from me, and I saw her thrust the knife into the chocolate cake. Her dark eyebrows plunged, a puzzled look on her face. "How odd. Something is..." She used a silver cake server to take out the thick piece she had cut. Instead of a complete triangle, a wedge, there was only the outside part of the cake, a chunk that left a notch showing in the cake. "I believe..."

Things happened so suddenly then that they remain a blur of impressions. Mrs. Lovejoy clapped her thin white hands to her face and screamed, a hideously loud and piercing sound, and staggered back. Violet shoved the cake away from her. Donald Wheelwright moved faster than I thought so large a man possibly could—he hurled his chair aside and backed away, knocking over one of the maids. Everyone else at our end of the table rose except for Holmes, who leaned forward, entranced.

Out of the opening in the cake had come the largest spider I had ever seen, a monstrous black thing, its torso an inch across, its slender legs giving it a breadth of four or five inches. Smaller brownish-black spiders poured from the cake, but they were not so fast as the big one. He ran madly for the other end of the table, the white linen providing a dramatic backdrop for his sinister, sable form. As he proceeded on his erratic path, chairs were upended and people backed away wildly from the table.

Half the people in the dining room—not all of them women—seemed to be screaming. "Oh God!" I heard Henry cry. More chairs fell over with bangs; water glasses, coffee cups, and saucers smashed.

Insects do not usually disturb me, but I was startled. Seeing them swarm from the cake like maggots from a corpse was unbelievably nasty. A wave of revulsion passed over me. For an instant I too wished to flee, but I forced myself to master my fear. Sherlock, Violet, and I were the only ones still near the table. Violet stared at me, then grabbed for her chair and sank down.

Sherlock's face was flushed, his eyes filled with excitement. "Incredible!" he exclaimed. "*Incredible.* I have never seen such a specimen of *tegenaria.*"

A hand grasped my arm tightly. "Lord, Michelle—get away!"

I turned. Henry was ashen.

"They cannot hurt us."

"For God's sake!—*humor me.*"

I stepped back. A brawny maid swept into the room; her stout hands raised a broom overhead, her grim eyes resolute.

"Kill them!" a man shouted, his deep voice shrill. "*Kill them all!*" It was Donald Wheelwright. He seemed to have completely lost his reason and reminded me of a frightened horse or dog, terror manifest in his visage.

The maid would have probably demolished the cake, but Holmes seized the broom handle. "Have a care—you must not disturb the cake!"

"Yes, sir."

She moved aside, bringing the broom down with a great *whoomph* on the table. Those few glasses left standing were knocked over, and the silver candelabrum at that end fell, some tapers breaking, others toppling onto the floor. "Got them!" She raised the broom, and I could see smashed spiders smeared across the white linen. The wrathful broom rose and fell several times, but Holmes stood guard over the cake.

Dr. Dyson appeared at our side, a glass of brandy in each hand. "Drink this." He offered Henry and me a glass each.

Henry snatched his, swallowed it down, then turned away from the table with a shudder. "Filthy buggers!"

I shook my head. "I do not need it. I have had enough to drink this evening." I was impressed with Matthew's composure. "You are so calm."

"I spent some time in the tropics. One grows accustomed to ungodly large spiders and beetles."

His wife nodded her approval at the maid. "That's right, dear—whack the little beggars!"

Matthew shook his head. "Luckily I brought along my bag, doctors. We have plenty of work before us. No strokes or heart failures, I hope, but several very shaken people."

"I shall be with you in a moment," I said. "First I must see to Violet."

"Don't get too near!" Henry exclaimed.

I put my hand on his cheek. "Please calm yourself, darling. You cannot help anyone when you are like this. You are being rather silly. The spiders cannot harm us."

He took a deep breath, and much of the wildness went out of his eyes. "I… One spider might be tolerable—but so many!"

"Hush."

He took my gloved hand and kissed my knuckles. His color was returning. "Next time I suggest remaining home for the evening, I hope you will listen to me."

I smiled faintly. "So I shall."

I walked around the table. Old Wheelwright stood surveying the crowd, his face pale. A ghastly, trembly smile contorted his lips.

Violet still sat in the chair staring at the wrecked table with the smashed spiders, broken glasses, and china. I pulled off my glove and put my hand on the bare skin of her shoulder. She glanced up at me. Her face appeared thin and flushed, a wild gleam in her eyes; her mouth twitched briefly into a smile that reminded me of Sherlock.

"How are you, my dear?" I asked.

"I shall never forget this birthday."

Holmes was bent over the cake. At last he stood up and thrust his hand into the opening where Violet had cut out the piece. "My God!" someone shrieked. He withdrew a small envelope smeared with chocolate, tore it open and withdrew a note. His gray eyes glared, but his mouth twisted into a frightful smile.

"Hah!" he shouted.

"What on earth is it?"

He handed me the note. Violet stood and read it with me.

Mr. Sherlock Holmes cannot save you from me and my little friends. Next time they will eat you, not cake.

A.

Michelle and I did not get home from the disastrous dinner party until well after midnight. It was a fortunate coincidence that three physicians had been invited. Many of the ladies—and gentlemen—young and old alike, suffered from hysterical shock. Others had been physically injured.

One lady, in her alarm, pulled the chair out from under her husband, and he landed hard upon his coccyx. This may sound comical, but if the bone breaks, it is extremely painful, and one cannot sit for weeks. The maid that Donald Wheelwright had bowled over struck her head against the wall and was briefly knocked unconscious. Old Mrs. Wheelwright had fainted dead away.

Perhaps the saddest case was the cook. She blamed herself for everything, although she was clearly not responsible. At first she insisted she would pack her things and leave at once. Both Michelle and Violet tried to calm her. Finally she agreed to remain, but she was inconsolable. Before we left, Michelle gave her a sedative to help her sleep. She kept muttering that she was disgraced, that she would never cook again.

Holmes wanted to question her about the cake, but Michelle would not allow it. She told Violet to make sure the cook went back to work in the kitchen the next morning; that would be the best thing for her.

I sympathized with the cook. My own actions during the cake cutting were a major source of embarrassment. True, I had not completely lost my reason like Donald Wheelwright, but my irrational fear seemed foolish and unmanly. It had taken Michelle's remarks—and her touch—to bring me to my senses. Early in our relationship I had grudgingly realized who was the stronger person. I was only a fair-weather physician, while Michelle would have made an excellent army surgeon.

By way of absolution, I resolved to return to the Wheelwright's house the next day. Someone needed to check on the casualties, and as usual, Michelle's morning schedule was full. The hansom pulled up before the townhouse shortly after ten. The rain had returned, the day overcast and gloomy. A footman let me in, and then took me to Lovejoy, who appeared none the worse for wear.

"Ah, Dr. Vernier, how good of you to come. Mrs. Wheelwright went to bed at last, while Mr. Wheelwright has just risen. Your cousin, Mr. Holmes, is in the dining room."

"When did he arrive?"

Lovejoy smiled. "He never departed."

"Good Lord—he has spent the entire night here? Well, I shall want to see the little maid that struck her head—Alice, wasn't it?—and the cook and your wife. How is your wife doing this morning, Mr. Lovejoy?"

"She is better, but still gravely shaken. She does not have a strong constitution to begin with, and such a disturbance... We men may laugh at spiders, but to a woman's fainter heart, the loathing is quite genuine."

I managed a smile. "No doubt, although you must have noticed that several of the men—especially your master—had an equal dread of spiders."

Lovejoy gave a reluctant nod. "It is true, sir. The fact was well known in our household, as I told Mr. Holmes this morning. Nothing infuriates the master more than finding a spider in the house. Mrs. Lovejoy always stresses this to the maids. Frightened though they might be, they must tell her, and she, poor dear, who loathes them herself, gets one of the footmen to destroy the creature. The point has been driven home many a time, and as a result, I can truly say this house has always been free of spiders. We have been ever vigilant."

"I am sure you have."

"Perhaps you would like a cup of coffee with your cousin before you get to work."

"That would be very kind."

We went upstairs. The enormous dining room appeared different, vast and mostly empty, the warm, subdued light of the candles replaced by the dull gray light of the cloudy sky. Gone were the white linen tablecloth and napkins, the splendid sterling silver settings, the vases and bowls of colorful exotic flowers, and the throng of guests and servants. The bare brown table had shrunk, many leaves no doubt having been removed.

Holmes sat at one end of the table, a cup of coffee before him, a cigarette in hand. He was pale, and the fatigue seemed to be setting in. His black tailcoat had been removed, but he still wore the dress shirt, waistcoat, and bow tie. They had lost the crisp, freshly starched look of the evening before and, like Holmes, appeared slightly wilted. Next to him, on the table, was the infamous chocolate cake.

"Good morning, Henry. You look much rested."

"I wish I could say the same for you. Did you sleep at all?"

"Of course not. I wished to think."

"I have told you before that one thinks better when one is rested."

"And I have told you that I disagree." He sipped at his coffee. A maid appeared with another cup and poured me some.

"Thank you." I turned to Holmes. I did not want to look at the cake. In spite of myself, it set my insides crawling again. "Have you discovered anything?"

"Yes, but it is most frustrating. Someone has gone to a great deal of effort to humiliate me, and..."

"Humiliate *you*?"

His gray eyes showed anger, and he stubbed out the cigarette in a huge crystal ashtray. "*Yes*." He pointed at the note from the cake. "This was meant for me as much as the Wheelwrights."

"Could this person have known you would be present?"

Holmes gave an annoyed snort. "Do not be obtuse. Of course they did. This has all the marks of an inside job. I always considered the gypsy story ludicrous, and this is further confirmation. It should be one of the servants, but what servant would go to such ridiculous lengths? Someone has a peculiar sense of humor."

"Humor?" I set down my coffee cup. "You call that *humor*?"

"It is very black humor, but humor all the same. Did it never strike you as amusing last night? To see the cream of London society, all those ladies and gentlemen in their finery, reduced to a hysterical mob, knocking furniture, glasses, and each other aside in their panic to escape? Once some time has passed and your own fears have dwindled, you will see the comical side."

"I do not think so. You have a peculiar notion of the comical."

He frowned. "You mistake me if you think I could ever condone such a thing. The people's fear was all too genuine. Comical it may have been, but cruel, as well. It was not a trivial matter to pull off. We are dealing with a very clever and determined person. I simply cannot believe it was a mere servant. Have you given any thought as to how the spiders came to be placed in the cake?"

"I... I suppose someone in the kitchen..." Again my intestines seemed to writhe. "Yes, it must have been one of the cooks who..."

"But how would this person have placed live spiders inside of a cooked cake? It would have been quite a project. To begin with, many spiders were captured—this in a house reputed to be free of spiders. Then the entire center of the cake was hollowed out so that it resembled a tube cake. The spiders and the message were put inside, then the open center was covered with a circle of stiff paper and the whole thing frosted over. Such a cake would take considerable time to prepare, yet the cook and her assistants made the cake in the early afternoon, working together. It was placed in the pantry off the kitchen. They all swear the cake was a normal one. Once made, you could not easily tamper with such a cake; sabotaging it would be a difficult and messy business. So how did the spiders get into the cake?"

I frowned. "I had not thought... I do not know." I could not repress a shudder.

"What is it, Henry?"

"I was thinking about someone trapping all those spiders, especially the big one. What a loathsome monster."

"They were all harmless, Henry, and they too are to be pitied."

"I hope you are joking!"

"Not at all. They were taken from their natural habitat, stuffed into a cake, and then most of them were slaughtered unnecessarily. They committed no crime. That theatrical performance last night says far more about the nature of humans than that of spiders. The big one was a beauty, an extraordinary specimen of *tegenaria domestica*, also called 'the cardinal' because one of its distant relations so frightened Cardinal Wolsey. At least the big spider appeared to escape with its life. This business with the cake was concocted to frighten and to appear supernatural. We were meant to think the spiders appeared in the cake by diabolical means."

I could not restrain another shudder.

Holmes laughed. "Come, Henry—you must know better! Does the devil stoop now to culinary maleficence? Brimstone in the biscuits, sulfurous sauces, and the like? No, no. The cook insisted last night and again this morning that the cake was not hers. This morning she was calmer, and I tried to stimulate in her a sense of outrage. She said the color of the frosting there is wrong; she tasted it and said it could not be hers, as it was made with lard, not butter. Now do you see how it was done?"

"No."

Holmes sighed, nostrils flaring. "They switched cakes. The pantry had a door to the outside; someone came in and substituted that cake with the spiders for the benign one."

"But that would…" I frowned. "You are correct about the trouble involved. Why on earth…? And it must have been someone in the household, someone who knew exactly what kind of cake was to be served."

"Yes!"

"But what servant would have the time—or the money—to construct such a cake?"

"Now you begin to comprehend my frustration. Of course, the results of this extraordinary effort were spectacular. One must grant our opponent that. No one who attended will ever forget last night's party."

"One can imagine an angry servant slipping soap in the potatoes, but the cake is on a different scale altogether. Who can have done it?"

Holmes took out his silver case and withdrew a cigarette. "There is a familiar suspect in affairs where the wife has been mysteriously threatened." I stared incredulously at him. "You do not catch my meaning?" He said softly, "The husband."

"You cannot be serious!"

"It is a possibility which must at least be considered."

"I have never seen a man so frightened in my life. He was nearly out of his mind. How could he ever devise such a plan? Moreover, he came to you."

"That could be meant to distract us. However, you have pointed out the main problem. I also doubt he could have ever willingly gone along with such a scheme given his dread of spiders. Quite a foolish dread–I cannot say they would not hurt a fly, but humans had nothing to fear from that batch. Perhaps Wheelwright had an accomplice, one whom he let improvise."

"I would not want to be that accomplice when Wheelwright gets hold of him."

Holmes laughed, knocking off a long cigarette ash. "Quite so, but who else might have the imagination–and the resources–to concoct such a scheme? None of the servants, except possibly Lovejoy or his wife, seems likely."

"But Mrs. Lovejoy was hysterical, and why would they do such a thing?"

Holmes suddenly slammed his fist against the table, rattling our cups and saucers. "How should I know?" He stubbed out his cigarette. "Pardon my bad temper, but I... Perhaps it is only egotism, but I almost wonder if *I* am not the real target of this business, the Wheelwrights mere pawns. Perhaps it is–" his lips twisted into a weary smile– "...my Moriarty."

I opened my mouth, then closed it. Again, I had the odd sensation of something crawling about in my belly, and I wanted to leave the Wheelwrights' house. Holmes had focused on the comical side of the infected cake, but to me the black side was far more evident. Only a deranged mind could have dreamed up so cruel a trick. Holmes had many enemies, and Watson had made him famous. What if a criminal genius had determined to humiliate and destroy him? I took a final swallow from my cup. "I do not think you are being egotistical."

Holmes stood, raised his long arms overhead, and yawned as he stretched. "I am truly tired. I wish I could leave."

"Why do you not?"

"I do not wish to postpone an unpleasant encounter with Mr. Wheelwright."

As if on cue, the door at the far end of the room opened, and Donald Wheelwright strode toward us. He was pale, and he had a small nick on his right cheek where he had cut himself shaving. One look into his eyes, and I knew we were in for trouble. His dress was immaculate: black frock coat and waistcoat, gray satin cravat with a diamond pin, striped trousers, black boots with pointed toes, everything brushed and pressed. I realized abruptly the difference between then and the first time I had seen him—he had been disheveled that afternoon.

"What have you to tell me, Mr. Holmes?" He folded his arms and remained standing.

"I cannot tell you who is behind this business, although that is surely what you want to hear."

"I have been humiliated—humiliated!—and in my own home. Whoever will dare set foot in my house again?"

Holmes sighed. "I share your humiliation. You have no comparable reputation to live up to, and if your friends are so easily frightened away, they are of the fickle sort hardly worth bothering with."

Wheelwright's hands formed those two massive fists. "I won't be talked to that way!"

"Then perhaps I should leave. It has been a long night, and I am rather fatigued."

Wheelwright's eyes showed disbelief. Given his size and his position, people would be deferential, but I had never seen Holmes back down before any man. He was brave, it is true, but reckless at times, and the owner of quite a temper. My own instincts were more conciliatory.

"He has not been idle," I said. "He has figured out how the spiders came to be in the cake."

A shadow passed over Donald Wheelwright, and his face grew paler still. He glanced down at the cake, and I saw the revulsion strike him anew. "I want that out of here!"

Lovejoy had entered the room behind his master, and he stepped forward, seized the silver tray with the cake, and walked briskly toward the kitchen. Wheelwright sat down and wiped his forehead with a handkerchief, his anger forgotten. Remembering how I had felt myself, I sympathized.

"Did you get much sleep last night?" I asked.

His head turned slowly toward me. "No. Very little."

"Let me leave you something to take tonight. You will feel better after a good night's rest."

"Thank you." He took a deep breath. "What was this about the cake?"

Holmes started to explain, but I stood up. "I must see to my patients."

"I shall join you when Mr. Wheelwright and I are finished," Holmes said.

"Very well. Oh, how fares Violet this morning? Michelle will want to know."

Donald Wheelwright lowered his eyes. "I have not seen her."

Holmes took out his cigarette case. "She was up all night. I spoke to her before she retired this morning. She appeared quite calm."

"Calm!" Wheelwright mouthed the word to himself.

I went to the kitchen and found Mrs. Grady, the cook, and her two assistants hard at work. She was a tall woman with large hands and broad shoulders, her black hair shot through with gray. One assistant was peeling potatoes, the other working on pie dough, but Mrs. Grady stood before a large cutting board. She held an enormous butcher knife, her hands bloody, two piles on the wood—one of chopped and one of whole kidneys. Close by sat a bowl filled with cubes of raw beef. Obviously dinner was to be steak and kidney pie, a dish I could not tolerate. Every since my anatomy classes, I could not bring myself to eat either kidneys or liver.

"How are you feeling this morning, Mrs. Grady?"

She gave a resolute sigh. "Much better, Doctor. That drink your good wife gave me made me sleep like a babe. And the mistress and Mr. Holmes both spoke to me this morning and cheered me."

"Mr. Holmes spoke with you?"

"About the cake. He explained what those devils did. By God— should I ever catch them!" By way of emphasis she brought her muscular forearm down quickly, the blade chopping a kidney neatly in two. "Somehow knowing... knowing it was not my cake—that my cake had nothing to with the frightful business—made me feel so much better. Saboteurs they was, Mr. Holmes said, saboteurs, and he swore he'd catch them."

"If anyone can catch them, Sherlock Holmes can."

"And Mrs. Wheelwright told me she would be lost without me, that every woman in London envies her. She is very sweet. She suggested I make the master's favorite dish by way of... by way of restitution. I pride myself on my sauces, but he likes a steak and kidney pie better than anything. Of course, when the crust is done just right and the gravy the proper thickness, it is a dish fit for a king. The trick is not to overcook the kidneys and make them tough."

"I am glad to find you so recovered."

"Someone has to look after the mistress, after all. Mr. Holmes said if I was to leave, who would make sure the food was fit? No saboteurs will meddle with my kitchen again, I promise you." Again the knife hit the board with a *thunk*, another kidney lopped in two.

"I shall see to Mrs. Lovejoy next and then Alice."

"I'll have Rose here show you to Mrs. Lovejoy's room. Poor little Alice. Of course Mr. Wheelwright didn't mean to knock her down, but she's a tiny thing. Do thank your lady for me, Doctor. I was most upset last night, and she was so kind to me."

"I certainly shall."

Rose wiped off her hands on a towel, then led me into the servants' wing. We paused before a stout door, and I rapped lightly. "Mrs. Lovejoy, it is Dr. Vernier. May I see you?"

"One minute, please."

"Thank you, Rose," I said.

She curtsied. "You're welcome, Doctor. Oh, and Alice is just there, four doors down."

"Come in," Mrs. Lovejoy said.

I turned the brass knob and opened the door. The room was dim; the curtains drawn. Mrs. Lovejoy wore her customary black dress, and she lay upon the bed, one hand across her forehead, palm up.

"How do you feel today, Mrs. Lovejoy?"

"Not well, Doctor." Her voice was tremulous, her eyes wild. "I fear we are all doomed."

"Surely not. Everyone has survived the evening."

She sat up abruptly. "The devil is loose in this house, Doctor! The Evil One—Satan himself! He toys with us!"

Her fear and excitement were somewhat contagious, her voice deafening, but I remained cool. "Calm yourself, madam. There are other agents besides diabolical ones."

"It was no agent—it was Satan, I know it! How else came those filthy vermin—those wretched spiders—into the cake? He breathed upon it! He touched it with his sulfurous breath and left those vile crawling things, his minions of…"

"Do not work yourself up, madam. There is a simpler explanation. Mr. Holmes is certain a cake was prepared with spiders and substituted for the cook's good one. The devil had nothing to do with it."

Her eyes abruptly came into focus. "What?" She drew in her breath, then a sharp laugh burst out. Her mouth twisted into a peculiar smile. She turned away, but another laugh slipped out. Her laughter had an ugly edge.

"Please, Mrs. Lovejoy." I seized her arm. "Please calm yourself."

"He thinks he is so clever, your Mr. Holmes. Well, I know it was the devil–I know it! There is evil here in this house, and now we must pay. The Fiend will not be satisfied until we are all damned–until we all burn naked with him in the fires of hell! All their pride and money will be no help, then, not against that fire–everyone will writhe and twist–and burn–and scream…" Her voice rose in a deafening crescendo.

"Stop it!" I cried. "*Stop that!*" I shook her.

Her eyelids fluttered, and she put her hand over her forehead. "What? Oh, yes. Yes…" She drew in her breath. "Forgive me, Doctor. I did not sleep well, and…"

"I shall give your husband something for you to take tonight, and I do not want you in here alone in this gloomy room."

She touched my hand with her fingers. They felt hot but faintly clammy. "Whatever must you think of me?" She stood. "I'll go and see how the mistress is faring. First I must wash up." I stared closely at her. "Have no fear, Dr. Vernier. I shall follow your advice."

She seemed to have recovered, and I was glad to leave her. I wondered about her sanity. Alice was quite a contrast. She appeared so young and healthy, her spirits so good, that I told her she could certainly go back to work. She had a nice goose egg on her head, but her youthful exuberance had shaken off the dark events of the prior evening.

I left the servants' quarters, turned down a hallway and saw Lovejoy talking with the older Donald Wheelwright. My frown was involuntary, but perhaps the old devil was kind enough to check on his son and daughter-in-law.

Lovejoy gave me a wary look, but Wheelwright smiled ferociously and approached me, his top hat in hand. "Good morning, Doctor."

"Good morning, sir. You seem fit today."

"It takes more than a few bugs to ruffle my feathers."

"Your son does not seem to share your attitude."

The old man's smile changed to a scowl. "He's a fool—a silly fool—a woman. I've told him so from the time he was a boy, but he won't listen to me."

"One cannot always control one's fears. It is not a matter of mere will."

"Nonsense." Wheelwright's jaw snapped at the air. "But that's not what I wanted to speak to you about."

"No? What then?"

"My daughter-in-law, Doctor. She is a lunatic."

"*What?*"

He smiled again. "Oh, you're taken in like all the others, but it's true, you know." He watched me closely, but I said nothing. "She's beautiful, I admit that, but quite mad. Soft and weak, too, like a woman. It wouldn't matter so much if she wasn't barren. Women aren't good for much else, not really, not if you don't care for the filthy business."

I gave him a look of utter astonishment, and my face grew warm.

"Come, come, sir—we are men, are we not?"

"I— I do not share your views."

"As you will. All the same…" His eyes watched me very closely. "My son's marriage is… ridiculous. Always has been. Your wife is her doctor. If he could be freed, I would be most grateful, most grateful indeed."

"What are you talking about?"

He sighed wearily. "I've misjudged you. I should have known. You're no better than all the others. Your cousin is worse yet. No help from the great Sherlock Holmes. Being able to resist a woman's charms is a genuine talent, one all too rare. Good day to you, sir." He nodded and walked past me down the hallway.

I stared dumbly at him. The brief conversation left me feeling oddly disgusted. I went downstairs and found Holmes and Lovejoy by the entranceway. Holmes had put on his black tailcoat. "There you are," he said. "How are your patients?"

"Mostly better." I opened my medical bag. "Mr. Lovejoy, this small vial contains a sedative. Give your wife about five drops in a glass of water at bedtime, twice that for Mr. Wheelwright."

Lovejoy nodded. "Very good, sir. Five drops and ten."

"And should your wife behave at all… strangely, send word at once to me or my wife. She should be better tomorrow."

"I am sure she will be. I shall try to persuade her we are in no immediate danger from the devil. I shall see to your coats, gentlemen, and have the carriage brought round."

I turned to Holmes. "Did you see Mr. Wheelwright, Senior? Count your blessings, if not. He behaved most curiously."

Holmes' eyes narrowed. "I shall want to hear about it."

"I see you survived your conversation with his son."

"Yes. Your mentioning the cake seemed to de-fang him. We discussed–" he looked around, but we were alone– "the Lovejoys and his household affairs. They have his complete confidence, although the wife is something of a fanatic. He also does not consider it unusual that Mrs. Wheelwright handles nearly all his finances. She also has his confidence." He smiled ironically.

Lovejoy and a footman returned with our coats and top hats. We put them on and stepped outside. The overhang of the roof sheltered us from the cold incessant drizzle. The doors behind us opened again, and a different footman rushed up to us, his face flushed. The Wheelwright footmen were spared gaudy antiquity, but this fellow had powdered hair, white stockings, a red jacket, and buckles on his shoes.

"Mr. Holmes—Mr. Sherlock Holmes? Ah, thank heavens! I tried Baker Street, but your landlady said you'd been out all night. Please, sir, you must come at once—the master is powerful upset. The house is just down the street—number twenty-seven."

Holmes' gray eyes stared wearily at him. "And who is your master?"

"Mr. George Herbert."

Holmes closed his eyes. "Blast it. We shall walk. Twenty-seven, you said?"

"But I can bring round the carriage straight away."

"I prefer to walk."

Holmes had long legs and set a quick pace; I always had to work to keep up with him, my own stride being more leisurely. "What can Herbert want?"

"Do not be obtuse, Henry. I must say he has acted quickly. He was probably at the jeweler's shop as soon as it opened."

"Good Lord," I murmured. "The necklace." The rain was cold on my face.

"Yes. He has had it appraised. Now he too will want miracles from me."

"Out of one madhouse and into another," I said. "Mrs. Lovejoy seemed close to a mental breakdown. She rather worried me. I wish I could have seen Violet. Did you spend any time with her during the night?"

Holmes abruptly stopped walking and stared at me, his eyes incredulous.

"I only meant—Sherlock, you know what I meant. As neither of you

slept, I only wondered… Forgive me, it was an impertinent question."
My face felt flushed.

Holmes gave a snort of laughter. "No, it was an honest one. She spent
most of the night in the library, while I was in the dining room smoking
and thinking. She did come to visit me at about four in the morning. We
shared a cup of warm milk in the kitchen. It was remarkably peaceful
after the pandemonium the evening before. I am sure Mrs. Grundy or
the Reverend Killington would not approve of my being alone with a
married woman, but I assure you I was the perfect gentleman." His
voice had a faint hint of irony or contempt.

"There can be no question of that."

"She said we must speak of other things than spiders and gypsies;
otherwise she would never be able to sleep. We talked about…
many things. Do you recall Michelle mentioning Mrs. Wheelwright's
occasional dyspepsia?"

"Yes."

"She tried to hide it, but she did appear to be suffering from some
pains. I noticed her pressing her hand against her side. The warm milk
seemed to comfort her."

I frowned. "I do not like that. She could have a stomach or duodenal
ulcer."

"She is quite a remarkable woman," he said. We had arrived at the
house numbered twenty-seven.

"In what way?"

"In *every* way."

Holmes used the ornate brass knocker to rap at the front door.
Another distraught-looking footman in the same ostentatious red livery
opened the door. We followed him upstairs. A door opened and Emily
Herbert stormed out followed by a matronly old servantwoman. Mrs.
Herbert had clenched her fists, and her eyes were furious. When she

saw Holmes, her lips drew back to reveal her large jagged teeth. She managed a nod, but said nothing.

The old woman dabbed at her eyes with a lacy handkerchief. "Oh dear, oh dear."

We stepped into the library. George Herbert was seated in a large armchair with the necklace on the table before him. Also present was an elderly man with wavy white hair curling over his outstretched ears. From his formal dress, I surmised he was the butler. He clasped the cupped fingers of one hand with those of the other, then repeated the motion with his hands reversed. He had brown age spots below his knuckles.

"Thank God you've come, Mr. Holmes." Herbert's face was pale, his thick neck ballooning out from the tight, starched wing collar. "It was exactly as you said. That thing is a fake, a well-made one, but a fake all the same. Whatever am I to do?"

Holmes' mouth drew into a tight line as he started to remove his overcoat. At this, the elderly butler staggered to his feet to help. The old man set the overcoat on a chair, then arranged the top hat and walking stick.

"You ask me whatever are you to do. Well, it is too late for me to tell you. You have already further bung… mismanaged things."

Herbert was surprised. "What do you mean?"

"I mean, sir, that by now everyone in your house knows the necklace has been stolen and the news is well on its way about the neighborhood. By dusk half of London will know of the theft."

"Surely you exaggerate, Mr. Holmes."

"Not at all, Mr. Herbert. Had you consulted me first I would have told you to pretend nothing was amiss. I could not have promised anything, but there might have been a chance, albeit a slight one. Now, however, if the thief is one of your household—the likely case—that person has his guard up."

Herbert's dismay was apparent. "I only thought…"

"You did not think, sir–that has been your problem all along, but we shall have to do the best we can. I am not hopeful. I believe you said you purchased the necklace five years go? Yes, then it could have been stolen almost any time. Where was it kept?"

Herbert raised his hand. "Behind the picture there."

Holmes grasped the pastoral landscape with cows by the frame and set it on the floor. "Yes, the safe is, at least, a decent one." He put an ear next to it and turned the knob. "In good working order. You have, I trust, committed the combination to memory."

Herbert's looked to the floor, then out the window. "Not quite."

Holmes ran his hand across his forehead and into his oily black hair. "I suppose you have it written on a piece of paper. And where is this piece of paper kept?"

"Locked away, Mr. Holmes–locked away in my desk drawer there." Herbert seemed pleased with himself.

Holmes' gray eyes shifted to the desk, and he struggled, visibly, with his temper. "In the desk. A child could pick that lock, Mr. Herbert–a child could force the drawer open. What is the point of buying an expensive, well-made safe if you leave the combination lying about? Why did you not just leave the necklace in the drawer along with a note saying, 'Please steal me?'"

Herbert said nothing, but his eyes glistened.

Holmes sat down, withdrawing his cigarette case from his pocket. "May I smoke?" He withdrew a cigarette, and then lit it, his fingers quivering. "I am tired, Mr. Herbert, and already… rather frustrated. As you may have deduced from my dress, I have not been home since the party last night."

"That wretched party. I wish I had never gone. I am ruined."

Holmes inhaled deeply on the cigarette. "Surely not, although you have lost a good sum of money. About a hundred thousand pounds, I'd wager."

Herbert groaned, then nodded.

"Good Lord," I murmured.

"But you still have your business and your home. You are not the first man to be robbed, nor the last. You are still a wealthy man."

"It was much of my fortune, Mr. Holmes. Twenty years work gone down the drain."

"Tell me, who officially knew—besides yourself—that the necklace was kept in the safe there?"

"My wife, of course, and Firth, our butler." The old man wearily raised his head; he seemed even more heartsick than his master. "No one else really."

"Who took the necklace from the safe when it was to be worn?"

"I did—oh, and Mrs. Dalton. I would take it from the safe and give it to her. She took it to my wife and helped her put it on."

"Did she watch as you opened the safe?"

"No, no—she waited outside the door."

"But could she have seen you with the key to the desk in your hand?"

"Possibly."

Holmes closed his eyes briefly. He walked to the fireplace and flicked off an enormous ash from his cigarette into the grate. "I shall want to speak with her."

"She was with my wife. You must have seen her as you were coming in. She has been with our household for over twenty years. I trust her completely. An amiable woman who reminds me of my old nanny."

"All the same, I shall want to talk to her—now, if that is convenient."

"Firth, could you fetch Mrs. Dalton?"

The butler slowly stood. "Very well, sir." He remained bent over as he walked. Holmes waited until the old man had closed the door.

"Who runs your household, Mr. Herbert? I doubt your butler is up to the task anymore."

"Emily has no head for figures, Mr. Holmes. Mrs. Dalton oversees the servants, the menus, our dealings with tradespeople, and the accounts. Firth used to do it, but as you noticed, he has declined over the years. I shall soon have to put a younger man in his place."

Holmes took a final draw on his cigarette, then tossed the remnant into the fire. "I take it your wife is quite angry?"

"Furious, Mr. Holmes. Furious. I... Some day that tongue of hers will get her into trouble. I am a patient man, but I shan't be vilified in my own home. She does not understand the benefits to us of mingling with the better classes. She forgets how little she had when we were married, what a good husband I have been, and how much she owes me."

Holmes gave me a quick, ironic glance. "Women can be most ungrateful."

"Mr. Herbert," I said, "were you at the Paupers' Ball at Lord Harrington's?"

He nodded gravely. "I was. I'm not superstitious, but a man has to wonder. Harrington cut his throat, Jenkins gone mad. Perhaps this gypsy..."

"Who is Jenkins?" Holmes asked.

"Richard Jenkins. Made his fortune in steel, owned the biggest ironworks in London. He used to live not three houses away. Went completely crazy and had to be put away. I heard about it at my club. Emily knew his wife, a friend of Violet's."

The door swung open, and Firth let Mrs. Dalton in. She was still dabbing at her eyes with the handkerchief. A stout woman, she wore the familiar white lacy cap and a white apron over her black dress. Her jaw was wide and permanently thrust forward, a dental defect that gave her the truculent look of a bulldog.

"Such a tragedy!" she exclaimed. "Such a tragedy."

"Mrs. Dalton, I am Sherlock Holmes."

"Oh yes, I have heard of you."

He gestured with his long fingers at the false necklace. "What can you tell me about this?"

"Nothing, I fear." Her face scrunched up, tears appearing in her eyes. "Except my poor master is heartbroken, and the mistress is very upset."

"Yes, yes, Mrs. Dalton. But what do you think happened to the necklace?"

"I'm sure I don't know, sir!"

"You know the household well. Whom might you suspect?"

"None of us, sir! Certainly not! Burglars it must have been, cracksmen. They must have come in late one night and opened the safe."

"How would they have known about the safe?"

"They has their ways, Mr. Holmes. Some are fearsome clever."

Holmes nodded. "No doubt. Mr. Herbert tells me you would take the necklace from the safe to his wife on those occasions when she wore it."

"Not from the safe—no, sir—from Mr. Herbert. I don't know nothing about the safe. I stayed outside. I wouldn't want to accidentally see what I wasn't meant to."

"And you always took the necklace directly to your mistress?"

"Straight away—and clutched to my bosom. No one could take it from me."

"And you put it around her neck yourself."

"Oh, yes." Her forehead became a mass of wrinkles. "Usually."

"There was an exception?"

"Let me see now. Yes, when we had that maid a year back, Gwendolyn Harper, she was named. She was with us only a few months, before I sent her packing. You recall, Mr. Herbert, the business with her young man. Shameless, that."

Holmes' finger drummed impatiently at the table. "You were about to explain the exception."

"Oh yes, she took the necklace from me at the mistress's door and insisted she'd put it on the mistress. Said it was her duty."

Herbert sat up in the chair. "I recall her now—a very surly girl of lax morals. She was insolent and was not with us for long. You don't mean to say you actually handed the necklace over to her?"

"What else was I to do?" Mrs. Dalton sobbed loudly, sniffled, then began to cry.

Holmes' gray eyes were fixed on her. "Calm yourself, madam. So you suspect this girl, do you?"

She nodded slowly. "I do, Mr. Holmes. She was a bad sort, that one. Always putting on airs, and so proud. She didn't like the mistress and the master or the rest of us."

"Why did she not like them?"

"She said…" She glanced warily at Herbert. "She complained about the wages and the treatment she got. She was lucky to have a roof over her head and three good meals a day! Ungrateful, very ungrateful—so many of these young girls are that way nowadays."

"What were her wages?"

Herbert stiffened. "I hardly think that has any relevance."

"Let me worry about the relevance. What were her wages, Mrs. Dalton?"

"If the master doesn't wish me to say…"

Herbert gave a resigned sigh. "You may tell Mr. Holmes."

She moistened her lips with her tongue. "Seven shillings a month."

Holmes stared at her, then turned to Herbert. "A month? Surely you mean a week?"

Herbert stared at his hands. "No, those were her wages."

Holmes looked at Mrs. Dalton. "And what are your wages, madam?"

"I cannot tell you, sir."

"I wish to know."

"Well, I'll not tell you." Her defiance was manifest in her eyes and her jaw, and she twisted the handkerchief with her big hands.

"I pay her a pound a month," Herbert said.

A sharp laugh escaped Holmes. "After twenty years service? Perhaps we had best discuss my fee, Mr. Herbert. I expect more than a guinea or two."

"Mr. Holmes!" Herbert struck the table with his fist. "You shall have whatever you wish. Within reason."

"Oh, thank you." He turned to Mrs. Dalton. "So you think this girl might have arranged the theft because of her... ingratitude?"

"I don't like to speak poorly of anyone, sir, but yes, I do." She glanced at her employer. "I could make inquiries. Someone may know where she is living now."

Herbert nodded. "That's very good of you, Mrs. Dalton. Please do so."

"Yes, sir." She stood, but Holmes was between her and the door.

"Tell me, Mrs. Dalton, have you many friends in the neighborhood?"

"Friends?"

"At other houses. Such as the Wheelwrights'."

She did not falter, but I sensed the wheels turning briefly before she answered. "A few."

"That is not surprising, since they live so close. And who might these acquaintances be?"

"The cook, Mrs. Grady, is my friend. She's the best cook in all of London."

"Anyone else?"

She hesitated and again moistened her lips. "Mrs. Lovejoy I know. A little."

He stared closely at her, but she would not meet his eyes. "Have you nothing more to tell me, Mrs. Dalton?"

"No, sir."

"Are you certain of that?"

She nodded, her jaw shifting as she briefly ground her teeth.

"Very well, you may go, but I shall wish to talk to you again soon."

She drew in her breath, and then seemed to notice the handkerchief in her hand. With a sniffle, she dabbed at her eyes. "A tragedy it is. I only hope I can be of help."

Holmes closed the door behind her. "Normally one tries to determine who might have a motive for a crime, but if these wages are typical, any of your servants might wish to rob you."

Herbert grew red in the face. "You do not know the entire story, and there are other compensations—such as the Christmas bonus."

"Oh, no doubt—no doubt." He pulled out his cigarette case again, then thrust it back. "I can do nothing more here. I shall return tomorrow." He picked up his overcoat, draped it over his arm, and then took his hat and stick. "One caution. Have someone keep an eye on Mrs. Dalton. I want her to be here when I return."

Herbert stood. "Surely you cannot suspect her? As I said, she has been with us for over twenty years—she is part of our family and does admirable work."

"We shall discuss my suspicions tomorrow, Mr. Herbert. We shall also discuss my fee."

"I assure you, Mr. Holmes..."

"Tomorrow."

Herbert tagged along behind us, puffing to keep up. From the sound of his breathing I knew his lungs were not in good condition. Holmes strode down the hall, taking the stairs two at a time, then put on his coat as he crossed the mammoth entry room, the black wool swirling about him. Firth nodded weakly at us, while the footman opened the door. Herbert mumbled an apologetic farewell, but his words were lost in a gusty wet wind that assailed us. The rain had stopped, and patches of blue showed in the gray sky as the sun struggled to appear.

"Imbecile," Holmes muttered. "Stingy imbecile."

"So you think that Mrs. Dalton might be the thief? She did remind me of my grandmother."

"That, I believe, is the desired effect. Yes, I suspect her."

"And not the maid?"

Holmes gave a snort of derision. "That was her mistake. She was too quick to bring up the maid. Far too convenient—a suspect who is not available to confirm or deny Mrs. Dalton's allegations. Herbert is busy thinking about the maid instead of the fact that Mrs. Dalton is the one person who regularly handled the necklace. Switching it would be a simple matter."

"Someone else might have opened the safe. You did say anyone might get the combination from the drawer. Why would Mrs. Dalton do such a thing?"

"Henry! Were you not listening? Because he has paid her a pittance for over twenty years! He decorates his wife as if she were a Christmas tree so all of society will know of his riches and success; yet he pays a maid seven shillings a month. And then there is his handling of the necklace. He *is* an imbecile."

I seized his arm. "Do slow down a bit. You are practically running."

"Oh, very well."

"Did you eat any breakfast?"

"Uh… perhaps. Nothing substantial."

"It is well past noon. You must be ravenous."

He took a deep breath. "Very good, Henry. A sound deduction."

"Unless you are going somewhere else in particular, we might stop for lunch."

"I am going nowhere but away from this wretched street and the homes of Mr. George Herbert and Mr. Donald Wheelwright. I have had my fill of their company. I know a restaurant close by, a twenty-minute walk, which serves a superb hot corned beef, boiled cabbage, and potatoes with horseradish on the side."

"That sounds delicious. Then I must be getting home. I shall have much to tell Michelle. I wish I could have seen Violet."

"Violet," Holmes murmured. He stopped walking, turned and stared down the street at the elegant row of townhouses with their immaculately groomed lawns and shrubbery, their neat walkways, their red brick and green ivy, their stately trees. He raised his stick and swept the end in an arc to encompass them all. "She does not belong here. She is better than any of them—she is wasted here, *wasted.*" He closed his eyes and let his stick fall. The iron tip clacked against the pavement. "I am weary, Henry."

"You will feel better after you have eaten." We resumed walking. I knew exactly how he felt. I would be happy to get home to Michelle.

Seven

The day after the party I was very busy with patients, but after a quick supper, I took a cab to the Wheelwrights' home. Henry did not want me to go, and truly, after the events of the past twenty-four hours, I would have been happy to spend a quiet evening with him. All the same, Violet was my friend and my patient—I felt I *must* go, especially since Henry had not seen her in the morning.

Lovejoy was surprised, but since I had my medical bag, he must have assumed it was a professional visit. Ladies of good breeding did not make social calls after supper. He told me Mr. Wheelwright was out, and then assured me that the cook, Alice, and his wife were all feeling much better and did not require my attention. A maid, Gertrude, led me up two flights of stairs to Violet's bedroom.

Gertrude knocked lightly at the door. It swung open. "Yes?"

"Ma'am, the doctor is…"

"Oh, Michelle—you need not have come. You must be exhausted yourself."

"I wanted to see you, Violet."

"Come in. Thank you, Gertrude."

The bedroom was an enormous one, easily larger than our sitting room, and very inviting. Many of my wealthy patients had terrible taste, their bedrooms overflowing with bric-a-brac, lace, gaudy drapes, patterned wallpaper and borders, and baroque furniture. This room was clean, bright, and simply done, the curtains and the wallpaper cream-colored, the carpet a reddish Persian pattern. The bed had no canopy, and the chairs were comfortable-looking but not ornate. A large desk sat near the tall windows, books and papers covering it. Violet's nightclothes were also simple, not the silk negligee or robes one might expect, but a white nightgown of cotton flannel which fell to her feet, and over it, unbelted, a pure white wool robe. She gestured at a chair near the fireplace.

"Sit down. You do look tired."

"I am weary. It was a very busy day. Where will you sit?"

"I shall bring over another chair in a moment. I do not want to sit just yet."

I was only too happy to rest. A chunk of glowing coal gave off welcome warmth after the damp chill of the cab ride.

Violet stared down at the black iron grate. She held out her hands, her long slender fingers spread apart. They began to quiver slightly. She made fists, then thrust her hands into the pockets of her robe. Her face appeared pale and thin, but her dark eyes were restless, agitated. Her long black hair fell nearly to her waist. I had not seen her before with her hair down; she appeared younger and slighter, oddly vulnerable. Perhaps it was only that I was accustomed to seeing her elegantly dressed with not a hair out of place. The robe and gown hid her woman's shape; she reminded me somehow of young waifs I had seen on the street.

"I fear I am hardly presentable," she said. "I hope you do not mind."

"Of course not. You look very comfortable. I envy you."

She gave me a smile that had none of her usual irony. "Take off your boots if you wish and join me in my slovenly ways."

"Thank you, I shall." I bent over and undid the buttons, then slipped my feet free. The boots were well made and did not have the high heels and pointed toes fashion decreed, but it was still a relief to have them off after a long day. I thrust forward my feet and flexed my toes before the fire.

"Ah…" I murmured. "This is the best I have felt all day."

The room was very quiet; the wind rattled the windowpanes gently. Violet took a step closer to the fire. Her bare feet protruded from under the lacy hem of her nightgown. Her feet were pale, her toes long and slender like her fingers.

"I am glad you came, Michelle. I was…" Her voice faded away.

I reached out and gave her wrist a squeeze. "How are you feeling, my dear?"

She raised her shoulders but said nothing.

"Lovejoy tells me Alice and the cook are perfectly well. And his wife is much better."

"Thank God for that," she said.

I sighed and closed my eyes. It would have been easy for me to fall asleep in that chair. With the bustle of the day done and the room so warm and peaceful, I could feel how fatigued I really was. "I wish there was something I could do, some way I could help you."

"Oh, Michelle, you have helped me—only… I cannot—I cannot bear your kindness—I do not deserve it. You are so… good. You are everything I am not." Her voice broke, and her eyes filled with tears.

"What are you saying? Your servants worship you. You are known throughout London for your kind heart and your good work. I have seen you at the clinic. Somehow you understand my patients; they sense it. You are one of the few women of your class I know who is completely free of prejudice and vanity."

"Oh, Michelle." The tears started down her cheeks, and she turned away. "If you only knew… what your friendship means to me… what…" She took a deep breath, her back straightening, and she rose up on the balls of her feet and clenched her fists as she struggled to master herself. Suddenly she wilted, knees bending, body twisting about as her right hand clutched at her side. "Dear God." Her face went white.

I was out of the chair at once. I did not try to make her stand but guided her to the chair. She collapsed and bent over with a groan. "Oh, it hurts…"

"Try not to fight it so," I said. "It will pass. Take a deep breath. Yes, that's good."

Slowly, she straightened up, a peculiar smile tugging at her lips. "That was the worst one ever."

I frowned. "Have you been having these pains for long?"

"For a while, but not so often. Since last night they come and go all the time."

"What kind of pain is it?"

"Very sharp. I imagine a knife slipping between one's ribs would feel that way."

"Is it better or worse on an empty stomach?"

"Worse."

"When did you last eat?"

"I… I am not exactly sure."

"You did not eat supper?"

"I could not face Donald—not today. I…"

"Violet, that is foolish! You must eat regularly. You may have the beginnings of a stomach ulcer." Actually, it was probably quite far along. "Where is the pull for the maid?"

She took a deep breath and sat up. "There, by the bed."

I walked over and pulled twice. I poured a glass of water from the pitcher on the nightstand. "Drink this. It should help."

"Thank you." Her color was coming back, but she still held her hand to her side.

There was a knock at the door. I walked over and opened it. Gertrude looked up at me; she was so small she made me feel like a giantess. "Your mistress needs some food. Could you bring some hot soup and bread up on a tray?"

"Certainly, ma'am."

I closed the door, then walked back across the room, picked up a chair and carried it over next to Violet and the fireplace.

Her mocking smile had returned. "Thank you, Doctor."

"Violet, you must take care of yourself."

She sighed, and then put her lip between her teeth. "I shall try."

I put my hand on her shoulder; she felt so bony, so slight. She was only five or six inches shorter than I, not tiny like Gertrude, but next to Violet I must resemble some brawny peasant lass. She brought out both my maternal and professional instincts: she needed to eat more—she was far too thin.

"Is the pain better?"

"Much better."

With a sigh, I sat down, stretched out my legs and flexed my toes again, warming them. "I shall want you to eat quite regularly, and every hour or two between meals you must drink some milk."

She made a face. "I do not much care for milk, Doctor."

"Consider it medicine and drink it down."

She let go of her stomach. "I suppose it could be worse. It could be cod liver oil."

"You take that after the milk."

She gave me an incredulous look. I laughed, and she smiled. "Thank you again for coming. I was so dreading this evening, this night. I…"

I waited for her to continue, but she did not. "You should have sent for me if you were having pains."

"I did not want to bother you, especially after last night."

"Violet—it is no bother. Even were you not my friend, it is my work. Promise me that if the pains change, if they grow… more severe, you will call me at once."

She looked up at me, her cheeks slightly flushed, her dark eyes bright.

"Promise me."

"Oh, very well."

"Ulcers can be quite serious if left untreated. I shall… I should speak with your husband."

Her hand clutched at her side. "You must not!"

"He should be told."

"*No.*"

"Why not?"

She said nothing, but glared at the fire.

The sadness caught me by surprise, my fatigue augmenting it. "Do you hate him so much?"

She glanced at me, and now her brown eyes truly seemed to burn, to smolder, like the red-hot coal on the grate.

"Oh, Violet, he must feel something for you—I know he does. When the cake was brought out…"

"You know nothing about it. *Nothing.*" Her voice was colder than I had ever heard it. I had an odd feeling at the nape of my neck; I turned away. "You are upset. Why?"

"Because you hate him—because you are unhappy, and it should not be that way."

She sighed. "It is as I said. You are too good."

"You are good, too."

She gave her head an emphatic shake, a hard, sharp laugh slipping from between her lips. "No, there you are wrong. I am not good. Quite the contrary."

"That is nonsense! I told you so. You deserve to be happy."

"Do I? Does anyone deserve happiness?"

"Everyone deserves happiness."

She smiled. "The Reverend Killington would be interested in your view. Does even Donald deserve happiness?"

"Yes, but perhaps... perhaps apart from you."

Her smile was cruel. "That is all rather beside the point. I could never obtain a divorce. As a man, his adulteries are excusable under the law, and my virtue is intact. However, if *I* could find a partner in sin, then Donald might be persuaded to divorce me. Unfortunately, I have neither the time nor the inclination."

My face felt hot, and I stared in horror at her. "What are you saying?"

"Oh, he has a mistress, a plump little blonde thing. No doubt that is where he is tonight, seeking consolation."

"Is this some... joke?"

"No joke, I assure you."

How would I feel if I ever discovered Henry had been unfaithful to me? I wanted to speak, but my throat seemed to have closed off.

There was a knock. I rose quickly and went to the door. "Thank you, Gertrude." I took the silver tray and carried it over to Violet, then returned to my chair.

The grief had come from nowhere, and it all whirled about—the look in Violet's eyes, the thought of how such a betrayal must hurt, the sense of what my life would be like without the love that sustained me. I did not trust myself to speak yet.

Violet frowned, then set the tray down before her chair and stared into the fireplace. "Oh God, how I loathe myself." Her hands curled into fists, and one slipped again to her side. "I had no right to tell you—to burden you with my shame. I knew it would disturb you, but I went ahead anyway. Can you forgive me?"

I gave an impatient sigh. "For God's sake, Violet—will you not believe I am your friend? There is nothing to forgive. The hurt, after all, is yours, not mine."

"Will you not understand? There is no hurt."

"The pain, then." I suddenly understood. "The shame—the rage, the anger—it is pain."

"Ah." She laughed once. "Yes, perhaps... You are perceptive."

I drew in my breath resolutely. "Now eat your soup. We are both too tired to know exactly what we are doing or saying."

She picked up the tray and set it on her lap. She removed the silver dome covering the soup bowl. "Perhaps there is something to what you say." She took a spoonful of soup, showing even then a certain graceful elegance.

I took a slow, deep breath. The thought that Donald Wheelwright had a mistress still shook me. I knew I was being foolish. So many men did. There were reasons, explanations, but none of that mattered. A thought popped into my mind—Sherlock saying Donald Wheelwright did not much care for his wife—then the glance he and Henry had shared. "They should have told me," I murmured angrily.

"What?"

"Nothing. How is the soup?"

"Very good. It does feel quite... soothing."

"That is what we want. I shall have to talk to the cook about what you should eat. No curries or extremely spicy food."

"I never much cared for curries."

The sudden grief had died away, and now I felt very tired. I knew if I closed my eyes I would be asleep at once. The fire felt so warm and good on my feet. They had been half frozen during the cab ride.

Violet's throat rippled as she swallowed the soup. She did have the longest neck I had ever seen. She too appeared exhausted, her eyes dull, the lids half closed. I thought of Donald Wheelwright off with some plump, insipid blonde, and again I felt an ache of sorrow. He should be the one with Violet now—the one to comfort her.

"You know," she said, "that I do envy you."

"I am flattered."

"Do not joke about it. You have everything, and I have nothing."

"I would not mind a room like this."

"Gladly would I give it to you—along with this entire house, all the servants, the furniture, the whole wretched lot. I have nothing that matters. I wish I could trade places with you for one day, but that would be worse—I could never bear to return."

"You are serious."

"Of course I am. I can see how you and Henry feel about one another." She smiled briefly. "I cannot exactly understand it, but I can see that it is genuine enough. Then there is your profession—to actually be doing something worthwhile, something using the brains God gave you—and there is your beauty."

At this I could not restrain a laugh. "Are you mad? You are one of the most beautiful women I have ever known, while I... You would not want paws like this." I held up my red hands with their thick fingers.

"I like your hands. My beauty, as you call it, is only fashion, mere convention. Every man at the party was staring at you, even the Reverend Killington."

"That dirty hypocrite. I know one man who could not take his eyes off you—Sherlock Holmes. You really are very lovely. That is why I cannot understand…" I did not mention Donald's name, but it rose like a dark cloud between us. "You know, if you wished—you are not too old—and you would make an excellent physician."

This set her laughing. She grasped her tray with both hands.

"I am not joking."

"I know you are not, but I haven't the stomach for it—literally—nor the inclination."

"It is good to use the brains God gave one, as you put it."

"I know." She kept laughing.

"Are you all right?"

"Yes." She caught her breath and managed to stop laughing. "It struck me as funny for some reason. I know because I do use my brains—I cannot help it. I cannot exactly turn off my brain, if you know what I mean." She took a piece of bread and buttered it, then set down the tray. "I was hungry, and I do feel much better." She began to yawn, covering her mouth with her hand. "Pardon me. I feel now like I could sleep."

"Did you sleep at all last night?"

"No."

"Perhaps I should leave and let you go to bed."

"Please do not go—*please.*" Her eyes were suddenly frightened.

"Of course, I shall stay if you wish."

She bit off a piece of bread. "I am being foolish. Go if you wish. I only… I am tired now, but when I lie down I grow so… restless. How can I be so weary and yet not sleep?" The question had an undercurrent of anxiety.

"You are overly tired. Let me give you something, and then I shall stay until you fall asleep."

"You would do that?"

"Of course."

Her eyes filled with tears. "You really are a generous person."

"Oh, do stop it, Violet! I assure you, I am no paragon, no angel in womanly form. You know better."

"Ah, but you *are* an angel in womanly form, that bearer of the divine spark, that divine vessel meant to guide the errant nature of your husband onto the spiritual plain."

"Now you are delirious. Whatever have you been reading?"

"All that is needed are the darling children, four boys and four girls."

"Rather more than I had in mind."

"But there will be children?" Her dark eyes were fixed on me.

"Oh, yes. When we are ready."

"Ah. The Princess of Wales was quite worn out when she was our age. She had borne the Prince, our future king, six children by the age of twenty-six. Her reward was that he took up with Lily Langtry, the first of his whores to be publicly flaunted. Have you seen Mrs. Langtry on stage? They say she is still a beauty but has gotten quite fat."

"Violet…"

"I am sorry. Please pardon me. My mind sometimes does cartwheels. Perhaps you should give me the magic potion so you can be off."

"I can stay as long as you wish."

"You are very kind, but I have imposed on you long enough. Besides, I am so exhausted I can hardly think straight. Do you ever wish you could shut off your mind? Mine just seems to go and go like some mechanical thing, the same tired thoughts repeating themselves endlessly." Her eyes had an unhealthy glint.

I took her empty water glass and filled it from the pitcher near the bed.

"All of life seems like clockwork," she said. "It all just goes, the wheels and cogs turning ceaselessly. The key has been wound, and now the machine must run. It is out of my hands. I thought I was controlling it, but I am only one tiny part, one more cog. There can be no retreat, no turning back."

I gave her so curious a look that she laughed.

"Surely by now you know not to pay any attention to my ravings."

I added a few drops of an opiate to the water. "Drink this."

She took the glass, swirled the liquid. "Will it keep me asleep? I… I do not like waking in the early morning."

"It will," I said, knowing that my firm pronouncements were often more effective than my medicines.

She raised the glass. "*A ta santé, ma chère amie.*" She drank it down.

"Now get into bed."

She stood up and swayed slightly. I stepped forward and seized her arm. Again I had a sense of being so much larger than she. She smiled at me. "I am only a little dizzy. It is nothing."

I led her to the bed and drew aside the covers. "Do you sleep with your robe on?"

"Yes, the sheets are cold—icy."

I thought of the familiar warmth of Henry beside me at night, and something seemed to catch in my throat. I drew the covers over her. She was having a hard time keeping her eyes open. I turned and walked toward the fire.

"Michelle!" She had sat up in bed, her eyes wide open.

"I am only getting a chair."

"Oh. Yes."

I brought the chair over to the bed and turned down the flame of the nearby lamp.

"Do not turn it off."

"I shall not."

I sat down by the bed. Violet smiled at me. The drug already seemed to have soothed her agitated mania. Her pale thin face showed all her weariness. She had dark circles under her eyes, her mouth pinched. She looked so ill it frightened me. I reached out and took her thin white hand in mine.

"You are so cold."

"I am freezing. It was nice by the fire."

I put my hand on her forehead. "You have no fever."

She gave a restless sigh. "If only I could sleep."

"You will, and I shall be here until you do. You have my promise."

She smiled. "Did your mother tuck you in when you were a child?"

"Yes, she did."

"I wish I had known my mother. My nanny tucked me in, and sometimes my father. He would tell me bedtime stories."

"I'm afraid I cannot remember any."

"His stories usually had insects in them. The ants were very good, very civilized, while the beetles were bad."

I laughed. "I would have liked to hear one of those stories."

"They were wonderful. I like stories, except ones with gypsies."

"We shall not talk about gypsies. Besides, Sherlock believes there are no gypsies involved. Whoever is behind it, he will catch them."

"Can you be so sure?"

"Yes. He is very tenacious. He will not rest until he figures things out."

The wind rattled the windows again. "Do you like the sound of the wind?" Violet asked.

"When I am inside, warm, and comfortable!"

"I do not like it. It makes me feel frightened. Mr. Holmes is very different from how I thought he would be."

"In what way?"

"He is not such a machine, and he is so interesting. And he has hungry eyes."

I laughed. "So you noticed that?"

"Yes. But it is not mere appetite as with the Reverend Killington or Donald's father. I thought women would not interest Mr. Holmes, but they do."

"You interest him very much."

"I wish… I wish I had not met him this way. I thought I had him all figured out. If only… But it is too late." She had closed her eyes.

I wanted to take her hand again, but she was nearly asleep. "Perhaps it is not so late," I murmured.

"It is too late. Years too late. It…" She paused mid-sentence, then she began to breathe very softly and regularly.

I sat back in the chair. "Oh, Violet, whatever am I to do with you?" My voice quavered slightly.

I walked back to the fire, then sat down and put my boots back on. Outside the wind had grown fierce. I wanted to stay awhile, but I could not keep my eyes open. Finally, I stood up. Violet was obviously sound asleep, but she looked so sick.

I closed the door softly behind me and went downstairs. Lovejoy insisted on fetching a carriage, and I had a wild, wet, windy ride home. As soon as I saw Henry, I rushed into his arms.

"What is it? You are so cold. Are you…?"

"Just hold me for a moment," I said.

"Gladly. I did miss you," he murmured gently, and his tone of voice, his touch, seemed to resonate through me as if I were a harp or other instrument, the feelings–the melodies–beyond my control, some mysterious law of harmonies guiding me. As we went upstairs, I told him I would talk about Violet in the morning. We lay together in the darkness, and I clung to him as if I were cast adrift in frigid waters. I fell asleep almost at once, but my dreams were troubled. Violet's ghostly face with its corona of black hair stared at me. I kept reaching out for Henry.

Eight

When the morning light fell on my face, I put a pillow over my head and went back to sleep. When I finally woke up, I rolled over and felt with my foot for Henry, but he was gone. I was very warm and comfortable, but then memories of the night before came back. I glanced at the clock.

"Good heavens!"

I never slept so late—it was after ten, and I had patients arriving before nine.

I slipped out of bed, dressed quickly in the frigid room, and then went downstairs. Harriet had the stove going and was making pie crust. Our black-and-white cat Victoria rubbed about my ankles. I scratched her forehead.

"Morning, ma'am. You look much rested."

"I should have been awake hours ago."

"Mr. Henry said you weren't to be bothered. He is seeing your patients for you. Let me pour your coffee and milk. And shall I warm up some of the leftover porridge?"

"Yes, I am famished."

I sipped my coffee and glanced at *The Times.* A column about the Prince of Wales reminded me of what Violet had said the night before. "Harriet?" The kitchen was empty, a small pan left on the stove. I rose and gave the porridge a stir, then burned my mouth tasting it.

The kitchen door swung open, and Henry came in wearing his best black frock coat and waistcoat.

"Good morning," I said.

He stared closely at me. "How do you feel?"

I kissed him lightly on the mouth. "Much better. Can you spare a moment?"

"Yes. Mrs. Scott sent a note saying she could not make her appointment." We sat down at the table. "Now tell me everything that happened to you last night. You were not yourself. You had quite a grip on me, you know."

"Poor darling." Harriet had returned, and she set a bowl of porridge before me. As I ate, I told him all that had occurred. His face grew more and more sober. When I had finished, he took my hand. We were both silent.

At last I said, "You should have told me about the mistress. I would not have been so shaken had I already known."

"I am sorry. I almost did, but… Sherlock did not want me to worry you."

"Let me be the judge of that! However did he find out?"

"He deduced it from the disorderly state of Donald Wheelwright's clothing when he visited Baker Street in the afternoon."

"Oh, no!"

"Yes. I… I shall not keep such a secret from you again."

We were quiet again, our hands still clasped. At last he looked up at me. "Do you think Violet is… mentally unbalanced?"

I shook my head. "I do not think she is crazy if that is what you mean. She is under a great strain, and..."

"And?"

"She is not telling me everything. She was so very... odd. She wanted to know if we were going to have children. She asked about it so frivolously, and yet she badly wanted to know. Why?"

"Is that not obvious? It is because she cannot have children of her own."

I shook my head again. "No, that is too obvious. She really wanted to know what *I* was going to do. I have never seen her the way she was last night. I always thought her the most self-assured woman I knew."

Henry's shoulders twitched. "That business with the spiders would disturb anyone."

"She said nothing about the spiders. I do not think it was them. I am worried about her, very worried. I shall have to keep a close watch on her. The ulcer would be problem enough, but..."

"You do have a kind heart, Michelle. She was right about that."

"So do you, my dear, and I hope you are not black and blue from all the squeezing I gave you last night."

He smiled. "You may squeeze me whenever you wish. Do not worry about squeezing too hard." Harriet had her back to us, and he raised my hand and kissed my knuckles.

"Oh, Henry. I hope–I hope we never hate each other–or tire of each other."

He gave his head a fierce shake. "We shall not."

I bit at my lip and stroked his cheek. "I have dawdled long enough, Dr. Vernier. Lady Brankenbury has an appointment at eleven, and she most assuredly will not be late. Duty calls."

We went downstairs together, and Henry went to check the morning post. He came back into my examining room with several letters.

"Here is a telegram from Sherlock. Damnation," he muttered, giving his head a shake. "Mrs. Dalton has flown the coop."

"Who is Mrs. Dalton?"

"George Herbert's housekeeper. She must have stolen the necklace after all."

"Oh dear–although you said she was frightfully underpaid."

"Yes, but that is not considered grounds for grand theft. On a more cheerful note, he wants to know if we would accompany him to Covent Garden tomorrow for the performance of *Il Trovatore.* He apologizes for the late invitation and pleads distraction. He even offers to pay for our tickets."

"How sweet of him. We must go."

I saw Violet late that afternoon. She had slept ten hours, was much improved and–like me–seemed embarrassed about the night before. I casually mentioned that Henry and I were going to the opera the next day with Sherlock.

Her eyes widened, and she seized my wrist. "Oh, but you must join me! Father Wheelwright has a box at Covent Garden, but he and Donald have some evening meeting, potted meat business. I was debating whether to go by myself. The seats are really very good. Tell Mr. Holmes to save his money. It would be wonderful to have you all as my guests–it would mean so much to me!" Her enthusiasm was catching, and I assured her I would pass on the invitation.

Sherlock, Henry and I–all three of us once again in our finery–paused before the door to Box Three at Covent Garden. Henry knocked. The door swung open, and Violet stood before us, radiant.

"Oh, I am so glad you could come!"

Her silk gown was two shades of blue, an elaborate lace framing her bosom, a split in the skirt revealing a darker blue fabric. Her shoulders were bare, and she wore a black silk choker about her slender neck, a single magnificent pearl in front. To my physician's eyes, she seemed pale and thin, her ribs showing near the sternum above the curve of her bosom. However, her beauty could not be denied; unlike so many of the women at the opera, her gown and jewels did not clash with her person.

I glanced at Sherlock and recalled Violet saying he had hungry eyes. "I think we are in for a splendid evening," he said. "Reports of the tenor are favorable, and the principals and the conductor are all Italian."

Violet laughed. "An oddly chauvinistic view for an Englishman."

"No, no—it is not chauvinism. *Il Trovatore* is the quintessential Italian opera, and as such is best left to the natives. One would not wish to hear Signor Vitelli attempting Irish ballads; similarly, *Il Trovatore* should be entrusted to those who know the language and have the music in their blood."

"Henry and Sherlock have been telling me something of the plot," I said. "It sounds very confusing."

Violet raised her right eyebrow, smiled and shook her head. "Oh, but it is not complicated at all. It is a simple story of revenge. I can explain it to you. I also have two copies of the libretto. Following it should help. Do you know Italian?"

"Some. Henry and I both took up Italian before a trip there. It does not *sound* like French, but the vocabulary is similar. I also studied Latin for years. I should be able to follow along. However, Sherlock reads Italian better than either of us."

Violet stared up at him. "Indeed? I am surprised, Mr. Holmes. Somehow I would have thought Italian a bit too extravagantly Mediterranean for a practical Anglo-Saxon nature such as yours."

"You are mistaken, madam. Even ignoring the Gallic side of my family, what lover of music could neglect the language of Petrarch and

Dante? '*Nel mezzo del cammin di nostra vita mi ritrovai per una selva oscura che la diritta via era smarrita.*'"

I frowned slightly. "In the middle of the road of our life, I found myself by an obscure wood that the direct way was marred."

Sherlock and Henry smiled, while a ripple of laughter slipped from Violet's lips. "Very close. Not obscure—dark, a dark wood." Her smile faded away. "'*Una selva oscura*'. 'In the midst of the path of our life, I found myself in a dark wood where the straight way was lost.' The first stanza from Dante's *Inferno*—Hell. '*A quanto a dir qual era e cosa dura esta selva selvaggia e aspra e forte che nel pensier rinova la paura.*'" The words sounded beautiful, but she spoke them sadly.

I shook my head. "I dare not try to make that out."

Sherlock smiled. "The second stanza. 'Ah, how hard to say how this wood was savage, bitter and dense; even thinking of it renews the fear.' The syntax is rather twisted, but there is nothing in English like '*selva selvaggia*'; 'savage wood' is not so melodious."

"Nor can fear compare to '*paura*'," Violet said. "You seem very familiar with Dante's *Divine Comedy*, Mr. Holmes."

"Yes. I read it while at university, and I still pull out my copy occasionally."

Henry gave his head a shake. "The Italian is beautiful, but I grew tired of all the misery in the *Inferno*. One must give Dante credit for making art out of poetic spleen and fiendish torture. A bit twisted, though."

Violet nodded. "Revenge is rarely so poetic or beautiful, nor does it often rise to the level of art, but Dante's language is sublime. I love the Italian country, too, all that sunshine and spontaneity, and of course the food."

"Did you not travel there just after your marriage?" Holmes asked.

Violet was smiling, but the right side of her mouth straightened, then twitched. She swallowed, the expression in her eyes suddenly changing.

"Yes. I... I came down with a common traveler's ailment and felt quite dreadful. I believe it was some bad fruit I ate in Venice. We... I had to come home early." She managed a laugh. "I fear it still makes me queasy just thinking about it! That was not my first trip. My father loved Greece and Italy, and we spent many summers there. Sometimes I long to just run away to some beautiful villa in Tuscany or perhaps by the sea. But come, we should be gazing at the other spectators, rating their apparel, and sharing the latest gossip. We have little time for this amusing sport, for the performance is about to begin."

"That does not stop most ladies," Holmes said.

Violet laughed. "Very good, Mr. Holmes. My sister-in-law is one of the worst offenders. We have this large box to ourselves, a blessed occasion—as you would know if you had ever endured a performance in the company of Donald and his relations! The worst was the time the Reverend Killington accompanied us."

Holmes' brow furrowed. "Whatever could have persuaded him to attend? And what was the performance—*Parsival?*"

"Oh, no—Wagner is the Antichrist. It was Saint-Saëns's *Samson and Delilah*. He approved heartily of the temple coming down at the end. Let us be seated. Michelle and I shall be in the middle where I can talk to her."

We sat in the front; Violet was on my left, then Sherlock, with Henry to my right. The chairs had red velvet seats and padding over the arms. They were much more comfortable than anything in the stalls below, and the view was perfect. The balconies swung about in a great U; we were up one level very close to the stage on the right-hand side. The orchestra in the pit began to warm up. Violet handed me a book.

"You and Henry may share one libretto, Mr. Holmes and I the other."

Holmes glanced overhead at the massive chandelier. "As usual, there is plenty of light. I would prefer the Bayreuth custom of dimming the lights in the auditorium during the performance."

Violet raised her right eyebrow. "Ah, but then one might be forced to watch the performance rather than the other spectators. And have you really been to Bayreuth? Oh, how I envy you!"

"You were going to explain the plot to me," I said.

"Yes." Violet put her gloved hand over mine. "The title, *Il Trovatore*–'The Troubadour'–is misleading."

Holmes nodded. "Verdi thought of calling it *The Gypsy*."

"That would have been better," Violet agreed. "Azucena is the gypsy in the opera. An evil count has burned her mother at the stake as a witch. In revenge, long before the opera begins, Azucena has stolen one of the count's sons. But I do not wish to give too much away. If you get confused, nudge me, and I shall untangle things for you. The three other main characters are part of a love triangle: the tenor Manrico–Azucena's supposed son–the soprano Leonora, and the baritone Conte di Luna, the old count's son and successor. Just remember, at heart the opera is about Azucena's vengeance and other dark passions. The music is sublime, although, in real life, human misery is never so beautiful."

Soon the brief overture began. The first scene with a chorus of soldiers did not catch my attention, but the second with the heroine Leonora, and the two men quarreling over her, was more interesting. Violet and Sherlock were clearly excited about the tenor and the soprano, but the high pitch of their voices sounded odd to me. I preferred the warm baritone of the count, and he was pleasant to look at with his black goatee, doublet, and tights. Henry and I shared a pair of opera glasses.

During the second act, the opera truly came alive. The anvil chorus of the gypsies (even I recognized it) was great fun, but then the chorus trooped offstage and the gypsy Azucena began to sing to her son Manrico. Her voice was very dark–smoky, even; she hardly sounded like a woman–but gripping. I peered through the glasses at her. The makeup on her face was obvious—the lines for wrinkles, the false shadows—but her dark eyes appeared genuinely haunted. She had on a white wig, and large golden circles dangled from her ears. She wore a red dress, a black handkerchief over her hair, and a black shawl over her shoulders. Truly she seemed possessed.

I followed her words in the libretto. She explained how she had struggled to get through the crowd with her baby, desperately trying to reach her condemned mother, "*ma invano.*" The music was low and ominous, the violins playing a plaintive, re-occurring sigh. Before the ghoulish crowd drove her mother into the roaring fire, she cried out to Azucena, "*Mi vendica*"—"Avenge me."

I would not have thought the gypsy could be any more intense, but then she sang how later she stole the evil count's baby. She was determined to throw the baby into a fire of her own, but she hesitated, disturbed by the child's crying. Then she saw the cruel mob and the flaming pyre again, her mother's pale ghost screaming "*mi vendica.*" She hurled the baby into the flames, but when the fatal delirium faded, she saw the count's baby next to her.

"*Ah! Che dici!*" sang the tenor Manrico. "What are you saying?"

The music built to a tremendous crescendo. "*Il figlio mio—mio figlio avea bruciato!*" The Italian was simple enough: "My son—I had burned my son!"

"*Orror! Quale orror!*" The tenor seemed genuinely horrified. So was I. She had thrown her own baby into the fire. A shiver worked its way up my spine.

I glanced at Sherlock and Violet. They were absolutely transfixed, in another world. I think that for them, Henry and I, the audience, no longer existed. Violet's cheeks were flushed, her pallor gone, but her excitement somehow did not look healthy.

The tenor repeated "*orror*" several times, and then the music died down even as flames would. Manrico asked who he was if he was not her son, but Azucena stubbornly told him he was her son. The moment was past; the story went off in another direction. When the scene ended, the tenor and the contralto, Azucena, were loudly applauded, but during her brief solo bow, shouts of bravo filled the hall.

I could barely restrain another shudder. "She was incredible."

"Yes," Holmes said. "Bravos are rare at Covent Garden. The tenor has a beautiful voice but not her histrionic talents."

Violet nodded. "I doubt even Donald could have slept through that. The end of the scene always strikes me as comical. Poor Manrico, always running off to save someone; always having to choose between Leonora and his mother. His grand moment in the limelight is coming up in the next act. I shall give you a nudge, Michelle, before he hits his high C. If done well, it is a thrilling moment. This is a splendid performance. The one in eighty-eight with Tomagno was good, but hardly on a par with this."

Holmes' gray eyes watched her. "You saw that *Il Trovatore*, did you?"

Violet hesitated only an instant. "Yes. What did you think of it, Mr. Holmes?"

"You are correct. This is far superior."

During the intermission Henry and I went outside together. Violet and Sherlock were talking and hardly noticed us leave. I held Henry's arm with both my hands and nodded my head against his shoulder. "It seems such a pity," I murmured.

"You mean Violet and...?"

"Yes. What is the good of forcing her to remain married to Donald Wheelwright? How is the public morality served by the misery of three people—or four, if you include the mistress?"

The first scene of the second act had the count's men catching Azucena and preparing to burn her at the stake, just as they had burned her mother. Again, the singer was remarkable; she made me feel apprehensive and trapped. In the next scene Manrico was about to marry Leonora, when his friend rushed in to tell him Azucena was about to be burned before the castle walls.

Violet nudged me gently. "Be prepared—here it comes."

Manrico had just sung a slow rhapsodic song, but the tempo picked up as a chorus of soldiers trooped on stage. The tenor's Italian was simple: "I was already a son before I loved you." "*Madre infelice, corro a salvarti, or teco almeno corro a morir!*" "…Unhappy mother, I run to save you, or at least I run to die with you!"

On the *teco* the tenor briefly hit the high note. The chorus sang "*all'armi*"—"to arms." I watched Manrico through the opera glasses. He swelled up like a frog, the sweat beading on his forehead, his eyes ferocious, then drew his sword and bellowed: "*All'armi!*" This was the high C to end all high Cs, the note piercing, filling the auditorium. He held it so long I thought his lungs would burst. The back of my neck felt prickly. The curtain dropped, and the audience applauded wildly.

Sherlock and Henry shouted bravo, while Violet and I clapped. She smiled. "Well?"

"It was not exactly a pretty sound, but it was very exciting!"

"Only one act left," Violet said. "The count has captured Manrico and locked him up with Azucena. Leonora makes a bargain with the count, offering herself in exchange for Manrico's life. The count accepts, but she takes poison, then goes to Manrico in prison and tells him to flee. However, being a man, he assumes the worst and berates her for her faithlessness."

Holmes was watching her. "Do you think, madam, that only men are capable of assuming the worst of the opposite sex?"

"I did not say that." Her smile was ironic. "But it is often the case."

Leonora was moving in the final act when she pleaded with the count for Manrico's life, then again when she begged Manrico to flee. However, as before, I found Azucena's mere presence spooky. One moment she raved of "*il rogo*," the stake, the next she sang longingly of escaping to the mountains. When Manrico realized the truth–that Leonora was dying–he sang mournfully, "And I dared curse this angel!" At that point I sympathized with Violet's viewpoint–how like a man!

At last Leonora collapsed and died. The music sped up. The count had Manrico dragged away. My eyes flickered back and forth between the libretto and the stage.

"*Madre! O, Madre, addio!*" Manrico sang.

Azucena awoke with a start. "Manrico! Where is my son?"

"He runs to his death," snarled the count.

"Stop!" screamed the gypsy. "Listen to me!"

But the Count dragged her to the tower window. "*Vedi?*" he cried. "Do you see?"

"*Cielo!*" Azucena sang. A loud bang, the dreadful sound of an ax hitting a block of wood, resounded through the auditorium.

The count said something, and then Azucena, absolutely mad, turned to him. "He was your brother!"

"*Ei. Quale orror!*" The Count sang the same words as Manrico had earlier.

Azucena's voice, already powerful, soared above the orchestra. "You are avenged, mother!"

With a final clash of cymbals and beating of drums, the music ended: the Count collapsing in horror and remorse, Azucena raising her clenched fists to the heavens, the curtain falling upon the scene. There was a second or two of silence, and then the applause began.

I gave a great shuddery sigh and turned to Henry, my eyes wide. He smiled but did not try to speak over the din. We all stood. Violet's brown eyes glistened with tears, and she tried to smile at me. Her face was flushed, and she looked almost feverish. Oh no, I thought. Holmes was more restrained, but his face was also flushed.

There were several curtain calls and a standing ovation. Worried now, I kept an eye on Violet. When the clapping finally ended, she sank down into her seat, and the rest of us did the same.

"Amazing," Holmes said. "I doubt we shall see its equal any time soon. Wagner's leisurely musical dramas simply do not have the sheer visceral appeal of a well-performed Verdi opera."

Henry nodded. "This is the only opera I have ever seen that compares with the *Faust* we saw in Paris."

Holmes' lips formed a brief smile. "That performance was... unique, especially its unexpected conclusion." He withdrew his watch. "It is not yet eleven. Thanks to Mrs. Wheelwright, my billfold has been spared thus far this evening. Perhaps you would all join me for some refreshments nearby?"

Henry nodded.

"Oh, I would love to!" Violet exclaimed. She stood up, but abruptly, tears flowed from her eyes. She made a choking noise, then twisted away and leaned against the railing.

Henry and Sherlock were astonished. I gave my head a shake. "Too much excitement."

"It is not that!" Violet tried to say.

I stood up and took a handkerchief from my handbag. I touched her shoulder. "The music—it was so..." she began. "The story is so dreadful, so sad, but the music is so very beautiful."

"Sit down, my dear."

"I am tired. My sleep is still... Oh Lord, I feel so foolish!"

"Please sit down."

She swayed. "I am dizzy." She sat, then dabbed at her eyes with the handkerchief. I noticed her other hand slip down and clutch at her side.

My own eyes filled with tears, and I glanced at Henry. It was so unfair—I had never seen her so happy.

He pulled at the corner of his mustache. "Perhaps we should make it another night, Sherlock."

"Not on my account!" Violet said. "I shall…" She took a deep breath, and I could see her will exert its customary force. "I shall go home. Collins is waiting out front for me, but you two must join Mr. Holmes. I only wish—how I wish…!" She paused. "I only wish I could accompany you."

Holmes looked at me, his face a mute appeal.

"I think it would be best for her to rest," I said.

Violet closed her dark eyes, the nostrils of her aquiline nose flaring. "I shall go home. You have had enough outlandish behavior from me for one evening." Her mocking smile had returned. She handed me the handkerchief. "Please, let us go." She stood up.

I followed her, ready to catch her should she stumble. Sherlock and Henry were behind us, two tall figures in their black tailcoats and trousers.

"Do not be glum on my account. I am quite recovered."

"Be sure to eat some soup or something when you get home."

"I shall, Doctor. Did you like the opera, Michelle?"

"Oh, yes, but it was sad. I see why you said it should be called *The Gypsy*."

"And the plot was not too difficult?"

"No. It was, as you said, a simple story."

"I also enjoyed myself." We reached the bottom of the stairs, and she took my arm with one hand, then half turned. "I know Mr. Holmes enjoyed himself." She slipped her other hand about his arm.

He stiffened slightly, allowing a brief smile. "I am in your debt, madam. The seats were perfect. It was a performance—an evening— which I shall always treasure."

Violet's smile softened. "I believe you mean it. As for me–you have no idea how wonderful it was. True, the box is a fine one, but if you had had to sit through so many performances listening to Father and Mother Wheelwrights' insipid chatter–at least Donald sleeps quietly and does not snore."

I smiled. "Poor Violet."

"It is very distracting. You understand, do you not, Mr. Holmes?"

"Yes."

We had lingered in the box, and most of the crowd had left by the time Henry and Sherlock got our coats and we had stepped outside. The rain had stopped, and the cool air felt good on my face after being inside for so long.

"Thank you so much, Violet," I said. "It was wonderful."

"Superb," Henry added.

Violet smiled, her eyes bleak. "You are welcome. There is Collins."

"I shall see you tomorrow," I said.

"Oh, Michelle, you need not."

"I shall be the judge of that."

Violet stared past me at Holmes. He had on his black top hat and greatcoat. His pale thin face stared down at her, but he did not speak. The gas lamps before the theater were bright enough that I could see the flush return to her cheeks. "Mr. Holmes," she began rather loudly.

"Yes?" He looked puzzled.

"I thank you–thank you–for a most pleasurable evening, and for…" Her voice died away.

"As I said, it is I who am in your debt."

"No–*no*–it is I who…" She drew in her breath. "Thank you for being so charming, for reminding me that not all men are–for reminding me that men can also be intelligent and love art and music and the beautiful." Her small hands quivered before her, then reached out and seized his big hand. I do not know which of them was more surprised. They stared at one another, their eyes devouring each other, briefly paralyzed. Henry looked at me in disbelief. Abruptly, Violet raised Sherlock's hand, squeezing it tightly, then releasing it. "Goodnight." She turned and fled, her heels clattering upon the pavement as she strode toward her carriage. Sherlock's lips had parted, his eyes still fixed on her.

Henry put his arm about me, shielding me from the wind and drawing me close. "This has been quite an evening," he murmured. "Sherlock, I could certainly use those refreshments—especially something liquid."

Holmes stared curiously down at his hand in its black glove and drew in his breath. "An excellent suggestion, Henry. I know a place close by if you would care to walk."

"Let us walk," I said.

We hardly spoke. I slipped my hand about Henry's arm and stayed close to him. The restaurant was warm, brightly lit, and full of opera-goers. We remained morose and silent until the drinks came. I sipped my liqueur and felt it heat my mouth and throat.

"I wish…" I began. "I wish Violet could have come. And I wish she felt better and—I wish this nightmare were over, the old gypsy woman found, and Donald…" I took a big swallow, then coughed. "Oh, pardon me, but I do hope, Sherlock, that you soon figure out who sent those terrible notes."

Holmes sat back in his chair and placed the tips of his fingers together. "I know who the gypsy was."

Henry leaned forward. "You do!"

Holmes smiled sadly. "Yes. It is rather obvious. Do you recall that the letters were signed with an A? The A stands for Azucena."

Henry and I stared at him. "Sherlock, what do you mean?" I could not keep the annoyance from my voice. "Azucena was the character in the opera. She is not a real person."

"Oh, I am quite aware of that, as was the person who played the gypsy. However, Azucena was the model for her character. I suspected some such scheme, but the realization struck me as a certainty in the second act. The gypsy at the ball was described as being almost exactly the same, her costume identical."

"You are only guessing!"

"I do not guess, Michelle." His voice was cold, but then he smiled and shrugged. "I rarely guess. I am absolutely certain Azucena was the inspiration for the gypsy and her curse. '*Mi vendica*,' remember? 'Avenge me.' This is more of the strange humor as with the cake and the spiders. Signing the letters with an A is some person's idea of a clever joke."

"It is not my idea of a joke—it is hardly funny."

He stared innocently at me. "You think not?"

"*No*. Is this just a game to you?"

Henry took my arm. "Michelle..."

"It is no game to me! Violet is my friend, and she is so sad and sick—oh, Sherlock, you must help her. I beg of you—the strain is tearing her apart."

"She is a strong woman," Henry said.

"You would not say so if you had seen her two nights ago! She is strong, yes, but so much of it is an act. I am worried to death about her. Please, Sherlock."

He had grown very pale. He ran his long fingers through his black, oily hair, and then set his hand on the table. "I shall do everything I can to save her, Michelle. Believe me, I would..." His fingers touched his glass, caressed it briefly, then circled the rim. "One way or another, she is in grave peril."

"One way or another—what do you mean?"

He sipped his whiskey and soda. "*La diritta via era smarrita.* I promise, I shall save her." He obviously meant what he said, but I had never heard such quiet desperation in his voice.

Nine

We had seen *Il Trovatore* on Wednesday evening. Saturday morning I went to Baker Street. Although I arrived at eleven, my cousin was only then confronting a boiled egg perched upright upon its holder. His dark brows sank inward, a smile flickered over his lips. He struck the egg sharply with his spoon, cracking it nearly in half. "Ah, Henry. Do sit down. Are you hungry?"

"I have already eaten."

"A shame. Mrs. Hudson is very good with a boiled egg. Four minutes and thirty seconds exactly. Overcook them, and they are a dry abomination. Undercook them, and they are repulsively gelatinous."

Mrs. Hudson gave me one of her long-suffering smiles. "Coffee, Doctor?"

"Please."

She poured a cup from the china pot, and I sat at the small table. Sherlock had removed the upper half of the eggshell and set it upon a saucer. Carefully, he spooned out some egg, leaving the top concave so the yolk would not run out.

He was so meticulous an eater I could not imagine when or how it had happened, but on the cuff of his purple dressing gown was what appeared to be prehistoric, dried egg yolk. Although I knew that he changed his linen every day and that he would discard a coat or trousers at the first sign of wear, the old woolen gown appeared decrepit. This one slovenly garment was the exception that proved the rule. No doubt it was like a familiar, comfortable old friend.

"I am glad you did not come yesterday, Henry. I was in a foul mood. Rarely have I been so frustrated. However, I have resolved anew to use those brains, those unique talents, which God has given me. I have been behaving... I have not been myself."

"This affair of the Wheelwrights is very dark. It has disturbed Michelle greatly, and I too feel uneasy."

Holmes had eaten the upper, uncovered half of the egg; now he carefully scooped some from the half shell remaining. "Very dark indeed. Michelle has a kind and generous heart. It does her credit, but I cannot—must not—let my sympathies cloud my reason."

I took a sip of coffee and smiled. "Reason and the heart are often at odds."

He took the last bit of egg from the shell. He chewed briefly, dabbed at his lips with a napkin and threw it aside. "I must be true to my nature, or I am lost. I am too old to change."

"Are you? It hardly seems that way. It seems as if you *are* changing and that fact disturbs you."

He sat back in his chair and extended his long arms before him, his gray eyes fixed on me. Abruptly he rose, strode to the fire, then stood with his back to me, his left hand clutching the wrist of his right arm. He was still for only seconds, then whirled about.

"You are very perceptive, Henry. All the same, reason—this brain—" he placed his forefinger on his temple— "has been my guide through the labyrinth of life. I must trust it still. The heart will only… leave me wallowing in the mire."

I laughed. "What a frightful metaphor! It is clear where your sympathies lie."

He returned to the chair and crossed his legs, revealing a bare bony ankle between the leather slipper and the black wool of his trousers. "Is it? Do you also presume I am some mechanical automaton incapable of genuine human feelings?" His eyes were hot and fierce.

"You know me better than that—I have never presumed any such thing. Quite the contrary."

He took a quick sip of coffee. "Forgive me. I do know that. All the same, it is my reason I must now follow and not my heart."

"Why divide yourself?"

"Because my heart might misdirect me—because it might make me betray everything I have ever believed in, everything I have fought for."

"How could it do that?"

He stared at me, and then lowered his eyes. "If you do not understand… that is good. Perhaps…" Briefly his gaze lost its focus as his thoughts turned inward; at last he seemed again to see me. "The lady in question is a married woman. How, therefore, can I trust my heart?" Despite his smile, his eyes were pained.

I stared at my cup and toyed with the spoon. "Perhaps there might be… some way."

Holmes laughed, a harsh, sharp sound. "Do you think if there was any real hope that I would not…?" He paused, his Adam's apple bobbing as he swallowed. "No, Henry. Even were I lacking in moral scruples—even if I did not respect the lady so much… Over the years, in my profession, I have encountered too many sordid and disgusting cases involving married men or women and a third person. The guiding force—despite protestations of great love—was rarely the heart, but another portion of the anatomy. I could never lower myself—or dream of lowering a lady—to the level of some vulgar, clandestine affair."

"I was not proposing any such thing! I only... Perhaps she could... obtain a divorce."

"On what grounds? Adultery in the male will not suffice. And Father Wheelwright would never tolerate such a scandal. Very bad for the potted meat business." Holmes shook his head. "Besides, this is all extremely presumptuous on our part. The lady may not share..."

"She is interested," I said. "Very interested."

Holmes started to speak, then hesitated. "Do you believe so?"

I laughed. "I may not have your powers of observation, but in this case I am certain."

A furtive smile pulled briefly at his lips, but he shook his head. "No matter, Henry. Futile reveries will not assist me now; mere feelings must not distract me. I must rely on my mental powers, as I have for all these years. There is a problem to be solved—many problems. This business with the Wheelwrights is only one part of a larger puzzle, the most complicated I have ever encountered."

"What puzzle is this?"

He scratched his bare ankle with his finger, then, abruptly, was up and pacing again. "You know about the theft of George Herbert's necklace. I have spoken with Lestrade, and some other acquaintances, at Scotland Yard. Crime is difficult to quantify, but they think they have been busier. Several thefts, as in the case of Herbert, were very skillfully done—not the work of crude, sloppy burglars or cracksmen. You know how Lord Harrington was blackmailed. I have had another member of the nobility approach me—a prostitute is threatening him with ruin. Lestrade has heard similar tales, and he suspects some high-class procurer is systematically putting the squeeze on his clientele. Other curious things have happened. The coal baron, Michael Welsley, died a week ago and left his entire fortune to a miners' hospital. It will be contested, but the nurse and a patient at the hospital witnessed him signing a letter requesting the change. And then there is the recent madness of Lord Wilson."

"Is he not known for his violent temper?"

"Yes. He has apparently been hearing voices, threatening voices. They keep him awake. They torment him. He is under his wife's care, but he may soon be sent to an institution in the country. Oh—so far all these unfortunates seem to have attended the Paupers' Ball."

I felt the dread squarely in my chest. "Good Lord."

"Hardly surprising, Henry. *Everyone* was at the ball."

"Do you think the gypsy...? Some evil presence seems at work in all of this."

He gave a fierce nod. "Yes—some evil *human* presence. One need not posit evil spirits or devils. Men are sufficiently wicked. I have encountered men who would outmatch any devil from hell. The gypsy is a fake—I am certain—but the evil is real enough. I believe a single person is behind this epidemic of crime."

Again I felt afraid. "Your Moriarty?" My voice was very soft.

Holmes gave me a wan, weary smile. "Yes. Whoever this person may be. And his 'Angels.'"

"And is he also behind the threat to Mrs. Wheelwright?"

"I believe so, but I have so few facts." He shook his head and sat again, drumming at the table with his long fingers. "My instincts tell me it is all related, all part of a vast pattern—a great web. Blast it! Watson's feeble metaphor *would* be the first that comes to mind! Some puppeteer is pulling all the strings. However, what I most need now are facts. I have several leads, which must be pursued. I have pondered idly long enough—I am ready for action."

"I hope these other crimes will not distract you from the Wheelwrights."

"They will not. I shall not rest until I discover the truth about the Wheelwrights." He stood up again. "I have several ideas, some of which are not… I need more information about the Lovejoys. I mistrust them both, especially the wife."

"Why?"

"Her hysteria is too convenient. She plays the part of a devout Christian, yet when I ask her what church she attends, she cannot tell me. I press the matter, and down she goes. When I returned to the Herberts', I questioned the servants and discovered Mrs. Lovejoy seems to have been more than just a casual acquaintance of Mrs. Dalton."

"I do not like that. But the husband seems a decent fellow."

"Perhaps a trifle too decent. He is like the perfect butler in some play. Oh, I have less to go on than with the wife, but I suspect him all the same. The fact they come from Liverpool bothers me."

"How can they possibly help that?"

"Again, it is too convenient. They have no past I can examine, no former employers whom I can question. Even their Liverpool employer is accommodatingly deceased. However, there is another person whom I wish to meet, a rather obvious suspect."

I pulled at the corner of my mustache, frowning. "Who?"

"Come, come, Henry. You must know."

I gave him a blank stare.

"Consider how Mr. Wheelwright spends his afternoons."

I sat upright, and then stood. "The mistress!"

"Yes. She has an excellent motive for wishing Violet harm."

"Of course! She must be the person."

Holmes laughed, then took off his dressing gown and threw it over a chair. "You have never met the woman, and yet you appear certain of her guilt. Many men have mistresses, but most mistresses do not plot against their benefactors' wives." He took a pair of black stockings from his desk drawer (I could see the gray blur atop the desk which was the web of his resident spider), and sat down on the sofa, raising one bare foot. "Would you like to meet her?"

"What? You are going to confront her?"

"No. I merely wish to meet the lady. You really must join me."

"When Wheelwright finds out, he will be furious."

"He will not find out."

A gentle rap sounded at the door, then it swung partly open revealing Mrs. Hudson. "Lord Harrington is here to see you, Mr. Holmes."

"Harrington? Why the devil would he choose now of…? Give me two minutes, Mrs. Hudson, then you may admit him." Holmes was wearing black trousers and a white shirt without the collar buttoned on. He snatched the dressing gown and retreated to his bedroom. From there he said, "As soon as we are finished with Lord Harrington we shall pay a call upon Miss Alice Ladell. I must confess to a certain curiosity."

He strode back into the room, collar done up, black cravat in place, his frock coat folded over one arm, his boots in hand. He put on the coat, tugged at the lapels, then flipped it back before he sat and pulled on a boot. By the time Mrs. Hudson opened the door, he was on his feet and looking as if he had been dressed for hours.

"Good day, Mr. Holmes." Lord Harrington gave Mrs. Hudson his stick, pulled off his gray gloves and put them in his top hat, then handed her the hat. He had not a hair on the dome of his head, but his beard and the hair in back were thick, curly and red. His large, light blue eyes had a wary look. He noticed me and struggled to recall my name. "Dr. Verner, is it not?"

"Vernier," I said, shaking his hand.

Holmes gestured at a chair. "Please sit down, Lord Harrington."

He sat before the fire and rubbed his hands together. His fingers were long and white; his hands oddly delicate for so large, broad shouldered a man. "It's beastly cold and wet."

Holmes nodded, then sat, watching him closely. Harrington gazed at the glowing coals. "I suppose frankness would be best. I'd as soon get it off my chest at once. Mr. Holmes, when you showed me that dreadful letter of my brother's, I told you I had no idea who the scoundrel was, the villain Joseph blamed for ruining him. I must confess I was being less than truthful."

Holmes stroked his chin with his forefinger. "I suspected as much."

"As well you might. The devil's name, Mr. Holmes, is Steerford. Geoffrey Steerford."

Holmes frowned, closing his eyes and putting his fingertips on his temple. "Steerford. I know that name." He stood up. "Something to do with investments? I heard the name at a party."

Harrington gave a reluctant nod.

"But there is something else. Steerford. Steer... Ah, Flora Morris, who gave us the suicide note, said the name crossed out had been Turnford—only a slip of the tongue away. This is very useful information, Lord Harrington. I am in your debt."

"I hope you can use it to save others from that blackguard."

"I certainly shall. What made you come to me?"

Lord Harrington had set his elbows upon his knees, leaning toward the fire. He gazed up at Holmes, then his eyes fell. "I did not want to come. My family name has been dragged through the mud because of this wretched business. Before you gave me that note, I had half convinced myself my brother had been murdered. Now it is clear that he was a very... disturbed man."

"I am sorry," Holmes said, "to have been the one to discover the note, but I thought..."

"You thought, quite rightly, that I should have it. After all, he was my brother. After some soul-searching, I have also showed it to Harriet,

Joseph's wife. The truth, dreadful as it is, is…" He looked up again at Holmes. "He tried to tell me, some six months ago, about his torment, but I was repelled by the little he revealed, disgusted. Had I heard him out…"

"You cannot blame yourself for his death."

"No? If he had had a sympathetic ear to share his troubles…"

Holmes' mouth was taut, grim. "It may have been closer to murder than you think. Someone knew his weaknesses only too well. His mistress, that pathetic child, did not come up with such a scheme."

I repressed a shudder. "It was that vile old monster, her 'aunt'."

Holmes folded his arms. "I shall want to meet this Mr. Steerford."

Harrington's jaw slid briefly forward, anger showing in his pale blue eyes. "I have not yet told you why I have come. I had thought of visiting you for the past week but always found some excuse for delay. However, yesterday I received a letter from Mr. Steerford, polite in tone, but most threatening. He apparently knows of your interest in my brother's death, Mr. Holmes, and he said all of London, including the newspapers, would discover more about Joseph's vices should I assist your investigations." His face had reddened, his voice hoarsened. "I'll not let the blackmailing dog who destroyed my brother threaten me. Regrettably, I cannot kill him with my bare hands, but I shall do all I can to bring ruin down upon his head." He drew in his breath, struggling to calm himself. His eyes were fixed on Holmes. "If I can be of any assistance, Mr. Holmes, I hope you will call upon me. Should you require additional funds…"

"You have already paid me generously, Lord Harrington."

"If you need money—or anything else—let me know, and you shall have it. I want this man brought to justice. I do not want him to destroy anyone else, as he has destroyed Joseph. He thought he could coerce me into silence—he thought I would put my pride as a Harrington above all else. Well, I do not wish to see Joseph's name further soiled, but I could not live with myself were I to sit idly by while other poor wretches and their families suffered. I shall see the villain in hell first." His voice shook, and his eyes were deadly earnest.

Holmes gave a nod. "You have chosen rightly."

Harrington stared down at his hands. "I hope so. Nothing can bring Joseph back, so whatever happens…" He withdrew his watch from his waistcoat. "I must go. I have another appointment." He stood up. "I meant what I said, Mr. Holmes. If I can help, please call upon me."

"So I shall."

We followed him to the door. Holmes assisted him with his coat, and then he shook our hands. He seemed embarrassed by the feelings he had shown us. "Good day, gentlemen."

Holmes closed the door behind him, then gave me an ironic smile. "Mr. Steerford seems to have misjudged Lord Harrington. I also misjudged him. I thought I had heard the last from him after I gave him the note."

"I do vaguely remember the name coming up at the Wheelwrights' party."

Holmes nodded. "Old Wheelwright did not like the smell of Mr. Steerford's enterprise. One shrewd devil no doubt recognizing another of his kind. Using an alias, I shall let Mr. Steerford know I have a substantial sum of money to invest and try to set up a meeting with him. However, this afternoon I shall visit Miss Ladell. Do you wish to accompany me?"

"I have no firm plans for the afternoon, and I too am curious."

"Excellent!" Holmes slipped out of his frock coat. "We must dress for the occasion."

"You are certain Mr. Wheelwright…?"

"We shall, of course, pay our visit in disguise. If you would care to join me in the bedroom."

"What disguise?"

"Our role will be one which I particularly enjoy and which has served me well in the past. We shall be plumbers."

"I know absolutely nothing about plumbing."

"An unfortunate gap in your education, Henry. We will cast you as my ignorant assistant."

To my way of thinking, Sherlock carries his desire for authenticity in his disguises too far. He produced soiled and foul-smelling clothing, which any true plumber would have been proud to wear. The touch of it made my flesh crawl, but I reassured myself with the thought of a hot bath when our charade was finished. Besides the dirty clothing, Holmes put on a red-haired wig and applied an enormous red mustache to his upper lip. He ruffled up my hair, then gave me a beard, which matched the color of my mustache. After adding a mole to his cheek, he blacked out a few of our teeth, then smeared some grimy black concoction on our hands and faces. When he was finished, we both resembled mangy sewer rats.

He strapped on a leather belt with wrenches dangling and handed me a wooden toolbox. On the way out, he tipped his worn bowler with a tear in the brim to Mrs. Hudson. "Guh'day, ma'am."

"Good afternoon, Mr. Holmes." She gave a slight shake of her head. "You both look absolutely dreadful."

Holmes laughed. "Excellent, Mrs. Hudson. I shall be home in time for supper."

We had some difficulty hailing a cab, as the drivers were wary of us. But Holmes finally flagged one down and paid in advance. When he mentioned the street to the driver, I said, "A modest, respectable neighborhood. How did you discover the woman's name and address?"

"I had a cabby whom I frequently employ wait outside Wheelwright's offices in the early afternoon. Mr. Wheelwright is impossible to miss.

On the second day at his post, my cabby was hired to drive him to the address we are visiting. Once I had the address, I sent one of the Irregulars over to get the name."

"It is odd to think that… such a woman should be installed in her own house in that neighborhood."

Holmes' smile was harsh. "Come, Henry. You are too severe. She has reached the summit of her profession. She bears no more resemblance to the toothless, diseased prostitute who spends the night on the street than an itinerant patent medicine peddler does to the royal surgeon on Harley Street. Mr. Wheelwright, whatever his other faults, is not a stingy man. Miss Ladell may not be respectable, but she leads a comfortable life which would be the envy of most of the women of London."

"It is disgusting!" I exclaimed. "When I think of the poor women who come to the clinic struggling to get by on a few shillings a week, their families crammed into a single filthy room, half of them married to drunkards or ruffians… They must suffer abuse and see their children half starved and sick. What is the sense of it all?"

Even under the red wig and mustache Holmes looked grim. "I do not know, Henry."

"That some vile woman…"

"First you were willing to make her the arch-conspirator, and now you portray her as the Whore of Babylon. She may be quite… respectable, in her own way."

"You are joking!"

"Not at all. Mr. Wheelwright does not strike me as a furtive sensualist. I expect he has found a woman better matched to his plodding intellect and leaden soul. You might also recall the frequently quoted—but rarely followed—exhortation: 'Let he who is without sin cast the first stone.' We shall shortly be meeting Miss Ladell, and I shall reserve judgment until then."

Holmes had the driver let us out a street away from the house; plumbers must not be seen arriving in a cab. The afternoon was cold and wet, the yellow fog dirty and heavy with the odor of coal smoke. Our coats were none too warm, and the toolbox was so heavy I had to keep switching it from hand to hand.

Irritated, I said, "What on earth is in this box?"

"More wrenches, cast-iron pipe, and a first-class snake."

"A *what*?"

"A plumber's snake, a device of coiled metal used to unplug drains. Henry, I shall do most of the talking. Remember to appear somewhat stupid."

The house was not large, but appeared pleasant, reminding me of a country cottage. Built of sturdy red brick, smoke billowed from its chimney. The rose bushes had been cut back for winter, and the hedge along the side was neatly trimmed. Holmes and I went to the door around back, and he knocked.

An elderly woman opened the door. She had on a plain black coat and hat and was obviously about to leave. Her eyes took in our filthy apparel and soiled faces, and her nose wrinkled in distaste. "Yes?"

Holmes tipped his ragged bowler. "Afternoon, ma'am. 'Eard you've 'ad some problems with the water closet. Yer landlord sent me and me mate 'ere to 'ave a look."

The maid still seemed unsure about us. "I was just going out for the afternoon, but the mistress will be here if…"

"Oh, we won't be no trouble, ma'am. Quiet as mouses, we'll be."

"Perhaps if you could come back next week?"

Holmes scowled horribly and shook his head. "No, ma'am, I can't recommends it. You'd be takin' a terrible chance, you would. Once a water closet is plugged up, they'll flood on you fer sure, and then yer done fer! The smell is powerful bad, and the dirty water and stinkin' muck soaks into yer fine oak floors and carpets. It's an 'orrible fate, one I wouldn't wish on me worst enemy. Best let us 'ave a look."

The maid had grown pale. "I shall ask the mistress." Her nose wrinkled again. "I guess you can wait inside."

Holmes held his hat before him, the brim clutched in his filthy hands. "Most kind of you, ma'am. Bitter cold and damp 'tis." He smiled; his blackened teeth truly appeared to be missing.

We stepped into the kitchen, which was gloriously warm and smelled like fresh bread. Two loaves sat on the table near the big black iron stove. I glanced at Holmes and repressed a shudder. "You do look terrible."

He smiled. "So do you. Most plumbers are cleaner than we are, but all this filth distracts from the rest of our appearance."

The maid soon returned with the mistress of the house. I was surprised. Holmes had been correct: I was expecting the Whore of Babylon—some voluptuous, painted creature in scanty garments. Miss Ladell resembled an ordinary woman of a respectable class, the wife of a well-to-do shopkeeper, banker, or merchant. She wore a plain blue muslin dress, and her blonde hair was braided and wound up at the back. She was pretty enough—fair skin tending toward rosiness; blue eyes and a small turned-up nose; a tiny mouth—but nowhere near so stunningly beautiful as Violet. Although not corpulent, her looks tended toward plumpness, her corseted waist rather thick. Her neck was short, full, and round; her jaw not well defined; her chin afloat on her fleshy white throat. She gave us a polite smile.

"So you wish to examine the water closet?"

"Yes, ma'am. Yer landlord thought we'd best 'ave a look. As I told yer good woman 'ere, what we want at all cost is to avoid a flood. I've seen deluges which would've frightened old Noah himself."

Miss Ladell laughed at this witticism. "We surely do. Your coming seems providential. I have had some difficulties but I hadn't said anything to Doh—to the landlord."

"Someone shorly did, ma'am."

"Well, do come have a look. I do not want to suffer this deluge of yours."

"Wise, ma'am—very wise."

The maid's brow was still wrinkled. "I can remain here until they are finished if…"

"No, no, Philomena—you must have your afternoon off. Baby Gerald will be waiting for you. These men, I am sure, know their profession and can be trusted."

"Thank you, madam." She smiled at her mistress, then regarded us suspiciously. "Mind you clean up after yourselves. If you leave a mess, I'll be after you."

Holmes gave her a reproachful look. "Ma'am, we're no sloppy pigs like some inferior plumbers. Part of the job is gettin' everything back spick and span." He held up his arms and his filthy sleeves. "We may get a bit on ourselves, but none gets left behind when we be done. Clean enough to eat off'uv, it'll be, the tile all a-sparklin'."

The maid nodded. "Make sure it is. Good afternoon."

"Goodbye, Philomena. The water closet is this way, Mister…?"

"Brownstone, ma'am. And this is my assoshut, Mr. Blackdrop."

I was holding my hat and bowed my head. "My pleasure, madam."

She gave me a curious look, and as she was not watching Holmes, he frowned and shook his head at me.

"Uh, nice place you 'ave 'ere, mum," I said.

"Thank you, Mr. Blackdrop." She led us out of the kitchen.

As I followed, I noticed that she smelled faintly of lavender. Two small black dogs rushed us, barking loudly, Scottish terriers by the look of them. Their two-foot long bodies were supported by six-inch legs;

their fur shaggy; their pointed ears standing upright.

Miss Ladell clapped her hands firmly. "No! Down, Blackie! Down, Reggy!"

One of the little beasts had his paws up on my leg, but at the command from their mistress, they both retreated.

The furniture in the sitting room was solid and well built, if not terribly expensive, and the carpet and drapes were of similar quality. However, every surface was covered with some bric-a-brac or knickknack: tiny glazed figurines of cheerful peasant lads and lasses (many I recognized as German); ornate china plates with patterns or paintings on them, all propped upright on holders, the place of honor going to Queen Victoria, whose dour visage showed alongside the number fifty. On the wall were the mass-produced productions of paintings and etchings which had become generally available: line drawings of trite London scenes; various languishing, voluptuous maidens who owed much to the pre-Raphaelites; and of course, a sweet, bare foot girl of about four, blonde and blue-eyed, with her faithful collie. Adding further to the clutter were the doilies and lacework covering all the furniture.

As Holmes and I glanced about, Miss Ladell smiled, glad to have all her treasures admired. Holmes stopped before the plate of Queen Victoria. "A good likeness of 'er majesty there." He took another step and glanced down at the cloth covering the round oak table. "But yer lacework is very fine, ma'am, very fine. So many doilies."

"Thank you, but how did you know it was my work?"

Holmes hesitated only a second. "Well, ma'am, I'm not Sherlock 'Omes." He gave a hearty laugh. "But I noticed the callous on yer finger. My wife does a good bit o' crocheting, and she 'as the very same callous. But what really gave you away was yer needles and yer work over there by the chair."

Miss Ladell laughed, the sound good-natured and lacking the artifice of many ladies. "Of course." She glanced down at her fingers. "There are those who think callouses are dreadful."

"But you know better, ma'am, I can tell."

She had a rather charming smile, which her rosy complexion and plumpness augmented. "I was not raised for idleness, Mr. Brownstone. I truly believe an idle mind is the devil's workshop. My knitting and crocheting keep me busy, and... I even make a few shillings selling my things."

Holmes nodded. "I can see 'ow. Fine work, 'tis. Very delicate, like. The missus's ain't half so fine, but never tell her so!"

Miss Ladell laughed again. "The water closet is here."

Holmes opened the door, and then let out a long loud whistle. "Wot a beauty, ma'am!" It was an impressive fixture, all dark oak, shining brass, and gleaming white porcelain. Holmes gave the brass chain a pull, and it flushed with a vigorous swirl of water. He scowled horribly. "Don't much care for the sound of that."

Miss Ladell stared at him. "Is it broken?"

"Not yet, but the water don't sound right. Well, we'll 'ave 'er good as new in a few minutes. Best to run the snake through 'er, unclog everything down below."

"I'll leave you to your work," said Miss Ladell.

I opened the toolbox. Holmes took out what appeared to be an enormous coil of metal rope, with a nasty-looking spiral of wire at the very end. "You are not really going to use this thing?" I whispered.

"We must earn our keep, Henry." He began to work the snake around the curve of the bowl and down the hidden drain. "This skill may prove useful to you some day if you cannot find a plumber."

I spent the next half-hour watching the snake unfurl itself into the depths, shake itself as he attempted to dislodge some obstruction, then slowly wind its way back up. The business was not too unpleasant until the snake re-emerged, soiling the water with black slime. The curled wire actually had some disgusting gook wadded upon it, the stench unbearable.

"I think we may have actually saved her from some trouble," Holmes said. He wadded the thing up in a rag, stuffing it and the snake back in the toolbox. He used another rag to clean up.

We stepped back into the sitting room, and I allowed myself the pleasure of again breathing through my nose. Holmes smiled proudly. "Good as new, ma'am. You needn't fear no deluge no more."

Miss Ladell set down her crochet needles and rose. "Thank you very much, Mr. Brownstone." She hesitated for a moment. "Would you care for a cup of tea in the kitchen before you leave?"

Holmes nodded. "Shorly, ma'am. That's most kind of you."

We started for the kitchen. The two terriers were seated together on a chair, but abruptly they leaped down and barked. Miss Ladell clapped her hands again. "*No*—stay, Blackie. Stay, Reggy." Reluctantly the dogs halted and watched us. "They are good dogs, but uncomfortable with strangers in the house." She closed the door behind us, then gestured at the table with her dainty white hand. "Please sit down."

The big black iron stove radiated heat, and the kitchen was much warmer than the rest of the house. Humming softy, Miss Ladell opened a canister, then put tea into one half of the tea ball and screwed on the top. She poured hot water from the kettle into a blue-and-white china pot.

"We must let it steep. Would you care for a biscuit?"

Holmes shook his head, but I realized I was hungry. "Yes, please, mum," I said.

Holmes glanced about the kitchen. The walls were painted yellow, lace curtains hung alongside the windows, the room clean and bright.

"Nice cheerful place y'ave 'ere, ma'am."

"Thank you, Mr. Brownstone. I am very proud of my little house."

"I'd wager you'd not trade it fer the biggest mansion in all of London town."

She gave her head an enthusiastic nod. "You would win your bet. I do not want some enormous house with servants underfoot. Philomena, Blackie, Reggy, and I get along perfectly here."

"And what about yer mister?" Holmes asked innocently.

Miss Ladell was so fair than any hint of a flush showed immediately; her face went quite pink. "I am not married, Mr. Brownstone."

Holmes appeared utterly surprised. "No?"

"No. This house is… My uncle was quite well-to-do and left me a bit of money when he died."

"Ah." Holmes nodded. "Fortunate for you, but I'm surprised some gent 'asn't snatched you up, so to speak, a fine young lady like yerself."

She gave a weak shrug. "There is a gentleman I see occasionally."

"Well, what's the matter with the bloke that 'e ain't married you at once?"

The flush deepened, and she shrugged. "I'm sure I don't know." She took the pot and began to pour the tea.

"I don't mean to embarrass you, ma'am. Fergive me if I've been rude."

She set down a blue-and-white cup of tea on a matching saucer before Holmes. "Not at all, Mr. Brownstone. You are very kind. Do you take sugar?" He shook his head. "And you, Mr. Blackdrop?"

"One lump."

Holmes drank his tea, slurping loudly. I frowned at him, but Miss Ladell hardly seemed to notice. "Fine tea, ma'am. Won't you join us?"

She hesitated, and then smiled. "Certainly."

She poured another cup of tea and dropped in three cubes of sugar. Holmes and I slid our chairs to the side, leaving more room for her. She took two digestive biscuits from a tin, then sat down and handed me one.

"Here's your biscuit, Mr. Blackdrop. I nearly forgot."

She sipped politely at her tea, ignoring the dreadful slurping Holmes made as he drank. He set down his cup. "I'll bet a lady like yerself could run yer own shop, all full of lace and doilies and fine things."

She stared incredulously at him. "You're a wonder, Mr. Brownstone. I have always wanted to have my own shop. My father is a shopkeeper."

"A fine trade fer a lady. Perhaps yer gentleman will marry you and set you up in such a shop."

She shook her head. "I think not. He does not approve of ladies in trade."

Holmes frowned. "The kind who wants to put you on a pedestal and 'ave you sit about being beautiful and queenly all the day long."

Again she stared at him. "Exactly so. He cannot understand all my handiwork. He thinks—he thinks I should be content to do nothing, grateful for the opportunity."

"A peculiar notion, ma'am. I'm shore he wouldn't wish to sit about all day. Of course, I could use a bit of idleness now and then, but not fer day after day."

She stared off into space. "All the same, I do believe he is fond of me."

"I'm sure he must be." Holmes said this so sincerely that she smiled.

"You are a philosopher, I can tell, Mr. Brownstone."

"Not me, ma'am. I'm only an 'umble plumber who sees wot he sees. I visits the rich all the time, and while I could do fer a bit of their quid, I'd not trade places with them. Why just last week I 'ad to clean out a drain at young Mr. Wheelwright's mansion—not the old man, the one on the meat tins, but 'is son. Now 'is wife didn't seem nowhere near as satisfied with 'er lot as you."

Miss Ladell snapped a piece of biscuit off with her teeth. "What... what was the lady like? I have heard of her—because of her charitable works."

"Oh, nice enough fer a lady, but 'ardly so friendly as you. She'd never 'ave tea with a couple of plumbers!" He laughed.

Miss Ladell's smile was forced. "Is she—is she not rather cold?"

Holmes frowned, his brow furrowing below the jagged edge of the red wig. "Maybe a bit. Of course, we 'ardly saw 'er. Our dealins was with the 'ousekeeper."

"And was she very beautiful?"

"No, she 'ad a face like a dried prune." Both Miss Ladell and I stared incredulously at him. He grinned, the corners of his mouth lost beneath the mustache. "Oh, you mean the missus—not the 'ousekeeper. She was a fairly fine specimen of a woman, but not enough flesh on 'er fer my taste. Too bony. As I say, I like a bit of flesh on a woman."

Miss Ladell's smile was genuine now. "I'd not trade places with her." Up until then, I had been favorably impressed with her, but I did not care for the smugness in her voice.

Holmes set down his cup. "Well, we've loitered about long enough. There's other drains to conquer. Drink up, Blackdrop, and let's be off."

We all rose, and she followed us to the door. Holmes had his hat in one hand, a congenial smile on his face. Abruptly he frowned and pointed at the wall beside Miss Ladell. "There's an ugly brute of a spider, ma'am. If you…"

Her eyes widened. She strode quickly around behind us, then seized Holmes' grimy arm. "Oh, please kill it—please do!" She would not look at the wall.

"I think it's gone behind that picture of the little girl."

"Oh, please kill it—Mr. Brownstone—please. I cannot bear a spider! *Please.*"

"Very well, ma'am. My missus 'ates 'em too." He withdrew a dirty handkerchief from his pocket, then raised the picture frame and proceeded to catch the nonexistent spider. "Got 'im!"

She raised her eyes, sighed, and put her small white hand over her bosom. "That's the second service you've done me today, Mr. Brownstone. Thank you, oh so very much."

"My pleasure, ma'am. Guh'day."

"Guh'day," I echoed. "The tea and biscuit was good."

"One moment, please." She seized a small purse and gave us each a shilling. We thanked her. She smiled again, opening the door to let us out. Holmes and I walked around the house. I put the shilling in my pocket. The fog and damp cold were cutting after the warm kitchen.

"That is a side of you I think I have never seen before," I said.

Holmes laughed. "I must confess that I sometimes find my disguises positively liberating. Well, Henry, do you think we have found our mastermind, the brain behind the spider-filled cake?"

I grimaced, shaking my head. "You need not remind me of my eagerness to jump to conclusions. I can think of no more unlikely suspect than Miss Ladell. She did seem somehow... well... positively wholesome."

Holmes laughed in earnest. "I warned you that might be the case."

"She was very candid with us. She does treasure her little house and her knickknacks."

Holmes nodded. "I agree. She has little capacity for subterfuge. Her emotions are transparent. She was genuinely curious about Violet Wheelwright. And her terror of spiders was not feigned."

"It's curious. I... she is nowhere near so beautiful as Violet, but she is appealing. I must admit I found her more likable than Donald Wheelwright."

Holmes gave a sharp laugh. "That is no great compliment, but yes, again I agree."

"Her taste is another matter. Those dreadful plates! Michelle has a horror of such things."

"Her doilies were well made, but her taste, although predictable, is not the best. She and Wheelwright are well suited for each other. A pity he did not marry someone like her. Of course, his father would have never allowed such a match."

I shook my head. "It is all so senseless. And we have wasted an entire afternoon."

"*Wasted?* Hardly! You have had your introduction to the snake."

"God save me from the snake!"

"And we have ruled out a major suspect. We are making progress. The goal must be to discover the perpetrator—not to have the perpetrator be the person we wish." The corners of his mouth vanished briefly under the red mustache. "That would be setting ourselves an impossible task. We are closer to the truth than we were this morning." We walked along in silence for a minute or two. "I must confess... I wish Miss Ladell could have her little shop and that Wheelwright could marry her. Well, we must try to hail a cab. I hope we have better luck this time. Would a bath interest you, Henry?"

"I have longed for one since I first put on these clothes."

"Let us return to Baker Street, fetch clean clothes, and then I know an excellent Turkish bath. We can spend the remainder of the afternoon soaking off the grime and cold."

"A heavenly idea!" I exclaimed. I shifted the toolbox from my right hand to my left. "Your snake is certainly heavy."

Holmes shook his head. "I fear we've a long ways to go before we make a real plumber of you, Blackdrop."

Ten

While we were sitting in the Turkish bath, the steam permeating our cold weary frames, Holmes appeared to doze. I was sleepy myself and closed my eyes.

"It might be worth the risk."

I gave a start, and then realized he had spoken. "What did you say?"

"I said it might be worth the risk. There is an unsavory fellow I have dealt with in the past, one Mortimer 'Ratty' Grace. He has been involved in every type of vice—cracksmen, pickpockets, fake revivalist preachers, and various swindlers—but his specialty now is prostitution. He owns several brothels. He might know something about the recent outbreak of blackmail and the mysterious Angels."

I gave my head a shake. "He sounds like a thoroughly despicable specimen of humanity."

"Oh, he is—although considering him human may be something of a compliment." He frowned slightly and stared at me through the steamy air. "We are not on the best of terms. I have frustrated certain schemes of his, but I also saved the life of his… friend, Moley."

"Moley? *Moley?* And Ratty? They sound as if they are characters in a children's story book."

Holmes smiled. "Hardly. One would not allow children anywhere near these two creatures." He closed his eyes and sat back.

"Well?"

He did not open his eyes. "'Well' what?"

"Are you going to arrange to meet with Ratty and Moley?"

"I am."

"But what of the risk you mentioned?"

"I shall take it."

Not being by nature one who relishes danger and adventure, I hesitated. "Do you want me to accompany you?"

Sherlock's dark eyebrows sank, a half-inch vertical line appearing on either side of the bridge of his nose. "Ratty favors a certain decrepit tavern in Underton, the worst rookery in London, and he holds a man's life very cheap."

I swallowed, my mouth suddenly dry despite the hot moist air. "Then I doubt you will want to venture into the lion's den alone."

Holmes was quiet for a moment. At last he opened his eyes. "No, I would not wish to go alone."

"I shall come with you."

"As I have said, the risk is considerable. Speak with Michelle before you hazard your life."

"Knowing her, if I do, she will wish to accompany us."

Holmes frown deepened. "Absolutely not."

"Do you think I would allow such a thing? I shall make some excuse and come with you."

Holmes opened his mouth, and then closed it. Finally, he said, "I should be grateful for your company, but do not feel obliged. Should you change your mind I shall certainly understand." He closed his eyes again and let his head rest back against the tiles.

"Will it be safer for two people to visit Ratty than for one?"

"Undoubtedly."

"Then I shall come."

Holmes said nothing, and I closed my own eyes and tried—in vain—to regain the warm, easy comfort I had felt earlier.

"Thank you, Henry."

Sunday was an uneventful day, and I worked to put our prospective visit out of mind. Perhaps, after all, "Ratty" would not wish to meet with Sherlock. Monday further lulled me into a sense of security. However, Tuesday I received a telegram asking me to be at Baker Street by eight p.m. should I wish to visit Mr. Mortimer R. Grace. My stomach lurched. I thought of backing out, but I knew I could never forgive myself should anything happen to my cousin.

I told Michelle that Sherlock wanted me to accompany him, but I did not mention the danger involved. However, I almost gave myself away with my farewell embrace. My eyes grew teary as I thought how much I loved her and as I reflected that I might not see her again. She knew me too well not to sense that something was wrong, but I rushed out before she could question me.

The weather was foul, a cold blustery rain, and Holmes' sitting room was so warm and inviting I would have gladly remained behind, even were our endeavor not so perilous. He sat in a wicker chair before the fire, legs crossed, a pipe with a long stem between his lips. He wore the purple dressing gown and his favorite slippers. One would have thought he was settled in for the night.

He withdrew his watch, noted the time and gestured at a chair with his long graceful fingers. "Have a seat, Henry. You are early. Warm yourself by the fire." He took a long draw from the pipe. "It is as I thought. We shall have to enter the singularly unpleasant Underton rookery and meet Ratty at the Sporting Tavern. There we have the exciting spectacle of some ratting to anticipate."

"Ratting?"

Holmes gave an ironic smile. "Although not as popular as in Dickens' day, it remains a favorite sporting event of the less fortunate. Rats are turned loose in a miniature circus and then the competing dogs, one by one, are set upon the unfortunate rodents. The dog who slays the most rats is champion."

"Good Lord—such things still go on?"

"One may sympathize with the bear, the cock, or the dog: hence the prohibition of their combats. Rats, however, have few friends." Sherlock exhaled a cloud of smoke, the bowl of the pipe nestled in his right hand. "We shall have to go incognito. I fear we must be nearly as filthy as our friends Mr. Brownstone and Mr. Blackdrop."

I gave him an annoyed look. "Oh, not again."

"Our journey will be dangerous enough disguised as ruffians, but were two prosperous gentlemen to pass through Underton after dark, they would not last five minutes." He stood, tapped the bowl of the pipe into the fire, and set the pipe alongside its companions in the rack on the mantel. "Come."

The clothing did not stink quite so much this time, but was still frightfully soiled. We put on black trousers, jackets, and hats. The bowlers were the same as before. I recognized the torn brim on Holmes'. His jacket had once been a frock coat, but all the buttons and the silk on the lapels were gone, the right sleeve badly torn at the elbow. The waistcoat had been a garish, black-and-white checkered affair, but now it was dirty gray. At least my shoes were still whole—barely, given the worn leather—but Sherlock's left boot was open at the toe.

"Your foot will be soaked," I said.

"No matter."

He dirtied our faces and hands, and then blackened a few teeth. He smiled and nodded. "Very good, even if I do say so." With his skeletal frame and that gaunt face with its piercing eyes and beaked nose, he did appear rather threatening.

"I would not wish to encounter you on a dark street."

His smile was reassuring. "You also appear rather intimidating. By the way, you are to play the part of my bodyguard. Try to appear as truculent and as fierce as possible."

"Your bodyguard? Who would believe…?"

"You are tall, your fists and shoulders large. I know you have histrionic talents. Use them. Be silent but threatening. We shall have other reserves." He pulled open a drawer, removed a revolver, the metal a sinister blue-black, and handed it to me. "Be careful with this."

"You know I cannot hit the proverbial broad side of a barn."

"There are no barns where we are going, and if you need to use it, I doubt it will be from a distance." He tried to close the drawer, but it was too full of clothing. From a second drawer, he took out another revolver, which he examined and put in his coat pocket. He was searching for something else, but I turned away.

Outside the wind had picked up, and the rain seemed ready to become a downpour. "I suppose umbrellas would be out of character," I said.

"Most assuredly. Ah, Blunt is waiting for us, our Charon with his black barque."

Across the street, in the pool of light from a streetlamp, sat a battered black hansom. Both driver and horse had seen better days. The black horse's ribs were showing, his weary misery evident in his drooping posture. The driver's black mackintosh appeared waterproof, but the rain had pooled and dribbled off his worn top hat. His face was gaunt and white, an odd leer twisting his mouth. The sight reminded me of those grim medieval paintings of Death or the Plague, a hideous skeleton upon his chariot pulled by a skeleton horse.

"Blunt!" Holmes cried. "As we arranged, you will take us to the Running Fox Tavern."

"Certainly, Mr. 'Olmes." Blunt's teeth, what was left of them, were brown and rotting. He coughed once, a sound that made me think of the wasted lungs and tumorous masses I had seen in anatomy cadavers.

"I thought I told you when I last tipped you to give your horse a decent meal."

"I did, sir."

"You did not. We cannot continue our profitable association should you persist in abusing your horse."

I stepped up into the cab, glad to be out of the rain. Blunt snapped his whip, and the cab started down the street, the wheel to my left groaning horribly. It must have been misshapen, for each time the bump or flaw came round, that side of the carriage rose up, then down, with a slight jar.

"This was the best you could do for a cab?"

A streetlamp briefly illuminated Sherlock's soiled face, the ironic, tight-lipped smile. "Blunt will drive us nearer the rookery than any other cabby, and he will wait for us to return. The less distance we have to walk, the better."

The cold rain fell in earnest, blurring the gaslight and taking the sharp edges off everything: the storefronts, the countless billboards and signs. The journey was less than an hour, but the rain and fog, the groaning wheel and the regular jouncing to our left, the torturous coughs of the driver, and the thought of the danger and the ugly slum we rode toward, all combined into a waking nightmare, a ride that I shall never forget. Near the end of our journey, the buildings began to appear shabby, the streetlights fewer and further between.

We came at last to the Running Fox Tavern, a decrepit place, the creature on its signboard so worn it resembled a mangy cat rather than a fox. Holmes stepped out first. The rain had abated somewhat, but I knew I would soon be soaked to the skin. The drops felt frigid on my face, and a gust of wind seemed to reach with chilling fingers for my bones.

Sherlock took a coin from his pocket and gave it to Blunt. "We should return in an hour or two. As the night is cold, you may wish to wait inside."

"Bless you, Mr. 'Olmes." Blunt stepped down from the cab, then coughed hideously. He was only about five feet tall. He started for the door of the tavern.

"Do not drink so much you cannot drive," Sherlock said.

Blunt's laugh sounded much like his cough. "'Ave no fear. It'd take an 'ole night before you'd lose me. Come fetch me when y're back."

Sherlock turned to me. "We have about a fifteen-minute walk before us. Whatever you see, whatever anyone says to us, say nothing and continue walking. British law and civilization do not apply within Underton's boundaries."

He set off at a resolute pace down the street, and I followed, struggling with my fear. Across the street from the tavern was a tall, stately home, the windows lit up with a rosy, yellowish glow. The edifice was in much better condition than its neighbors and appeared inviting.

I raised my hand and pointed. "That place seems out of character for this neighborhood. It even has two functioning streetlamps."

Sherlock gave a sharp laugh. "It is a well-known bawdy house, Madam Irene's. You can have one of the girls for a mere seven shillings."

"That is the last thing I would want!" My voice was shrill.

"Henry, surely you must know that I would not actually suggest…"

"Forgive me. Yes, I do know that. My nerves are…"

"Well, let us go—the infernal regions await us." Sherlock turned down an alley.

Within a few yards, the rainy stinking darkness swallowed us up. The black walls rose on either side, only a window or two showing a flicker of light from within. The odor was a dreadful blend: human excrement, a rancid fatty smell, wood and coal smoke, something faintly rotten. I was glad I could not see what I was stepping in. These tenements had no plumbing; the refuse of the people packed into the dark cold rooms ended up in this foul alley. The frigid rain made a constant, gentle murmur.

"What a stench," I said.

"You should try a visit in the summer. This is nothing."

"What is it? It seems more than…"

"There is a rendering plant not half a mile from here, and next to it, a slaughterhouse."

We came out of the narrow alley and turned onto a wider cobblestone street. Here and there a streetlamp cast a feeble halo of rainy light. The buildings were mostly brick, the windows smashed out or boarded up. A group of men huddled about near a lamp, and a few pedestrians, all men in groups of two or more, walked the streets. Somewhere above us I heard a woman wailing.

"This is better than that alley," I murmured.

Sherlock's beaked, blackened visage was grotesque in the dim light. "We were safer in the darkness there."

The air was so damp that the rain seemed to come from every direction, to swirl from the side, to even fall upwards. My face was wet and very cold. I kept my hands in my pockets, my arms pressed to my side. The rain had penetrated the toes of my pathetic boots, and my stockings felt soggy.

Sherlock crossed the street to avoid passing too near any group of men; hence our path zigzagged back and forth. After about five minutes, I saw before us a particularly vile-looking man, much taller than his companions, a dilapidated top hat augmenting his height. His nose was bulbous, a mass of scar tissue covered his right cheek, and his complexion was sallow under the streetlight. I could imagine butter, rather than fat, filling that bloated, fleshy neck.

I turned away from that visage and was relieved (prematurely) when we had left behind us the man and his companions—four short, black, beetle-like creatures.

"'Ey, you two ugly crows! Come back 'ere!"

Something icy slithered up my spine, the muscles in my groin tightening.

"I mean you two stinkin' turds! Come 'ere—*now*."

"Damnation," Sherlock muttered. With a sigh, he gazed up at the solid brick facade of a building, and then walked over to it. "Keep your back to the wall," he whispered. "And do not use the revolver until I tell you to."

I watched the big man and his four compatriots approach us. He had a horrible smile on his face. With them was a mangy little black dog. "I told you nice-like to come 'ere, didn't I?" His malice was gleeful.

Sherlock's mouth twitched, his eyes widening. "You stinkin' lousy swine—you dirty fat pig—I'll cut open yer stinkin' rotten guts and feed 'em to yer dog, I will! By God, I will!" As he screamed these words, he withdrew an evil-looking knife, the blade over six inches long, and a leather-covered club.

The dog whimpered and retreated. The big man's smile had vanished, and his companions backed away. "'Ere now, mate. I…"

"Don't mate me!" Holmes yelled. "You want trouble—you can have it! Step closer and I'll cut the fat off you—I'll slice you wide open!"

I stared in horror at Holmes. His eyes were those of a madman, his face totally contorted with rage.

The big man took a step back. He had pulled a cosh from his own pocket, but it seemed more a defensive reflex that a threat. "Easy now, mate."

"Call me mate again, and I'll cut out yer liver and feed it to the rats."

The big man smiled, his fear obvious. "Easy now." He realized his friends had deserted him. "I'll just be off."

"Yer damn right you will! Get away, all of you—get away from me!" The other men and the dog fled, and their chief walked as rapidly as his massive bulk allowed. "Stinkin' pig! Come back 'ere if you want trouble! I'll make stinkin' bacon strips of you!" Sherlock stepped forward.

"For God's sake." I seized his arm, convinced he was going after them.

He brusquely shook me off, and then turned, a playful smile pulling at his lips. His eyes, however, did not appear quite normal. "Rather convincing, I trust?"

"Good Lord, yes!"

"Hurry, before they change their minds." He pocketed his weapons and strode away.

My hands were still trembling. "Truly, I thought you had gone mad."

"Excellent. That was the impression I wanted. Even a base ruffian fears a true lunatic, especially one with a knife. There is no predicting what such a man will do."

The rain had let up, but the foggy mist still soaked us. A breeze assailed my nose with some fatty rancid odor, and I thought of the rendering plant and slaughterhouse.

"Is it much further?" I could not keep the desperation from my voice.

"We are nearly there, and you have done quite well."

Holmes turned right at another alley. The walls were only ten feet apart, and the stench of excrement returned. I remembered Sherlock's open-toed boot and shuddered. My feet were damp, but at least *that* could not get inside. High above us was a forlorn strip of grayish-red sky—even it appeared unclean—and ahead to our left a gas fixture hung from a bracket on the brick wall. The light shone on a sign for the Sporting Tavern.

Sherlock stopped to hand me the cosh and knife. "You may want to wave these about. Remember to appear truculent. Ratty knows me too well for me to play the lunatic with him."

I shook my head. "He comes to a place like this for amusement?"

"Yes. A former denizen of Underton, he still has a sentimental fondness for the old neighborhood."

Holmes opened the sturdy oaken door and went inside. The air was warm and so thick with smoke that one could have saved one's own tobacco and simply inhaled deeply. The din was dreadful: loud talk, laughter, drunken singing, glasses being slammed down on tables, chairs scraped across the floor. The men were a rough lot, most wearing worn gray or black coats, bowlers or cloth caps. Sherlock had certainly dressed us appropriately; no one paid us any attention.

"Would you prefer...?" A curse drowned out his words, and he leaned closer and shouted, "Gin or beer—which would you prefer?"

"Neither."

"I shall get you something for appearance's sake. You need not drink it." Sherlock clapped a coin on the counter. "Two pints of stout." Behind the bar on the wall were photographs of several pugilists, many with faces as battered as the bartender's. "Ratty will be upstairs," Holmes said, handing me my glass.

We managed to cross the packed floor without spilling too much of our beer, then went up the rickety stairway to a big open room. At its center, a gas fixture with several branches and lamps hung from the ceiling illuminating the circus. The round wooden circus was painted white, its diameter about ten feet, its sides about three feet high. Men were crowded about, most of them talking, many holding small dogs. Several of the dogs barked or yapped, their voices generally high-pitched. To one side was a raised platform where several worthies sat. Two of them were so striking I knew at once who they must be.

"Ratty and Moley," I murmured.

"Yes." Sherlock weaved through the crowd toward them.

I brushed against a man; his dog–a nearly hairless white-and-black creature–gave a bark and snapped at my arm. "Watch yerself!" snarled his owner, equally vicious.

Holmes bent closer. "Stay as far from the dogs as you can. Most of them know what is to come, and they have worked themselves into a frenzy."

Sherlock stepped up onto the platform. Another former pugilist–this one in a dark suit of a respectable cut and fabric–stood.

Ratty seized the man's wrist. "Leave him be. They are friends." He rose and extended a hand, the smile on his face turning my already queasy stomach. "Good evening, Mr. Sherlock Holmes. You are looking well, but I can't say much for your tailor."

Holmes shook his hand. "Good evening, Ratty." He nodded at the man behind Ratty who slowly stood, rising higher, ever higher.

Their nicknames were appropriate, although Moley was a monster mole, one closer in size to an elephant. He was as tall as Donald Wheelwright but terribly fat. He must have weighed nearly four hundred pounds, perhaps over four hundred. His face was oddly diminutive, and the thick lenses of his spectacles shrank his eyes, making them appear tiny. His head was quite bald, the curved pate narrower by far than his massive neck. He wore the only black frock coat in the room, one that must have taken yards of worsted.

Ratty was only slightly over five feet tall. The outspread ears, the pronounced overbite, the thin face with its pointed chin, and above all, the small, malevolent eyes did create the impression of a large rodent. He wore a brown tweed suit and a black bowler. Brownish-gray curls fluffed out from under the brim, vainly attempting to conceal his enormous ears. His companions, except for Moley, also wore dark suits and bowlers; but none had so fine a suit, or a hat so spotless, the nap so new.

Ratty gestured at the wooden chairs. "Have a seat, Mr. Holmes. And who is your friend here?"

"This is Herr Heinrich Verniger, originally of Berlin. He is a talented man with a knife or cosh. I brought him along as a precaution."

Ratty squinted at me, a smile baring his slender, sharp teeth. "Have a seat, Mr. Vinegar."

For a native of Underton, Ratty's diction was fairly good—he must have had some coaching from a teacher of elocution—but the German "Verniger" was too much for him.

We sat in the front row, the place of honor, surrounded by Ratty's gang. Holmes was next to Ratty, and beyond loomed Moley's massive bulk, his bald head rising above all else like the dome of a church.

"Well, Mr. Holmes, it has been a while. It is good to see you under more pleasurable circumstances."

Holmes nodded. "Yes. My note suggested the reason for my visit. I wished to discuss any unusual activities you may have noticed."

"That's why I'm only too happy to see you. I was hoping *you* could tell me what's what. Someone's out there, Mr. Holmes. Someone's stirring up things and causing trouble, especially with the whores. My peers..." He seemed to relish the irony of this word so much that he repeated it. "My peers and I generally get along, and we have our ways of knowing what each other is up to, but some new bloke has entered the game, some sly devil. Can you tell me who he is?"

Holmes shook his head brusquely. "No. Unfortunately I cannot."

Ratty leered. "I'm disappointed in you, Mr. Holmes."

"Do you know about the girl connected with Lord Harrington's death?"

"Of course. Stupid little baggage. Auntie Carlson was the brains behind that—or the front for the brains, anyway."

"Does Auntie Carlson have a large and intimidating presence?"

"She surely does. She's the one what was living with her two 'nieces.'"

"And do you know what has become of her?"

Ratty gave a sharp laugh, inhaling through his nose as he did so. "Now that is the interesting part. In general, if I want to find someone—especially someone as obvious as Auntie Carlson—I can. But she's vanished."

"Have you also heard of the theft of George Herbert's diamond necklace?"

Ratty nodded. "Same kind of business. The housekeeper's also vanished, but the necklace itself is for sale. The dealer is hoping to find someone who will buy it as is. It'd be a shame to cut up such a beauty. Must be some swell willing to keep it locked up, secret like, only take it out once in a while to admire. Maybe put it and little else on his doxie." He laughed again, and I had the irrational, suicidal urge to strike him. "I tried to find the housekeeper. Thieving is a dangerous occupation, not fit for an old woman. She could fall prey to all sorts of villains with such a trinket. I could offer her my protection." Again he relished the irony of a word. "I'd've given her a fair cut, but someone beat me to it."

"How do you know that?"

"How else would it've got to a dealer so fast? Many servants steal things, then realize they don't know how to dispose of the merchandise. They're shocked when they find they can get back only a fraction of the value. This old lady was with the Herberts twenty years or so. Where's she going to make the contacts to unload a hot necklace? She's not, but it was up for sale two days later. Some clever bloke planned the whole thing. A nice bit of business that—very professionally done. No breaking and ent'ring, no stupid cracksmen having at the safe. From what I hear, if it wasn't for you, Herbert wouldn't even know the necklace was gone."

"That is so." Sherlock's voice revealed his pride.

"You and me, Mr. Holmes, we know better than to leave valuables lying about the house. I keep my money and any special goods in the bank."

The crowd of men began to cheer, while the dogs simultaneously barked or howled. Approaching the ring was a man holding before him an enormous wire cage some three feet tall. Inside, packed to the top, was a writhing, shifting mass of small gray, brown, and black forms. He set the cage into the ring, then swung his legs over the wall. I watched in horror as he unfastened some latches and raised the top, letting the rats swarm into the small circus. Some ran about; others washed at their whiskered snouts with tiny paws. Some stood against the walls seeming to reflect on how they might escape. Many must have come from the sewers, for the stench was terrible.

Ratty leaned forward. "They're about to begin. Nothing like the good old sport. Care to place a bet, Mr. Holmes?"

"I am not familiar enough with the dogs to make a wager."

"I could give you some good counsel. It's only for small stakes here—a pound or two is a big bet. And it's all honest and above reproach, more so than with the horses."

Holmes shrugged, then reached into his pocket and withdrew a sovereign.

Ratty turned to his companion who had been listening silently but attentively to the conversation. "What do you say, Moley? Which dog will it be?" He put his hand briefly on the other man's thigh then quickly withdrew it. I had an odd sensation at the back of my neck.

Moley's voice was a rolling basso profundo which contrasted with Ratty's shrill tenor. "Curly is the favorite, but Prince Albert is 'ere tonight and looks 'ungry. I says Albert."

Ratty nodded. "Albert it is." He took two gold coins from his coin purse and beckoned to the burly former pugilist. "Put these three sovereigns on Prince Albert, Jack."

The pugilist nodded, stepping into the crowd.

"Tell me," Sherlock said, "earlier you mentioned something about prostitutes."

Ratty frowned and nodded. "Someone's stirring them up. I own several houses myself, as you know. There's no man neither rich nor poor in London that can't get a bit of satisfaction. If a bloke has only five shillings, there's a place not half a mile from here, and if he's got a few pounds, well, I've got nice clean, high-class girls. They'll give him a night he'll never forget, and all in well-furnished, respectable homes in the West End." He shifted his glance from Holmes to me. "If your German friend here would care for a bit of gratification…"

Outraged, I gave him a look of absolute disgust, which he severely misinterpreted. "Of course, if you're of the other persuasion, I could…"

"I am a married man!" I exclaimed.

Holmes frowned, and I tried to get hold of myself. The smoke and the din made my head hurt, and Ratty and Moley were like two creatures from a bad dream.

"I mean… *Ich*… I have a… *weibchen,* my *kleine weibchen,* who is… very dear." I struggled to produce a German accent.

Holmes nodded. "Mr. Verniger is newly married, so he reluctantly declines your generous offer. He comes from a very respectable background for a person of his occupation."

Ratty nodded. "Ah. Well, he's lucky then. I've had to work hard to pass in more respectable circles, and they still look down on me—and especially Moley. I don't care anymore. I've finally understood that they're no better than me. Let them loiter in their finery at Ascot. The boys and I know how to have a bit of fun at a fraction of the cost. Nothing like a night of drinking and ratting, huh, lads?" He clinked glasses with Moley, and all his henchmen voiced their cheery agreement. "As for you, Mr. Holmes, my offer still stands: a night at my very best house with my star performer, a veritable legend–Miss Jeanne du Baisers. It's an offer worth a good hundred pounds."

Holmes face stiffened, but he forced a smile even as he shook his head. "No. As I have told you before, I have certain moral scruples."

Ratty shook his head sadly. "A pity that. I must admit I cannot understand moral scruples, but I respect them all the same."

"We have wandered off the subject. You said someone is stirring up the prostitutes."

Ratty frowned and nodded. "Someone is putting most peculiar ideas in their heads, telling them that they shouldn't work for men like me–that it's a disgusting profession because men are disgusting–or worst yet, that they should set aside their earnings and retire as soon as possible! All sorts of oddities. Then there's all the blackmailing."

Holmes nodded emphatically. "Ah–there has been an increase."

"Most assuredly! Such news travels fast, and it's very bad for business indeed. Your police and the average citizen don't understand, but running a brothel is like running any other business. Why, I don't mean to boast, but I am one of the largest employers in London. Do you know how many women would be starving in the streets if not for me?" He must have noticed the expression on my face. "Think what you will, Mr. Vinegar. I treat my girls far better than most employers. Visit one of those textile mills if you doubt me–machines going day and night, with all those poor females working as hard and fast as they can for the paltriest of wages! If one of my girls is good at her trade, she can move up the ladder to a better house. Why, one of my best girls took up with a royal relation and retired happily! I was sorry to lose her, but…"

"We were discussing blackmail," Holmes said.

"Ah—yes, and as I was saying, it's very bad for business—just as is roughing up the customers. Volume and happy customers are the key to my success. I want the man who visits one of my houses to go away smiling and eager to return. I want him to tell all his friends about my girls. Sure, you might make a few quid blackmailing some bloke, but word gets around—it always does—and then trade drops off. That's why any girl who robs a customer or tries a bit of blackmail is out the door at once. And that's why I'm concerned, Mr. Holmes. I've had to dismiss three times as many girls this past year as before, and that's most unusual. Until now, the rate always stayed about the same, and I've been involved in the trade for twenty years."

Holmes' fingers stroked his chin. "Curious. Have you…?"

His words were cut off by the boisterous applause greeting a fat man who had stepped up onto a rickety chair. He had a huge gray mustache and wore a purple velvet vest. "Welcome, gents! Welcome, one and all, to the Sportin' Tavern, and now it's time for our sport. Everyone placed their bets? If not, see Fred over there in the corner. Raise yer hand, Fred. Now let's get to it. You all know the rules. Whichever dog kills the most rats in two minutes wins the grand prize. First up'll be the current champ, Curly Joe."

A toothless old man at the front held up a truculent little brown bulldog whose face had many folds. Curly's partisans cheered loudly. The dog nearly writhed from his master's arms, so desperate was he to get at the rats. I had a sick feeling in my stomach and took a swallow of the foul stout. I did not care for rats, but I did not enjoy seeing any creature slaughtered.

Holmes started to question Ratty again, but his eyes were fixed on the ring. "Hold off, Mr. Holmes. I want to watch Curly. He was a wonder in his prime, but he's a bit old now. He's put on weight, hasn't he, Moley?"

"A regular little pig," rumbled his companion.

The master of ceremonies had withdrawn a gold watch and raised his hand. "Ready—set—*go!*"

Curly fell upon the rats like an avenging angel, catching them by the throats and shaking them. One he caught by the hindquarters and flung against the wall. The rats raced about, vainly attempting to escape. Some tried to work their way into the crack between the wall and the floor. One of the bolder ones leaped at Curly and clamped his teeth into the dog's ear. The dog released another rat and gave a howl, then shook his head wildly. The rat swung about, his long pink tail whipping through the air, but his teeth held their grip.

Ratty's smile was fierce. "He'll never win now. Too slow by far."

Seeing that shaking would not dislodge the rat, Curly changed his tactics and swung his head around, smacking the rat against the wall. With a squeal the rat let go, and Curly was on him at once.

"Time!" The man in the vest raised his hand.

"'Ere, Curly." With some difficulty, the elderly owner managed to pull the dog from the ring.

Two men in black aprons stepped into the circus and began gathering the dead or dying rats, while the master of ceremonies conferred with another man.

"Twenty-one rats it is for Curly!"

There was some feeble cheering, but the groans of disappointment were louder.

"No, he'll never win now. I recall one time he killed nearly fifty. Of course, that was the best night of his life."

I drank my stout and glanced at the men all around me, their faces hot and flushed from drink and excitement, and I felt, as never before, the incredible gulf between us. How could anyone enjoy this spectacle? It was so vile, so base and vicious. The Roman crowd at the Coliseum must have resembled this mob. My stomach twisted, and for a moment I feared I might vomit. I wanted to stand up and flee, but that was foolish. Getting away from Underton alive would be difficult enough even with Holmes' aid.

Ratty sat back and turned to us. "Now, then, Mr. Holmes, what was you asking about?"

"Have you no idea who is stirring up the prostitutes?"

"I have my suspicions. There is a certain revivalist church group made up of females. Angels of the Lord, they call themselves. Most of the preachers who come round are harmless fools. One such minister came to the house near here, and the girls got so tired of listening to his whining and lamenting about hellfire that they finally jumped him and pulled off his trousers. Gave him a blanket and told him to be gone or they'd strip him naked then start on themselves. I saw that part. You should have seen his face. A big gangly fellow, a blanket wrapped round his scrawny legs."

Moley's face reddened and his shoulders began to quake. He rumbled but nothing much came out. Glancing at him, Ratty began to laugh. Moley finally released some air, the sound something like an ill-firing engine, "puh-puh-puh."

"He was out the door in a flash and ran down the street. What a sight!"

Moley finally opened his mouth, emitting a veritable shriek of laughter, but the cheers and shouts of the crowd soon drowned him out. Another dog careened about the ring, snatching madly at the rats.

"Anyway, these Angels of the Lord are far cleverer than most preachers. They sound like... suffragettes or socialists. They tell my girls they are being exploited and that they need to unite and demand better wages. Now, as I've said, any of my girls who wants better wages can get them by moving up the ladder. It's survival of the fittest, after all. These Angels are a tough lot; a tight group, very secretive. Many of them are former prostitutes or dismissed servants. They tell the girls once their looks are gone they'll be cast out on the streets. They tell them how bad all men are and how the females have to stick together. It's very sad. I remember one bright smiling lass who had a great future before her. One of the Angels talked to her, and next thing you knew she was all sullen. Became a regular rotten apple. She tried a bit of blackmail with a poor clerk, and of course I had to let her go."

Holmes frowned. "And you think... some person is behind the Angels?"

Ratty nodded. "Oh, yes. I know talent when I see it. The head Angel is clever, whoever he is. The Angels may be righteous, but they're making a good take. The person is misguided: blackmail and theft are a dangerous way to make money. Oh, I've tried them both, as you know, Mr. Holmes, but my houses are safer and more reliable."

"And none of your—" Holmes smiled ironically— "peers knows who is behind the Angels either?"

"No one knows. Like I said, I was hoping you could tell me."

Holmes' upper lip curled. "Not yet."

"Look at that pathetic thing!" Ratty said.

A roar of laughter went up as a fat little terrier was set in the ring and gazed wearily at the rats.

"Get 'em, Tiger!" The owner was heavy himself, with protruding eyes and clenched fists. "Get 'em!"

"'E's too fat to move."

"Try starvin' 'im for a week or two next time!"

The humiliated owner withdrew the dog even before the two minutes were up. Holmes' long fingers made fists, and he pounded lightly at his knees, his jaw thrusting forward. He glanced at me and must have seen the desperation in my eyes. "There is little point in remaining." He turned to Ratty. "Tell me, have you ever heard of Geoffrey Steerford?"

"Something to do with finance and speculation, isn't it? Heard of him, but risky investments are not for me. My profits go straight into a good sturdy English bank."

Holmes took off his hat and ran his fingers through his damp hair. "Ratty, thank you for your assistance. I hope to remove this thorn from your flesh. I must be leaving."

Ratty's jaw dropped, again revealing his narrow sharp teeth. "So soon? But Prince Albert hasn't even had his chance yet! Won't you at least stay for that?"

"I have… other business. And Herr Verniger wishes to return to his wife."

"Ah." Ratty gave me a conspiratorial wink, which made me want to slap him. "It seems a shame. Not very polite, it is." His eyes narrowed, suddenly dangerous. "I could make you stay."

Something in his tone of voice made my flesh crawl, and I thought if I had to remain in that stinking, noisy, hellish den for even a minute longer, I would go mad. I slipped my hand into my pocket and seized the revolver handle while trying to look ferocious, not frightened out of my wits. Holmes stared coldly at Ratty, who was the only one smiling now. His men had all gone silent. Moley was frowning, his squinting eyes appearing even tinier behind the thick lenses.

"I think not," Holmes said.

"No? My pals are good men."

"Then it would be foolish to risk their lives—or your own."

Ratty's nostrils flared, and he gave a sharp laugh. "Oh, very well, be off with you then! I can't force you to share in our good times." He laughed again, and his companions joined in. They seemed as relieved as I. "What about your sovereign? I'm sure you'll win two on it."

"You may keep them, Ratty. After all, the tip was yours, and you have told me a great deal this evening." Holmes stood up.

"That's good of you." Ratty seemed genuinely pleased although he must already have had a fortune. He rose and nodded at me. "A pleasure making your acquaintance, Mr. Vinegar." Moley loomed up behind him.

I nodded and tried to smile. "Yah, yah."

We set down our glasses on our chairs then stepped off the platform. "Keep me informed!" Ratty shouted. He turned to the pugilist who'd taken his bet. "Jack, another round here—my mouth is positively parched."

A dog leaped into the ring, teeth bared, and seized a big gray rat by the throat, releasing a spray of blood. Small red splatters now covered the white paint of the floor and the wall.

I shoved aside a man who blocked my way, cursing him angrily. I made it to the stairs and went down them two at a time. My eyes burned from the smoke; they watered and stung.

"Henry!" Holmes shouted. "Henry!"

I strode through the pub, which was half vacant now because of the ratting upstairs, and pulled open the oak door. The cold wet fog enveloped me. After the heat and noise of the ratting den, it was like plunging into a quiet icy stream—a fetid one. The fatty, rancid smell of the rendering plant and the muted decay of the slaughterhouse mingled with the mist. My stomach lurched, and I tasted something hot and foul, which I fought to keep down. My hand groped out as I sagged against the brick wall.

"Henry—what is it?"

"I think I am about to vomit."

"Little wonder. I should never have brought you with me."

"Are you mad? You would have faced that odious little vermin alone?"

He seized my arm. "Try walking. It may steady your stomach."

"Yes. My God, let's get out of here." I lunged forward, but his grip tightened.

"I said walking, not running. In another quarter of an hour we will be out of here. In an hour or two you will be with Michelle."

I made a loud sound between a sob and a laugh. "Can it be? Shall I ever see her again?"

"Of course you will."

We were in the blackest part of the alley now. Most of the windows on either side were dark. The rain had already soaked my clothes again, and I started to shiver. Holmes still held my arm. "The trip was well worth it, Henry. He told me little I did not know or suspect, but confirmation of one's theories is of value in a case like this."

"He is not really a man, is he, Sherlock? He was truly a rat, and the rest of them were not men either. They were dogs—or pigs. Someone—Circe, I suppose—had turned them into swine. Or maybe rats. Did you ever see so many rats? It is the tails I cannot abide. Their bodies are all furry, but those pink hairless tails…"

"Please stop that, Henry. You have shown your bravery. Now show some good sense. Ratty is only a man. Were you to strike him down, another Ratty would arise. It is only a business to him, and he does treat his 'girls' fairly well. I thought he might know… If even Ratty and his friends are in the dark, then no one knows."

We had turned onto the cobblestone street. The rain poured down, drenching us to the skin. A few men were out, but they huddled under the shelter of the eves. I was shivering so hard my teeth wanted to chatter.

"Aren't you cold?" I asked. A streetlight lit up the steamy vapor of my breath.

"Yes, but this rain is a good thing. The roving bands like the one we met earlier will prefer to stay indoors until it lets up. It is time to consider what we might have to eat and drink when we return to Baker Street. We deserve some reward for this evening's work."

"Nothing for me. I shall never eat again."

"Perhaps curried rats tails?"

"Sherlock!" In spite of myself, a strange, outraged laugh burst from my lips.

He gave a great roar of laughter, drowning out the steady sound of the rain on the dark stones about us. "Forgive me, it was a very ill jest, but one I could not resist." He stopped before an alley. "And here is the gateway back to the surface, back for me—I who have no Michelle—to *Il Purgatorio*, while you pass upward to *Il Paradiso*."

We started down the alley, the featureless brick walls rising on each side. "You had your chance," I said. "Ratty offered you a night with the lovely Jeanne du Baisers."

Holmes was briefly silent, and I could barely see the black shape of him beside me, let alone his face. The alley was quieter and somewhat sheltered from the downpour.

"Ah, yes, the lovely Mademoiselle Du Baisers. One can imagine how lovely, how radiant, such a woman must be." His voice was full of loathing.

"When we reach the end of this alley are we almost to the Running Fox?"

"Yes, it is just around the corner."

The light from the street ahead of us spilled into the alley, and I could see the raindrops' slanted fall. Perhaps it was only my imagination, but already it seemed to smell cleaner. I staggered out into the street and swung my arms about, staring up at the cloudy heavens. The raindrops stung my cheeks and eyes. My hat fell off.

"Saved!" I cried. "Shall I kiss the ground?"

Holmes smiled. The rain had smeared the blackening on his face, and his dark clothing was soaked. All the same, he seemed as oddly happy as I. "I cannot recommend it. While not the equal of the alley, the pavement here is none too clean."

We started down the street, and abruptly the rain diminished. A great quiet seemed to settle about us. A lone carriage passed, the horse's hooves clopping regularly on the street. It stopped ahead of us at the stately old house with the two streetlights.

"I am so glad to be out of there," I mumbled. Never again would I volunteer for any insane adventures!

Holmes grabbed my arm and pulled me back against the wall, clapping his other hand over my mouth. All my fears returned at once. "What?" I tried to say, but could not speak through his hand.

"We are in no danger. Be quiet and still. Do you understand?" I nodded, and he lowered his hand. "Look over there."

We were in the shadows and behind a hedge of bushes and a thick tree trunk. Across the street, two women stood in the doorway talking. One was older and wore a gaudy, elaborate gown; the other was a slight figure in a black dress, bonnet, and coat. The older woman seemed to be thanking the younger woman.

"That is Madam Irene," Holmes whispered. "The brothel is hers."

I frowned. The younger woman was twisted partly away, and the light on the porch was not good. Still, she seemed oddly familiar.

"Good night, and bless you," exclaimed the older woman, her voice ringing out. "Truly you are an Angel of the Lord!"

The woman in black turned and started down the walkway to the waiting hansom. The light from the streetlamp fell full on her face, showing her pale skin, thin nose, and tight lips. The bonnet sat back on her head so that we could see the black hair parted in the middle.

"Good Lord," I said.

"Hush!"

She seemed almost to hear me, for she hesitated and gazed about. We did not move. She went to the end of the walkway where she was hidden from us by the cab. The driver climbed back up, then snapped his whip and started down the dark, barren street.

Holmes took a deep breath, then released my arm. "Mrs. Lovejoy?" I asked.

He nodded. "Yes. Mrs. Lovejoy."

Eleven

Henry had behaved so strangely before he left that I resolved to wait up for him. He returned just before midnight, murmured, "Thank God," and gave me an embrace that took my breath away. I demanded to know where he had been, and when he hesitated, I told him we must not try to deceive one another. Clearly, he was relieved to tell me the truth.

The mention of Underton made the back of my neck feel cold. I listened silently as he related the whole nightmarish story—the tubercular coachman, Sherlock's performance as a lunatic, the encounter with Ratty and Moley, the disgusting spectacle of the ratting, and the unexpected appearance of Mrs. Lovejoy. My anxiety grew, manifesting itself as a tightness in my throat and chest. When he was finished, I began to weep, an action that surprised us both.

He tried to comfort me—I was not only fearful but outraged. "How could you do such a thing and not even tell me? How could you?"

His own eyes filled with tears as he apologized.

We sat together by the fire a long while. Henry was badly chilled from being wet and cold for so long. We actually fell asleep, and only later did we wake and go upstairs.

The next day, Wednesday, was my day at the clinic. Violet was there although I had told her not to come. She was not squeamish, but the harried pace and the frightful condition of most of the patients were agitating and disturbing. She did not look well. She had grown thinner, gaunter, and although she was still undeniably beautiful, she appeared oddly fragile, vulnerable even—qualities I had never associated with her.

She lasted until mid-afternoon, but then, as I was stitching up a nasty wound in a man's leg, I noticed her turn absolutely white. The patient, a large, heavily muscled workman, lay unconscious from the ether on my improvised operating table.

I turned to Jenny. The contrast between her and Violet was striking. With her youth and rosy complexion, she radiated health and well-being. "See to Violet, my dear. She is about to faint."

"I am not." Even as she spoke, her brown eyes grew glassy, and she swayed.

"Hurry," I said to Jenny.

Violet let her lead her away. Jenny returned almost at once. She shook her head. "Is Mrs. Wheelwright ill? She does not seem herself."

"She is ill. I told her I thought she should remain at home."

Jenny's concern was obvious. "Is it serious?"

"Not yet, but it could be."

Jenny shook her head. "I cannot understand it. She has everything, has she not? She is beautiful, wealthy, and clever. And yet, she has always seemed so... sad."

I glanced at Jenny's blue eyes, the clear, youthful innocence reflected there. If I could not fathom Violet's torments, how could I begin to explain them to Jenny? I prayed silently that Jenny and her young man might truly learn to love one another. Recently we had talked again, and at least she knew what the whole business was about.

Jenny nodded at the unconscious man. "Can I help?"

"Yes. We are nearly finished. I am going to wash the wound in carbolic one last time, and then I shall be ready for the dressing."

She handed me the bandage, keeping her eyes focused elsewhere as she did so. I wondered why—bloody wounds and ugly sores did not seem to bother her—then smiled as the answer came to me. My patient was mostly covered, but his thigh was exposed. Jenny had never seen a man's bare leg before, that pale skin with the short curly hair. My cultivated medical detachment had inured me to such sights.

Violet did not want to leave, but I resolutely had a cab sent for. She stared so forlornly at me that I gave her thin white hand a squeeze, my own hand rough and red from the irritating disinfectant.

"What is it, Violet? What is wrong?"

"Nothing. I only... I look forward to this time with you, and I was hoping... We must go to Simpson's again soon."

"Certainly we shall. But you really should not have come today."

"No?" The mocking smile pulled at her lips. "I like to come here. It makes me feel... It is the only truly good thing I do. Everything else is..." A laugh slipped from her lips. "It gives me a context for my own ills, my own suffering, and it reminds me how wrong everything is."

"Wrong?"

She laughed again and stood. "Come and see me soon, Michelle, and perhaps I shall explain." The evasiveness in her eyes contradicted her words.

It was well after six when I got home, the streets dark and wet, and I had a sudden longing for the sun, for warmth. My patients needed me then more than ever, but it would have been wonderful to flee to the south of Italy or France, somewhere clear and sunny without fog or the stink of coal smoke and soot. However, a delightful smell greeted me as I climbed the stairs—roasting meat, probably a joint of pork. Coming home to a warm comfortable house and a good meal was no small consolation in the dark, wet cold of a London winter.

Henry rose to greet me. In the large purple armchair, his long thin legs thrust straight out, his boots up on the matching ottoman, sat Sherlock Holmes, a wary smile on his gaunt face. Abruptly I was struck by the similarity in appearance between him and Violet—the same unhealthy intensity, the sense of some dark obsession consuming them.

"Sherlock stopped by to tell me about his inquiries, and I invited him to stay for supper."

"Very well, but I have a bone to pick with you, Sherlock Holmes." His smile flickered weakly then vanished. "So help me, if you ever take Henry off to a place like Underton again, you will no longer be welcome in my house."

"Michelle…" Henry began.

"It is one thing to risk your own neck, but it is unforgivable to drag Henry along. I will not have it—do you understand? If anything had happened to him…" My voice shook, and my eyes were awash with angry tears.

Henry took my arm. "It was my choice, Michelle. He told me I need not come—he warned me it was not wise."

I wrenched free of him. "Then he must have known exactly how foolish you are! Such advice would only convince you all the more."

"Michelle, it is not fair to blame him."

"Is it not? Whose wretched plan was it?"

Holmes drummed nervously at the chair arm with his long fingers. "You are harsh, madam." (I could not remember the last time he had addressed me so formally.) "You forget that he is my cousin and my good friend. Desperate circumstances require desperate measures. This is a dark business, and the risk to everyone involved is considerable.

Do you recall what you said to me concerning Mrs. Wheelwright after the opera? 'I beg of you to save her.' And I promised you that I would do everything in my power. Our visit last night was part of my effort to honor that promise, and Henry, very bravely, offered to accompany me. Had he not, it is quite possible I would not have returned from Underton alive. Your friend and I are deeply in his debt."

I clenched my fists, drew in my breath, and all my rage seemed to melt into grief. I took out my handkerchief, sat down and wiped at my eyes. "You always know what to say."

Henry put his hand on my shoulder. "Michelle, I..."

"Next time please have the simple decency to tell me when you are about to risk your life."

"I promise I shall." He stroked my cheek in a way that made me want to cry simply because I did love him. "You must be famished. Perhaps if we ate..."

I stood and put my handkerchief in my pocket. "Yes, I am starved. Let us eat."

Henry helped me off with my coat. Holmes watched me sadly; at last he stood. I had taken Henry's arm, and as Sherlock started by, I slipped my other hand about his arm. I felt him stiffen, and then he gave a tired, yet relieved sigh.

"Next time I shall come along," I said. "Henry is not the only one with dramatic abilities."

Holmes smiled briefly. "I know that."

We all laughed. "I could play the part of a prostitute. I have seen enough of them at the clinic."

We sat down at the dining-room table. Harriet had put out the silver candelabrum that my mother had given us, as well as our best silver and china.

"You may have your histrionic opportunity sooner than you imagine,"

Holmes said. "However, the part is suitably respectable."

Harriet filled my bowl with the rich bean soup in broth, which was her specialty. "Thank you," I said. "It smells even better than usual."

"I put in a bit more pepper," she said.

I took a quick spoonful then turned to Holmes. "Of what role are you speaking?"

Holmes opened his linen napkin with a flourish. "That of the respectable wife of a wealthy merchant dealing in Scottish whisky."

Henry's eyebrows sank inward. "What merchant?"

"You are to play the merchant. After Mr. Blackdrop and Heinrich Verniger, I thought it well time for you to portray someone of a higher class."

"And what part will you play?" I could feel each spoonful of hot soup improving my spirits.

"I shall be Henry's elderly father."

"And who will be the audience for our performance?" Henry asked.

"Mr. Geoffrey Steerford."

Henry set down his spoon. "You have arranged a meeting so quickly?"

"I have, although it took me much of the day. Mr. Steerford is a hard man to see. He appeared in London about two years ago and has been selling shares in some enterprise, which has attracted considerable capital. The venture is both secretive and exclusive. I could not discover its exact nature, but the minimum investment is one thousand pounds, although ten thousand is not uncommon."

"Good Lord," Henry murmured.

"I began the day with a visit to Lord Harrington. He gave me the names of several investors, one of whom owed me a favor. I visited this person and obtained a letter of introduction for a prosperous merchant—a fictional one. Next I went in the guise of a servant to Steerford's residence, which is not half a mile from those of the

Wheelwrights' and the Herberts'. Steerford was out, but I arranged an appointment for my master tomorrow afternoon."

"Who is this master?" I asked.

Holmes smiled. "The wealthy whisky dealer Mr. Robert Carlyle."

Henry choked back a laugh, barely keeping his soup down. "Am I any relation to Thomas?"

"No, but we do have Scottish roots."

"Perhaps I shall wear a wig," I said. "I have always wanted to try black hair."

Henry shuddered. "God forbid."

"You and Henry need not bother to disguise yourselves, but I must alter my appearance. Steerford may be someone I have met before under a different name. Then too, Watson's narratives and Paget's drawings–highly idealized though his renderings may be–have made me much too well-known."

"When are we to meet Mr. Steerford?" I asked.

"Would tomorrow afternoon at four be possible? I know you are very busy, Michelle, but Mr. Steerford had few openings and is unavailable in the evenings."

"I shall manage somehow."

Henry glanced at Holmes. "And what of the Lovejoys?"

"I have discovered nothing. Their having no traceable past is, in itself, suspicious. I have telegraphed a police detective of my acquaintance in Liverpool and asked him to make some inquiries. I am not hopeful."

Henry shook his head. "I have never been so surprised to see anyone in my life. What could Mrs. Lovejoy have been doing in a brothel?"

Holmes took a spoonful of soup. "It must be as Ratty suspected. She was stirring up the employees. Madam Irene must be a partisan of the Angels."

I frowned. "I cannot believe... Perhaps Mrs. Lovejoy was only there on a visit of mercy. She is a religious woman."

Henry again shook his head. "But the hour—that is not the time one would choose for a charitable visit to a brothel—not during the prime shift, so to speak."

"Please, Henry."

"Well, it is true. And her manner was furtive. I wonder... That woman has never seemed quite sane. The morning after the spider cake she was positively deranged. Maybe she is mad but dissembles well. She could have some irrational grudge against Violet."

I bit at my lip. "I suppose it is possible, but Violet treats all her servants so well."

"The person behind this business is quite sane," Holmes said. "Only a capable mind of extraordinary power could have concocted these schemes. And as I have noted before, the person has a peculiar sense of humor, not mad, but... deviant."

"Who can it be?" Henry could not keep the exasperation from his voice. "The Lovejoys seem so plain, and neither Donald Wheelwright nor his mistress is a mental giant. Perhaps none of it is related—the gypsy's curse, Lord Harrington's suicide, the theft of the necklace, and the threats against Violet."

Holmes smiled coldly. "Ratty knew better. A rat has a remarkable sense of smell."

"Is that why they sniff about so?" Henry repressed a shudder. "Let us not discuss rats—not after last night. Perhaps... Old Wheelwright is very shrewd and would like Violet out of the way. Could he be behind all this villainy?"

Holmes was briefly silent. "It is certainly possible. I consider him a suspect in the Wheelwright affair, but it is nearly inconceivable that he has any connection with the Angels of the Lord. Even in the case of the Wheelwrights alone, I sense a powerful and curiously subtle intellect.

Then there is the dark humor I have commented upon. Old Wheelwright is simply too vulgar—too grasping and rapacious—too dull."

"It might be best," I said, "to simply ask Mrs. Lovejoy what she was doing near Underton last night."

Holmes set down his soupspoon and shook his head curtly. "That is the one thing you absolutely must not do. It would put her on her guard."

"We could question Violet about the matter."

"*No.*" He gave his head another resolute shake.

"But why?"

He hesitated, licked his lips, and then dabbed absentmindedly at his mouth with his napkin. "It is… too risky. Mrs. Lovejoy would certainly notice any change in Mrs. Wheelwright's manner toward her."

Harriet marched in bearing the steaming joint on a platter and set it before Henry. He inhaled deeply. "Superb, Harriet—truly superb!"

She smiled at him. "Thank you, sir."

Henry ran the long blade of the knife over the steel a few times, then began to carve. Harriet was a wonderful cook (unlike me), and we ate very well, although we spurned elaborate sauces and many courses. If one ate everything served at a dinner like that at the Wheelwrights', indigestion—or worse—was guaranteed.

Henry put the brown meat from the outside on my plate; he knew I liked it best. Then he heaped meat on Holmes' plate. "We must fatten you up, Sherlock," he said. "You are looking thinner than ever."

I nodded. "Henry is right. I saw Violet today and thought the same thing: I wanted to bring her home and let Harriet help me fatten her."

Holmes paused, fork in hand. "Mrs. Wheelwright did not look well?"

I sighed. "She did not."

His gray eyes somehow stared through me. "This case may be the high point of my career, and at last I sense the threads coming together.

All the same, sometimes I wish I had never heard of the Wheelwrights."
His voice was suddenly harsh, and he paused. "Other times I feel that
I would have missed…" His eyes shifted and noticed us both staring at
him. "Forgive me. I too am weary. And hungry." He cut off a piece of
meat and put it in his mouth.

Henry stepped up to the front door of Steerford's house and rang
the bell. He was magnificently dressed in his best black greatcoat and
silk top hat. A diamond pin pierced his gray silk cravat, a loan from
his cousin. As an old man with a miserly streak, Holmes appeared
almost shabby—and virtually unrecognizable. He had colored his hair
white, then added bushy white eyebrows and curly white sidewhiskers,
which blossomed out from under the brim of his top hat. A huge white
mustache somehow shrank his nose and hid his lips. He wore spectacles
with thick lenses.

The door swung open, and an elderly man in formal attire opened
the door, his watery eyes scrutinizing us. "Good day, sirs. Madam."

"Mr. Robert Carlyle to see Mr. Steerford," Henry said.

"He is expecting you, sir. Please come in."

The butler gave our coats to the housekeeper then led us down the
hallway to a cozy sitting room. The dark, elegant furniture and carpets
were all new. Standing before the fire was a man in a black frock coat,
his hands clasped behind him, his back to us.

"Ah, good… day." As he turned, his voice skipped a beat, his eyes
narrowing ever so slightly. His smile wavered, then recovered and
became earnest. His hair was black, but his sidewhiskers were grayish,
as were his mustache and goatee. He wore thick spectacles low on his
nose, his eyes peering over the rims, and his hair was combed straight
back and had an oily shine. His dress was impeccable: a double-
breasted black frock coat with silken lapels (nearly identical to the one

Henry wore), black waistcoat, and gray-and-black striped trousers, the glossy toes of his boots gleaming. As he extended his hand to shake Henry's, I saw a pearl-and-gold cuff link.

"Robert Carlyle," Henry said.

"A pleasure to meet you, Mr. Carlyle. And this charming lady must be your better half. I hope talk of financial matters will not bore you too much, Mrs. Carlyle."

I managed a smile. "I shall do my best to keep awake."

Steerford's brow sank as he turned to Holmes. He had extremely bushy, black eyebrows, which extended across the bridge of his nose. "And who are you, sir?"

Holmes extended his hand. "I'm a Carlyle, too. James Carlyle, this lad's father. Someone has to keep an eye on him. Can't have him squandering the family fortune." Holmes' faintly querulous voice had the quaver of age and a slight Scottish burr.

"I am glad to meet you, Mr. Carlyle. Rest assured, we are not talking of squandering fortunes here, but of increasing them many times."

"Easy words to say, Mr. Steerford."

"Hopefully before you leave, you will be confident I offer more than mere words. To those select few my partners and I feel are worthy, we offer the financial opportunity of a lifetime." Mr. Steerford's voice flowed smoothly, almost like a caress, but its tone was pitched high for a man.

"Please sit down and warm yourselves by the fire. Mrs. Carlyle, I think you will find that chair most comfortable. Gentlemen, if you will take either end of the sofa, I shall soon show you certain documents and tangible evidence of our enterprise."

We did as he suggested while he turned and walked over to a desk. He dimmed the lamp slightly then picked up a thick leather-bound book, which appeared to be a photograph album. He walked over to the fire and turned toward us. With the lamp low and his back to the fire, his face was in shadow.

"Gentlemen, could one of you tell me what the dominant fuel of our century has been, what fuel has made possible the great flowering of British industry and the rise of steam-powered machinery?"

Holmes cackled. "That's easy enough. Coal."

"Exactly so, Mr. Carlyle. Very astute."

"Astute? Hardly. Any fool could figure that out."

"You would be surprised, sir. Now, can either of you tell me what fuel is likely to dominate the coming century?"

Henry and Sherlock shared a glance. "Coal again," Holmes said.

Steerford shook his head. "No, sir. Petroleum—oil."

Holmes scowled. Henry said, "Do you think so?"

Steerford's right arm swung out expansively. "Have you heard of Herr Benz's horseless carriage, constructed in 1885? A humble start, but already Mr. Renault has begun constructing more advanced machines. He has refined the internal combustion engine, adding a second cylinder. These engines all use petrol, a distillate of petroleum, and one considerably lighter than kerosene. Kerosene has already captured a major portion of the lamp business. It burns better than coal or whale oil and can be produced more cheaply. Given the existing market for kerosene and the potential market for petrol as the internal combustion engine and the motorcar grow in use, we are confident the market for oil will dramatically increase in the twentieth century, eventually far surpassing that for coal."

Holmes cackled again, an annoying sound. "What about the electric light, sir? What happens to your market for kerosene then?"

Steerford smiled and nodded patronizingly. "A very apt question, Mr. Carlyle. It is true that the electric light will someday replace light produced by gas or oil, but the process will be a lengthy and costly one. Electricity requires expensive generating and distribution facilities. Wires must be strung up everywhere and run into houses, which must then be retrofitted with further wiring. The growing petrol market for engines should more than compensate for the gradually declining market in kerosene. Does either of you gentlemen know the current source of most oil?"

"Another easy one," Holmes said. "The United States of America."

"Very good, sir!" He turned to Henry. "You are well served by having so knowledgeable an advisor. And has either of you heard of Mr. John Rockefeller?"

Holmes nodded. "Certainly."

"Perhaps you could tell your son and his wife about Mr. Rockefeller."

"He's an American millionaire and the owner of Standard Oil." Holmes had an avaricious glint in his eye. "He started with practically nothing in the seventies, and now he is one of the richest men in the world. He has a virtual monopoly on oil production in the States."

"Quite so. Mr. Rockefeller is proof of the extraordinary opportunity which the oil business provides." He let his right hand drop. His left hand still held the leather book. The fireplace seemed to be his stage, we the audience. "What I am about to reveal now must remain confidential. I must have your word on it."

Henry had been stroking thoughtfully at his mustache, his gray leather gloves in his other hand. "You have my promise."

"And mine," I said.

Holmes cackled again. "I'll not make any promises beforehand! What's so blasted secret?"

Mr. Steerford squinted gravely at him through the thick lenses. "If not, I shall have to ask you to leave."

Holmes' smile turned to a scowl. "An outrage! I've never had to make such a promise in my life."

Henry gave him a severe look. "Father, I think we should hear him out."

I restrained a smile. "Yes, Father Carlyle."

Holmes scratched fiercely at his nose. "Oh, I suppose so."

"I have your word you will not say a word to another living soul?"

"You do, sir." Holmes emphasized the "s" with a sibilant hiss.

Steerford nodded. "Excellent. You will not regret your promises. I have a brother slightly older than myself, a learned man, who studied chemistry and geology at Oxford. He spent some time in the United States working in the oil business. His education and his work there convinced him of the possibility that petroleum reserves might exist in Britain itself. If so, our country would no longer be dependent on American oil, and of course, such a discovery could lead to very great wealth indeed. Some five years ago my brother returned to England and commenced his quest. Two years ago we began some test drilling. The results have exceeded our wildest dreams. The first well began limited production a few months ago. We had a few investors provide capital for our initial foray. They have already quadrupled their money–*quadrupled it.*"

Holmes regarded him warily, as if he suspected a snake-oil salesman. "Who are these investors?"

"Lord Russell, the former Lord Harrington, and Mr. Lawrence Hawke. Any one of them would be only too happy to confirm their profit in this enterprise."

Henry nodded. "So that is where Harrington got the money. He was reported near bankruptcy."

"He borrowed all he could and put every last penny into the well." Steerford sighed gravely. "How tragic that he left us before he could enjoy his profits."

Holmes shook his head. "Foolish, foolish! Never put all your eggs in one basket. That's sound advice."

"My brother is certain that the entire region near our first well abounds in oil. We hope to construct some fifty wells in the next ten years as well as extensive facilities for refining and processing the crude oil. We shall have the largest production facilities in Europe. To make our dream possible, we are selling shares in our venture for the price of one thousand pounds per share. We hope to raise a million pounds."

My jaw dropped, and Henry gave his head a slight shake.

"We are very near our goal, but should you wish to invest, there are still shares available for purchase."

Holmes stared suspiciously at him. "Where is this well?"

Steerford gave a mournful sigh. "You certainly must understand that I cannot possibly reveal the location. Negotiations are underway to purchase the surrounding land over the petroleum reserves. If the news were to get out... No, no—once our goal is met and the deeds are in hand, I shall gladly tell you—but I must remain mute until then."

"And how do I know you are not making this all up? Tell me that, sir?"

"Father!" Henry exclaimed. "Surely you can see that Mr. Steerford is a gentleman."

Steerford gave an appreciative nod. "Thank you, Mr. Carlyle. Your confidence is appreciated, but your father's skepticism is understandable. In some cases, we have actually arranged visits to the well in a completely shut-up carriage, in order that the route remains secret. But hopefully, these documents will suffice. I have here photographs of the well, the signed testimonials of several worthy gentlemen who have seen it, and the bills of sale from a refinery which received our raw petroleum and produced petrol and kerosene. May I?"

He sat down on the sofa between Henry and Sherlock, and then opened his book. "Here is the well itself."

I rose and walked over behind the sofa. I saw a picture of an oil derrick, its metal frame silhouetted against the sky. As he turned the pages, Steerford provided a running commentary—which soon grew tiresome. There were several photographs of the well, including one showing a wagon loaded with the metal barrels, and the testimonials he had mentioned. Both the nobility and the wealthy merchant class were represented. When he had finished, I returned to my chair while he stepped before the fireplace. Again it was as if he were on stage, we the audience. To emphasize a point, his already high-pitched voice would soar higher still.

"Well, gentlemen, I hope you realize the incredibly lucrative opportunity being offered to you."

Holmes licked his lips, almost drooling with greed. "And may we interview some of these gentlemen, should we wish to?"

"Oh, yes. Any of those whose testimonials were included."

"And how many shares might we purchase?"

"As many as you wish—within reason."

Holmes cackled. "Reason has little to do with it! I'll be talking to some of your people there. We'll see, we'll see."

Henry nodded. "Indeed we shall. It seems a splendid enterprise."

"I have put every pound of my own modest income into this venture." Steerford slipped his watch from his waistcoat pocket; the gold had a reddish glow in the firelight. "I shall be happy to answer any further questions, but I do have another engagement soon."

Henry discreetly stared at Holmes, who gave his head a quick shake. "We need not keep you any longer," Henry said as he stood. "You have given us nearly an hour of your valuable time." He shook hands with Steerford.

Holmes leered at them, his frame stooped. "And will you need your answer soon?"

"I do not wish to rush you, but the shares are going quickly."

"I heard you needed the money by the fifteenth of November. Heard that was the absolute deadline."

Steerford smiled politely. "There are those of an indecisive nature whom I might have wished to hasten. That might explain your misapprehension, but I wish you to be comfortable with whatever sum you choose to invest."

Henry nodded. "That's decent of you. I feel confident we shall purchase some shares."

Holmes made his annoying cackle for what I hoped was the last time. "If this is on the level, we surely will."

Henry stared severely at him. "There can be little question of that."

I smiled and nodded. "Certainly not, and when the profits begin to come in, you will no longer be able to deny me the new brougham I want."

Henry smiled. "You know I can refuse you nothing."

Steerford rang for the butler, who, after another round of farewells, showed us to the front door. A rented four-wheeler waited for us across the street. The fog drifted lazily before the streetlamp; in the muted, dying light the carriage itself seemed almost a mirage.

Henry and I sat together on one side, Sherlock opposite us. "What a dreadful old man you make!" I exclaimed.

Holmes' cheeks rose, the corners of his mouth hidden under the mustache. "I thought I was rather charming in a miserly sort of way. And what did you both think of Mr. Steerford's proposal? Would you invest your every pound?"

"I must confess," Henry said, "that I found his presentation quite persuasive. I would, of course, wish to confer with some of the people who have actually seen the well, but I was favorably impressed." He laughed. "As I have no thousand pounds to invest, it hardly matters."

Holmes' thin face went in and out of light and shadow as the carriage made its way along the street. He had taken off his spectacles. "And you, Michelle?"

"It was, as Henry says, impressive, but all the same, something about Mr. Steerford did not please me. I did not exactly mistrust him, but... His voice was odd."

"In what way?"

"It was curiously high-pitched and yet so mellifluous, so... polished. I suppose he has given the same speech dozens of times–that would explain why he almost seemed to be saying lines in a play."

Holmes gave a sharp laugh. "Very good, Michelle! I suppose it is to be expected. Neither of you has had my experience with frauds, cheats, and charlatans. All in all, the higher classes of society are more gullible than the lower ones. If some polished rogue appears to be a fellow gentleman, he can spout almost any nonsense and be believed."

"But the photographs," Henry said, "and all the testimonials. He said we might even visit the well."

"It would not be so terribly difficult or expensive to construct a false well and stock it with real petroleum."

"But what about the men who have already made their fortune off the well? Surely if it were fraudulent...?"

"Bait, Henry–bait. Once such a scheme is going well, one can pay off the earlier investors to make the business more convincing. As I said, a certain class of people rashly assumes that a fine-speaking man with a good tailor cannot lie; and when they hear that simple Mr. Bull has already made his fortune and that Lord Twitterly has invested, all remaining doubts vanish."

"Do you think..?" Henry drew in his breath loudly through his teeth. "Is there no possibility that he was telling the truth?"

"There might be a possibility–a slim possibility–but for one thing."

"What one thing?"

"The fact that Mr. Steerford was not who he appeared to be–the fact that he was in disguise."

"*What?*" Henry and I exclaimed in unison.

Holmes laughed. "Can you both be so blind? Did you not notice his resemblance to me? I refer to the spectacles, all the false facial hair—mustache *and* beard in his case. I must admit, his disguise was well done, a professional job. The beard hides all manner of distinctive marks on the chin."

"Ah…" I said. "And his voice…"

"Exactly. Pitched far higher than normal. He used falsetto for emphasis."

Henry made one hand into a fist and struck his knee. "Oh, I feel like a very idiot."

"As I said, he is quite good, and you are certainly not the first to be duped. I do believe he is close to his goal of a million pounds."

"Good heavens," Henry murmured. "There has never been such a theft."

"Whoever can he be?" I asked. "And why would he need to disguise himself?"

A patch of yellow-white light suddenly illuminated Holmes' face, revealing the fierce glee in his eyes. "I believe I know exactly who Mr. Geoffrey Steerford is."

"*Who?*" Henry asked. "*Who?*"

"I really must verify my suspicions. It is a bit premature to tell you."

I reached out and squeezed his bony knee. "Sherlock—you must tell us!"

"All in good time, Michelle. All in good time." He gave a short laugh. "And of course, I shall have to be on guard myself."

"Why?"

"Because our friend, Mr. Steerford, undoubtedly recognized me, even as I recognized him."

Twelve

I had not seen Violet since Wednesday afternoon when she had left the clinic; Friday, after supper, I resolved to visit her. Henry was surprised but did not try to dissuade me, probably because he knew how headstrong I could be. He only said, "Try not to be too late."

Since I worked during the day, I was spared many boring hours and the snobbish warfare of ladies' afternoon social calls. I could avoid spurning or being spurned, and no silver tray sat near our door for ladies' cards. Because Violet was a patient, I had a ready excuse for calling at so odd an hour.

The rain of the past week had ended, giving way to a cold, blustery wind, which howled mournfully and sent flying everything not fastened down. Someone's newspaper had escaped, and the pages were scattered about the street. The wind seized a page and hurled it onto our neighbor's lawn. The barren black tree branches swayed. I shivered, thought how nice it would be to spend the evening with Henry, and then stepped into the waiting hansom.

Once we were off, I leaned against the side of the swaying cab and closed my eyes. My feet hurt, and I had the beginning of a headache. The week had been so busy, and I was still tired from being up so late Tuesday night. A quiver of fear flickered about my chest as I remembered the risk Henry and Sherlock had taken. How I wished the whole wretched business with Violet were resolved, the threat against her lifted.

If only she were free. She was one of the few women whose company I enjoyed. I need not try to hide my intellect; I need not titter or giggle; I need not feign a fascination with the latest fashions from Paris or the latest gossip about Lord and Lady So-and-So. And Sherlock was a sweet man, although I could never tell him such a thing to his face. Such a curious blend of intellect and innocence. The worst of it was that they needed one another: each seemed strangely incomplete. The law and custom that bound Violet in her marriage were wrong; no good could come of it, I was certain.

Such thoughts made my head hurt all the more, and I tried to set them aside. The wheel of the hansom went through a pothole; the cab sagged, then threw me to the left, the springs groaning. I thought longingly of Violet's carriage. No doubt she would offer to have me driven home.

The wind was even stronger before her house. The giant maple groaned and shook. A crow rose cawing from a limb, black against the pinkish-gray sky. The ivy along the brick front rustled and fluttered. I wrapped my coat tightly about me.

A shapeless, muted cry merged briefly with the wind, taking on a human timbre. I stopped and wondered what it might be. The sound ceased abruptly, leaving only the moan of the wind. It had been so faint, I wondered if I had only imagined it. My hands felt cold. I made fists with them.

I strode quickly to the front door and pressed the bell. Up close the rustle of the ivy was even louder, as if each leaf were alive and struggling to escape. Hurry, I thought, and rang the bell again.

I waited and waited, but at last I turned the knob and pushed open the heavy door. Glancing over my shoulder, I stepped in and closed the door behind me. Strangely relieved, I set down my medical bag and pulled off my gloves. "Hello?" I cried. "Good evening!" The entrance way was very dim, an oil lamp burning in the room next door.

At last I heard the rapid patter of footsteps, and the little maid Gertrude came toward me, her handkerchief clutched in one hand. "Oh, thank heavens!" she cried. "It's Providence surely! Oh, please come in—someone's been murdered!"

"Murdered! Are you certain?"

"Oh, just come, ma'am! Please!"

I took my bag and followed her to the hallway. A group had formed before the library door: the footman Collins, Mr. Lovejoy, Mrs. Grady the cook, and looming over them all, Donald Wheelwright. He hammered at the door with his massive fist. "Open up, I say! Open up!" He put his hand on the brass knob, and then slammed his shoulder into the wood. "It's no good. It won't open."

"What has happened?" I asked.

Wheelwright glanced at me, puzzled. "What are you doing here?"

"I came to see Violet. What has happened?"

Lovejoy appeared only faintly perturbed. He had on his usual black morning coat and striped trousers; his black hair was parted neatly on the left side, not a hair out of place. "Mrs. Wheelwright was reading in the library, and I was speaking with Mr. Wheelwright when we heard a dreadful cry."

Mrs. Grady sobbed loudly. "Someone's killed, I know."

"Oh, I hope not!" said Gertrude.

I looked about. "Where is Mrs. Lovejoy?"

Lovejoy swallowed once. "She may be in there."

"We must break in the door!" Wheelwright exclaimed.

Lovejoy shook his head. "There is no need. Collins and I can go around the outside. The library windows are only about five feet above ground. We shall be able to enter."

"For God's sake, then–hurry!"

The two men went quickly down the hall. Wheelwright ran the thick fingers of his right hand through his hair, then slammed his fist against the door, a rumbling snarling sound issuing from between his lips. I took a step back–he always made me uncomfortable. A blend of fear and anger showed in his eyes. He had on evening dress–a black coat with tails, white shirt and tie, and glossy patent leather pumps of a size so large I had never before seen their like.

"I thought I heard something from outside the house," I said.

The cook shook her head. "I never heard such a sound before in my whole life! Horrid it was–simply horrid. Oh, what if the mistress is…?"

Gertrude began to cry.

"We must wait and see," I said.

Wheelwright lashed out at the door, striking it with his palm. "What the devil is keeping them?"

Again I stepped back, a cold feeling at my neck. The door swung open, revealing Lovejoy's pale face. Wheelwright hesitated, suddenly frozen, and I stepped past him. A tall window at the far end was open, and the frigid wind touched my cheek. Papers from the table had already been blown on the floor. Collins stood at the end of the table, fear showing in his eyes. On the floor lay Violet and Mrs. Lovejoy, both of them unconscious.

"Turn up the lamp!" I cried, then went to Violet and knelt beside her. I pressed my fingers against her throat and felt a pulse. "Thank God!" I stood.

Light from the lamp on the table flooded the room, revealing the rich brown of the oak table and chairs, the deep hues of the oriental carpet. Another gust of wind swept into the room, moving the draperies on either side of the open window.

"Close that window," I said. "It is freezing."

Collins nodded, then his face suddenly scrunched up, even as his eyes widened.

"*Uhhhh...!*" a man cried behind me.

I turned and saw the expression of absolute terror on Donald Wheelwright's face, even as he staggered backwards out of the room. I looked about, expecting to see blood pouring from Mrs. Lovejoy's skull, but the movement was what caught my eye, the impression of something black scuttling across the floor. The spider was the twin of the big one in the birthday cake. The creature darted under the table, vanishing into the shadows.

Collins grabbed a heavy volume. "Filthy bugger!" he snarled, then dropped down onto his knees and pursued the spider under the table.

"Forget the spider!" I knelt beside Mrs. Lovejoy and put my fingers against her throat.

"Is she...? Lovejoy's voice broke, and for once his impenetrable calm was gone.

"She is alive. Help me get her up."

Her head lolled about as we lifted her, and she moaned softly. We set her in one of the big red-velvet chairs. Her face was pale, the part in her black hair revealing the gleaming white line of her scalp. She wore the usual severely cut black dress.

I turned to Collins, who had reluctantly set down the heavy book. "Help me with Mrs. Wheelwright."

We lifted Violet gently and set her on another plush chair. Her undergarments rustled, but she seemed so light, so little of her under the blue silk of her dress and all those petticoats. Long strands of black hair had come loose—one hung down across her face. I touched her neck, and she winced and opened her eyes.

"Michelle—what are you doing here!"

"I came to see you, my dear."

"Oh, no! Oh, no!" She closed her eyes and tears seeped from under the lids and down her cheeks. Her mouth half opened, then twisted and clamped shut. I felt her thin chest quake under my hands.

"Violet—what is it? Where do you hurt?"

She said nothing, only turned and tried to hide her face in the side of the chair.

I sighed and glanced about. Collins appeared as consternated as I. The cook and Gertrude had come into the room, and the cook was sobbing loudly again.

"Go fetch Mr. Sherlock Holmes," I said to Collins. "He lives at 221B Baker Street. Get him here as fast as you can."

Collins was relieved to have a course of action. "Yes, ma'am—I'll take the very best pair and be back before you know it."

I sighed again and turned to Violet. "What is wrong, Violet?" I set my hand lightly on her shoulder. "No one will hurt you, I promise. Are you in pain?"

I saw the familiar signs of her struggling to master herself, but for once her will did not seem up to the task. "My neck hurts." Her voice was hoarse.

The collar of her dress was high and tight; my big fingers fumbled at the tiny buttons as I softly cursed their manufacturer. When I had the dress unfastened down to her bosom, I spread the blue silk apart. "Dear God," I whispered. The fear and loathing I felt were like a pain, a wrenching spasm deep inside me.

The entire side of her throat was bluish-purple, the bruise forming the pattern of a hand. Very gently I tipped her head the other way and saw the same pattern on the other side. Her face had a strange, wild smile, which made her almost unrecognizable. I closed my eyes, then stood up and turned away. For the first time in my life, I thought I might actually faint. Mrs. Grady was still crying.

"Do stop that!" I snapped at her.

"I'm sorry, ma'am," she sobbed.

"Go into the hall, please."

Gertrude appeared frightened but not hysterical.

"Gertrude, could you get me some brandy and bring it here?" She nodded.

Violet turned away again and buried her face in the chair. I put my hand on her shoulder and felt her body quiver from the force of her silent weeping.

"Violet—*please*. You mustn't. You are safe now."

"Is she hurt?" Donald Wheelwright had appeared in the doorway.

"Not seriously." I could not keep the contempt from my voice. His terror of spiders was ludicrous. For such a giant to fear a harmless insect... I turned to Lovejoy. "How fairs your wife?"

"She appears to be breathing normally."

I probed at Mrs. Lovejoy's skull but found no bumps. "Perhaps she only fainted." I took some smelling salts out of my bag, unscrewed the cap, and passed them back and forth under her nose. Her eyelids sprang open; she gasped and looked about.

Lovejoy clasped her hand tightly and pressed it to his chest. "Oh, my dearest, oh thank God!"

"Oh, Jonathan," she murmured, her eyelids fluttering. She smiled, then closed her eyes. Abruptly, she sat up and stared about. "The mistress! The mistress! Oh, God help us all!"

"Calm yourself, Mrs. Lovejoy," I said. "She has not been harmed."

She stared up at her husband. "Not harmed? But where is… *it*?" She shuddered and covered her face with her hands.

Lovejoy and I looked at each other in confusion. "Abigail, dearest, to whom do you refer? What is '*it*'?"

She let her hands fall, her brown eyes opening wide. "Father in Heaven, protect us! Angels of God defend us!" Her voice was loud and piercing.

I glanced at the doorway. Mr. Wheelwright still stood there, filling the frame. Behind him was Gertrude. She obviously did not dare tell him to move aside.

"Please come in, Mr. Wheelwright," I said, "or go into the hall."

He frowned and took one reluctant step forward, then another, his eyes searching the floor. Gertrude walked past him and set down the silver tray bearing a decanter and glasses on the table.

I poured half a glass and gave it to Mrs. Lovejoy. "Drink this."

Wearily she shook her head. "I do not drink spirits."

"Consider it a medicine." I gave her my most authoritative stare. "Drink it. *Now.*"

She took the glass reluctantly. Lovejoy said, "Drink it down, dearest. The doctor knows what is best." She took a sip, coughed once, then took another sip.

I poured another glass and walked over to Violet. She was turned about in the chair, her face pressed against the velvet back, her right hand gripping the top. "Violet." I put my hand on her shoulder. "Violet." I tried to turn her forward, but her hand clutched at the chair. "Violet, what is wrong with you? Look at me. This is foolish."

At last she let me turn her. Her face was red, her eyes swollen. "I feel so… awful." Her lips twitched and started to form a grimace.

"Do not smile that way." My voice was sharper than I intended. "Drink this."

She took a big swallow and began to cough, her hand clutching her side. "Sip it. No…" I pulled the glass away. "Take small sips."

I took a deep breath myself. Gertrude stared in horror at her mistress's neck. "What… what did that to her?"

"The fiend!" shouted Mrs. Lovejoy. "The fiend from hell!"

Gertrude gave a sharp cry and stepped back. I heard other cries and talking in the hallway. Much of the household staff must have gathered there.

"The black man—I saw the black man—I saw the devil!"

My skirts trailed behind me as I spun about. "You keep silent! Not one more word, or I shall gag you myself!"

Mrs. Lovejoy's eyes shone with fury, but it vanished at once. "Yes, Doctor."

I took Gertrude by the shoulder. "Your mistress will soon be well again. I want you to go into the hall and tell everyone that she and Mrs. Lovejoy are in no danger. Everyone should go back to what they were doing. Can you do that for me?

She drew in her breath and squared her shoulders. I doubted she was even five feet tall, and again I felt like a giantess alongside her. "Yes, ma'am—Doctor, I mean."

"Very good." She did as I told her. "Close the door," I said to Lovejoy.

Donald Wheelwright came close enough to the table to pour some brandy, and then he backed quickly away and downed the glass, the muscles of his massive neck rippling. I went to the table and poured some for myself. The brandy was very smooth, but burned slightly. Lovejoy stood beside his wife who sat in one chair, while Violet sat in the other, her mouth twitching as she struggled not to smile.

The door opened, and Sherlock Holmes strode into the room, his top hat and gloves in hand, his black greatcoat sweeping behind him. "What has transpired?"

I had never been so relieved to see anyone in my life. "Thank heavens you have come." I leaned against the table, supporting myself with my right hand, suddenly aware of how exhausted and disturbed I felt.

Holmes was at my side at once. "You had better sit down."

"There is nothing the matter with me."

He pulled out one of the stout wooden chairs. "All the same, there is no reason to remain standing."

"Thank you." I sank into the chair and realized my feet were hurting again, despite my sensible shoes. If I had remained at home, I could have slipped out of the beastly shoes and warmed my feet before the fire. Henry was usually only too happy to massage my feet. At the thought of him, something seemed to catch in my throat. I looked up and saw Collins standing near the doorway, his rugged face flushed with excitement, his hands grasping the brim of his top hat.

"Collins?"

"Yes, ma'am?"

"Could you do me another service and go to my house to fetch my— Dr. Vernier? It is near Paddington Station."

He laughed. "Have you forgotten how often we've driven you there?"

"Oh, of course—forgive me. Do not alarm him, but bring him here at once."

"Certainly, ma'am."

Holmes draped his greatcoat over a chair. He wore his usual black frock coat, the gold chain of his watch dangling between the pockets of his black waistcoat. He glanced at Mr. Wheelwright, who stood before one of the bookcases. "Would you not prefer to sit, sir?"

He shook his head.

"The spider must be gone," I said. "He would not have lingered."

"I'll stand." The tone of his voice was glacial.

Holmes set one hand on the oak table, his long fingers spread slightly apart. "Collins told me the spider was enormous, no doubt another fine specimen of *tegenaria domestica.* They can grow nearly six inches across. Quite harmless, however."

Donald Wheelwright went paler still, his eyes shifting toward the doorway.

Holmes' eyes swept about the room, his fingers tapping lightly at the table. "Collins told me all that happened. It is regrettable that everyone has gone stampeding through the room and grounds obliterating any hint of a footprint or other evidence."

"Sherlock, I thought someone might be badly hurt. We could hardly..."

"I understand, Michelle. All the same, it is a pity. Collins said the window was still wide open when he came around the house."

Lovejoy gave an emphatic nod. "So it was, Mr. Holmes."

"And the two ladies were lying on the floor. Where exactly were they?"

"Violet was near the open window there," I said, pointing to the one in the far corner. "Mrs. Lovejoy closer to the door."

Holmes walked over to Violet. His presence seemed to steady her. She smiled once, a brief twitch, and then stared up at him, brushing aside a strand of black hair.

"Do you feel up to a few questions, Mrs. Wheelwright?"

She nodded. I joined them. "Are you certain Violet?" I put my hand on hers.

"Yes."

Holmes seized a chair, then sat and leaned forward, his elbows resting on his knees. She looked down and raised her hands to pull together the collar of her dress. "What do you remember?"

"It was blowing hard, and I thought I heard something outside. I went to the windows, and then…" Her voice grew fainter still. "…someone… choked me. From behind. Someone… very strong." Her mouth tried to smile, but then she slipped her lower lip between her teeth and bit down.

"May I show Sherlock the bruises?" I asked.

She nodded but did not look up. Her hands slipped away from her collar, and I pulled the silk aside. The bluish-green outline of a hand was clearly visible, the fingertips spread slightly apart just before her larynx. Holmes' eyes widened, his lips pulling back, and he stared up at me. He extended his finger and touched her chin. She averted her eyes and turned the other way. For only an instant, his guard was down. He ran his fingertip along her jaw, his eyes full of longing. Immediately he dropped his hand, stood and swiveled about, putting his hands in his frock coat pockets.

"And you remember nothing more after someone choked you?" His voice had a hint of strain.

"No." Violet closed her eyes and let out a long sigh.

Holmes' fingers tapped again at the table. Wheelwright watched impassively like some great sullen mountain—or perhaps a volcano. Holmes glanced at Mrs. Lovejoy. His nostrils flared, then he gave me a conspiratorial glance. He took the brandy decanter and poured more into Mrs. Lovejoy's glass. "And what can you tell me, madam?"

Her hands began to tremble violently, and suddenly she spilled brandy all over her dress and onto the floor.

"Oh dear," whispered Lovejoy. He knelt down and sponged at the liquid with his handkerchief.

His wife stared up at Holmes, her hands clenching at the chair arms. "I saw…"

"Now I wish you to remain calm, Mrs. Lovejoy—there is no reason to become distraught."

"No reason? No reason?" She gave a sharp strained laugh. "No reason—if you had seen what I have…" She closed her eyes, then opened them and stared intently into space. "I was walking down the hallway when I heard a noise coming from the library, a very peculiar sound which made me uncomfortable. I knew the mistress was in there, so I opened the door to see if anything was amiss. The room was very dim, the lamp low, the fiery orange embers in the fireplace hardly visible. Outside the wind was howling. The mistress… was not at the table. The… noise was coming from near the window. *She* was making that sound!" Her voice had grown steadily louder, and she raised her entire arm and pointed with her forefinger at Violet. "The black thing had its hands about her throat—the sound I had heard was her choking to death!"

"Please calm yourself, Mrs. Lovejoy."

"I'll not calm myself—do you not understand what I am saying? The fiend was strangling her! I screamed and screamed! The blackness of hell was about that thing, and it was so tall and had black horns, and—oh, dear God!—it had a tail!" Again her voice had risen to a deafening crescendo, and she gave a shriek, which made me start, and clapped her hands over her face. "Oh, God!" she shuddered. "Oh, *God!*"

"Please, Mrs. Lovejoy…" Holmes began.

She slowly lowered her hands. "You do not believe me."

Lovejoy put his hand on her shoulder. "Of course we do, but Mr. Holmes is right—you must not upset yourself."

"You do not believe me." Abruptly she stood and stared defiantly at Holmes. "Do you!"

"Abigail—*please.*"

She swung about. "You don't either! Can you not understand? I saw him! I saw the devil himself—with his long rat's tail. The devil—it *was* the devil!" She was nearly screaming again. "Oh, someone help me—please help me! Oh, save me—save me! Do not let the fiend take me! Oh, God— *God!*"

Abruptly, she collapsed into the chair, covered her eyes and sobbed loudly. Holmes and I stared wearily at each other. I had nearly clapped my hands over my ears because Mrs. Lovejoy's voice was so very loud. Any servants close by would have heard her every word, and such news would spread instantaneously.

Holmes turned to Lovejoy. "I shall defer further questions. Could you entrust your wife to another servant's care and return shortly? Later I am sure Dr. Doudet Vernier can prescribe something to help calm her."

Lovejoy put his hand gently on her arm. "Come, Abigail."

She let him lead her, still weeping, to the door. "They do not understand," she muttered. "They do not. Oh, we are all doomed. What is the use? We are powerless against the forces of hell."

"She must not talk to the other servants," I said sharply. Someone had doubtlessly tried to strangle Violet, perhaps a man all in black, but I could not believe it was a devil with horns and a tail.

Holmes ran his hand through his hair. "Lovejoy and Collins have no doubt tramped the lawn under the window to mush, but I shall want to have a look. The grass is wet, and a solitary footprint may remain. The intruder must have locked the door, then escaped through the window." He looked up and noticed Wheelwright still standing. "*Tegenaria domestica* is as frightened of humans as you are of her. No doubt she has retreated to some crevice. You may as well sit down."

Wheelwright did not move. Finally, he said, "You have been on the case for nearly a month, and we have gone from one disaster to another. I cannot take much more of this."

Holmes drew himself up to his full height, which still left him a few inches below Donald Wheelwright. "I have tried to explain to you that I am not a miracle worker. I am making progress, but you must be patient."

"You ask me to be patient when my wife is nearly strangled to death? We will both be dead and buried by the time you figure things out."

Holmes' eyes narrowed, and his face went red. He glanced briefly at Violet. "Perhaps you have a point. I... I shall personally see to it that there are no further attacks upon your wife. With your permission, I or one of your male servants shall remain close by her."

Wheelwright did not appear mollified. He went to the table, poured more brandy, and sank into a chair. The massive oak chair looked like child's furniture with him sitting in it. He took a big swallow of brandy. Outside, the wind was low and steady.

"I cannot... This is like some terrible nightmare. This has been the worst month of my life."

Violet gave a sharp, shrill laugh, which made my flesh crawl. "It is a nightmare for *you*? My nightmare has lasted for more than four weeks—it has lasted for months—for years—and it grows worse and worse. Oh, whenever will it end?" Her voice broke, and she turned away from us to hide her tears.

Again I felt as if something had caught in my throat. Wheelwright stared dumbly at Violet, his eyes pained and confused. I wanted to shout, "Go to her for once—comfort her, you blockhead!" But he did not move.

Holmes took a step forward, then stared at me, his hands clenched into fists. "See to her," he managed to say.

I rose and put my hand on her shoulder, then touched her black hair with my other hand. "Please, my dear..."

She almost leaped to her feet, turning and twisting away. "Michelle, I cannot bear your kindness! Can you not understand? Oh, God." She bit savagely at her lip, her right hand clutching at her left side. "I must get away from here! I must. Donald, you must take me away—away from this wretched house—from London—you must." Her voice was raw and hoarse.

Surprised, Wheelwright looked at her. "Where?"

"Anywhere!"

He drank the rest of his brandy. "We could go to Norfolk. If not for the family business, we would have gone there by now, but father wanted me close by because of his dealings with Atherton. I think after all that has happened he would understand."

"Yes—any place. Norfolk will do fine." She gave a harsh laugh.

Wheelwright stared vacantly at her. It was as if he could not really see her. "We could leave tomorrow."

"Yes. Oh, yes." She laughed again, then her hand clasped at her side, and her face went ashen. "Oh Lord, it hurts so."

I took her arm and drew her back to the chair. "Do sit down." She might have fallen had I not had hold of her.

"Thank you. I have to get away. I must get away." She was crying again. Sherlock's eyes were anguished.

"The brandy has probably irritated her stomach. I shall have to get her some milk."

Holmes turned to Wheelwright. "Norfolk may or may not be safer than London. With your permission, I shall accompany you there."

Wheelwright had refilled this glass. "As you wish."

"So shall I." The words were out of my mouth before I could reflect on what I was saying.

Wheelwright raised his head. "What?"

"She is ill. Someone needs to look after her."

Violet appeared truly surprised. "You cannot mean it. Your practice..."

"I can be away for a week or two, if need be."

Holmes stared intently at me. "I shall want Henry along as well. He will be of assistance."

"Someone can fill in for us."

Violet put her small white fingers about my big red hand. "I shall be glad for your company. You are the only person who is not part of the nightmare, the only one who is free. I... I did not mean it about your kindness. I..."

Wheelwright took another swallow of brandy. "Mr. Holmes, there is one thing you must understand." His face was ruddy, his broad forehead wrinkled. "This is your last chance. No more talk about patience or the difficulties of the case. Any more disasters, and you will be dismissed, and I'll find someone who can do a proper job."

Holmes' lips curled into a smile, gray eyes smoldering. He hesitated, no doubt struggling with his pride. "I accept your terms, sir."

Wheelwright emptied the glass and rose. "If we are to leave tomorrow, I must see to a few things."

Violet let go of my hand, then withdrew a handkerchief and wiped at her eyes. "The Lovejoys can join us later, or perhaps Abigail should come. She also needs to get away."

Wheelwright gave a short rumble of a laugh. "She needs a stay in a madhouse."

Violet sat up, her right hand still holding her side. "She is not to blame for this business. It has taken its toll on her."

Wheelwright shrugged. "We can discuss it in the morning." He started for the door.

"One moment, sir," Holmes said. "What were you doing when you heard Mrs. Lovejoy scream?"

Wheelwright blinked dully. "I was in the smoking room talking with Lovejoy and Collins."

"How long had the three of you been there?"

"Half-hour or so."

"Thank you, Mr. Wheelwright."

Wheelwright closed the door behind himself. "His hands are far too large, anyway," Holmes said softly. "Mrs. Wheelwright, may I have another look at those bruises?"

Violet nodded. "Certainly."

Holmes walked over to us, raised his hands, then hesitated and looked at me. "Michelle, would you be so kind…?"

I opened her collar, pulling the material aside. The sight of those bluish handprints on her white skin still disturbed me. She must bruise easily to have it show so distinctly. Her throat was so very long, and the finger marks came around the front; the fingers separated only slightly at their tips, but the hands had not quite met. There was a gap of over an inch, which was lucky–otherwise, her larynx might have been crushed. The palms in back had made little impression, but the thumbprints were clearly visible.

Holmes' hands hung tightly at his sides, and again I saw longing in his eyes. He had an excuse for staring at her so, but I knew he was appreciating the beauty of her throat, the curve of her jaw. His eyes briefly met hers. Then they both looked away.

"Curious," he said. "Very curious. Mrs. Wheelwright, would you care to retire?"

She shook her head. "I shall never sleep."

"I can give you something, Violet. And you must drink some milk."

"I feel better now." She tried to smile, but her brown eyes still had a wild glint. Briefly, she bared her teeth. "Mr. Holmes?"

He sat back against the edge of the table. "Yes?"

"Have you… have you ever thought you might be going mad?"

I put my arm on her shoulder. "You must not say such things."

She laughed. "Michelle is far too healthy–far too sane–to understand, but you… Has the possibility ever occurred to you?"

He stared gravely at her. "Yes."

"*Ah*–I knew it."

"But I do not allow such thoughts to linger. I do not allow myself to indulge in such fancies. They are a form of… self-deception. Self-punishment."

"Do you think so?"

"Yes."

She put her hand over her forehead. "If only I could stop my thoughts… It grows so tiresome!"

"No storm lasts forever. It is the penalty we pay for our intellect, for our ability to think better and more intensely than our fellow men. Once our mind undertakes a problem, we cannot rest until it is resolved, until we have our answer, and the wearier we grow, the more frantic our thoughts become. When it is all over, exhaustion and black melancholy often follow."

Her hand shot out and touched his knee. "Oh, yes–*yes!* You do understand–you do."

I could see his fingers tighten about the table edge, the tendons rising to the surface. "You shall not go mad, Violet. I promise you. Your sufferings will end."

It was the first time I had heard him address her as anything other than Mrs. Wheelwright. She laughed, a strained sound, but her relief was audible. "Oh, thank you. I hope–I wish…" She put her hand over her forehead. "Oh God, I am so exhausted I cannot…"

I shook my head. "As well you might be. You should go to bed."

"I shall, but first…" She looked again at Holmes. "Would you do me a favor, Mr. Holmes?"

"Anything you wish."

"My violin is on the shelf there. Play me something–play some Bach" Holmes frowned. "*Now?*"

"Yes."

"But… will it not appear somewhat strange to…?"

"Everyone will think it is me. If anything, it will reassure the servants. They are used to music emanating from this room at odd hours. No one has enough of an ear to tell your playing from mine."

Holmes gazed at me. "Will you go upstairs," I asked, "when he is finished?"

"I promise I shall. I merely… I am not up to playing myself, and I want… I want to think about something else."

I hesitated, and then nodded. Holmes shrugged and walked over to the shelf where the violin sat. He plucked the strings, tuning them, and then tucked a handkerchief and the violin under his chin. The bow slid across the string and swelled into a resonant note, which his quivering fingertips gave a warm vibrato.

"A wondrous instrument," he said.

The door burst open, and Henry rushed into the room. He wore a bowler hat and his black overcoat, but his shirt collar was unbuttoned. "What on earth has happened?"

I walked over to him and slipped my arm about his waist. "Hush, for a moment, and then I shall tell you everything. Just now we must listen to Sherlock play."

Holmes raised the bow, then began. I do not much care for Bach's music. All those melodies going at once frustrate me because I can only hear one thing at a time, only bits and pieces. Nevertheless, Holmes played beautifully. I had always been struck by the passion of his music; only then did he give his emotions full rein.

Violet had closed her eyes and seemed to melt into the chair. Holmes was the only other person I had known who brought such utter concentration to listening; briefly her dark thoughts were forgotten. He finished the piece. She did not open her eyes. "One more, please. Do you know the saraband from the third partita?"

This was more languorous than the first—stately in its sorrow—but I hardly heard it. I was so sleepy. I leaned against Henry, and he drew me close. "Oh my dearest," I murmured softly. How I wished the long evening were over.

At last Holmes lowered the violin, sighing deeply. "My Stradivarius is no better. It may not be its equal."

Violet moistened her lips and opened her eyes. "Bring it with you to Norfolk, and we shall see. Thank you very much, Mr. Holmes. Your playing is inspired." She looked at me. "I am very tired."

"As well you should be."

There was a polite knock at the door. "Come in," Holmes said.

The door opened and Lovejoy stepped into the room. "I am sorry for the delay, but Abigail was distraught. You wished to see me, Mr. Holmes?"

"In a moment. I want to have a look about the grounds. Would you fetch a lantern? First, however, we need Mrs. Wheelwright's maid. She is ready to retire?"

"Certainly, sir."

Henry slipped free of me and put his hat on the table. "What has happened here?"

"You will hear the whole story soon enough." Holmes gestured with his hand at Violet. "By the way, would you be so kind as to have a look at Mrs. Wheelwright's throat?"

Henry frowned, then walked over to Violet. She drew in her breath and looked elsewhere. "Good God!" Henry seemed to jump back. "Who has done this?"

Holmes gave a sharp laugh. "That is the question I would most like answered. Have a good look, Henry. I shall want your professional opinion."

Henry's examination was more detached than Sherlock's, but his revulsion was obvious. Brutality disturbed him.

Another brief knock at the door, and Lovejoy reappeared with Gertrude. I helped Violet to her feet. Her eyes were red and puffy–she was utterly worn out. Her fingers brushed aside a strand of black hair. She winced.

"My throat hurts."

"Have Collins go upstairs with Mrs. Wheelwright and the maid," Holmes said to Lovejoy. "Collins should examine the room, especially under the bed and in the closets. He should only remain outside while Mrs. Wheelwright is dressing. She is not to be left alone under any circumstances. Have a cot brought up for the maid."

"Me, sir?" Gertrude's eyes opened wide.

"Have no fear, miss. You will not be alone. I shall be in a chair in the same room."

"The same room?" Lovejoy's voice was faintly incredulous.

Holmes frowned. "Yes. There will be no more mysterious assailants. Please fetch me that lantern now."

Gertrude and I led Violet to the door. She walked stiffly, stumbling slightly. I released her arm, and she turned, her face a mute appeal. "Michelle…"

"I shall be up in a moment to say good night."

She smiled weakly. "Thank you." She turned to Holmes. "Good night, and thank you again for your playing."

He nodded, then closed the door behind her. Henry took off his coat. "Now, will one of you please explain what has happened!"

Holmes took out a cigarette, which he smoked while I told Henry all that had occurred. When I was finished, Henry shook his head.

"Who–or what–can have done this?"

Sherlock's lips twitched briefly into a smile. "You think it was the devil, then?"

"I no longer know what to think."

I shook my head. "Why should the devil need to go around strangling people? I would also expect him to be better at his work."

Holmes laughed loudly and threw his cigarette butt into the fireplace. "Oh bravo, Michelle! One would assume the fiend could choke someone to death if he were really determined to do so. Did you notice the unusual nature of those bruises on her throat?"

"They were so distinct," I said. "She must have fragile blood vessels."

Holmes shook his head. "No, no—I refer to the gap in front."

"The gap?" Henry asked.

"Given the size of the hands, the person could have wrapped them entirely about her throat, but he did not. He carefully avoided her larynx. I doubt he wanted to severely injure or kill her."

My hands clenched into fists. "You mean someone only wanted to frighten her? How absolutely beastly!"

"I must question the servants, but the most obvious and interesting suspects—Lovejoy, his wife, Mr. Wheelwright—cannot have done it. Lovejoy and Wheelwright were together, and of course Wheelwright's hands are far too large to have made those marks."

"You do not actually think Mrs. Lovejoy could have done it?" I asked incredulously.

Holmes shrugged. "I know not what to make of her mental state, but she is the single most obvious suspect. She gave quite a performance. We have only her word for the 'black fiend,' and she could have crept up behind Mrs. Wheelwright and tried to throttle her. Unfortunately, she has very small, weak-looking hands. She, too, could not have made those marks. So we are left with a mysterious assailant who conveniently fled through the window." Lovejoy reappeared with a small lantern. "Ah, thank you. Henry, would you care to join me?"

"Do you think it is safe outside?" I asked.

"I only wish our strangler were loitering about." Holmes and Henry took their hats and left.

I seized my bag and went upstairs to Violet's room. She had on her nightclothes. She was visibly trembling. "There is nothing to be afraid of now," I said.

She gave me a grotesque smile. "Yes, there is."

I prepared several drops of an opiate in a glass of water for her, and then sat beside her on the bed. She fell asleep almost at once. The fearful tension slowly faded until her face was utterly relaxed, her lips half parted, her forehead a smooth blank. Her hair was aswirl, the snaky black coil contrasting with the white sheets and her pale skin. Even asleep she appeared thin and exhausted.

I went back downstairs to the library. The wind had finally died away, and Henry had pulled one of the plush red chairs near the fireplace. A big log crackled nicely. He raised his arm, and I squeezed into the chair beside him, a tight fit.

"This will teach you to go visiting at odd hours."

"I am so tired," I said. "And did you find anything outside?"

"Only many of Collins' and Lovejoy's footprints."

"No cloven hooves? Perhaps the fiend does not leave footprints." I felt him stiffen. "I am sorry. It is not really amusing."

"Sherlock told me we are going to Norfolk."

"Yes. You do understand why?"

"Of course I do. We might get a spot of nice weather there. It should be lovely."

"No, this cold and fog and rain and darkness will last forever." My voice nearly broke.

"Hush." Henry touched my cheek and slipped out of the chair. I shifted about, resting my head on the soft curved back. The warmth of the fire felt good, and he stroked my shoulder. "You are very brave, and I love you very much."

I wanted to say something or touch his hand, but I was so sleepy, my limbs so heavy. My thoughts drifted elsewhere. Henry's voice changed to that of Sherlock, but I could not make out his words. Sleep was a welcome refuge from black fiends and the memory of Violet's throat marred by those vivid, hand-shaped bruises.

Thirteen

Holmes took off his gloves and overcoat, then set them on the table. He stretched out his hands before the fire, warming his long fingers. He glanced at Michelle. She had shifted sideways and was fast asleep in the chair.

He gave his head a shake. "She is quite extraordinary, Henry. Rarely have I seen such grace under pressure in any man, let alone a woman." His voice was nearly a whisper.

I smiled wryly. "Much more so than her husband, you mean."

"I meant no such thing."

"You need not worry about waking her. Once under, she is a very sound sleeper. It would take considerable effort to rouse her now."

Holmes nodded. He took out his cigarette case. "Good. I have several important matters to discuss with you in private. Let us leave the fire to Michelle." He lit the cigarette, then walked to the far end of the table near the window through which the assailant must have come.

I pulled out a chair midway along the length of the table and sat down. Stifling a yawn, I withdrew my watch. There was barely enough light to see the face. "It's after eleven. No wonder I feel like sleeping myself."

Holmes bent over and flicked the cigarette ash into a potted fern. "I found no sign of anyone having left through this window. There should have been some trace. The earth near the house is wet; the lightest touch would have left a print. I suppose Lovejoy and Collins might have trampled the remnants underfoot. As if this case were not frustrating enough, without them stampeding about like elephants."

"It certainly is baffling." Recalling the bruises on Violet's throat, I could not repress a shudder. "He must have been a brute indeed to choke her that way."

"Mr. Wheelwright has been generous enough to give me one final chance." His voice was heavy with irony. "Another such incident, and I am to be dismissed."

I shrugged. "His impatience is understandable."

Holmes gazed out the window, his back to me. The wind had died away, and now the large, dim room was enveloped in a heavy silence. Holmes turned, then put more cigarette ash into the potted fern. "There shall be no further attempts on his wife's life. I will see to that." His eyes were dangerous. "Unfortunately, I have other important business here in London. I would like you to remain behind for a few days and stay in contact with Inspector Lestrade of Scotland Yard. It is regrettable; he is a man of mediocre ability who requires supervision. You can communicate with me by telegraph if necessary. I assume it will also take time to arrange things with your practice."

I nodded. "We certainly could not both leave tomorrow. I can cover our patients—who are mostly Michelle's. What is this business with Lestrade?"

"I have loosed him on our Mr. Steerford and the Angels of the Lord. The Steerford matter is the simpler, being as it is a traditional swindle. Its uniqueness comes from its many illustrious participants, its sheer audacity, and the sum of money involved. I have revealed Steerford's true identity to Lestrade, and he will be closely watched from now on."

"Who, then, is Steerford?"

Holmes' lips twisted briefly into a smile. "Lovejoy."

I stared at him, the name taking a second or two to sink in. "*Lovejoy.*" Unconsciously, I had risen to my feet.

"Keep your voice down. None other."

"How can you be so sure? He was nothing like Lovejoy. His voice, his appearance…"

"You are not trained in the art of disguise. I recognized him almost at once, as he most likely recognized me."

"Can you be certain of such a thing?"

"Any lingering doubts were resolved this morning when I made a brief visit here and spoke with Lovejoy. Since they were not hidden, I had studied Steerford's ears and hands closely, noting certain distinguishing characteristics. Lovejoy's were identical."

"But how…? And why?"

"The 'why' is simple. He was talking about raising a million pounds. As for the how, as the head servant he is not closely supervised and can frequently be out on business. He maintains the Steerford establishment conveniently nearby, but is rarely at home there. As Steerford he can use the oil well as his excuse for being absent."

"And is Mrs. Lovejoy a party to this scheme?"

He smiled. "It is not likely they came up with two such devious schemes independently. Devious and lucrative—the Angels of the Lord dabble in at least robbery and extortion. The Lovejoys' positions give them access to valuable information. At dinner parties they no doubt keep a sharp ear open, and the servants in higher-class households maintain a network of gossip. A talkative footman can spread a rumor about half the households of London in a mere week."

"Then you think Mrs. Lovejoy's hysteria is only an act?"

Holmes gave a gruff laugh. "I thought so from the first. She is a bit *too* histrionic."

"But... but this business with Violet—is it also their doing?"

Holmes frowned. "That is a puzzle. It makes little sense, as it draws attention to them and there is no profit in it. If not for the threats against Mrs. Wheelwright, I most likely would never have discovered Mr. Steerford or the Angels of the Lord. As for this evening, neither of them could be the perpetrator; a third person must be involved. However, none of the male servants were alone at the time."

"Could the Lovejoys have some grievance against Mrs. Wheelwright?"

"If they do, they are the only people in the house—with one exception—who do. As you know, I have questioned the servants extensively. They genuinely like their mistress."

"Who is the exception?"

"Her husband. Then, of course, we must not forget her father-in-law. I believe the old man is paying Lovejoy for information about his son's household."

"What!"

"This came out in my interviews with the servants. Old Wheelwright is a frequent visitor, and after his arrival he always speaks briefly and privately with Lovejoy."

"Then it must be the old man—he is behind the threats against Violet. And perhaps it goes further still..."

"Let me remind you that the last time you were equally certain the person in question was Miss Ladell."

"But I had never actually met her, while old Wheelwright is obviously despicable. Spying on his own son! Even so, this thing tonight remains baffling, and I suppose the old man has so much money he could not be involved in the Lovejoys' schemes."

Holmes gave a dry, hollow-sounding laugh. "There you are wrong. Men such as Wheelwright can never have too much money. There is no limit to their greed—it is bottomless and irrational. All the same, the Angels do not fit his style, nor does Steerford. Direct annihilation was always his stratagem in the potted meat trade, a full frontal assault upon his opponents."

We were both silent. I could hear Michelle breathing deeply and regularly. At last I spoke. "Perhaps it is time to confront Lovejoy and his wife."

"Absolutely not!" His voice was sharp. "Tell no one except Michelle."

"Not even the Wheelwrights?"

"Especially not the Wheelwrights. Mr. Wheelwright would want to thrash someone. Let us keep the Lovejoys guessing. They do not know for certain whether I recognized Lovejoy." Holmes ran his fingers back through his hair. "I shall write Lestrade a note, which I want you to deliver. He will be keeping Lovejoy under surveillance and preparing to spring a trap before the fifteenth. I am hopeful that we may finally discover the Lovejoys' true identities; Lestrade's clerks are searching the police files. When you depart in three or four days, Lestrade should have some news for me. He will also be pursuing my suggestions concerning the Angels of the Lord."

"What if Lovejoy does not remain behind?"

Holmes laughed. "He will find some excuse to stay here. I only wish I could do the same."

"Why?"

"Because Lestrade is a mediocrity! The whole thing could slip through his clumsy fingers. And there are too many details unresolved. If I had another week… I shall also have you visit a brothel." He smiled at my look. "For information only."

"Oh." There was a faint stir of wind, which rattled the windowpanes. "You have made considerable progress in this case. I would not have believed it."

Sherlock frowned, the fingers of his right hand drumming relentlessly at the table.

"What is the matter?"

He finally raised his eyes. "Things still do not add up."

The attack on Violet had occurred on a Friday night. Michelle, Holmes, and the Wheelwrights left the next day. I was busy over the weekend with Holmes' tasks, then on Monday and Tuesday I handled our combined medical practice and prepared for my own departure. From morning to evening, I saw one patient after another.

A few days without Michelle always made me morose, and my last patient on Tuesday was a sweet old lady who was slowly dying of cancer. After she had left, I sat alone in my examining room, my head slumped wearily, my elbow on the desk, forehead against my palm, fingers in my hair. A rap sounded at the door. "Yes?"

Harriet's face appeared, a crease between her dark brows. "Doctor…" Behind her I saw the pale thin face of old Wheelwright, a faint smile pulling at his bloodless lips.

Oh Lord, I thought, a twinge of fear flickering through my chest.

"Come in, Mr. Wheelwright. Thank you, Harriet."

He silently stared down at me, his top hat held in his aged, trembling fingers. "I do not suppose you have come to see me about a medical problem."

His smile intensified. "*I'm* not sick, if that's what you mean."

"I thought not. What, then? Have a seat if you will."

He slowly sat down upon the edge of a heavy oak chair. "It's about my daughter-in-law. Do you believe me now?"

"Believe what?"

"That she is a lunatic."

I had the sudden urge to strike him, to plunge my fist into that smiling mouth of brownish-yellow teeth. The intensity of my repulsion caught me by surprise, and I had to compose myself before I could speak. "No, I do not. Someone tried to strangle her last week."

"She imagined the whole thing."

"She did not—I saw the bruises on her throat. They were shaped like hands."

"No one told me about any bruises—that's impossible."

"I saw them, sir. They were real enough."

His white brows had bunched up over his nose. "No matter, no matter. She is still a lunatic."

Again I had to restrain my anger. "It has been a long day, Mr. Wheelwright. What exactly do you want from me?"

He stared closely at me. "I want your assistance in committing my daughter-in-law."

My eyes widened, and a peculiar fear now contended with my fury. "*You* are mad, not her! Most asylums are still in the Dark Ages. I would not have my worst enemy committed, let alone a beautiful and intelligent young woman like Violet."

His smile grew contemptuous. "Beautiful, eh? It always comes back to beauty, doesn't it?"

"I can well believe you have no feeling for beauty." My voice shook.

"What good is it, Doctor? Tell me that. My age has finally freed me from all such snares. You are a respectable man, a married man. Her beauty is of no use to you—all it does is stir you up and make you behave stupidly. Otherwise, you would realize that I could make it very much worth your while to help me. If my son were free, he could marry again, marry someone who could bear him a child. What do you want? Money, prestige? They are yours for the asking, and believe me, it would be for the best. She is quite mad, you know."

I lowered my gaze, unable to bear his leering visage. "Mr. Wheelwright, you had better leave."

"Your cousin is a hopeless case. I could see that at the dinner. The great consulting detective—the finest mind in England, as the newspapers put it—reduced to quivering jelly by a mere woman. I had hoped for better from you, Doctor. You have a woman of your own, a pretty enough one. She need never know…"

"Get out of here!" I roared, leaping to my feet. "Get out before I give you the thrashing you deserve!"

His smile vanished, uneasiness appearing in his eyes: he saw that I meant it. "Very well, sir." He stood. "There is no reason to be abusive. You need not take that tone with me."

"No? You are the most morally repugnant… You spy on your own son, do you not? How much are you paying Lovejoy?"

His smile was wary. "I suppose Holmes discovered that. Maybe he is worth his fee. I'm Donald's father after all. Someone has to look after him, the poor fool. He can't seem to take care of himself."

"Why do you not simply talk to your son instead of spying on him?"

Wheelwright seemed genuinely surprised. "Because I want the truth."

"Oh, I doubt that. And is Violet mad, or are you only trying to drive her mad?"

"There's no need for me to do anything. She's been that way for many years, ever since her marriage. She hides it well, but I can see—I can see."

My head had begun to hurt, and I put my hand on my forehead. "Go away—leave *now*."

His contemptuous smile returned. "Very well, sir, but you might tell your cousin that if he gets in my way I shall crush him. I have broken far better men than he."

"And he has been threatened by far better men than you—good day, Mr. Wheelwright."

He turned and walked out of the door.

A decanter of brandy, usually reserved for medicinal purposes, was on my desk. I poured a large glass, my hands shaking, and took a big swallow. I stared out the window at the gray, rainy sky and tried to calm myself.

"Deliver us from evil," I murmured. A shiver snaked its way along my spine, and I took another swallow of brandy.

The next day, Wednesday, I arrived at Norfolk on the three-fifteen train. Collins and Michelle were waiting at the station. Collins smiled as Michelle gave me an embrace that would have crushed a smaller man. It seemed as if we had been apart much longer than four days.

The sun was out, the day cold and clear, the air marvelously fresh after London. Michelle wore a beautiful purple coat with sable collar and cuffs. Her face was slightly sunburned, the few freckles on her nose and cheeks clearly visible. She wore black leather gloves, which hid her powerful hands. Looking at her made me briefly forget Sherlock, the Wheelwrights, and Lovejoys—I was only conscious of my desire for her.

"You look well," I said. "The country air must agree with you."

She slipped her hand about my arm. "How I have missed you! Now everything is perfect. We have been having a wonderful time. Violet seems much better. It is good for her to be away from London. Donald Wheelwright tramples about the woods every day with his dogs and shoots at various birds and animals. In the meantime, I..." She stopped abruptly, glancing sideways at Collins, who was carrying one of my bags.

Noticing the silence, he turned to us. "I'll fetch the cart, ma'am. No need to walk all that way."

"Thank you, Collins."

We watched him start down the cobbled street. "What were you saying?"

She smiled wryly. "I have been chaperoning Sherlock and Violet. They are such good company. They have brought along their violins, and they play beautifully together. We've gone for walks in the woods. The forest is so beautiful. We saw a deer yesterday. The two of them have also been playing chess. Violet won the first game."

"*What?*"

She laughed. "You should have seen the expression on his face. He was ahead by a rook, when she checkmated him."

I glanced quickly about, and then kissed her on the lips. She pressed her fingers into the small of my back. "I have been longing for you," she said.

Collins came down the street driving a dogcart. He stopped, then hopped down, opened the door, and helped Michelle up. I got in and sat across from her. Since the carriage was open to the air, I could savor the sunny weather. Within five minutes we were out of the village following a country road winding about a pastoral setting.

We entered a forest of gnarled, ancient oaks, their trunks massive, a yard or two across. Many of the leaves were still on the trees, all bronze, russet, or reddish; others had fallen and formed a thick carpet. The air had a moist, fecund smell, a heady odor of fresh earth and rotting leaves. The branches themselves were long and twisted, nearly black. It seemed the kind of forest where Oberon, Titania, and Puck dwelt, where fairies would dance under moonlight. Gradually the trees thinned, the road dropped and curved, and ahead at the summit of a vast expanse of lush green lawn was an enormous house of gray stone.

"Good Lord," I murmured. "That is where we are going?"

"It has only fifty rooms or so. Somewhere they will find a place to put you. The great hall appears to be something from *Ivanhoe.*"

I shook my head. "There are those that aspire to great wealth and such houses, but I keep thinking in practical terms of the difficulties in maintaining such a residence."

Michelle nodded eagerly. "The rooms are cold and drafty. Already I miss our little house and Harriet and Victoria. How are Harriet and Victoria, by the way?"

"They are both well, but they miss you. Victoria wanders about the house yowling pathetically."

"Poor dear." She reached out and took my hand. "I am glad you do not wish to be horribly rich. Violet is the first wealthy friend I have had, and I do not envy her."

I glanced at the back of Collins' neck. "You would not want your own huge room far from mine, and your own bed?"

She frowned. "Absolutely not!" She smiled and squeezed my hand.

The house was imposing, but melancholy. The gray stone was colorless and forlorn, and the rooms inside were huge—and as Michelle said, cold and drafty. The fire burning at one end of the great hall was large enough for roasting an ox, yet it hardly cut the chill. Somber, uninspired paintings hung from the walls, mostly bucolic pastorals in gaudy antique frames. Portraits of several generations of ancestors would have been more appropriate, but the Wheelwrights were a youthful dynasty. However, before the dining table in the place of prominence was a painting of the elderly Wheelwright and his wife. The artist had the features exactly right, but as there was no hint of malice or avarice, the Wheelwright on canvas appeared to be only some saintly relative of the old scoundrel.

As we crossed the chamber, our footsteps echoed faintly. "Most of the rooms are still closed up," Michelle said. "There are only about twenty servants here. The rest are coming down early next week with the Lovejoys."

"I would not expect the Lovejoys." I tried to keep my voice low, but the room seemed to echo my words. Before we had parted, I had briefly told her what Holmes had revealed about the butler.

Michelle had pulled off her gloves. She gave me a curious look. "No?" One of the maids was nearby polishing the silver. "We shall have to have a talk," Michelle said.

Collins had left us earlier. I took her hand and kissed her palm. "Talk is not exactly what I had in mind."

She stroked my cheek and gave me a look, which made it plain that she was of like mind. "We should go see Sherlock and Violet."

"I suppose so," I said reluctantly.

She took my hand and led me up the massive stone staircase. "Violet has a knack for finding a comfortable room and appropriating it."

"This house has some comfortable rooms?"

"Our bedroom is rather nice."

"Why do you not show it to me?"

Her fingers tightened about mine. "Do not tempt me."

"Sherlock once told me the afternoon was reserved for loose women and their customers. I told him that he was... ill-informed."

"Harriet is only too happy to have the afternoon off, but with so many maids..." Her voice was wistful.

Violet's sitting room did seem different from the rest of the house. It faced south and had been converted to a sunroom, a row of windows letting in the warm autumnal light. A wood fire blazed in the fireplace, and a thick, reddish, patterned carpet covered the cold stone floor. A velvet sofa was against the wall with all the windows, and two matching chairs were close by. Sherlock and Violet were seated at a cherry-wood table, a chessboard between them. Gertrude sat on the sofa embroidering, her white apron and lace cap contrasting with the black dress.

Violet smiled at us. Her color was better, and she wore an electric blue dress with a high collar, no doubt selected to hide the bruises on her throat. Holmes' brow was furrowed, and he kept his eyes fixed on the chessboard. His heavy tweed suit had a gray herringbone pattern. He was playing black, and he was down to two pawns, a queen, and a rook, while Violet had her queen, two rooks, and a pawn.

"I found this man at the train station, and I thought I would bring him home with me." Michelle slipped her hand about my arm.

Violet kept smiling, but a faint wariness showed in her dark eyes. "Perhaps he will make some impression on Mr. Holmes, who has been staring at the board for some ten minutes. He would be saving himself some grief if he simply resigned."

"I never resign." Holmes slid his rook the length of the board and raised his eyes. "Henry, how good to see you." His smile was warm. "I trust your time in London was well spent?"

"Very well spent."

His gray eyes narrowed. "I am eager to hear about it."

Violet moved her queen. "You did exactly what I wanted. Check."

Holmes glanced at the board, his smile vanishing. "Blast it! How could I have…?"

Michelle folded her arms. "It is most impolite to play chess when you have guests. You must both be charming now."

Violet smiled. "Of course you are right, Michelle. Our game can wait. I shall give Mr. Holmes a respite, although I fear it will be of little help." She stood up.

"Sherlock," Michelle said sternly.

Reluctantly he turned away from the board. "Oh, very well."

Violet stepped over to the windows. The view was stunning, the long expanse of lawn and the foliage of the oak forest all golden and glowing from the sinking sun. Her violin lay upon a window seat, and she reached out tentatively and touched it with her white fingers. She was turned from us. Holmes was watching her, an unfamiliar longing in his eyes.

"If you would like to play, that would be nice," Michelle said.

Violet picked up the violin and the bow. "I would have thought by now that my playing had lost whatever meager charm it possessed."

Michelle shook her head. "Not at all." She led me to the sofa. Gertrude started to get up. "Oh, stay put, my dear—there is room for all three of us."

Gertrude was surprised. "Thank you, ma'am."

Violet closed her eyes and drew the bow across the strings. The note was like a long, tremulous sigh. Something softened in Violet's thin face, the tension easing. She had been so weary or ill the last few times I had seen her that I had forgotten what a lovely woman she was. Her fingers were long, delicate, and graceful as they moved across the strings.

Michelle's beauty was somehow robust and muscular—cheerful, like her. She radiated health, strength and—although this may sound biased—goodness. There was nothing delicate or refined about her, although she was quite pretty. Her skin was very fair, her hair a light brown verging on red. Violet also had fair skin, but her hair was absolutely black, her aquiline nose, brown eyes and full lips strangely exotic. Somehow, despite her beauty, intelligence and strength of character, she remained oddly vulnerable.

She began the Bach partita I had heard her and Sherlock play in London. The instrument did have a warm tone, but that particular afternoon the music had a plaintive, even sorrowful, resonance. Holmes could always close his eyes and be swallowed up by music, but I was too earthbound, too easily distracted. All the same, that day I was moved. It was not merely the music, but the sight of Violet, the languorous tenderness in her beautiful, pale face as she caressed the strings of her Guarnieri.

When she finished, she lowered the violin but did not open her eyes.

"How beautiful," Michelle murmured.

Holmes was staring at Violet, his gray eyes consuming her. Anyone could have seen that he was totally and hopelessly in love. I stroked the end of my mustache. How ever would this end? She probably felt the same way, but she was a married woman. I knew my cousin too well to think he could ever be part of some sordid, adulterous affair.

Holmes stood and seized his own violin from the end of the table. Hearing him, Violet opened her eyes. He pulled out a handkerchief, and tucked it and the violin under his chin. "Play the partita again," he said.

Violet closed her eyes and played. Holmes hesitated, and then began. I knew he played well, but I had not realized he could improvise so spectacularly. He picked up fragments of the melody, spun them out, raised or lowered them an octave, slowed them down or sped them up, all the while managing to harmonize with Violet. The Bach was difficult enough, but his contrapuntal accompaniment was that of a virtuoso, truly inspired. Near the end, his melodies merged with hers, and the final notes were in unison.

Michelle clapped her hands loudly. "Oh, bravo!"

Violet opened her eyes and stared up at him, a faint flush lingering on her cheeks. "That was very good, Mr. Holmes."

Oh, dear God, I thought—she does love him.

We dressed for dinner and ate that evening in the great hall, our conversation drifting into the vast expanse overhead, echoing back faintly. The room was chilly, all the courses tiresome. Donald Wheelwright was silent, his great sullen presence casting an air of gloom over the meal. Holmes and Violet were reserved, and I was relieved to see that the feelings, which had seemed transparent earlier, were well hidden.

Wheelwright might have a mistress whom he had set up in her own house; he might no longer love his wife; yet I was fearful of what he would do should he discover that Violet loved another. His size certainly contributed to the impression, but he had always seemed dangerous to me, someone I would not wish to anger.

The evening dragged on, and at last I pleaded fatigue from my journey as an excuse to retire early. Michelle looked at me, then made a similar excuse. Holmes appeared faintly amused. It was some time before Michelle and I were in a mood for conversation. I told her of the realization that had struck me that afternoon.

"I am so happy for them," she said with great enthusiasm.

I stared curiously at her. "Why? I cannot see any way that they might..."

"Somehow they will find a way, I know it."

She seemed so pleased, so happy, I did not want to tell her outright that the situation seemed hopeless. Michelle was the optimist, while I had a jaundiced view of humanity. All in all, we balanced each other out, and her cheerfulness was one of the very qualities that had attracted me to her. Nevertheless, I felt I must warn her.

"It would be very difficult for them. Wheelwright does not seem the type of man to ever willingly step aside. And Sherlock would never..."

She frowned and regarded me curiously. "Would he not?" I gave her such a look that she blushed, which was rare. "I only meant... It is only convention, after all, especially if Donald has a mistress, and... Oh, Henry—you know I am not a wicked person, and they are not wicked either! It does seem so wretched."

"Perhaps... They might be content with a Platonic relation." She stared at me so that I laughed, then took her hand and kissed her knuckles. "I know it is hard for you to conceive of such a thing, but there are people, especially women, who lack your passion. Not every man is as lucky as I."

She smiled, her face still flushed. "I am glad you feel that way, but you saw how they looked at each other. I do not think a Platonic relation would satisfy them. Besides, I have always considered such arrangements absolutely beastly—as if an illicit love were perfectly acceptable, so long as it was not technically consummated! Were you to love another, it would not much matter to me whether... It is the loving itself which would hurt, regardless."

I kissed her gently. "You needn't worry."

"Oh, Henry. I wonder..." After a brief silence, she said, "Perhaps you could speak with Donald Wheelwright and try to probe his thoughts."

"You are joking."

"I do not mean you should ask him directly. However, you might sound him out. The poor fellow must be rather lonely, although he seems happier here. He is fond of his dogs and his sport. I do believe he likes the outdoors, and he has never seemed happy in formal dress. You could accompany him when he goes out tomorrow."

"Possibly."

My lack of enthusiasm amused her. She had let down her hair, and it spilled onto the pillow. I stroked the thick strand nearest me.

"I must speak with Sherlock tomorrow and give him some papers from Lestrade."

"There will be plenty of time for that in the morning. Then you and Donald Wheelwright can be off together on the hunt. It may even be agreeable." She laughed at the expression on my face. "You might bring home a pheasant for our supper."

Thus it was that after reviewing matters with Holmes in the morning, I found myself plodding through the woods with Donald Wheelwright and his two retrievers in the afternoon. The day was again very fine, another golden autumn afternoon, the clean fresh air invigorating. Given the weather and the retrievers' canine enthusiasm, it would have taken an effort to be gloomy, and my companion's spirits lifted once we had left the house.

I realized I had never had a real conversation with Wheelwright or actually been alone with him. He was more at ease in his aged brown tweed jacket, canvas trousers, and battered, shapeless wool hat with almost no brim. I had seen hunters on my country walks whose apparel was as fashionable and spotless as their citywear, but Wheelwright obviously preferred worn and comfortable clothing. He carried his shotgun breech open, and the pockets of his jacket were stuffed with shells. He had offered to lend me one of his shotguns, but I told him I would accompany him as a spectator only. Not only the birds and animals would be safer.

Two or three times I tried to start a conversation, but Wheelwright obviously did not believe in idle chitchat for the sake of avoiding silence. He had a leisurely stroll, yet his legs were so long that each step covered a great distance. I was over six feet tall myself, but I had to work to keep up. In the woods it was cooler, the light dappled, yellow, on leaves or bark or fern where it penetrated the foliage above. My breath formed a white mist, and everything about us seemed damp and decomposed, the odor rich and earthy, overpowering.

"What exactly are you hunting?" I asked.

"Nothing much." He had relaxed, the customary tension, which showed in his eyes and furrowed brow, completely gone. "If we're lucky we might scare out a pheasant or a cony. I'm more just walking, as I said earlier. If I really wanted to get a few ducks, I'd go down by the pond and sit, but Goldie and Chieftain like to keep moving. So do I."

The path opened up, and we came out into a clearing, grass and ferns sloping downward to a big pond below, its waters blue and still under the autumn light. By the pond was an ancient oak, six feet across, its limbs all gnarled and twisted, the lower branches each as thick as the trunk of a normal tree. Most of its leaves were gone, many floating on the waters below. Black forms were perched about the branches, and we could hear the din of the crows, the caws, of their convocation.

Wheelwright stopped to enjoy the view. The golden retriever saw the water and was off like a shot down the hill. She plunged into the pond with no hesitation. The Irish setter trotted down, but only stared curiously at its companion. Wheelwright leaned his gun against a stump and took a silver case from his jacket.

"Care for a smoke?"

"No, thank you," I said.

Wheelwright took out a very long cigar, then put the case back in his jacket. He glanced at me, the hint of a frown briefly showing. He hesitated, bit off the end of the cigar, spat it out, and struck a match. As he inhaled, he continued to regard me closely. I was again struck by the size of his fingers; they were thicker than the cigar, a good inch across above the knuckles.

"I hope you don't mind seeing a man bite off a cigar." From his tone it was difficult to tell whether he was apologizing or warning me not to take offense.

I smiled. "Not at all. Gentlemen are supposed to use cigar cutters, but surely one must make some allowance for this rustic setting." He stared curiously at me. I glanced down at the pond. "This is a beautiful spot."

He nodded. "It's my favorite hereabouts. Care to sit for a moment? We've been walking for a while." He sat on the tree stump. "I usually sit here and have a cigar. I like a cigar. Violet hates cigars." His eyes clouded over. "It's one more thing about me she can't abide." His voice was bitter.

I sat on another stump—several trees had been cut there—and picked up a small twig. I began to snap off pieces.

Wheelwright sighed. "Yes, this is a good place. The rooks surely like that big tree. Some days when I'm sick of their cawing, I have a shot at them. I'm not really trying to harm them, just scare them off. It works, too. Today they aren't so noisy."

I nodded and carefully pulled off a strip of bark from the twig. "I can see how they would get on one's nerves."

We both remained silent for a while. The sun felt very warm on our faces, and a faint breeze rustled the dry leaves in the trees behind us. One of the crows spiraled upward from the tree; another followed. With a caw, the higher one swooped and dived at the other. Wheelwright knocked off the cigar ash and ground it into the earth with the toe of his enormous boot. I could smell the oiled leather; the boots were beauties and had been well cared for, no doubt by his valet.

"Tell me, Dr. Vernier…"

"You might as well call me Henry. 'Doctor' sounds too formal for this setting. Besides, I grow tired of hearing 'doctor' all the time."

His brow furrowed, then he stared closely at me. He shrugged. "Tell me, Henry, do you ever feel like chucking it all?"

"Chucking it all?"

"Your doctoring, your friends, your family, your house. London. Just giving it all up and going somewhere else—somewhere like this." His head swept about.

"Well, yes, I have thought about that. Being a physician really is such a hopeless business. We can diagnose, but we simply cannot cure many diseases. And then you have to deal with the hypochondriacs who are not sick at all, but who are always coming to see you. It's not charitable, I know, but some of them… I almost wish they would get truly sick. It would serve them right."

Wheelwright laughed. I could not recall ever having heard him laugh before. "I can see that. All the same, your doctoring can't be worse than the potted meat business." He smiled grimly. "I promise if I ever have a son—which isn't likely—that he won't have to work for me. No one should have to work for their own father. At least not for my father. He just can't understand…" He drew in deeply on the cigar, then exhaled the pungent smoke. "He can't understand that it bores me. He thinks of nothing else. He's shrewd, and he's rich, but he still badly wants to make more money. I told him once I didn't see the point. We have enough." Wheelwright laughed, this time harshly. "He gave me such a look, then started yelling at me. I stood there and took it, just as I always take it, but…" He stubbed out his cigar, then ground the butt savagely underfoot. "What's the use of it all?"

I stared at him in amazement. "I… It does get tiresome, doesn't it?"

He nodded. "I'd like to be outdoors more. Not in London, of course. Half the time you can't breathe there. Lord, how I hate going to that office every day. He won't trust me with anything important. I can't blame him. I'm no businessman. All the same… It seems so foolish that we have to pretend all the time, pretend we're something we're not."

"Couldn't you…? Do you have money of your own?"

"Some, but he'd cut me off without a penny if I tried to leave the firm."

"He cannot—he cannot live forever, at any rate—cruel as that might sound."

Wheelwright gave a gruff laugh. "Sometimes I think he will outlive me."

"Of course he won't."

Wheelwright shrugged. He stared down at the dog swimming about in the pond. "It's funny how happy a dog is. It doesn't take much to please them. Some meat and a bone, running about outdoors, and a bit of affection." He smiled briefly, his mouth taut under the neatly trimmed mustache. "Yes, sometimes I think I'd like to chuck it all. Go somewhere and start over. Just take…" He glanced at me and stopped abruptly. He was probably thinking of his mistress; she would be the one person he would wish to take with him. Or was she only one more unwanted obligation?

He stood up, put his fingers in his mouth and gave a deafening whistle. "Goldie, come on!" He glanced at me while we waited for the dogs to come back uphill. "It's all just dreaming, anyway. I guess I'm stuck with houses and servants and the whole business. Most men would envy me, I suppose."

"I do not envy you."

He laughed again. "That's wise."

"My practice does grow tiresome. I know something of what you must feel. One wearies of burdens and responsibilities. At least if you make an error, no one may suffer terribly for it."

Wheelwright's mouth twisted into a smile. "No?" Goldie appeared before us and shook the water eagerly from her coat, splashing us. "Goldie, you stupid dog! You bad dog!" Wheelwright bent over and tousled the fur on the dog's head, then brought his enormous hand around and scratched at the ruff of her throat. "You are a stupid dog." Chieftain, the setter, watched forlornly, until Wheelwright beckoned with his hand. "Here, boy. You want some, too. That's a good dog. Yes, you're much smarter than Goldie." He rubbed the dog's head and stroked its back. He picked up his gun, and we started down the path.

I wanted to ask him about Violet, but I could not. He had confided in me, and I could not bring myself to probe, to manipulate and spy.

"We all have our burdens," he said. "You're right about that, but you are a lucky man, Henry."

"Me?" I could not think why.

"Your wife loves you, and you love her. Anyone can see it."

"I... Your wife does not hate you." I licked my lips. "You may have your differences, but surely..."

"She hates me, and I hate her, but I'm not as good at it as she is."

It was as if a dark cloud had blotted out the sun, dimming the beauty all around us.

"Have you…? Perhaps if you tried to talk with her about the situation. It does neither of you any good to be so miserable."

"Lord, that's true enough." He gave his massive head a shake. "It's no use me trying to talk to her. I've never been much good with words, while she… She can talk and talk. She makes a net with her words and catches me in it. I'll not try talking to her. Sometimes she makes me so angry…" And indeed, his face had grown quite red, that sullen anger showing in his eyes and brow.

I wanted to say something that might help. "Perhaps I could…? If someone else tried to talk to her…" I felt confused and stupid. What was there for them to talk about? They had little in common, and both of them now loved another.

"No, no." Wheelwright drew in his breath. His lung capacity was immense; he seemed to inhale for a minute, trying to fill himself with the clear clean air. "As you say, we all have our burdens and responsibilities."

The path skirted the pond. I saw the reflection of the oaks shimmering on the blue-gray surface and closer up, floating leaves and bits of grass.

"I wish I could help." My voice was plaintive. His pain was so obvious.

"That's decent of you, but I'll get by. I suppose. I wish this gypsy business were done with. It's only when… when I think about the future, that this might go on for years and years, my father getting older and meaner, and Violet…"

Again he drew in his breath. We were both silent. The dogs had run far ahead out of sight. Abruptly, something came out of the brush before us.

Wheelwright moved very quickly. His gun was up, the breech locked, then he raised it and fired, the boom of the shell so deafening I clapped my hand—too late—over my ear. It would be ringing for hours.

"Did you see?" Wheelwright's blue eyes were wild, and his teeth showed below the mustache. "A pheasant! A beauty, I think." The dogs came barking down the path toward us. "Get her, Chief!" His rumbling voice was loud.

The Irish setter came up to us, the bird hanging limply from his jaws, the brilliant feathers spattered with blood. Wheelwright took it and held it up by the neck. The sun glinted off the feathers, the iridescent shades of gray, red, green, and gold. I could see the tiny wounds made by the shot.

"Well, we've something to show for our walk this afternoon, Henry. I'll have the cook serve it, and we'll have the choicest portions for ourselves."

I smiled, but I felt a strange dread that I could not quite understand. My ears rang. The sunlight seemed faint and feeble, and I felt cold even though we stood in the sun. The blast had disturbed the crows. They filled the sky with their caws, shards of blackness against a vast blue.

Fourteen

When we were alone that evening, I told Michelle about my conversation with Donald Wheelwright. As she listened, the creases in her forehead deepened. For once she was at a loss for words.

"I wish we could leave this place," I said. "I wish we could leave Sherlock, Violet, and Donald. I... I am sick to death of the whole business." My vehemence surprised us both.

"I cannot abandon Violet, my dear."

I sighed wearily. "Oh, I know. Nor can I abandon Sherlock. All the same... there is something unhealthy and disturbing about the Wheelwrights."

Michelle stared at the candle flickering on the table. "Surely... surely not with Violet."

"Her, too."

Michelle's hand tightened about my arm. "But... she is only tired. This is all such a strain. If we could get her away from here—away from Donald and the Lovejoys and the gypsy's threats—then she would be well again. I know it."

"Perhaps." I was not convinced, and my face showed it.

Michelle's eyes filled with tears and she turned away.

That night my uneasiness kept me awake. Michelle was asleep in minutes, but I was up at least two hours longer. As a result, I slept later than usual. After a solitary breakfast I went to the sitting room.

Michelle rose to greet me. Sherlock sat on the window seat playing an informal air on his violin. Violet sat close by, a book on her lap. Gertrude was at a chair by the fire. The day was again spectacularly fair, the green expanse of lawn and the oak forest visible, the light different this early in the day. A small clock showed it was nearly eleven.

"Welcome, slug-a-bed." Michelle kissed my cheek. "I thought you would never get up."

Violet seemed more interested in Sherlock than her book. He set down the violin. "This country air does not make one industrious. Rather it has a soporific effect." He played part of Brahms' *Lullaby*. Michelle and Violet laughed.

"You seem full of energy," I said. "What project will you undertake today?"

He raised his long hand, gesturing at the table. "Mrs. Wheelwright must offer me another game of chess. We are tied at one game apiece."

"You actually managed to win the second game?" I said. "You were losing."

"I was lucky."

Violet gave a sharp laugh. "No, I was stupid—I made a very ill-considered move. You may be full of energy, Mr. Holmes, but I do not know if I am quite ready to start another game. Chess takes such concentration."

Michelle gave her head a shake. "It is far too lovely a day to be playing chess indoors, especially in November. The weather could change at any time."

A sharp rap came at the door, and then it opened. Collins was dressed in his formal footman's garb, and behind him were Donald Wheelwright and old Wheelwright. The two Wheelwrights strode into the room.

Violet's eyes narrowed, but she stood and smiled, a faintly glacial expression. "Father Wheelwright, what a pleasant surprise."

The younger Wheelwright gazed about the room. He did not appear particularly happy himself, and I remembered him saying how much he disliked working for his father. "Father had some business to discuss."

The old man nodded. "We can't all retreat from our everyday affairs. The potted meat trade requires constant attention. I'd never be where I am today—this house would never be in the family—if I had gone running off to the country all the time." He turned to Holmes. "And have you discovered who attacked my daughter-in-law, Mr. Holmes?"

Holmes shook his head. "No."

The two men stared at each other. Old Wheelwright wished to compel some explanation, but Holmes would not speak. "It's a fine business when a lady can be attacked in her own home. Fleeing to the country hardly seems much of an answer. I hope you have not been overrated, Mr. Holmes."

Violet's smile had vanished, but Sherlock only smiled. "I hope not."

Old Wheelwright glanced about angrily, and his gaze fell upon Gertrude. She sat quietly in the chair by the fire, her knitting untouched in her lap. Something about the old man's thin neck and jerky movements reminded me of a bird, one with a white head and black body. He stepped forward, walking over to her chair. She did not move.

"Here now? What's this?"

I could see that Gertrude had fallen asleep. Her eyelids fluttered, then opened.

"Sleeping—*sleeping?* I cannot believe it! Get up, girl! Where are your manners?"

Gertrude leaped up, her knitting tumbling from her lap. She clutched at her black skirts and managed a feeble curtsy. She looked pale and tired. "Good day, sir." Her voice was hoarse. She made her tiny hand into a fist, and then coughed into it.

"If you worked for me, girl, I'd have you go pack your things." He turned to his son. "Lax. Very lax. Parlor maids sleeping and staying seated when their master enters the room."

"The girl is ill. Anyone can see that." Michelle's voice was steely and she stared sharply at the old man.

His upper lip curled into a brief smile. "Ill? *Ill?* That's no excuse. Servants have no business being ill—not on our time." He glanced about, but no one said a word.

Gertrude swayed slightly, as if she were about to faint. She coughed again. Michelle went to her side and took her arm. "Sit down, my dear."

"Oh, ma'am!" Gertrude shook her head, sagging against her.

"Outrageous!" Wheelwright turned to his son. "I hope you'll deal with her. If you let this kind of behavior go by, you'll soon have all your household making faces at you behind your back."

Donald Wheelwright slowly drew in his breath. "She shall be punished."

"See to it." The old man strode from the room.

Donald started to follow, then turned to Violet. "See to it."

Violet's face was red, but her voice was like ice. "See to what?"

"He's right. We can't have servants falling asleep and ignoring our visitors. Make certain it does not happen again."

"Oh, I shall." Violet gave a savage laugh.

Wheelwright's eyes were sullen. He turned and left the room.

Gertrude began to cry. Michelle lowered her into the chair.

"I couldn't help it," Gertrude said. "My chest hurts and my head. If I was awake... Someone shoud've nudged me." She turned to Violet. "Oh, ma'am, I'm so sorry! Honestly I am." She began to cough in earnest.

Michelle put her big hand on her shoulder. "There is nothing to be sorry about. You just sit and stay quiet."

Violet had not moved from where she stood. Her fists were clenched, and her thin arms shook beneath the silken sleeves. Her upper lip had drawn back, so that I could see her clenched teeth. Holmes' eyes were full of concern, but he did not move.

"That old... lizard," Violet managed to say.

Michelle went to her. "The girl has a fever. She should be in bed. Violet?" She seized her arms and felt the violent trembling. "Oh, my dear—it will be all right. Do not..."

"What if she is sick?" A ghastly smiled appeared on Violet's face. "She must continue to work. She must stand and curtsy. She must... As if she were a machine—as if she were not even alive! They must smile and bow and scrape and serve us like slaves, and if they make the least bit of unpleasantness, they must be thrown out on the street without references and made to starve and suffer." Her voice was raw with rage. "Of course they are not real people. They are only animals—only insects—grubs."

Michelle's big hands gripped Violet's shoulders. "*Stop it.*" Violet's brown eyes lost some of their wildness.

"You must not let them upset you so. Let's go for a walk. The air will do us all good."

Violet nodded. Tears seeped from her eyes, but she rubbed angrily at them. "Oh, yes—let's do that. Let's get outside." She was still trembling.

Michelle had her by the arm. "We shall get our coats and some comfortable shoes. And we must put Gertrude to bed."

Gertrude was crying and coughing. "Oh, I mustn't."

"You will!" Violet exclaimed. "By God, you will."

She and Michelle led Gertrude out of the room. Michelle turned to me.

"Meet us downstairs."

I nodded. Holmes' face was pale, his gray eyes showing anger and concern. "He is a foul old serpent," I said, "full of poison. No wonder Donald does not like working for him."

Holmes stared at me. "He told you so?"

"On our walk yesterday."

"Indeed? I want to hear about this walk, but I must change my clothes. If you would care to accompany me?" I told him about our talk near the pond while he changed from a frock coat and striped trousers to a Norfolk suit. At one point I hesitated, then mentioned Wheelwright's saying I was a lucky man. Holmes smiled.

"Perceptive of him. Did he say anything more of interest?"

I hesitated again. "He said Violet hates him, and he hates her, but…"

Holmes raised his eyes from his boot. "But?"

"But he is not as good at it as she is."

Holmes lowered his gaze. "Ah."

Holmes and I went downstairs and through the great hall. Luckily we did not see either Wheelwright *père* or *fils*. Rather than waiting in the gloomy entranceway, we went outside. A gravel road ran before the house, a small roof providing shelter for carriages, but the vast expanse of lawn was lush, green, and still wet. The moisture glistened on the toes of our boots.

A tin bucket full of the gardener's hand tools stood near one of the roof columns, and Holmes poked about in the bucket with his stick. He had on his cloth traveling coat and deerstalker hat; somehow the cap made his nose appear even larger. He looked washed-out under the bright sunlight.

I heard an odd scrambling sound: A youth on a bicycle pedaled vigorously uphill, standing almost upright as he did so. He came to a stop a few feet from us, and then withdrew an envelope.

"Does either of you gentlemen know where I might find Mr. Sherlock Holmes?"

Holmes raised his stick. "I am he."

"I've a telegram for you, sir."

"Thank you." Holmes handed him a shilling.

The boy grinned at the coin. "Thank *you*, sir."

Holmes slipped his long finger into one end of the envelope, then tore it open and withdrew the paper. His lips formed a smile and he laughed sharply. "Imbecile."

"What is it?" I asked.

"The chickens have flown the coop. It's from Lestrade. The Lovejoys have vanished." Sherlock whacked at the gravel with his stick, then drew a line. "I expected as much."

"I wonder if we shall ever see them again."

Holmes shrugged. "I wager we shall, and probably sooner rather than later." He withdrew his watch and opened it. "I wonder what is keeping the ladies."

"Their clothing is more complicated than ours. Violet was surely angry."

Holmes' nostrils flared as he whacked at the gravel. "Yes. I wish…"

I waited, but he did not finish. "What do you wish?"

"I wish… I wish I could help her. I wish I might break the enchantment and rescue her from this–" he raised his stick and pointed at the gray stone walls of the immense house– "this castle, this tower, where she is imprisoned. If she is imprisoned."

I smiled. "You wish to save her from the giant. And the old ogre."

"I only wish to save her. And I wish this case were over and done with."

"I told Michelle the same thing last night."

"One way or another, it will be over soon." He stared down at the gravel. "I have never been so caught up in a case, never felt so..." Again he struck the gravel. "It makes everything so much more difficult. Usually I pursue the truth. That is my guiding light, my main principle, but now I am not certain I want the truth. All the same, there is no other way. First I must have the truth. Then we shall see." He stared out across the lawn.

Wanting to comfort him, I blurted out, "She does love you."

He winced as if I had struck him and turned away.

"I am sorry. I only..."

"That also makes everything more difficult." He would not look at me.

"I wish I could help you."

He raised his eyes and smiled at me. "You and Michelle have been invaluable. I am glad you are both here."

"Michelle thinks you will find a way."

"She would. I have never met a more generous spirit." His eyes were sad, his smile pained. "But you know better."

I opened my mouth, but I could not lie to him.

He shrugged. "So do I." He raised his stick and rested it on his right shoulder.

We heard a noise behind us. Michelle and Violet had changed their shoes and put on their hats and heavy coats. Michelle carried a wicker hamper with two handles. She was flushed with excitement while Violet appeared pale.

"I'm sorry we were so long," Michelle said, "but we had the cook put together a picnic lunch. It is almost noon, and this way we can stay outside longer."

Violet gave a curt nod. "And we can avoid the ordeal of lunch with my father-in-law, an event which would be a dyspeptic extravaganza even for those with stomachs made of stronger stuff than mine."

I could not help but laugh at this. "Let me carry the basket." I took it from Michelle. "Goodness—how many people did you tell her you were feeding?"

Violet smiled. "I fear the dear cook wants to fatten me up. If we cut across the grounds, there is a pleasant path into the woods."

Michelle slipped her hand about my left arm. Her face was radiant, her happiness apparent. Violet seemed to have recovered her spirits. Her full lips formed the customary ironic smile, but her dark eyes had an almost haunted look.

"What a beautiful day," Michelle said.

Violet nodded. "It is good to be outdoors." She stared up at the sun.

"I put Gertrude to bed," Michelle told me. "The poor girl. I did not like the sound of her lungs."

Violet sighed. "Her health has never been good. When she first joined us, she was sick all the time, but she has been much better the past two years." She stared past me at Michelle. "Promise me you will look after her."

Michelle laughed. "You know I shall."

Violet stepped before us. We stopped, and she seized Michelle's arm. "I mean *promise me* that you will look after her—that you will not forget—no matter what."

Michelle's smile wilted, but did not quite vanish. "Of course I promise. You know I am fond of Gertrude."

Violet realized we were all regarding her. The ironic smile returned; she forced a laugh. "Forgive me, I... Because of Father Wheelwright I may not be able to keep her with me for much longer."

Michelle's smile was gone. "He would actually have you dismiss her, even if you told him she had been ill with a fever?"

Violet laughed harshly. "Without a doubt. You must have seen that."

"You were right, my dear. He is an old lizard." We were all walking again. Michelle stared resolutely ahead. "I shall find her another place, I promise you. She is such a sweet girl. Oh, it does seem monstrous."

"Hush," I said softly. Michelle gave me a wrathful glance. "We must not spoil the day." Nor must we get Violet all worked up again.

She caught my meaning, even though I did not say the significant part aloud. "Oh, I am sorry," she said. "Things are barely calmed down, and..."

Violet smiled wearily. "If only you knew what it means to me to have friends who understand, friends who do not snivel and whimper about the 'servant problem.' But it is too nice a day, and I must be good. I must think soothing thoughts and put that vile old scoundrel out of mind. Even Donald cannot bear his company—I know no one who can. But there I go again!" We had nearly reached the woods. Violet slipped her hand about Holmes' arm, then started down the path into the trees. "You are very quiet, Mr. Holmes. Have you nothing to say? Nothing pleasant to say?"

"Idle pleasantries are not my strong point."

"Oh dear, I do hope you have not been overrated," she said. A loud laugh burst from Holmes. "Oh, sorry." But Violet sounded pleased with herself.

We were all silent for a while. The forest air and the sunshine were like a tonic. Violet was the shortest of our group, and she set a leisurely pace. The breeze overhead ruffled the dry leaves, and a few of them came drifting down to join their departed brethren on the forest floor. It felt much damper and colder amongst the trees. We could see the blue sky through the branches, but a few high thin clouds had appeared.

Holmes and Violet stopped abruptly. A squirrel ahead of us on the path dug about and produced an acorn. He glanced up and sprang to the nearest oak, running around and up the massive trunk. The tiny head with the acorn in its mouth stared warily at us.

Violet laughed, then resumed walking, her hand still holding Sherlock's arm. "That squirrel reminds me of a time I went walking with my father long ago, oh so long ago." She was briefly silent. "Somehow... something about you reminds me of him."

"I fear," Holmes said, "that I know more about footprints, bloodstains, and tobacco ash than flora and fauna."

"Oh, but it is the same love of minutiae in either case. A walk with him could be tedious, a kind of school lesson. He would be telling me the name of that moss there and what side of the tree it typically grows on. His specialty, however, was spiders—or beetles, rather. He knew everything about them both. Oh, and he was a very good chess player. He taught me the game."

"Ah—then, he was a *very* good chess player indeed."

She laughed. "I remember the first time I beat him. I was only about twelve years old, and I think he was even more surprised than you were." She was silent again. "I took up with Donald shortly after he died. I must have been truly desperate." A hint of sarcasm had crept into her voice. "I do miss him—my father, that is. Not every day, but often. Is it not odd—how you can still miss someone after almost ten years? How can you still love someone after all that time? If you truly love someone, you cannot ever stop, while if you have never loved someone..." Her voice broke. "Forgive me—I–I'm being so foolish today. I cannot understand..."

"Your feelings for your father do you credit," Holmes said. "I am certain he was a worthy man."

We were behind Violet and could not see her face; she made a sound between a laugh and a sob. "There are so few."

The path came out at the same pond Donald Wheelwright and I had visited the day before. I recognized the gigantic oak, but the crows were gone that day.

"What a lovely spot!" Michelle let go of my arm and looked about. "A perfect place for our picnic. Is anyone else hungry?"

Sherlock and Violet stared at her curiously, too polite to say no. I laughed.

"Michelle is not a woman of delicate appetites." I squeezed her shoulder, then set the basket on a tree stump and opened it.

Michelle blushed. "If no one else is hungry…"

"But I do not like women of delicate appetites," I said. "There are very good-looking sandwiches here. Ham and cheese, or boiled beef and mustard."

"Nor do I," Violet said. "I shall have ham and cheese."

We divided up the sandwiches. The cook in her wisdom had also packed four bottles of beer (which explained the basket's weight). We sat—Michelle and I sharing one stump, Violet and Holmes another—ate our sandwiches and drank our beer. There were pippin apples and russet pears for dessert. I cut them into quarters and passed them out.

When we had finished, Violet put her hand over her mouth and fought back a yawn. Her gloves lay on the ground; her skin was white, her fingers thin and delicate. "I am so very tired. I could lie down here and sleep for the rest of the afternoon."

"So could I," Michelle said.

Holmes smiled. He had removed his hat and the sun gleamed off his high forehead and black, oily hair. "Does Morpheus also beckon to you, Henry, or does he only tempt the gentle sex?"

"Having slept until nearly ten, I am immune to his charms."

Violet had scrunched up her nose at the phrase "gentle sex," but she again covered her mouth and suppressed a yawn. "This is a lovely, lovely place, and the picnic was a wonderful idea, Michelle. Thank you so much."

Michelle smiled. "You're quite welcome." The intensity of Violet's gratitude left her puzzled.

"I only wish it could last forever—that we could stop time at this instant."

Holmes smiled.

"What is it?" she asked.

"I fear we would grow frightfully bored."

"But we would also be frozen."

"Then why bother—what would be the point?"

Violet gave him a mocking smile. "I see you insist on being logical and literal. It is so splendidly beautiful here, and I am enjoying your company so much—all three of you. It is nice not to have to pretend, not to have to work at being a fine lady, and... Oh, I suppose it is only because I do not want to go back—not ever—it is so perfect!" She clenched her fists and said this rather fiercely. "Forgive me, but my life is such a nightmare, and I feel as if—for once—I am awake. Only it cannot last. The nightmare will return." Her face had grown flushed, and her eyes had an unhealthy gleam.

"Oh, Violet," Michelle said. "Is it truly so terrible for you? I cannot... I cannot understand."

Violet laughed—a pained, hollow sound. "No, you cannot. It is all one rather ghastly dream everywhere I look. There is my life with Donald: people always watching me—all those servants—and then our whole dreadful social set. The business with the spider cake has one good side: I may never have to give another dinner party! Who would come? All that planning and arranging; all the pretentious menus and food; all that polishing and cleaning—so that a few vicious, rich, ugly people can meet and compare jewels and finery. The men smoke and boast, the women gossip and titter. It is all so banal—so petty—their minds so hopelessly trivial and polluted."

We had grown very still, but she hardly seemed to see us. "But I have no right to complain. There are all those others—the poor, the sick, the miserable—the great mass of London that we see at the clinic and on your rounds, Michelle. For every woman in her fine gown and jewels, there are a thousand malnourished wretches in rags. Families living in rat holes too dark and filthy for animals—for rats, even!" She laughed. "Then there are the lucky ones with jobs, the masses who slave in the factories day after day for a miserable pittance, or people like the woman who drugged her own babe to keep him silent so she could do her sewing work. Do you recall, Michelle?" Her dark eyes burned. "Do you?"

Michelle nodded. Her eyes were full of tears.

"Poisoning her own baby to keep it quiet. And then there are all the thieves, and our miserable prisons, and the workhouses. Their humanity has been taken from them. We treat them worse than slaves. 'Lax, lax!'" She laughed savagely. "They call this the greatest nation on earth. They speak of evolution, progress, and survival of the fittest. They boast so, and it is only a cesspool, a filthy cesspool.

"Oh, but I must not forget the whores." She rose slowly to her feet. "All the whores—old or young; fat or thin; inexpensive or very dear; male or female—someone for every taste, every appetite. No act is too vile or disgusting that you cannot pay…" She choked off her words and clenched her fists. "Lord Harrington, the great Lord Harrington, had his little whore—they all do, every one of them! That is why it is all part of the same nightmare—all the same—all the same!"

Michelle groaned and hid her face against my shoulder. I put my hand on her hair. "Don't," I said both to her and Violet.

Violet put her hand to her mouth. "Oh, God—oh…" She bit into her hand so hard I thought she would draw blood, but Holmes yanked her hand away. She stared up at him.

"One can always find reason to despair. One can always transfer the inner darkness to the outside."

Some of the fury went out of her eyes, and she grew pale. "But it is so dreadful."

"Of course it is. Men do have a great capacity for evil. At least we no longer hang a man for stealing a loaf of bread. Nor do we cut off his right hand."

"Oh, no, we only lock him up for years in some stinking prison."

Holmes drew in his breath and set a big hand on each of her shoulders. "My mistake. I cannot win such an argument. No one can. I happen to believe—fitfully—in progress, but it certainly cannot be proven. One can always find examples of evil and cruelty, but there are other examples as well. Kindness is possible. Honor is possible."

"*Honor?*" she laughed. "Falstaff was right about honor."

"No, he was not. Had Hamlet or Lear no honor? Shakespeare believed in honor. His plays are full of it. And there is…" He paused abruptly. "There is goodness, there is… the love between parent and child, between members of a family." I saw the tendons in his hand tighten.

Violet swayed slightly. "Is there?"

"Did you not say you still loved your father?"

The tears flowed from Violet's dark eyes. She managed to nod.

"And there is…" He turned to me and Michelle, his eyes hot. "Look at them."

"Oh, God," Violet moaned.

"And does Michelle not love you? Can you possibly doubt she is your dearest friend?"

Violet's hands clawed at his sides, and she clamped shut her eyes, her teeth. He held her back for an instant, and then she collapsed against him, her hands clutching desperately at his back, her face hidden against his chest. I could see her body quaking, but she made hardly any sound. Holmes' face was pale, the oddest expression in his eyes, as he held her to him.

Michelle had sat up. She pulled a handkerchief from her coat pocket and wiped resolutely at her eyes. She stared at Sherlock and Violet, frowned slightly, then looked at me. I took her hand and kissed her knuckles.

The high thin clouds had covered most of the blue sky, and the sun was noticeably lower. It was very quiet, the only sounds the murmur of the wind in the nearby trees and the faint splash of a fish down in the water.

At last Violet straightened up and drew away from Holmes. He did not try to hold on to her. "Oh, we must not—I cannot. I'm sorry." She turned away from us. "You must all be convinced I am a lunatic. I must go."

She almost ran to the path. Michelle glanced at me, then rose and rushed after her. "Wait, Violet—*wait*."

Violet turned and regarded her warily. She waited until Michelle was almost to her, then reached out and embraced her.

They drew apart, and Violet rubbed at her eyes. "You will not always have to put up with my nonsense. You deserve better from me. Whatever happens—and I shall not ask you to make any more promises—always remember... A sister could not be dearer to me than you." She looked at Holmes, biting at her lip. "Oh, I must go back." She started down the path, and Michelle followed.

I took a deep breath, then sat back down on the stump. I felt rather lightheaded. Holmes stood silently beside me, his fists clenched.

"I wonder..." I murmured, "if she is quite sane."

Holmes laughed. "Few people are *quite* sane. *Mostly* sane is the best one can hope for. Violet is mostly sane." He put his hand on his forehead, and then let it drop. "Whatever am I thinking of? Could you follow them, Henry—please? She must not be left alone."

I stood up, fingers of dread caressing my heart, my lungs.

"I would go," he said, "but I want to be alone for a few minutes." His voice was suddenly anguished.

"Are you certain you want to be alone? I…"

"Yes—*go!* I doubt there are black fiends lurking in the forest, but we must not take chances."

I strode off at once. The shadows of the oaks were longer. Less light reached the forest floor, and the sky was nearly all gray. It was probably the spell Violet had woven with her voice, but I was immensely relieved when I caught sight of the two women, especially the taller of the two.

I followed them silently, not wanting my presence known. The wind picked up, shook the trees, and sent dried leaves hurtling down to earth. With the sun gone, the wind was very cold. When I reached the lawn, I leaned against a gnarled trunk, watching them.

The afternoon had begun so well, the lunch delightfully casual after the fussy, overabundant meals at the house. However much I sympathized with Violet, I was angry with her for spoiling everything and upsetting Michelle. I tended to agree with Violet's view of life. It was a sordid business, and the self-importance and self-righteousness of Victorian England grew tiresome. The poverty and suffering of the urban poor were certainly depressing. It wore on me. Somehow the work at the clinic invigorated Michelle. I, instead, felt overwhelmed, exhausted and disheartened, but some notion of duty kept me at it. Perhaps I wanted to show that I was different from those who either ignored such misery or who, like the Reverend Killingsworth, considered it part of some divine plan. God could not be such a sadist.

When the women were halfway to the house, I started after them. They were almost to the door when Michelle turned and saw me. We smiled at one another. Violet is wrong, I thought. It need not be a nightmare. Violet's face was pale, but she had again mastered herself. With a smile, she gave Michelle a nudge and went inside.

Michelle walked toward me. "I think Violet is better."

"And how are you?"

She smiled and shrugged her shoulders. "She made it all sound... so horrible. I felt so bad for her."

I grasped her hand. "I wish I could take you away from here."

"I wish you could, too. But you cannot."

I stared up at the stone facade rising before us with its dark slate roof. "It is an ugly house." I lowered my gaze. "Sometimes when I wake up late in the night, I have thoughts like hers, a sense of how weak and evil we all are. Usually the brightness of day dispels my dark mood." I looked up at her. "You dispel it."

"Oh, Henry."

I sighed. "I suppose the old man will be joining us for dinner. Lord, I hope he leaves soon."

Neither of us wanted to go back into the house. The wind rose, soaring in over the grass and rattling the many windowpanes overhead. A faint uneasiness, a sense of having forgotten something, made me frown.

"Are you cold?" Michelle asked.

"Yes."

"So am I. I think it may snow."

The cold, unyielding sky made me shiver. "I do not doubt it. Oh, good Lord!" I started for the house at almost a run.

"What is it?"

"We must not leave Violet alone—Sherlock said she must not be left alone!"

"Surely there can be no danger?" Michelle did not sound convinced.

The door was open, and I went quickly up the stairs. The great hall echoed with our footsteps. Under the dim light it seemed positively medieval. Collins saw us, grinned, and raised a hand.

"Where is your mistress?" I asked.

"She went upstairs to her room."

"You should not have left her alone—Mr. Holmes told you she was not to be left alone."

Collins' grin weakened. "But I didn't leave her alone. Mr. and Mrs. Lovejoy went with her."

I stared dumbly at him; dread caught in my throat. "*What?*"

"The Lovejoys're back from London. They… Sir?"

I ran up the stone stairs and heard Michelle behind me. "Henry— wait. *Henry!*" Violet's room was on the third floor. I strode down the hallway. Michelle seized my arm. "Please wait—my feet hurt so."

I took a deep breath and slowed down. "When will you find some sensible shoes that work?"

"My feet are too big."

"Your feet are perfect. I admire them greatly. They are among the parts of you I most treasure."

Her hand slipped down to mine. "Oh, don't talk that way—not now, you silly fool." We had come to the door. "They would not harm her, Henry. I am sure of it."

I wrapped loudly at the door. "Violet? *Violet!*"

The door swung inward, and Lovejoy gave me his most polished smile. If this was only a role, he had it down to perfection. "Good afternoon, Dr. Vernier, Dr. Doudet Vernier. How good to see you both again. The country air obviously suits you. Do come in."

We stepped into the bedroom. Violet had removed her coat and hat. She sat in a chair by the window. Mrs. Lovejoy stood nearby, a figure in black—her face pale and severe as ever, her dark hair parted down the middle.

"I am quite weary," Violet said, "but I need to discuss some household matters with Mr. and Mrs. Lovejoy. They are finally up from London. The rest of the staff will be joining us soon. Is anything the matter?"

I said nothing, but my expression must have been grim.

"Nothing." Michelle smiled. "I only wanted to check to see how you felt."

Violet's mocking smile returned. "I feel embarrassed, and you look tired, Michelle. If you wish to nap, I shall see that no one disturbs you. Lovejoy?"

He gave a nod. "I shall pass along the word, madam."

I did not move. "Sherlock said you were not to be left alone."

Violet laughed. "I am not alone."

I licked my lips, uncertain how to proceed. Luckily, Collins appeared at just that moment. "Is anything wrong, sir? You looked as if…"

"No, nothing is wrong. Would you stay with Mrs. Wheelwright until Mr. Holmes returns?"

Collins' grin returned. "Surely."

Lovejoy nodded. "And I shall see that no one disturbs you both. You also look fatigued, Dr. Vernier."

Michelle and I walked down the hallway to our own room. I removed my coat and dropped it over a chair. "Lock the door," I said.

"Are you sure, Henry? It seems…"

"Lock it."

She did and turned to face me. "It seems wrong somehow."

"Wrong?"

I kissed her. Never had I loved or desired her more, and I could tell that she felt the same way. Her large strong fingers sank into my back, and she seemed to melt into me. Finally, I drew away from her and kissed her throat, tugging her collar downward with my fingers.

"Oh, Henry—I do love you so."

"Why did you say it seems wrong?"

"Because of Violet—because of what she said."

I kissed her again. "It is not wrong. I want to show that she is... mistaken. A nightmare is only a dream. It is to show that life can be beautiful—that you are beautiful—and that I love you more than anything in the world."

Her skin was red from the sun and wind, and her face had a warm glow. She drew me to her, and all her strength seemed to flow into that all-consuming embrace. For a time I forgot about Violet, Donald, the Lovejoys, and Sherlock Holmes.

Later, we dressed for dinner. I folded over my cuff and put in the stud. The bureau mirror was not flattering. My hair was a tousled mess, and I appeared haggard. I did my other cuff and picked up the hairbrush.

"Would you fasten me up, Henry?"

Michelle turned her back to me. Her gown was yellow satin, and, regretfully, hid her arms and shoulders. I could not blame her, given the cold hall. I began to fasten the tiny hooks. When I was about six inches from the top, I kissed her bare skin. "It seems a shame to fasten you all up."

She laughed. "It is curious. You never seem to tire of me."

"That would be correct." I finished with the last hook. "Is it not better having your husband fasten you up than a maid?"

"Oh, yes. Far better."

I tightened my bow tie, arranging it before the mirror, and then brushed my hair. Michelle put on her earrings and then helped me into my black tailcoat. She kissed me quickly.

"Was it not better having your wife help you with your coat than a valet?"

I laughed. "You are much prettier than any valet." I unlocked the door. "I must confess that I am not looking forward to dinner."

She slipped her hand about my arm. "Neither am I. It was nice to be alone with you."

"It is not yet five, but I suppose we should be sociable."

We walked down the hallway to the stairs. The house had no gas lighting, and the hallway was already almost pitch black. "It grows dark so early," Michelle said. "Oh, I wish we had not even had to get up."

"I must confess that I am ravenous. For food. Perhaps there will be some appetizers."

The great hall had been fitted with a crystal chandelier, a glaring anachronism that did not provide much light. It also had to be raised and lowered by a rope so the candles could be lit. A fire crackled in the enormous fireplace and lamps were lit on the dinner table; but the massive chamber still seemed mostly dark, the light feeble and flickering, with black shadows everywhere.

Before the fireplace in his formal attire, Holmes stood smoking a cigarette. He smiled languidly at us, tossing the cigarette butt into the flames. "Did you see that it has begun to snow? Only a few scattered flakes thus far, but I'll wager we have several inches by morning."

"Let's go and see," Michelle said, "just to a window."

I glanced at Holmes, but he did not seem inclined to venture from the fire. Michelle and I stepped through a doorway to a small room, which had ancient, mullioned windows, the thick wavery glass panes set in lead cames. We were up a story, and all we could see was the cold gray sky, a few large white flakes drifting slowly downward. The wind was faint—a low, constant sigh.

Michelle drew closer to me. "It looks so cold. I am glad we are indoors."

"This room is even colder than the hall. You can feel the chill coming from the glass. It will soon be dark out there."

We were only too glad to rejoin Holmes by the fire. The bricks within the six-foot enclosure were blackened with soot, and a huge log sat on the grate. The tile floor, of course, was clean; no doubt a maid scrubbed at it on her knees early every morning, long before the lord of the manor stirred.

"It seems to me," I said, "that a deer or an ox should be roasting there."

We heard footsteps on the stairs and turned. Violet approached through the shadows, her black hair done up elegantly; diamonds at her throat and ears; her dress a vision of white, cream, and lace. It was difficult to believe this could be the person who had told us her life was a perpetual nightmare, but when she came closer I could see the tension about her mouth and eyes. All the same, she was very beautiful. The dress had sleeves that ballooned out at the shoulder and tapered at the elbow; it emphasized her slender waist and hips. Behind her, ever vigilant, was Collins.

"I see," Violet said, "that you have all found the warmest spot in this icy cavern. I have tried, in vain, to convince Donald that it would be both pleasant and sensible to dine in a different room. In fairness, it is his father who insists this is the dining hall. Perhaps when icicles form on his long nose, he will change his mind."

The image was so ludicrous that we all laughed. Holmes appeared his usual cool and detached self, but occasionally, as he watched Violet, something in his eyes gave him away. Lovejoy approached us with several slender glasses on a silver tray.

"Would anyone care for sherry?"

"Hot cider might be more appropriate," Violet said with a smile, then reached for a glass. Her fingers trembled slightly. She seized the stem and swallowed half the sherry. I took two glasses and handed one to Michelle. She was staring at Violet, her forehead creased. No doubt she was reflecting that sherry on an empty stomach is not wise for a person with an ulcer.

"At least," Violet said, "this fireplace is big enough for a crowd to share."

I realized that she had not once looked at Holmes. Perhaps she was embarrassed about what had happened that afternoon. "I was just saying," I said, "that you should have a deer or ox roasting on a spit here."

"I shall have to suggest that to cook, although I doubt she will like the idea. She may have difficulty concocting a sauce to serve on a side of beef."

We heard more footsteps on the stairs, echoing faintly through the hall. Donald Wheelwright and his father were descending. They appeared almost comical side by side: the one all thin bone, his features sharp and predatory; the other all muscle, flesh and fat, towering above his progenitor. They were like a pair from an Aesop's fable–the stork and the ox, the weasel and the elephant, or the rat and the plow horse, both animals in formal attire.

Violet's distaste was obvious. She finished her sherry, and then said, "I must speak with Donald." She set down the glass, nearly knocked it over, but caught it and set it upright. She started for the two men. The Lovejoys hovered about the dining table.

Sherlock's eyes were fixed on Violet. His mouth twitched, and he turned away toward the fire and sipped his sherry. Michelle gave me a pained look. I stepped nearer to my cousin. The flaming log cast a reddish glow, tinting his white shirt and bow tie, his pale thin face and prominent nose.

"I think," I said, "that we will all be happier when dinner is finished."

His eyes watched the flames. "I cannot bear it. I feel as if..." His voice was a hoarse whisper.

I seized his arm. "I believe I am supposed to say, 'Steady now, old man,' or some such thing."

Holmes laughed, and then looked at me. "I have faced physical danger many times. Sometimes I was fearful, sometimes not, but I have never fled from hazard."

I nodded. "Your bravery has always amazed me. I have watched you in awe, even as I quaked in my boots. There were all those times in that dark maze beneath the Paris Opera, and then the way you faced down that mob in Underton. I wish I had a fraction of your courage."

Holmes smiled. "But you never ran away either." He watched the fire. "That is what I would like to do now—run away—flee. And not because I am afraid, but because…" His free hand formed a fist even as he drank. "It pains me so. It is as if I were starving to death—some street urchin with a feast spread before him, but absolutely forbidden to touch anything."

Michelle had wandered away, no doubt thinking Sherlock and I wished to be alone. I could think of no easy comfort. "You said it would be over soon."

"So it will." He drew in his breath, then turned and stared past me.

Donald Wheelwright and his father were taking glasses of sherry from Lovejoy's silver tray, while Mrs. Lovejoy fussed over the table's floral display. Michelle stared up at a boring painting, even though it was so dark you could hardly tell whether sheep or cows were in the meadow. Donald Wheelwright stepped toward us.

Something smashed on the tile at my feet—Sherlock's half-empty sherry glass. He drew himself up on the balls of his feet, his eyes sweeping about the room. He strode forward, and I followed.

"Where is Mrs. Wheelwright?" he asked.

Donald stared curiously at him. "She had something to tell the cook."

"Oh, good." I was relieved, but Holmes was not.

"You let her go alone?" Holmes did not wait for an answer, but headed for the doorway. I was right behind him.

A dim corridor led toward the back of the house, the only light a solitary oil lamp. We descended a narrow stairway. At the bottom was a door to the outside. We were only halfway down when we felt icy air sweep about us.

The door stood open, a few flakes of snow swirling about in the muted gray light.

"Oh, Lord," I whispered, suddenly afraid. "Could she...?"

Holmes pushed open the door and stepped outside. It was bitterly cold, and the sky had almost no daylight left. However, because of the cloud cover, we could still see fairly well. The snowflakes stung my cheeks and made me blink. The snow had not yet accumulated on the ground, but it would before long.

"Perhaps she is still inside," I said. We had passed the door leading to the kitchen.

Holmes said nothing, only peered about trying to decide where Violet might have gone. We had come out at the back of the house. A few feet from the gray stone facade was a jungle of darkling foliage—ferns, trees, and rhododendrons. A stone path wound around the house.

"Perhaps..." I began, but a scream interrupted me, a sharp pained cry.

Holmes turned right and ran along the side of the house, turning right again at the corner. "Violet!" he shouted. "Violet!" The wind was worse on that side, but I hardly felt it.

He stopped at the front of the house. "I think the cry came from that way." He pointed away from the dwelling where the gravel driveway sloped downward. Before us the lawn was an unfamiliar dark sea, which ended at the black oak forest on the horizon.

"I could not tell," I said.

We heard a faint noise, perhaps a sob, from the direction he had pointed, and he was off at once. "Violet!"

We found her only a few feet away slumped against the stone wall. She was crying, her right hand clutching at her shoulder, her white shoes with the pointed toes and her legs sprawled out before her on the cold gravel. There was not enough light to see much color, but something black stained the sleeve of her dress where her fingers grasped her shoulder. She looked up at us, her mouth a pained O in the oval of her face.

"Thank God," Holmes murmured. "Oh, thank God."

We helped her to her feet, but he did not let go of her.

"I thought you were gone—I thought you were lost forever."

She stared up at him, her hair all disheveled, her eyes wild. "Did you?"

He said nothing. One hand grasped her uninjured shoulder; the other slipped about her waist. I took a step back. She put her arms about him. I shall never know who moved first, but she rose up onto her toes, her head twisting about as he drew her to him. The kiss had a fearsome energy, some desperate, long-repressed passion on both sides released at last. I stepped back, unsure what to do. The left shoulder of Violet's gown had been almost completely torn away: the white flesh of her slender upper arm gleamed in the dim light, three dark, bloody wounds marring her shoulder. Fear slithered quicksilver through my belly, and I turned away.

"Violet!" someone shouted. It was Michelle's voice.

The two of them must have heard, for they drew apart, although they still held one another.

"Forgive me," Holmes murmured.

A pained sound burst from her lips. "Oh, it is too late. I am lost. I was lost long before I ever met you."

"*No.*" Holmes' eyes almost glowed in the dark. He shook his head. "You cannot be."

"Violet!" Michelle was nearer.

"Here!" I shouted.

Holmes and Violet started at my cry, then he released her. Their hands touched, his fingers lingering briefly about her palm. She bit at her lip. Blood had oozed from the wounds, and she clutched at her shoulder, wincing with pain

"Who has done this to you?" I asked.

"Henry!"

"Here, Michelle!" I cried again.

Violet stared at me, but seemed unable to speak. Michelle, Collins, Lovejoy, and Donald Wheelwright all came running down the path. Behind them, the house was a looming black shadow, a few of the windows feeble squares of yellow light in the dark monstrosity. The wind swept about us, the snow heavier than before, and I was aware of how cold I felt. All about us, the ground had at last begun to turn white.

Michelle took Violet by the arm. "Show me," she said.

Violet slowly opened her hand, revealing the three bloody marks on her bare shoulder. "Merciful God," Collins muttered.

"Who did this?" Michelle asked.

Violet stared past her at Donald Wheelwright, his tall form rising above all the others.

"The gypsy," Violet whispered. "It was the gypsy."

"Good heavens!" exclaimed Lovejoy. "Not *here.*"

"She was at the door, calling to me, beckoning to me. When I stepped outside, she grabbed me. She was... so strong." Violet stared into the darkness like a woman possessed; I do not think she saw any of us. "'Now I've got you,' she said. She dragged me away, and I fought her, but she was too strong. She pulled me here, and then I heard someone call my name. She was angry. Her eyes were red and glowing. Her fingers were like claws with long ugly nails. She... she scratched me." Violet's breath caught; she almost choked and began to weep. "It hurts—it hurt me so."

Donald Wheelwright stared dully at her, his eyes wider open than usual. His mouth twitched to the right.

Michelle put her arm about Violet. "We must get you inside. It's freezing, and I shall treat the wound."

"You won't hurt me?" Violet sounded suddenly like a child.

"Of course I shan't hurt you."

Wheelwright folded his arms. "Mr. Holmes, you are off the case."

Holmes stared at him, but said nothing.

Violet bared her teeth briefly like a dog. "He has done a better job protecting me than you ever have!"

Wheelwright thrust his jaw forward and lowered his big hands. He turned again to Holmes. "You are to leave. Immediately."

Violet laughed harshly. "You cannot just send him off into a blizzard! You cannot!" Michelle had to hold her back. As if to reinforce her words, a sudden gust blew snow into our faces.

"I'll do whatever I want. He can leave—they can all leave."

"But you cannot!"

"Mr. Wheelwright." Holmes' voice was loud, but restrained. "This is your home, and should you wish us to leave, that is surely your prerogative. I can well understand your frustration. This is the most baffling case I have ever encountered."

"But, Sherlock...!" I began angrily, aware of all he had discovered about the Lovejoys.

"Please do not interrupt, Henry. As I was saying, Mr. Wheelwright, I shall gladly leave, but I respectfully request that you let me remain until the morrow. I would like to have a look about. Then too, I would not care to face the road on such a foul night. All I ask for is simple courtesy. I shall leave first thing in the morning."

Wheelwright drew in his breath. "Oh, very well."

Violet laughed, then said sarcastically, "'Very well'?"

Holmes turned to her. "Please remain silent, madam. You are not well."

Wheelwright shivered and clutched at his arms. "I wouldn't put a dog out on a night like this. But I want you gone in the morning. All of you." His gaze encompassed Michelle and me. "I'll have my house to myself at last."

"Certainly," I said, relieved.

Michelle glared up at Wheelwright, her arm still about Violet. "But I am her physician."

Wheelwright shook his head. "I don't care about that. She isn't dying. We'll be back in London soon. No point in staying here now. It doesn't seem to much matter where we are." Fear had crept into his voice. He turned and stalked back toward the house.

"For God's sake," I said. "Let's all get inside before we freeze solid."

We started up the path, the snowflakes stinging our cheeks, the gravel faintly slippery from the snow. Violet began to cry, softly at first, then in great sobs. Even Michelle could not comfort her.

We went in the front door, and the calm and warmth were a relief. Michelle led Violet upstairs to the great hall. Holmes took Collins by the arm. "I shall need a lantern, possibly two of them. Bring them back here in about five minutes."

"I'll see to it, sir."

"Wait, Henry."

Sherlock and I were alone in the alcove, the feeble light from the great hall up the stairs spilling out near our feet. Holmes had blood on his formal clothes, vivid red splotches on the white shirt—Violet's blood.

From above we heard old Wheelwright's shrill voice. "Outrageous—

outrageous–I'll not stay a minute longer in this madhouse, not a minute longer!"

"What is it?" I asked.

"Would you help me search the grounds?"

"*Now?*" My dismay was obvious.

"Yes. The snow will soon hide everything; we must get to work at once."

"But what…?

"On the other side of the stone wall where we found Violet is a tangled slope of vegetation–ferns, rhododendrons, and other growth. I want to have a good look about."

A sudden dread caught at my throat. "The gypsy! You do not think…?"

His laugh was harsh. "No, it is not the gypsy we seek. Get your overcoat, a hat, gloves, and some decent shoes, and meet me back here."

"But what are we looking for?"

When he told me, I thought he was joking.

It was cold, dark, and snowy when we went back outside, a regular blizzard commencing. As we trampled about in the brush, lanterns in hand, I wondered if the strain had finally been too much for my cousin. I managed to thwack myself in the face with a rhododendron branch and was ready to go back inside, but I decided to humor him. We had been out for about forty minutes when he stumbled across exactly what he had told me we were searching for.

Fifteen

I could do nothing with Violet. I thought it might help once we were alone together, but she continued to weep loudly. "Can you tell me anything?" I asked. She said something about being lost. I could understand how frightened she must have been.

Because Gertrude was ill, another maid had joined me, a girl only a little older, whose name was Daisy. She was so upset that she was of little help. Violet's shoulder was a bloody mess, her lovely dress ruined.

At last I managed, with Daisy's feeble assistance, to remove the dress. Daisy choked out "Lord" and turned away. I gave my head a shake. Violet's slender throat still had those ghastly handprint bruises, their color now dark and purplish, and her left shoulder was torn open, the cuts beginning in back, coming all the way over the shoulder and extending to the pectoral muscle above the breast. Gently I bathed the wound with hot soapy water. Bad scratch marks I had seen before, but these appeared too narrow and deep to have been made by fingernails. Perhaps they should be stitched up, especially the center one, but I was uneasy about anesthetizing Violet and working on her. Certainly they needed to be disinfected, but that would sting badly. "You won't hurt me?" Violet had pleaded. I considered asking Henry to care for her.

The tears continued to flow from Violet's eyes, but she seemed somehow calmer.

"What is it?" she asked.

"I should put something on those cuts, but it will hurt."

"Oh, go ahead if you must." Her mouth formed an ugly smile. "I deserve it."

"Do not say such things!"

I was genuinely angry, and it sobered her. "Go ahead then."

"Perhaps I shall ask Henry."

"I'd rather you did it. Just get it over with."

I drew in my breath, doused a clean cloth from my bag with an iodine solution, and then said: "Hold on."

The muscles of her arm went rigid, and she moaned through clenched teeth. Involuntarily she tried to pull free of me, but I had her firmly in my grasp. I worked as quickly as I could. When I was finished she began to tremble, her thin arm quaking. I put some gauze over the cuts and taped it in place. My hands were steady, but I felt terrible.

The maid had collapsed on the bed, her face hidden in her arm. "Daisy," I said, then more sharply, "*Daisy*." She looked up. "Get me a robe for Violet, something warm—wool, not silk." I handed her a clean handkerchief.

"Yes, ma'am." She sniffled loudly.

"It is finished." I helped Violet to her feet. She swayed, then reached out and embraced me.

"Thank you, thank you for everything."

There seemed little of her left. I stroked her hair briefly, struggling with my own emotions.

Daisy brought me a cream-colored robe made of very soft wool. We helped Violet into it and put her in a chair before the fire. Daisy added a piece of coal. Violet sat huddled in the chair. She was still crying—she had never really stopped. Her right hand was pressed against her stomach.

"Get me some brandy," I said to Daisy, "and something to eat. Some bread and soup. Enough for two." She started to leave. "Thank you, Daisy. I know this is very hard."

She smiled and curtsied. Her eyes were puffy.

After she was gone, I sighed deeply and glanced at Violet. Slowly, I walked over to the window. "Very hard," I whispered to myself. My hands never shook, but somehow I wished they would. The windowpanes rattled from the wind. Outside everything was whiteness: the sloping lawn before the house covered with the snow, the blank featureless sky, the shreds of snow hurtling slowly past the glass.

I swallowed and thought, yes, for once you are truly afraid. Sherlock had seemed so certain the gypsy could not be real, and yet somehow she had dragged Violet from the house and ripped open her arm. The Lovejoys had been in the hall the whole time—I had seen them. And how could an old woman be so strong? Perhaps there was some evil power that... My mouth went dry, and I clenched my fists.

No—*no.* I would not believe such a terrible thing until I had absolute proof. It was curious. I believed in a loving God, but tales of the devil, of witches, ghosts, and the supernatural, had always made me skeptical. Perhaps the gypsy had been a man dressed as a woman—that would explain the gypsy's strength. And Violet was not strong—it would not be hard to pull her about. I could do it easily. I stared out into the white chaos whirling beyond the glass, my fists tightening. Try it with me, I thought. Show yourself and try yanking me about.

I heard the door open, and I turned away from the chill of the window. Daisy had a large tray, and I could smell the soup—something with leeks, if I was not mistaken. I realized I was starving.

I took a drink of brandy, considered offering Violet some, but decided against it. I did not like the way she clutched at her stomach. The soup was a vichyssoise: chicken broth, leeks, and cream, just the thing for Violet. She resisted briefly, but finally took the soup and ate very slowly. Mine was gone almost at once, and I thought briefly how hot food would mitigate most of life's pains and tragedies. My appetite whetted, I sent Daisy back to the kitchen. The dinner in shambles, the cook was happy someone was hungry; Daisy returned with pork tenderloins in a mushroom sauce, which I gobbled up while Violet worked on her soup.

Full at last, I set down the tray, unfastened my wretched fashionable shoes, and slipped them off, sighing contentedly. Violet ate mechanically, her eyes fixed on the glowing coal in the fireplace. I felt warm and comfortable now, much better, and my eyelids grew heavy. It was selfish, I knew, but it would be so good to get back to my own home and my practice. There was something... suffocating about the Wheelwrights' household. No wonder Violet could not bear it. I closed my eyes and began to dream at once, something where the blue of the pond was obscured by falling snow... I jerked open my eyes and sat up. If I fell asleep, I would be out for the night.

Violet had put down her soup bowl and was staring at me. She looked dreadful—pale and ill—her eyes were red, their lids swollen. At least she had finally stopped crying.

I smiled sadly. "How do you feel?"

Her lips tried to form the usual mocking smile, but she hardly seemed herself. "My stomach still hurts, almost more than my shoulder. I do not think I was cut out for..."

"Let me give you something to help you sleep."

She shook her head resolutely. "No. I do not want anything. I do not deserve it."

"What has deserving to do with anything?" My voice was sharp.

"No. I shan't take anything. Not tonight." She stared wearily at me. "How I shall miss you." She bit her lip, struggling to hold back her tears.

"But you will be returning to London soon, and I shall see you straight away. You are my patient, and you will find I am not easy to shake off." She smiled, but the tears began again. "Oh, Violet." I had a sudden longing to see Henry, to talk to him—and to Sherlock. Perhaps they had discovered something. "I shall be back in a little while." I stood.

Violet appeared genuinely frightened. "Promise me—*no*—no more promises! Please stay with me tonight—do not leave me alone. You can go, but please come back."

"I certainly shall, and before I go I'll have Daisy fetch Collins."

Daisy sat up. "Oh, he's in the hall, ma'am, right by the door."

"Good. I shall send him in." Violet stared forlornly at me. I squeezed her hand—she felt icy. "I shan't be long." I took a candle from the table.

Collins was leaning against the wall near the door. I asked him where I might find Henry and Sherlock, and told him to go into Violet's room. As I went down the corridor, the flickering candle cast strange shadows upon the wall, its light a feeble thing. Briefly I thought of the gypsy.

Holmes and Henry were in Violet's sitting room on the second floor, the room in which I had spent many a pleasant hour. Henry sat near the fire, half asleep, while Sherlock paced. Rarely had I seen him so agitated. He reminded me of one of the big cats at the London Zoo, nervously circling its small cage. He still had on evening dress, but he and Henry both wore heavy, soiled boots.

I took Henry's hand. "You look tired. Where have you been?"

He related how they had spent nearly an hour outside searching the grounds and what they had to show for it.

I frowned in confusion. "I don't understand."

"Neither do I."

"Sherlock." He strode by, hardly seeing me. He was circling the table where the wooden chessboard was still set up, hands behind his back, one grasping a bony wrist. I stepped before him. "Sherlock, do you understand any of this?"

His gray eyes glared furiously, and I thought briefly he might push me aside. He drew in his breath. "Yes."

"But you told Donald Wheelwright you were baffled."

His mouth formed an ironic smile. "I did not want to be cast out into the wilderness. Not yet."

"You know who the gypsy is?"

"Yes."

"And who has attacked Violet?"

"Yes, yes," he said impatiently.

I stared at him. Henry had sat up in the chair. "Please explain."

"I shall tell you everything in the morning." He stepped around me and started pacing again.

"Sherlock—please!"

He stopped and turned, placing one hand on the table. His face was pale, his eyes anguished. "Michelle, do not disturb me—not now of all times. I have it all, everything that matters. You will hear the truth in the morning. But for now, leave me be—leave me in peace!"

"Oh, very well." I went past him to the door.

"Michelle!" Henry cried.

I started down the hall, my hand holding the candle before me. Henry caught up.

"Wait," he said.

"He has never spoken to me that way before." My voice was shaky.

"You are lucky—but he is not himself. He will be sorry in the morning."

Abruptly I set down the candle and embraced Henry. I laid my head against his face and touched his cheek with my hand. The skin felt bristly from the stubble of his beard.

"Are they both mad? Whatever is the matter with them?"

"I do not know." His voice was gentle. One hand was clasped high against my back, the other just below my waist. His breath felt warm.

"I wish we could just go to bed," I said. "I am so tired."

"Go to bed, then."

"I promised Violet I would stay with her. She is most dreadfully upset."

Henry sighed; I could feel the movement along my chest and abdomen. "And I must remain with Sherlock," he said.

Neither of us moved for a while. The house was quiet and still, and we could not hear the wind or the snow there, where the outer and inner walls sheltered us.

"If he has figured it all out," I said at last, "it does not seem to have made him very happy."

Henry gave a muted laugh. "No."

We stood holding each other until I felt the fatigue settling about me. So much of the day had been disastrous. The house was so cold, Henry so warm.

"I must get back to Violet." I kissed him, briefly relaxing into his arms, letting him support me. At last, I stepped away and took up the candle.

Violet was still curled in the chair before the fireplace. With a yawn, Collins stood and was about to step into the hall. "Don't be silly," I said. "You can have Daisy's chair. She is ready for bed." They both protested, but I would not hear them.

Violet glanced up at me, her dark eyes tormented. I put my hand over hers.

"How are you?" The question was a foolish one.

"I feel cold—so cold."

"I hope you have not caught a fever." I put my hand on her forehead, but she was not hot. "Please let me give you something. You really should sleep."

She shook her head. "Not tonight." I went to the bed, took an afghan throw and put it over her lap. "Thank you."

My shoes still sat before the other chair where I had left them. Under my stockings, my toes were freezing; I sat and stretched my feet toward the fireplace, curling and uncurling my toes. Violet smiled weakly. I closed my eyes, opened them, and then fell fast asleep.

My dreams were restless. Henry and I wandered amidst the oak forest, but the sunlight kept turning to snow. I knew we needed to return to our house in London before the blizzard, but we had lost something—or someone—first Sherlock, but then he was beside me in his traveling cap, so it must have been Violet. But she was beside me wearing an evening gown and diamonds, a curious choice for the woods. Holmes must be missing... Then they were both there, but someone was chasing us. Donald Wheelwright? No, the gypsy. She was cackling in the midst of the dark green rhododendron leaves while the moon slowly rose, and now both Sherlock and Violet were lost again.

"Damn them both!" I cried. I thought Henry would admonish me for my language, but he only nodded. "We must find them," I said. "They must not loiter here in the dark wood."

We searched everywhere: beside the pond, the dark country house, the Wheelwrights' London mansion, Henry's and my home, the clinic for the poor, and even Simpson's. I looked under the table where Violet and I had eaten our roast beef dinner.

We could not find them, but some black shadowy thing—it lurked just out of sight—was also pursuing them. When I held up the lantern, it quickly scuttled under the table.

"Come out—show yourself!" I cried. "Filthy thing."

We were on the fourth floor of Violet's house before the rickety stairway to the attic. I held up the lantern. "They are up there," I told Henry. "Come."

He smiled but shook his head. Something strange was happening to his face. I turned away and started up the stairs. The door hinges creaked as I opened it.

"Violet? Sherlock?"

I held up the light, but it grew dimmer. My heart felt peculiar, its beat desperate and arrhythmic. "Violet? Sherlock?" Their faces were so gray. They must be dead. I wanted to run but could not move. As my eyes gradually adjusted to the darkness, I could see more and more. They were bound in a gray, sticky substance—threads which cut more tightly even as they struggled and tried to escape. The web was in their mouths and noses; they could not possibly breathe. They must be dead, but still they writhed, two mummies in their suffocating bonds, every futile breath drawing the gray poison deeper into their lungs and their hearts.

Something laughed overhead—a woman's voice. I did not want to raise my head, but something made me. It lurked in the corner, a part of the darkness, its form barely discernible: a spider—bigger than a man—bigger even than Donald Wheelwright. It had red eyes and wore golden earrings even though it had no ears. More dreadful laughter: I realized she was laughing at me.

It would get me and weave its deadly threads about me, but I could barely stir. The harder I tried, the slower I moved. It would get me—I could not escape.

"Michelle," it said.

I tried to scream but nothing came out. I knew that voice.

"Michelle."

It was Violet's voice—it was Violet.

Someone shook me, and I bolted upright. Violet stood before me, her hand over her mouth, her dark eyes fixed on mine. I was breathing hard and my heart thudded against my ribs. My eyes took in the bedroom: the solid, well-built furniture, Collins sleeping in a chair, the clock on the mantel. It was one thirty in the morning.

"You had a nightmare," Violet said. "You could not seem to move."

I put my hand on my face. "Oh God, what a horrible dream."

Violet hesitated, and then stepped closer. She gave my hand a squeeze. "Poor dear."

I moistened my lips. My throat was dry. "Have you slept?"

She shook her head.

I stood slowly. "You really should. You feel warmer anyway. Sit down." I covered her with the afghan. "What have you been doing?"

"Thinking. Watching you."

"It is a new day," I said.

She nodded. Her lips drew back into a smiling grimace. "Today is my wedding anniversary."

I stared incredulously at her. "What?"

"Eight years," she said. "Eight years." She laughed.

I recalled the gray filaments binding her, suffocating her, filling her mouth, nose, and lungs, and I could not repress a shudder.

"What is it?" she asked.

"The dream—it was so dreadful. "I think... I shall go downstairs for a moment. I shall be back in only five minutes or so."

I took the candle. It was shorter now. Walking—being able to move—felt good, but the house was quiet as the tomb, and I was thinking about spiders. Henry was asleep in the chair, slumped to the side and breathing loudly. He looked odd sleeping in evening dress. Holmes sat in another chair smoking a pipe, and the room stank of tobacco. Although he was seated, he appeared as restless as when he had been pacing. He smiled weakly, the expression gaunt and forlorn.

"I suppose you have been awake all this time," I said.

He shrugged. He would not meet my gaze. I turned to go.

"Michelle." His eyes watched me. "I am sorry if I behaved rudely earlier. You will understand all in the morning."

I smiled wearily. "Maybe I should send Violet down. She will not sleep either. Perhaps you could play chess."

I was only joking, but he shook his head forcefully. "*No.*" As I stared at him, his nostrils flared. "I must not. I... I shall see her in the morning. Oh God, how I wish I had never laid eyes on her."

I was too sleepy for more mysteries. "Good night," I said.

Violet, of course, was also wide awake, the afghan wrapped about her shoulders. She managed a wan smile. I thought of trying to talk with her, but again I fell asleep. My dreams, while still troubled, were not so bad as before.

When I woke, a cold white light had filled the room, and the coal in the fireplace was nearly gone. Violet was still in the chair, and the clock on the mantel said seven thirty-five. I glanced slowly about. Violet had obviously not slept, and she seemed more fragile than ever, as if one more blow would shatter her.

The door opened, and Daisy looked in. When she saw we were awake, she came into the room. She gave Collins a playful push. He stirred and sat up. "What a night," he muttered, stretching.

Daisy walked over to Violet and me. "Mr. 'Olmes'd like to see you in the sitting room whenever you're ready."

Violet sat up stiffly, raising her chin and showing her long slender neck. The bruises were so ugly. "Get me my lavender dress, the silk one with the lace collar."

"Very well, ma'am."

Collins stepped outside. I blinked my eyes, stared distastefully at my shoes. I slipped my feet into them.

"How does your shoulder feel?" I asked.

"It throbs some."

Violet went to the washbasin and splashed ice-cold water on her face. I felt chilly merely watching. Daisy helped her out of her robe. I went to the window. The snow had stopped, but the sky—and all else—was white, the landscape totally altered, the golden autumnal vista seemingly gone forever. Daisy fastened Violet's dress in back, helped her with her hair, and then we two went downstairs to the sitting room.

It was faintly cold and smelled of tobacco, but a wood fire roared in the fireplace. Holmes stood before a window. He had changed into his frock coat and striped trousers. Henry wore a tweed suit and looked rested, despite the night in the chair. The Lovejoys sat on the sofa, polite yet wary smiles on their faces.

Holmes stared for only an instant at Violet. She stiffened, and a faint blush showed on her high cheekbones. "Please be seated, ladies." He gestured at the two plush chairs near the fire. "It is time for me to relate what I have discovered."

Lovejoy was clean-shaven, his linen white and crisp looking alongside his fine black morning coat. "I do not see why you wish us to be present, Mr. Holmes."

Holmes gave him a frightful smile. "You will soon learn exactly why. You are my special guests."

Lovejoy was unperturbed, but his wife gave a quick, desperate glance at the door.

"Should not Donald be here?" Violet asked, her hand holding her side.

He looked at her, then looked away. "Not yet." He stepped over to the fireplace and prodded the logs with the black iron poker, making them flare up. Violet and I had the comfortable chairs near the fire, but they were turned outward, toward the room. The sofa where the Lovejoys sat was before the windows, that long, southern expanse of glass. Henry was seated by the cherry-wood table and the chessboard. Holmes prowled about upon the carpet with its vivid, scarlet pattern. He had changed from his muddy boots to shoes of a glossy black.

"I fear, Mrs. Wheelwright, that I have made some unpleasant discoveries about the two persons who oversee your household."

Mrs. Lovejoy wore one of her plain black dresses, and she scowled. "We've done nothing wrong."

Lovejoy nodded. "Someone has misinformed you, Mr. Holmes."

Holmes gave them such a look I was glad not to be in their places. "I think not. You, Mr. Lovejoy, I have already seen first-hand playing one Geoffrey Steerford and attempting to sell shares in imaginary oil wells. Your research was well done, your references excellent, the whole business handled with the utmost skill. Yesterday was the deadline for investors, and in spite of my warnings to Inspector Lestrade, you managed to give him the slip. He was supposed to track down your bank accounts and seize the funds, but I am certain you did not come here empty-handed."

Lovejoy gave us a very sorrowful look, although his wife had gone paler still. "I honestly have no idea what you are talking about."

Violet stared at Lovejoy, her mouth a taut line. "Can this be true?"

Holmes continued to smile. "As for your wife, in her guise as an 'Angel of the Lord,' she has been stirring up prostitutes and servants, enlisting them in blackmail, theft, and extortion."

Mrs. Lovejoy rose to her feet, her brown eyes blazing. "I...!"

Her husband's hand shot out and seized her wrist. "*Abigail!*"

She glanced at him, then nearly collapsed onto the sofa. I would not have thought she could lose any more color, but her face was nearly white. "It's not true," she whispered.

Violet licked her lips. "Have you proof of these allegations, Mr.

Holmes? The Lovejoys have been with me many years, and I... I must confess I find these accusations difficult to believe."

Holmes' mouth twitched. "You are too trusting, madam. As I said, I myself saw Mr. Lovejoy in disguise, and Henry and I saw Mrs. Lovejoy coming out of a brothel near Underton."

Mrs. Lovejoy gave him a look of absolute hatred. "I often visit brothels as part of the Lord's work. The poor sinners need our pity."

"My cousin Henry went to the same brothel and discussed your activities there with one Lucy Jennings. She said it was widely known that you would pay for any sordid and disgusting information, that you were only too happy to blackmail the clientele, especially those of a higher class. She also said you had unusual... ideas about her trade."

Henry nodded gravely. "She told me all that and more."

Mrs. Lovejoy's upper lip curled back. "She was lying!"

"Lestrade also found that you and your associates were well known," Holmes said. "I am certain you are responsible for the theft of Herbert's necklace and for Lord Harrrington's death."

Mrs. Lovejoy leaped again to her feet. "*No!* I did not kill anyone."

Lovejoy seized her wrist again. "*Abigail!*"

Holmes stared calmly back at her. "You only drove him to it."

"*No.*"

Lovejoy stood and took her by the shoulders. "Please, Abigail."

Violet had also gone very pale. "Why... why would she do such a thing?"

Holmes' fingertips tapped at his thighs. "There was a great deal of money involved. But let me tell you who these two really are. Lestrade was kind enough to set his clerks to work and sent descriptions of the finalists in the contest down with Henry. The clerks were looking for a man and woman briefly involved in crime, five to ten years ago, who had no subsequent record of arrests. I provided a detailed physical description of the Lovejoys, and I told Lestrade to be especially alert for any persons with a background in the theater."

"*Theater?*" Henry said.

Mrs. Lovejoy's teeth clamped together, while Lovejoy gave a sharp, involuntary laugh.

Holmes nodded. "Yes. It had become obvious that both Lovejoys were consummate actors. I had seen Mr. Lovejoy do Steerford, and then there was Mrs. Lovejoy's remarkable performance last week after seeing the supposed fiend. Do you recall her excellent diction and impressive volume? Unlike Mrs. Wheelwright, whose voice was hoarse, weak, and strained, Mrs. Lovejoy was deafening. She has a very big voice and has been well trained. Her religious fanatic is quite convincing, but of course it is only another role."

Mrs. Lovejoy could not repress a brief, savage smile.

"Of course, the high point of her career, the performance of a lifetime, was that of the crazed gypsy at the Paupers' Ball."

Mrs. Lovejoy dug her nails into her knees, and I drew in my breath sharply. "Dear God," Violet murmured, her hand still pressed to her side.

Holmes smiled. "The old gypsy was always the most preposterous part of the whole business, a character from a second-rate melodrama. After I saw *Il Trovatore* I became convinced she was modeled after Azucena. Tell me, madam." He stared sharply at the woman in the black dress. "Did you ever study voice as well?"

She said nothing.

Henry nodded. "She could have left the note in the library—and substituted the cake before the party. She knew everything that went on in the house. And she must have watched while someone else tried to strangle Violet."

I leaned forward in my chair and stared at the woman. "How could you do such a thing? What has Violet ever done to you?"

Her guilt seemed obvious, and she lowered her eyes. Lovejoy had hold of her arm. "I... I do not know what you are talking about," she said.

Holmes gave a sharp laugh. He was pale himself and caught up in a strange fury. "Do you not, Miss Abigail Farnsworth?" She drew in her breath, her eyes widening. "It was unwise to retain your actual first name. And this is Mr. James Farnsworth. They are not man and wife. They are brother and sister. The descriptions fit perfectly, and there are even photographs from their days on stage. She had lighter hair then, but it was only dye."

No one spoke for about a moment—the air was charged with tension.

"These two come from a theatrical family, having joined their parents as children on tours. They worked in the serious theater. Miss Farnsworth had a career as the blonde ingénue, while her bearded brother—who is six years her senior—specialized in Shakespeare. Unfortunately, Miss Farnsworth decided to supplement her flagging career with some extortion. She became involved with several wealthy and indiscreet young gentlemen. Miss Farnsworth would lead them along so far, but then Mr. Farnsworth would appear as the outraged brother and threaten both bodily injury and public denunciation. They were only too happy to pay a hundred pounds or so to have him off their backs. Two disgruntled suitors finally compared notes and went to the police."

Already I felt relieved. "But why would they want to hurt Violet?" I asked.

The Lovejoys—or Farnsworths—stared at one another. He still held her arm in his hand. She turned to me and gave a sharp laugh. "You don't understand, do you? You are like all the others. I hate you—*hate you all*." She clenched her fists, her face contorting horribly. She laughed again. "Have you ever had to bow—to scrape—to fawn and beg? You are no better than she! Your kind treat us like dirt—you do not even see us!"

"No mistress is kinder than Violet!" I exclaimed.

"Kind—*kind!*" She drew back her lips, baring her teeth at me. "I do not want your kindness—your charity! I want you and all your kind to suffer—to suffer as you have made me and so many others suffer. And all those filthy young men! Curse you—curse you all!"

Lovejoy shook her arm. "What are you saying, my dear? Stop this, I beg of you! Please, *my dear.*" He shook his head. "Your nonsense has disturbed her, Mr. Holmes. You are absolutely mistaken—I have never heard of your Farnsworth, but you have upset my wife. Her mind is... unbalanced." He seemed genuinely distressed.

Holmes raised his long white hands, then clapped politely three times. "Bravo, Mr. Farnsworth—bravo, Miss Farnsworth. Another superb performance. It is truly a shame you did not continue on in the theater. What a pair you might have made. You could have challenged Henry Irving and Ellen Terry. Alas, I fear it is now too late."

Violet's left hand clutched the arm of the chair, the tendons standing out. I was glad to have the threat to her life lifted, but I feared what this added strain might do to her. She did look ill, her eyes feverish. She stared at Holmes. "Are you... are you quite sure about this, Mr. Holmes?"

As he looked at her, the smile faded from his lips, and I could see the fatigue about his eyes. He had also been up all night, and the two of them were beyond mere exhaustion. "Yes," he said.

Violet put her hand over her eyes. "I... I cannot believe it."

Henry appeared as relieved as I. "You must tell Donald Wheelwright. He will have to eat some crow."

Violet moaned and turned away toward the window. I stood up and went to her. "Oh, my poor dear." I touched her unhurt shoulder, and she clutched desperately for my hand. "It will be all right now—it is all over with."

The Farnsworths said nothing. Sherlock's mouth jerked briefly into a smile, and then it was gone, his gray eyes bleak and desperate.

"Not quite," he said. "A few details remain."

The fire had died down. He picked up a log, dropped it on the flames, then seized the poker and thrust viciously at the blackened wood. "Obviously an accomplice was involved, the person who attempted to strangle Mrs. Wheelwright last week and who attacked her last night. The first event would seem to require a man, the second a woman."

"It could have been a man disguised as a woman last night," I said. "The gypsy must have been strong."

Holmes laughed, a sound that set my teeth on edge. "Very good, Michelle. So we have an accomplice to account for, and one very curious fact." He paused and looked first at Henry, then at me. Neither of us spoke.

Holmes began to pace. "The Farnsworths in the police records do not amount to much. Their crimes were petty and uninspired. Decent actors they might be—even splendid at times," he gave them an ironic glance, "but there is nothing to prepare one for the scope and genius of what they have done in the last year or two. You have heard me jokingly refer to my Moriarty, but all along I have sensed a truly first-rate mind at work. The oil scam was cleverly designed to pull in the cream of London society, to embarrass and even ruin many. I am quite certain Mr. Steerford got his million pounds, and then there was the peculiar business with the Angels of the Lord. A very odd sensibility was involved, one with an insidious twist. My Moriarty wanted to arouse the prostitutes and servants, to inflame them, to turn them against their employers and their clientele. Money—mere avarice—was not what motivated Moriarty. We are dealing with a complex and disturbed mind, but a brilliant one. To have conceived of so many plots, to have spun so many webs, cast so many threads, found so many allies, all consumed with the same hatred of high society and the same hatred of... of men."

Violet still held my hand, and I could feel her trembling. A strange, subliminal dread coalesced out of the air and settled about my heart.

"Could the Farnsworths—could two hack actors—have ever dreamed all of this up? Never—*never*. My Moriarty is made of stronger stuff." He laughed.

My eyes were fixed on him. His face appeared grotesque and twisted, his anguish apparent in his terrible smile. He ran his long fingers through his oily black hair, leaving his arm raised and bent.

"Who?" I asked. "Who?"

Holmes stared out the window at the bleak white landscape. "She might have gotten away with it if only she had kept me out of it. The note made Wheelwright call me in. He was never much of a suspect. I sensed something wrong, but the Farnsworths were her agents and a shield before her. If not for the spiders... But she could not resist the spiders. They were a cruel touch. Wheelwright has a mortal fear of them—there can be no doubt of that. But she was an entomologist's daughter, one who took after her father."

I felt a very odd sensation at the nape of my neck, and while my face felt hot, my hands were suddenly cold as ice. "Oh, dear God—no. *No*." I stared out the windows at the whiteness. Small black dots began to swim about and fall slowly downward, while the blood in my ears roared like a waterfall. Very distantly, I heard myself saying, "Oh God!" again.

Someone shook me hard, and briefly I saw Henry, his blue-gray eyes intent, the flat bone running down his nose, the brown thick hairs of his mustache, and the creases in the dark skin of his lower lip. "Sit down—you must sit down." I nearly fell into the chair. He was massaging my hands. "Keep your head low. Damnation, Sherlock! Next time don't do this to her after she has been up half the night and has had no breakfast!"

My eyes came back into focus upon Violet. She was staring at me, her dark eyes full of concern. "I am sorry, Michelle." She looked up at

Holmes, the mocking smile pulling briefly at her lips. "I knew from the first that I could never deceive you." She appeared somehow relieved.

Lovejoy—or Farnsworth—or whoever he was—shook his head grimly. "Mr. Holmes, you have no proof of any of this. You have upset my wife; you have driven my mistress half mad. When will you be satisfied?"

Henry still had hold of me, and I could not see his face. His voice was grim. "Are you certain of this, Sherlock—are you absolutely certain?"

Holmes drew in his breath. He looked very tired, dark circles under his eyes, his face gaunt, his lips grayish. "Yes."

Violet was smiling at him. "Tell them what proof you have."

Holmes reached out with his long arm and sagged against the wall next to the fireplace. "It was those attacks which gave you away. The first was brilliant, the second merely desperate."

"But the bruises…" I moaned. "Who choked her?"

"That was Mr. Farnsworth." He turned to Farnsworth, whose genteel front suddenly wavered, his alarm apparent.

"But he was with Wheelwright!" Henry exclaimed.

"Yes, but he had choked Violet a few minutes earlier. He did it quite carefully, not wishing to injure her, and then he went downstairs. The two women did the rest. Violet is not a professional actor like those two, and as a result, I… was more easily taken in." He was staring at Violet. "All the same, it must have hurt. Other women might have dreamed up such a scheme, but to actually sit there and let him put his hands about your throat…" He let his arm drop. "This would be quite easy to verify. Mr. Farnsworth's hands should perfectly match the handprints on her throat. Enough of the bruises remain to make such a comparison."

No one said anything. I felt dizzy again and faintly nauseous. What kind of woman could possibly…?

"This attack was followed by your desperate plea to escape—to go somewhere else—anywhere else. This happened the day after we met

Mr. Steerford. Farnsworth had recognized me, even as I recognized him. You knew I was getting very close, and you wanted me out of the way, out of London and far from Steerford and the Angels of the Lord. I was forced to rely on Lestrade. Yesterday the Farnsworths arrived, no doubt with an enormous sum of money, and it was time to send me packing. Mr. Wheelwright had given me one more chance. What better way to get rid of me than by staging a final attack? You did your best to make your husband send me away at once—you baited him—but the storm complicated matters. You three planned to depart today with the money, no doubt heading for the continent. England would be far too hot for you. However, that final attack was clumsy. It confirmed all my suspicions and made everything fall into place."

Violet's head was held high, her brown eyes glistening and chin thrust forward. "And your proof?"

Holmes walked over to the small desk, opened the top drawer, and held up a common garden fork, less than a foot long, with a wooden handle and three curved tines. I had used such a fork many times to prepare a bed for flowers.

"Last night I found this near where you were attacked. You had laid it upon your shoulder like this." Holding it in his right hand, he set the three metal claws back behind his left shoulder. "You pulled it forward and down, ripping open your dress and cutting yourself. You then hurled the fork over the wall as far as you could."

"Oh, Violet!" I could not keep the revulsion from my voice. "How could you do such a thing to yourself?"

She gave me a pained smile, and then looked again at Holmes. "The fork might have been misplaced by the gardener. One would expect to find it amidst rhododendrons and ferns."

Holmes gave a savage laugh. "This particular fork was in a bucket before the house with several other tools yesterday morning. The fork was not in the bucket last night. You seized it when you ran from the house." He held it upright again, his hand shaking. "Shall we examine your lovely white shoulder and verify that the spacing of the tines matches that of the wounds?"

Violet sighed. "That will not be necessary Mr. Holmes. As I said, I knew I could never deceive you. And I could no more have ignored you, than you could have ignored your Moriarty."

I felt curiously empty inside. I made a sound, which I recognized as a sob. "But why, Violet? Why did you do all these terrible things and hurt yourself and…?"

She lowered her gaze. "Mr. Holmes?"

"Her all-consuming hatred of her husband. She has hated him for many years, and that hatred has grown into a hatred of his entire circle of acquaintances, of his entire class. It has become a hatred of life itself. She began by wanting to revenge herself upon her husband, to frighten and humiliate him; then she determined to destroy all those who seemed equally shallow, vicious, and cruel. Perhaps… perhaps there was an element of jealousy as well."

"Never!" Violet leaped to her feet, her voice a sudden clap of thunder, both hands raised. "*Never.*" She glared fiercely at him.

Holmes shrugged. "Comprehending female sentiments has never been my strong point."

"His little blonde shopkeeper is welcome to him—welcome to him!" She sank into her chair.

I put my hand over my mouth. My throat hurt, and I felt almost as if I had been physically assaulted, kicked, or slapped. "I don't understand," I managed to say.

"No," Violet said sadly, "and you never shall."

Henry stroked my hair lightly. "How could you… waste…? Oh, what is the use of questions."

Holmes dropped the fork abruptly and pulled a revolver from the pocket of his frock coat. "Please do not move your right arm, Mr. Farnsworth—no sudden motions whatsoever. Very good. Now slowly withdraw your hand. Set it on your lap. Excellent. Henry, I believe he has a pistol of some sort in his inner jacket pocket. Would you be so kind…?"

Henry walked across the room to the sofa and carefully reached into Farnsworth's pocket. He was on the opposite side from the sister. He withdrew a small, ugly weapon.

"A derringer, Mr. Farnsworth. Wherever did you find it? Do you realize how difficult it is to hit anything? They are totally useless beyond a few feet."

Violet shook her head angrily. "You did not tell me about any guns, James."

Farnsworth glared at her. "His proof does not amount to much."

"What is the use?" Violet sighed. "You have it all exactly right, Mr. Holmes." Her smile slowly faded. "I must confess I don't much care for the idea of prison."

"You cannot!" I cried. "You are too sick!" I turned to Sherlock. "For God's sake—you cannot let them lock her up—*please!*"

Holmes flinched. "Calm yourself, Michelle," he said. Henry came back across the room. I grabbed for his hand. He sat on the chair arm and put his other hand on my shoulder.

Holmes and Violet were staring at one another. She appeared sick again and utterly exhausted. The Farnsworths were frightened now, both of them. The fire had died down, but with a sudden crackle, an ember flew out and landed on the hearthrug.

Holmes lowered the revolver and closed his eyes momentarily. His mouth twitched. "If you will return the money—every penny—I shall let you go."

Violet stared at him. "*What?*"

"You must give back all the money and call off the Angels of the Lord and the others. It must all cease."

Violet smiled. "My own father-in-law has paid James for years to spy on me, and Harrington—he was such a pig. Abigail was only one of his victims. If you had known him, you might have understood."

Holmes opened his mouth, his face reddening. "You presume too much, madam. Never speak that way to me—*never*. I will not tolerate such talk from you or anyone else. You are beautiful and have great charm; you are a genius; but you do not know everything. You are not God. Do not try to be a deity—do not try to judge and punish the guilty. The world will always have an abundance of fools and scoundrels. Now then, as I said, if you will return the money, dismiss these two, and call off your Angels, I shall let you go free. If you will only give me your word, I shall leave this house and never set eyes on you again."

Violet stared silently at him. The corners of her mouth slowly rose. "Free?" She laughed. "You still do not understand."

"For God's sake, Violet." Farnsworth leaned forward, a man I had never seen before. "Say yes!"

Violet shook her head. "None of you do. You simply do not understand. I would rather die than spend another day with my husband. This is my eighth wedding anniversary." She laughed, baring her teeth. "It was to be the day of my escape—my triumph. I'd rather die than stay with him—I'd rather die." She was smiling, but there was no doubt she meant it.

"Damnation." Holmes shook his head, teeth clenched. "Whatever am I to do with you?"

The door swung open, and Holmes jerked about, the revolver ready. Donald Wheelwright froze in the doorway, looming there like some great brown mountain, and stared at the gun. Holmes lowered the barrel. "What is going on in here?" He had on his worn tweed jacket and his enormous walking shoes.

Violet began to laugh. A red flush appeared on her cheeks. "I was just explaining to Mr. Holmes that I would rather die than spend another day with you."

Wheelwright's brow furrowed, the sullen anger showing in his eyes. "What are you talking about?"

"You must congratulate Mr. Holmes. He has solved the whole mystery—the spiders, the gypsy, everything. He is worth every pound you paid him. You must assure Father Wheelwright that he is most assuredly *not* overrated."

"What is this?" Wheelwright asked.

Holmes and Henry stared blankly at him. I knew how they felt. Not only did he appear dangerous, but whatever could we say to him?

"I am the mastermind—I am the evil genius." She laughed harshly. "I made the whole thing up—along with the Lovejoys' assistance. Abigail was the gypsy at the Paupers' Ball, and she left the note in the library."

Wheelwright turned his gaze on Miss Farnsworth, and she went ashen, her fear obvious. "No, no," she murmured.

"But you must not blame her—it was my idea—it has all been my idea. I dreamed up the cake with the spiders, and I helped choose them. I knew what a coward you were, how they would reduce the big, strong, masterful Donald Wheelwright to quaking jelly. Watching your face that night made it all worthwhile—watching you run away like some silly little servant girl. And it was Lovejoy who choked me last week after I had found another spider. The spiders were a nice touch. Abigail and I pretended I had been attacked. And last night I tore open my gown with a garden fork and pretended to see the gypsy. It hurt—it hurt dreadfully." Her voice wavered for a moment. "But I thought of you as I did it. Mr. Holmes was clever enough to find the fork. It's there on the floor. I've also been busy robbing all the pretentious, arrogant fools whose company I have had to endure all these years. I have used a good deal of your money in my schemes, but I have invested so wisely that you are a rich man. Of course, if you had tried to manage the money yourself, we would no doubt be in the poorhouse by now—you could not manage the boiling of an egg." This struck her as funny, and she began to laugh.

None of us had moved. Donald Wheelwright's face was red, his eyes fixed on her. "Is this some… joke?" He glanced at the rest of us.

Holmes grimly shook his head. "No."

He stepped slowly through the doorway, then closed the door and locked it. "You did all this?" He reminded me of people I had treated who had been badly injured but who did not seem to understand that they were hurt.

Violet choked off her laughter. Her face was red, her eyes aflame, and she hissed, "Yes!" and jerked her head in a nod.

"You did?" He could not seem to believe it. "But why?"

"*Why?* You dare to ask why? Because I hate you!"

"Why?" His voice was a rumble.

"Because of what you did to me—because of the filthy, nasty thing you did to me—again and again. I told you not to touch me! I told you I could not bear it! But you were a brute—an animal. You hurt me so—again and again." The hysterical mania that had seized her faltered; her lips quivered, her eyes filling with tears.

"Oh, no." I sighed softly. "Oh, I should have know—I must have known."

She had married in her early twenties, and like most women of her class—like Jenny—she had known almost nothing. Some women were lucky, but if the man were rough and cruel, the results could be disastrous, akin to ravishment. And there was no escape for the unhappy woman—no way out—legal or otherwise. The man might do whatever he wished with her.

Wheelwright glanced nervously about the room. "I haven't touched you in years."

"Thank God for small favors." Violet laughed harshly. "But you did—you kept at it that first year even though you knew how I loathed it—*loathed it.* You kept pawing at me. I thought I would go mad each time you touched me. I did not know what to do. I seriously considered suicide. Spiders are no more frightful to you than you are to me. I wanted to die, but then I decided that was foolish. What I really wanted was for you and all your kind to suffer—to feel the same pain and humiliation as I. That was when I decided upon revenge. I would wait and plan and gather you and all the others in my web. I pretended to submit, I seemed to make peace, but all the while I consoled myself by making my plans, by imagining how you and the others would suffer even as your wives, your servants, and your pathetic whores had suffered." She bared her teeth in a cruel, joyful smile. "Oh, yes, and I made sure I could not bear your child."

Frightened, I leaped to my feet. "What have you done!"

Violet bit at her lip, surprised. "It was only a simple… device, but it prevents…" Embarrassed, she looked away.

My fists were clenched. "Oh Lord, this is all so pathetically foolish—so absurd."

For a moment I had feared she might have mutilated herself, but I knew the device she spoke off. Now I understood. She had nearly fainted at the clinic when I had discussed human biology with Jenny and again when I had been stitching up a man's brawny thigh. Childbirth also made her uneasy. The signs had all been there. I had suspected all along, but I had suppressed the knowledge—driven it from my awareness because I did not want to believe it of my beautiful, brilliant friend.

Wheelwright looked like someone had struck him. "You did not want... a child?"

"No—never—not *your* child." Her repulsion was obvious.

Holmes seemed ill—and simply embarrassed. The Farnsworths sat stiffly on the sofa, no doubt glad not to be the center of attention, but still fearful.

Wheelwright made a choking noise. "You call me a... brute... a monster. Look at yourself, woman. Good God—look at yourself."

Violet glared at him, fierce as ever, but the wild joy was gone. For the first time she appeared truly ugly, her face twisted and deranged by hatred. Holmes had been correct—it was all-consuming. It would devour and destroy her.

"You are the monster." Wheelwright's massive hands had begun to tremble. "You. You do not deserve..." Abruptly he lashed out and struck her across the face.

"Mr. Wheelwright!" Henry exclaimed.

I went over to her. She sat in the chair, but her entire body quivered under my hand. Holmes had also stepped forward, a resolute look in his eyes.

Violet's mouth was bleeding, her laugh pained and sharp. "Go ahead—kill me and be done with it once and for all. Kill me—but don't bully me ever again, you ugly freak."

Wheelwright's blue eyes no longer appeared human, and I crouched down, trying to shelter Violet with my arms. "Do not touch her."

"You..." His eyes focused on me, along with his rage. "Meddling witch—keep out of this. All of you keep out of this!" he roared, and then his big hand caught me square in the chest, on the sternum, and sent me flying backward.

Violet screamed, "No!"

I landed hard on my backside, the breath knocked out of me. Henry rushed Wheelwright; I heard a sickening thud as the big man's fist struck him. Henry half turned, toppled, and fell near me.

"Henry!" I cried. I went on my knees to him. "*Henry.*" I touched his face; I saw the red mark on his chin and jaw that would become a bruise. I took his shoulders and shook him. "Oh, Henry."

Holmes knelt beside me, his black frock coat spilling onto the floor, and touched Henry on the throat. "The blow has only stunned him."

"Watch out!" I cried.

He had dropped his guard, and Wheelwright came at him, kicking out with his enormous boot. The revolver flew through the air; Holmes cried out and clutched at his hand. Wheelwright's head swept back and forth, then he turned and yanked Violet up out of the chair by her arm. She screamed, the sound raw and strained. He hit her face again, twice, his big hand like a flat club.

"Stop it!" I shouted.

Holmes stepped past me and his thin arm in the black sleeve rose, his fist striking Donald Wheelwright on the side of the jaw. Holmes groaned from the impact. Wheelwright released Violet, and she collapsed at his feet. Wheelwright shook himself dully, his nostrils flaring. Holmes stepped back and raised his fists in a boxer's stance.

Wheelwright's breathing was labored, and he touched his chin with his fingertips. "You bastard. I've seen how you look at her. You were in on it all." His eyes were half closed, ominous slits with blue slivers in them.

Sherlock was very pale. "That is nonsense—utter nonsense."

Wheelwright's hands formed fists. "So you want to box?" He rushed Holmes, a right jab thudding off his shoulder, and then he had him wrapped in his arms. Wheelwright staggered forward.

"Stop!" I cried. I glanced about. The Farnsworths had risen, but they were terrified and would be of no help.

"Michelle." Violet held out her hand to me. I helped her up. Her mouth was bleeding, her eye starting to swell. She swayed and I caught her.

Holmes writhed about, managing to slip one arm free. Wheelwright crashed him into the table, sending chess pieces flying. Sherlock's long legs and shoes thrashed about. Wheelwright grabbed him by the hair and slammed his head twice against the wooden surface.

"He will kill him!" I cried. I let go of Violet and went to them.

Wheelwright was bent over Holmes, his huge hands wrapped about his throat. Holmes was unconscious from the blows to his head. His face was red, and Wheelwright's thick ugly fingers were choking the life from him.

"Stop!" I shouted. "*Stop.*" I pulled at Wheelwright's arm, but I could not budge him. I struck him once with my fist, but it was as if I were a mosquito or fly, hardly worth his notice. He did resemble an animal: his mouth open, teeth bared, nostrils flaring, and that terrible, all-consuming rage in his eyes.

"Please!" I cried. "*Please*–you are killing him! He did nothing–I swear he didn't! Let him go!"

I do not think he even heard me. I glanced in desperation at the Farnsworths, but James appeared paralyzed, unable to move, while Abigail had hidden her face against him.

I heard a dull thud, and something splattered my face. Wheelwright's jaw dropped, and his frame quivered. I looked about. This time I saw Violet's arms swing around in a great arc, both hands holding the black poker from the fireplace, her own lips drawn back, teeth bared, her dark eyes raging. The poker again struck Wheelwright at the base of the skull. More blood flew, and this time he fell. The table collapsed, Holmes sliding off, and the two men lay unconscious on the floor.

I knelt down and fumbled at Sherlock's collar. I felt a pulse and could tell he was breathing. He would have a terrible bump at the back of his head. Wheelwright lay on his side. His eyes were open but blank, all the anger and hate and life gone from them.

"Oh, dear God," I murmured. I tried to turn him, but I could not move him. I felt at his throat but could find no pulse. I used both hands to pull at his arm, and he flopped onto his back. I opened his jacket and put my ear against his chest. My own heart was throbbing, but all was silent.

With a sigh I rose onto my knees. "He is dead." I looked up at Violet. "He is dead, Violet."

She gave a sharp terrible laugh and let the poker fall. "Oh, good," she said. "Oh, *good*." She laughed again, then bit savagely at her hand and staggered back.

I stood slowly. "That part of the brain controls unconscious functions like respiration and the heartbeat. The first blow must have been mortal." My words sounded strange, curiously remote. "I cannot believe it." I touched my face and felt something damp. Glancing down, I realized blood had splattered my yellow silk dress, my fancy dress, which I had worn since yesterday afternoon.

Someone began to cry loudly—Miss Farnsworth. She was on the sofa, her face in her hands. Her brother tried to comfort her. Violet made a pained noise, something between a laugh and a sob. She bent over and picked up the revolver, which her husband had kicked from Holmes' hand. "I did not even see this." She put her left hand over her bloody mouth while her right held the revolver, the barrel pointed at the floor.

"Violet, we must get away from here at once," Farnsworth said. "There is not an instant to lose."

Violet looked at me. She said, "Go ahead and leave. I always meant to give my share to the Angels. I am staying here. It does not matter now."

Farnsworth shook his head. "Are you mad? There is over half a million pounds. You said you wanted to be free. This is your chance. Come."

She shook her head. "No." She laughed. "I can never be free now." She stared down at Wheelwright's corpse.

Abigail Farnsworth rose, but she appeared weak. "Please come, Violet—before it is too late."

"*No.*"

Farnsworth stared at Violet. "We cannot leave you here. You could be tried for murder."

"No!" I said. "It was—he was killing Sherlock—he would have killed him."

Farnsworth gave a pained smile. "I would not want to argue the point with the police." He slowly approached Violet. "You must come with us—you'll thank me tomorrow."

His sister nodded. "Yes, Violet. We have accomplished all that we intended. The wretched men got what they deserved—all of them."

Violet's hand seemed to rise of its own accord, floating lazily upward so that the revolver pointed at Farnsworth. He stopped moving. Violet smiled. "Thank you, James, but I have other plans." She motioned toward the door with the barrel. "Our acquaintance has been a pleasant one, of mutual benefit, and I shall miss you. You both shared my hatred of injustice and played your parts well. Now please go."

Abigail was distressed. "But, Violet…"

"Will you leave me be!" Violet cried. "Do go! I would not want to shoot you, but I am so tired I cannot think well. My father taught me about revolvers. And Abigail, I know I can rely on you—distribute my share amongst the Angels. Now goodbye."

Farnsworth shook his head. He had played the butler for so long he tended to slide back into the role. "A pity. Mr. Holmes was correct. We are only two hack actors. We could never have managed without you. Goodbye, Violet."

He strode toward the door, drawing Abigail Farnsworth after him. "My gypsy was not hack work," she said. Farnsworth unlocked the door, then carefully shut it behind them.

I felt dizzy. Everything had happened so fast. Only about fifteen minutes had passed since Donald Wheelwright had come through the doorway.

Violet smiled briefly, her hand trembling. She walked over to a chair by the fire and sat. "Michelle…" Her voice shook, and her eyes were full of tears again. "Oh, God." She raised the revolver and put the barrel under her chin.

"Violet," I moaned as fear swept through me, a sudden chill at the nape of my neck, "whatever are you doing?"

"Do you not see? This is the way it was always meant to end. I understand that now."

"No." I shook my head. "No, it was most assuredly not meant to end this way." My mouth felt dry, my hands icy. The dread had returned.

"I'm sorry, Michelle, but…"

"Violet—in God's name, if you apologize to me one more time, I swear I will strangle you!"

We stared at each other, and then she laughed. "My poor Michelle. I cannot blame you. I shall… I shall try not to apologize again. Can I not make you understand? He hurt me so many times—*again and again.* I could do nothing. My life has been a nightmare, and now… I am glad I killed him, but I am sorry he is dead. Does that make sense?"

"Yes." I took a step forward.

"If you come any nearer I shall surely press the trigger. Perhaps I shall press it anyway. My head does hurt, and my stomach. Oh, it will be good to be dead, to be free, finally, of hate and fear and pain—all this pain."

"No, Violet." My own eyes were full of tears. "It is not good to be dead—it is good to be alive. You are free now, if you want to be."

"No—I told them the truth—I can never be free." Her right hand held the gun, but her left hand slipped over to her side. "Oh, God, this hurts so. My cursed stomach has hurt me forever—it wakes me in the night and spoils my days."

"The burden is gone, the truth known. You will heal now."

She shook her head, smiling wearily. Her left eye was badly swollen and bluish. Unaware of what she was doing, she wiped her mouth on her sleeve, leaving a bloody smear on the silk. Her eyes could not seem to focus properly, and I saw she was near the point of collapse. The barrel of the gun quavered continually. I took a step closer.

"No, Michelle." She drew in her breath, and I saw her struggling to master herself, to find the will for that one final, desperate act.

"You will not go to prison," I said. "I promise you. What you did was terrible, but necessary. You saved Sherlock. Donald very nearly killed him—and he might have killed you as well. Please put down that revolver."

"I should not have struck him the second time. That was cruel. I have no reason to go on living. Can you not see the justice of it? Mr. Holmes accused me of playing God, but all I ever wanted was justice." She sighed. "My justice may seem suspiciously like vengeance. I shall make amends now. I honestly cannot think of why I should live."

"Because you are my friend!" I cried. "And I should miss you ever so much if you were dead!" I could not restrain my tears, but I kept talking and took another step forward. Violet's dark eyes were stark against her bruised white face. "You are such a wonderful person, my dear, that it would be a terrible waste, the worst crime of all. You are barely thirty. You are young and you are beautiful, witty, and charming. I have few female friends whose company I can tolerate, and I will not have the best of them blowing her brains out! You said you would not apologize again; well, show me, for once, that you are my friend–show me that you love me even as I love you. And there is Sherlock–he also loves you."

Violet sobbed and shook her head. "No, no–it is too late–I am lost. I deceived him not once, but many times. And you–I deceived you. It has torn me apart. Oh, I did not want to!" She was crying so hard.

"Oh, my dear, I forgive you–you know I do. I only wish you had confided in me about... Oh, Violet–*please.*"

I walked over and took the gun from her hand.

"Michelle." She stood and embraced me, her arms feeble.

"It is over now," I said. "It is finished."

"Oh, thank God." Her body swayed, then went limp in my arms as she finally found the unconsciousness she longed for.

Afterword

I woke up early that morning and had to think for a while to remember that I was not at home in London, but near a small village, high in the Alps. February was only two days away. Henry lay beside me, breathing slowly. I moved nearer to him. The room was icy cold, and he gave off heat like a steam radiator. The window behind the curtains was a fuzzy square of grayish light.

I closed my eyes, ready to go back to sleep, then remembered that Violet was with us and that she was still miserable. The thought was like a reoccurring pain, some dull headache. Henry and I had been weary of rain and fog, the winter even gloomier than usual, but we had also made the trip because we had hoped it would improve Violet's spirits.

Over two months had passed since the disastrous climax at Norfolk. Physically and mentally exhausted, Violet had come down with bronchitis. She had been gravely ill, and I had spent many nights by her bedside. She had a high fever and grew delirious. In her sleep she would talk to Donald Wheelwright. When she became frightened, I would bathe her forehead and try to calm her. Between my practice during the day and the long nights with Violet, I too became exhausted. Henry finally took me aside and sternly told me that even though I had the constitution of an ox, I would eventually wear myself out or fall ill, and then I could help no one. Gertrude and the other servants shared the nursing with me after that, and Henry took on some of my patients. Several elderly ladies found him quite charming.

Violet had recovered from the bronchitis, but then the inevitable depression set in. At least the physical illness had let her sleep, the body overpowering the mind and asserting its demand for rest. Her stomach ulcer had also been better. But once her fever lifted, her spirits sank, and her insomnia returned. Try as I might, I could not distract her from black thoughts.

She, who had run a household of over thirty servants, handled all the accounts and investments, and overseen a vast, secret organization, now spent most of her days idly brooding before the fire. She had been a witty and charming conversationalist, but now I could barely get her to talk to me. I could not recall the last time I had heard her laugh. She had become pale, thin, and weak, a prime candidate for pneumonia—which would kill her quickly—or tuberculosis, a disease of lingering horror.

I turned restlessly in the bed, then stroked Henry's shoulder and arm, feeling the muscles beneath his nightshirt. He mumbled a word that I could not make out.

Old Wheelwright had been a devil, but we had managed to shield Violet. Holmes had resolved that we would, as much as possible, be truthful, and I had told Lestrade that Violet had struck her raging husband just as he was about to kill Sherlock Holmes. The fact that we had all obviously been assaulted—especially Violet—supported our story. However, because we did not want Violet to go to prison and because the Farnsworths had safely escaped, they took the blame for the oil well scheme, the Angels of the Lord, and the evil gypsy. We were all questioned, but in the end no charge was brought against Violet. I think her poor battered face influenced Lestrade.

Old Wheelwright had been doling out money to Donald for years, and he cut Violet off without a penny. However, unbeknownst to her father-in-law or her deceased husband, Violet had built up a small fortune of her own. She had had complete control of Donald's finances (a fact which astonished me, as I have no head for figures), and she had invested shrewdly.

The major newspapers were restrained in their coverage, but not so some of the sensational dailies. We made sure Violet never saw any of these, but Sherlock was not so lucky. One paper actually ran the headline, "Famed Detective Smitten at Last." My mouth twitched, my anger flaring briefly like an ember someone had blown upon. It was ironic because the famed detective was hardly behaving like a conspiratorial lover.

Although he was obviously deeply concerned, he had refused to see Violet since that fatal morning. When she had bronchitis, he had come to inquire of her health every day, and even now, he asked Henry or me about her at least once a week. On the worst night, as she lay burning with fever, he had paced about her library until morning, but I could not get him to come upstairs to the bedroom.

At first I had been willing to leave him alone, but when Violet finally recovered, I went to see him at Baker Street. I pleaded with him for over an hour to simply go to see her—but in vain. He appeared colder and more gaunt than ever before, his face thin and imperious like some marble Caesar. I asked if he might somehow excuse her actions, even if he could not forgive. All I received were remarks like, "It would be neither to her benefit or mine were we to meet again. I have nothing more to say to her." Always before, I had felt certain that Sherlock's better qualities outweighed his eccentricities; now I was not so sure. Perhaps he was cold—and selfish.

I had asked Henry to talk with him, but he gave me an odd look and asked if I really thought Sherlock could simply forget everything Violet had done.

"That is not the point!" I had exclaimed.

"Oh, but I'm afraid that is the point."

I ran the sole of my foot along Henry's foot to his ankle bone and onto his calf muscle. He stirred, and his hand sought mine even though he was still fast asleep.

Violet had not mentioned Holmes until one evening about two weeks ago. I had brought her violin to her room and urged her to play. She took the violin and the bow, and then considered my request, her gaze turning inward. "The last time I played was for Mr. Holmes at Norfolk." Her lips formed a smile, but one totally lacking in warmth or humor. "How he must despise me." She gave a sharp laugh. "I deserve his disgust." She set aside the violin.

She had caught me at a weak moment. I was angry and told her that instead of morbidly dwelling on her past sins, she might think about how she could atone for them—think what good she could make of the rest of her life. By the time I returned home, I was ashamed of myself and tearfully told Henry all that I had said.

"She needed a scolding," he said. "You have been so patient. And I think you are nearly as worn out as she." He suggested that a change of scenery might help us all, and the clear mountain air would be beneficial for Violet's lungs.

Well, the air was wonderful, the scenery spectacular, but Violet was gloomy as ever, and Holmes was back in London, no doubt sulking before the fireplace at Baker Street.

"How can they…?" I said.

Henry stirred abruptly. "Michelle?" He did not sound awake.

"Go back to sleep." I stroked his arm again.

Henry was so still I thought he was still sleeping, but at last he rolled over—his hair was tousled, his eyes closed—and slipped his arms about me. He tried to kiss me, but his mouth was so wooden I could tell he was still half asleep.

"Are you fretting?" he asked. I said nothing. "Are you?"

"Yes."

"Violet and Sherlock are grown up. Ultimately they must take care of themselves."

"Well, they are not doing a very good job of it."

"When we have children of our own," he said, "we shall be responsible for them. Violet and Sherlock are not our children. Perhaps they will come round some day."

"I wish I could believe that."

He drew me closer. The room was very cold—my nose was freezing—but we lay under a heap of quilts wearing our thick flannel nightshirts, and it was warm and comfortable. I could feel him fall back asleep, his breathing subtly changing. I watched the window square grow brighter and yellower, and then closed my eyes. But sleep eluded me.

I decided to get up—an adventure in the frigid room. I put my heavy wool robe under the covers to warm it before venturing forth. At last I sat up. I slid my feet into my slippers, not wanting my bare skin to touch the icy planks, then stood and wrapped the robe about me. I could see my breath.

I drew the curtains aside, and a shaft of bright yellow sunlight shot into the room. The light on the snow was blinding, and the vista spread before me was straight from a travel book. The Alpine mountains were sharp, jagged crags of white—winds stirring the snow on their glacial tops—and the sky was an absolute dazzling blue. There was an icy purity to everything, an austere and terrible beauty.

"How can anyone be gloomy in a place like this?" I was happy to be away from London, from its squalor and dark ugliness. We had only been in the Alps a little over two days; such a setting must, in time, help even Violet.

I put some kindling on the grate and started a fire, then added a large log so Henry would not have a similar adventure getting out of bed. Violet was sleeping in a chair before the fire in her room.

"She was up half the night, ma'am," Gertrude whispered.

Although Gertrude was frail herself, she had been a great help. She was fiercely protective of her mistress. Soon Violet would be moving out of the enormous townhouse, and Gertrude and Collins would accompany her. She had no desire to live so ostentatiously, and her house was full of bad memories and dark shadows.

Gertrude and I had breakfast together, and a sleepy Henry eventually joined us. The stove threw off heat—the tiny kitchen was the warmest room in the house. I teased him about his bedraggled appearance, but he only grinned and said something about the inevitable results of a night of wild abandon. Gertrude was making tea at that moment, so I smiled back at him.

By noon Violet was still not up, and Henry resolved to walk into the village proper to inquire about trips to the nearby glacier. Violet finally came down and picked at her breakfast while I ate lunch. She was pale, but less tired looking. I suggested a game of chess in the sitting room, but I was such a poor player that she could easily beat me without paying attention to the game. Afterwards I tried to read a tedious book on diseases of the heart and circulatory system, but always I was aware of Violet staring obsessively into the fire.

At about three, I grew restless. I set down my book, stretched, and then stood up. "Would you like to go outside for a while? If you do not feel up to walking, we could bundle up and sit on the balcony."

Violet smiled weakly. "Like all the tubercular patients at the inn. I saw them the afternoon we arrived. They appeared so sad, all of them: flushed, yet ill, wrapped in scarves, bundled in mittens and hats and coats and blankets, all of them waiting to die. No, it is too cold for me even when I bundle up, and the sun hurts my eyes. It makes my head ache."

"But I have some dark glasses."

She shook her head. "No. It is too cold and too bright."

It might make you feel better, I wanted to add. "It seems foolish to have come all this way to the beautiful sunny Alps and then to spend the days indoors before the fire." I could not keep the irritation from my voice.

She sighed and lowered her gaze. "Perhaps later I shall go out."

"Perhaps later I shall drag you out."

She looked up, and for an instant her lips formed the mocking smile that I had not seen for so long. "I do not doubt it."

No sooner had I picked up my heavy and tedious book, than I heard a rap at the front door. "Who can that be?" Violet did not much care. She continued staring into the fire, lost in some dark reverie. I frowned, then rose and left the sitting room.

Framed in the doorway, against the brilliant exterior light, was a familiar silhouette, a tall form in a black greatcoat and top hat.

"Sherlock!" I exclaimed. I strode forward. "Oh, at last!"

Gertrude gave me a puzzled glance, then said, "Won't you please come in now, sir?"

Holmes' eyes searched the room, his nostrils flaring, and then he released his breath in a great white cloud of vapor. He seemed frozen at the entrance. He was very pale, and the brilliant light emphasized his pallor. Dressed all in black, he resembled some type of night creature, some cave dweller, caught in the unaccustomed brightness of day.

"Do come in," I said.

He thrust forward his leg in the dark wool and his black boot, then crossed the threshold. "*Lasciate ogni speranza,*" he mumbled to himself. He tried to smile. "I... I had to come."

"It took you long enough! But I am glad you did. Violet will be happy to see you."

He took off his hat and gripped the brim with his long fingers in the black leather gloves. Despite his smile, his gray eyes swept anxiously about the room.

"Perhaps you can cheer her up. She is so despondent. And it is wonderful to see you. I... I'm sorry about last time." I took his arm. The muscle was hard and stiff. "Violet needs all the friends she can get. She would never admit it, but I know she was hurt that you would not see her."

Holmes' lips drew back. "It was never my intention to be unkind. I may on occasion be curt, blunt, or insensitive, but never deliberately cruel."

I smiled. "Well, it is good you are here. You could obviously use some fresh air and sunshine yourself."

"I shall not... I have some business in Geneva, and I thought I might stop on my way. My visit must be brief."

Holmes was skilled at deception when he wished to be—when he was playing a part or uncovering some hidden fact—but that afternoon he did not seem to be trying very hard. He appeared almost ill, what with his pallor and the shadows under his eyes, and he was so thin. All in all, he, disturbingly, resembled Violet.

Still holding his arm, I started for the sitting room door. He moved reluctantly and quite slowly.

"You must promise me one thing," I said. "You must not upset Violet. You must not be curt, blunt, or insensitive today."

He stopped and gave a quick shake of his head. "Do you know me so little, Michelle?"

He seemed so hurt that I was sorry and immediately backtracked. "Of course I know you would not deliberately be cruel, but you must…" I smiled. "Today you must be charming."

He made a frightful grimace. "I have never been charming in my life."

I laughed. "Yes, you have, although it is a charm peculiar only to you. Oh, pay no attention to me, but do be gentle with Violet. She is sorry for what she has done, I can tell you that. Can you not…?" I paused before the door. "Oh Sherlock, can you ever forgive her?"

"Yes."

I went through the doorway. "We have a visitor from London."

Violet turned slowly and saw Holmes. Her eyes abruptly widened, her lips parting, a fierce energy animating her face. Holmes froze again. The two of them stared hungrily at each other, their inner passion revealed only for an instant, as if two suns had suddenly flared up in the confines of the small room. Violet bit at her lip. She lowered her gaze, her eyes desolate. Holmes had not moved, but seemed paler than before. I gave him a nudge, but he seemed made of stone and incapable of motion.

The vast silence which had filled the room made me uncomfortable.

"Henry has just stepped out. He should be back shortly. He will be glad to see you, Sherlock." Sensing an opportunity, I added, "Perhaps I shall go and fetch him."

That moved them, but not as I had hoped: The prospect of being alone together clearly terrified them. Holmes' eyes had opened wide in disbelief, and Violet's delicate, shapely hand gripped at the chair arm.

"You need not trouble yourself," Holmes said weakly.

"Oh, very well." I walked over to a chair near the fireplace and sat down. My moving seemed to stir Holmes. He slipped his top hat under his arm, then pulled off his gloves and put them in the hat.

Gertrude stepped into the room. "Let me take your things, Mr. Holmes."

He nodded solemnly, handed her the hat, then took off his greatcoat. "Thank you, Gertrude." He strode to the fire and rubbed his hands briskly before it. Neither Violet nor I could see his face.

"What's the news from London?" I asked.

"Nothing of interest. The weather is even colder and drearier than when you left, the rain and fog unceasing. Good cheer for the New Year is difficult to come by. And there are no cases of particular merit, nothing to divert me now that..." He squared his shoulders, drew himself up, and then turned to face us. "And how are you faring, Mrs. Wheelwright?"

Violet shrugged. "As well as might be expected." She would not look him in the eye.

"I hope you will soon be recovered."

As soon as his words faded away, I sensed the all-encompassing silence lurking nearby. "I doubt," I said, "that you have remained completely idle."

"No, thank heavens. Ennui has always been the bane of my existence. Lestrade needed some help finishing up what he had bungled." He had begun to pace, but he glanced warily at Violet. "I managed to dredge up Herbert's diamond necklace. It cost him about a third of its purchase price to get it back, and now he has it up for sale." He smiled. "This time it is safely stowed in the bank. Would it disturb you ladies greatly if I smoke a single cigarette?"

Violet shook her head. "It is a beastly habit," I said, "but go ahead."

He withdrew a cigarette from his case and struck a match. "There has been work to do, but not enough, and nothing of real complexity. I have been..." He was pacing again. "Solving a challenging case is always satisfying, but the inevitable disappointment soon follows. The greater the challenge, the greater the disappointment. Rarely does anything of equal interest turn up. One is weary, one is restless, but there is little of merit to occupy the brain. Instead it continues to race on, to spin out lunatic reveries or veer off into odd, dark corners."

Violet had raised her dark eyes and was staring intently at him.

"There are times when my powers seem more a curse than a gift, when I would gladly... But such idle thoughts are useless. One must play the cards one is dealt. I only hope something of interest turns up soon. Patience is not one of my virtues."

Violet's cheeks had a faint flush, the first color I had seen there in some time. "I understand exactly what you are saying. At least..." She stared at him. "At least you have the possibility of another interesting case. I have spent so many years, so much time and energy... And now there is nothing, nothing at all. Am I to take up knitting or watercolor painting?" The ironic smile appeared.

Holmes gave a sharp laugh. "I think not. There is, however, the violin."

Violet lowered her eyes. "I have not played since... Norfolk."

"That is a waste," Holmes said. "I do not know what I would do without my violin. It soothes the troubled spirit. You must play again."

I nodded. "I have tried to tell her the same thing. She must not sit and brood all day long."

Violet was gazing at the fire. "I do not want to be soothed. I do not deserve it. At least, Mr. Holmes, you have the consolation of knowing your talents have been put to good use, that you have righted wrongs and helped the unfortunate. You have not been corrupted—you have not let hatred and the desire for vengeance drive you to terrible deeds." Her eyes filled with tears.

Holmes was distressed. "It is not so simple as you think. I deal with vicious and unsavory people all the time. Frequently they are my aids and accomplices. You said that you wanted justice. Your goal was a worthy one, although you took... the wrong path."

"Was it?" She laughed sharply. "As they say, the road to hell is paved with good intentions. You accused me of wishing to be God, and you were absolutely correct. I thought I could be judge, jury, and one of the avenging Furies. My crimes were monstrous, but worse still was my arrogance, my phenomenal arrogance." Her cheeks were flushed, her dark eyes smoldering, and she had run out of breath.

"Do not torment yourself," I said. "It does neither you nor anyone else any good."

She did not seem to hear me. "And Donald, poor Donald. During our eight years together, I never felt any pity for him, not one ounce. I pitied only myself."

"He was cruel to you," I said. "He hurt you physically. Your hatred was understandable."

"But it was as he said—he had not touched me for years! He turned to his little blonde, and he tried to leave me alone. Still I hated him—I would not let him be—I baited him. He was a fairly normal man of no great intelligence, but by no means a cretin. And he was nowhere so cruel or spiteful as his father. Yet my mind made him into an absolute monster. Surely he deserved some pity? He was unhappy too. Other men marry women more intelligent than them, yet they are not… murdered."

Holmes stared at her in horror, a long ash dangling at the end of his cigarette. I felt my face grow hot.

"Oh, Violet, why must you talk so? I was there—whatever else it may have been, it was not murder."

Her mouth twisted into a frightful smile. "Whatever else it was does not much matter now. He is just as dead. And his only crime was that he married a woman with ice in her veins, a woman who could not love."

"Stop that!" I had stood up, my fists clenched. "In God's name, Violet, you are no saint, but you are no such devil either. Can you not see? Now you are making yourself far worse than you really are."

She stared up at me, her eyes black whirlpools of despair, which would suck into their depths the entire world. "Do you think so?"

"Yes. I know there is much that is good and loving in you." I sat down.

A tear trickled from her left eye, and she wiped quickly at it. "Oh, I hope you are right."

"She is," Holmes said softly. When Violet looked at him, he walked to the fire and flicked off the ash of his cigarette. He had his back to us again. "You are beautiful and... charming. You are... It was very hard for me to expose you. I hope you understand that."

"I do," Violet said.

"And I was... hurt that you deceived me for so long, but that is not fair on my part, because I think we both always knew how things stood. The realization was always there at the back of my mind. Henry and Michelle had no suspicions, but you and I knew better. We were not fooling one another, not for much of the time." He turned about to face her. "Were we?" He raised the cigarette to his mouth.

She smiled, her eyes still glistening. "No."

"You certainly had me fooled," I said.

Her smile grew sad. "It is as I have said—it is because you are too good. I hope you understand that my greatest regret is for deceiving you, for betraying your trust and your friendship."

I sighed. "And I have told you repeatedly that you are forgiven."

Violet laughed softly. "I do not seem to want to be forgiven."

Holmes turned again to the fire. "You are a woman of extraordinary talents. Unfortunately, they were wasted—there was no worthy outlet for them. And there is your... phenomenal beauty. Even I cannot resist it. But what have I to offer? I have reached my fortieth year, but it feels more like my seventieth, my three score and ten. I am a confirmed bachelor like those old men with long white sidewhiskers, black cloaks, and tall hats—everything long out of fashion—who totter through the park clacking at the walkway with their sticks. My hours are irregular, my habits fixed and eccentric, and my interests bizarre and fantastical. I could not, in good conscience, wish one such as myself on any woman, let alone one so remarkable as you. I have spent my life pursuing evil and dealing with perverted and deranged creatures. It has taken its toll. I am not... I am barely fit for company such as yours. My heart is not capable of normal human affections, and then there is my appearance." He laughed sharply. "Perhaps it is my occupation which has made me resemble some lean and hungry bird of prey with a monstrous beak."

I stared at him in disbelief. Violet appeared exhausted by her own earlier outburst. The silence filled the room, a great gray, deadening thing that reminded me of the web I had dreamed about at Norfolk, the web binding and suffocating Violet and Sherlock. I waited, hoping one of them might break free, but it was no use.

At last I said, "That is utter and complete nonsense, Sherlock!"

He took a final draw on his cigarette and threw the butt on the fire. His shoulders were slumped, his long thin hands dangling at his sides, white alongside the black frock coat. "The truth is rarely pleasant."

"The truth? *The truth?* You dare to call that ugly drivel the truth? You are no such homely freak, and besides, women are intelligent enough not to love men only for their appearance. Have you forgotten how Susan Lowell could love the maimed Erik?"

"Because she was blind."

"Do you think so little of her? Do you think she could not have loved him otherwise?"

He shrugged. His eyes shifted briefly to Violet, who had, almost reflexively, turned again to the fire. "What I think does not particularly matter." He took out his watch and glanced at it. "Mrs. Wheelwright, I wished to pay my respects and let you know I hold no grudge against you. To the contrary, I admire you greatly, and you did save my life.

Unfortunately, as I told Michelle, I have business in Geneva, and I fear I cannot linger."

Violet stared dully at the fire. "I understand."

I was astounded. "You are not leaving? You have not even seen Henry."

"I had hoped to catch the four-thirty train so I could be in Geneva before eight. If you would be so kind as to have Gertrude fetch my coat."

I stared at him, but his eyes would not meet mine. The silence began to settle again, gray and terrible. I would still breathe, but the filaments were slowly settling, winding about Sherlock and Violet, slowly binding them. It was only a matter of time. A sense of dread washed over me. I wanted to rise from the chair, but I felt suddenly as if I could not move.

"I shall fetch her. You need not trouble yourself." He started for the door.

Can they both be so blind—so ridiculously stupid? I asked myself, the silence gathering again, somehow more deafening than a clap of thunder.

"No—*no*! It shall not be—I will not let it!" I stood and savagely pushed over my chair. The crash made Violet start. She and Sherlock stared at me.

Gertrude appeared in the doorway. "Ma'am, is anything…?"

"I have matters under control, Gertrude. Please close the door."

"Yes, ma'am."

Neither Violet nor Sherlock could meet my gaze. "I cannot bear it. You two will drive me mad! I cannot believe a grown man and woman can be so foolish. Perhaps you deserve to be the poor shriveled-up, desiccated creatures you pretend to be, for that is certainly where you are headed. I will not allow it because I know you love one another. You talk as if you had ice in your veins and withered hearts when your love is obvious to anyone with eyes in their head. I could see it. Henry could see it, and even Donald Wheelwright could see it. Both of you have fire in your veins, not ice."

Holmes' face was flushed. "I was not meant for a conventional life."

"Of course you were not! And neither was Violet! You could not abandon consulting detection and become a banker living in a tidy house in the suburbs, nor could Violet take up knitting and raise a dozen angelic children. I would not wish such a fate on you—no more than I would wish it on Henry and me. Neither a conventional marriage nor what Sherlock calls a vulgar affair will do—you are both too decent."

Violet laughed harshly, her face flushed. "'Decent?'—*I?*"

"Yes! Your decency was what drove you to your crimes. What more is decency than the desire for justice and the hatred of injustice? Your acts came more from an excess of decency rather than a lack of that virtue. No, I do not expect the ordinary, but neither do I expect you to throw away your one chance for happiness—for love. You are nearly there! Do not suffocate yourselves. It is not so difficult as you believe."

I turned to Violet. "You made a dreadful mistake—you took the wrong path, but you are being offered something few people get—a second chance. *Take it*—redeem yourself. Make something of your life. Sherlock will help you. Your husband was a brute, but you must know Sherlock would never hurt you. Again, these things are simpler than you think if you will but love one another."

I paused to draw in my breath, my eyes sweeping about. I walked over to Sherlock. He wanted to retreat, but he watched me warily.

"Do you love Violet?" I asked.

"What?"

"A simple yes or no will suffice."

His tongue flickered across his lower lip. "I... I am not sure I know what love is."

"I think you know very well what love is, and I want an answer, not more equivocating, or quibbling, or philosophizing. *Yes* or *no*?"

His eyes stared past me at Violet. At last he said softly, "Yes."

I strode over to Violet, who shrank back into the chair. "Do you love Sherlock?"

"I... I honestly do not know if... if I can love any man."

Her confusion appeared genuine, but I would have none of it. "Well, if you could love any man, would Sherlock qualify, or is he too peculiar—too homely—too eccentric—to put up with?"

She shook her head. "Oh, no—*no*."

"Very well, then I shall vouch for you." I folded my arms. Both of them were staring at me. "Now then, it is customary after a declaration of love to embrace the beloved. Sherlock?" He stood with his big thin hands hanging awkwardly at his sides, his face still flushed.

I went over to Violet and put my hand on her shoulder. "Violet?" She stared up at me, her lips parted slightly, her dark eyes still anguished. "I... cannot. I..." Her voice was barely recognizable.

Holmes drew in his breath through his nostrils and squared his shoulders. "I really must be going."

I bit at my lip and shook my head.

He was nearly to the door when Violet's breath seemed to catch in her throat. She stood and strode quickly forward. Holmes heard her, paused, and then turned. Her arms swung about him, and she buried her face in his chest. I thought he might fall over, but he caught his balance and embraced her. Violet's shoulders were shaking.

"Don't," he murmured. He touched her hair, the back of her neck, with his slender fingers.

"Oh, my heart will break," she said. "I do love you—I swear I do—almost from the very first. That was why it was so hard—so dreadful. If there had been any way—if I had not been married to Donald—I would have stopped it—stopped everything! But now... You must believe I love you—*you must.*"

I sighed. "I am going out," I said softly.

Violet drew back slightly from Holmes, her head turning toward me. "No, Michelle." She stared up at him again, her arms still clasped about his back. "She cannot understand—she never will—but you can. I am not worthy of you—I…"

His gray eyes widened. "Not worthy?"

She shook her head. "No—not now. I am so very sorry, but that counts for nothing. I cannot… I must find some way to make up for what I have done. I do not know how I shall do it or how long it will take, but I must find a way. I was married to him for eight years, and although I hated him and was never happy—although I was miserable every minute—absolutely trapped—I still cannot… One cannot wave a wand and make eight years and all my crimes vanish. I must—I shall try to find a way, but…"

Her back was to me, but her eyes were obviously fixed on him, and they both seemed to have forgotten me. "I can wait for you," he said.

"Could you? I cannot tell you how long it will be—it may be years—but…"

"I shall wait."

"Thank you." Again she pressed her face against his chest.

He closed his eyes, his gaunt face relaxing, his arms tightening as his big hands drew her closer.

"If you will wait," she said, "then I shall find a way—somehow I shall find a way to live again and to make up for all the grief I have caused. But it may… It seems so unfair to you. Surely… surely you could do better than…?"

"No," Holmes said with a quick shake of his head. "There is no one else—not now—nor will there ever be. I had thought I would go to my grave without… So long as I know that some day you will send for me, then I can wait—then I can hope."

"I promise you," she whispered fiercely. "I promise."

Again his arms tightened about her, and I turned away, not wanting to intrude at such a moment, sorrow washing over me. The room was absolutely quiet, no one stirring for a long while.

"Go now," Violet said at last.

Holmes held her hand. "Goodbye, Violet." He hesitated, then raised her hand and gently kissed her knuckles.

Violet let her breath out in a tremulous sigh. He turned away, but she seized his arm, then rose up on her toes, touched his cheek with her fingertips and kissed him on the lips. "*Au revoir,*" she said.

Holmes opened his mouth, and then closed it. He turned and walked through the doorway. I followed him slowly. Violet caught my arm and kissed me on the cheek.

"Thank you, Michelle—for everything. And… try to understand." Despite her tears, I saw a strange wild joy in her dark eyes.

Sherlock was at the front door putting on his greatcoat and gloves. His eyes softened when he saw me. "Do not pity me, Michelle. I have more than I ever hoped for."

"You are easily pleased."

He laughed. He pulled on his gloves and held his top hat in his right hand. He hesitated a moment, his eyes fixed on mine. "It is Violet I love, but then, every man cannot be so fortunate as Henry." He immediately turned and stared out into the sunlight. "There is the promise of an interesting case in Geneva. Nothing so spectacular as that of the web weaver, but a bank vault mysteriously—and impossibly—empty. Give Henry my regards and tell him I shall see him as soon as he returns to London." He stepped into the icy air and closed the door behind him.

I felt curiously numb, my emotions aswirl, but I badly wanted to see Henry and get some air. I was pulling on my heavy boots when Gertrude appeared, a frown on her face.

"Is everything all right, ma'am?"

"I do not know, Gertrude. I hope so. I am going out for a while."

She helped me into my fur coat. I put on mittens, a hat, and dark glasses, and stepped out into the bracing air. To the left, the snowy road curved sharply into the trees and led to the train station, half a mile away. Holmes would have gone that way, but he was a brisk walker, and there was no sign of him.

To the right, toward the village, children were squealing and hurling snowballs, darting in and out of the firs. They reminded me of children in London, the same high voices, but with the guttural consonants of German. The boughs were heavy with the snow that had fallen two days ago. The light was dazzling on the snow, blinding, and the sky overhead was still absolutely brilliant blue.

I started for the village and had walked for about twenty minutes when I saw Henry coming from the opposite direction. I ran to him. His face was red from the cold, a thin layer of ice covering his mustache.

"What is it?" he asked. "What is wrong?"

"Sherlock has come—and gone. He and Violet told each other what dreadful, hopeless, unloving, dried-up people they were."

"Oh, no—I can imagine what they might have said."

"I lost my temper and gave them a talking to."

"I'll wager you did." I slipped my hand about his arm and told him all that had happened.

When I finished he was silent for a while. "After all that has occurred, do you think they could simply…? No, Violet was right, but I think she will someday go to him. It is as you said: They do love one another. And she is the only woman who could ever happily raise pet spiders with him."

"Do not joke about it!"

"I am sorry, Michelle. You are so generous with your love that you simply cannot understand." He stopped, then set his hand on my shoulder. "Diseases of the heart are difficult to treat—I am not joking now. You have done as much as anyone could, Dr. Doudet Vernier. Time must do the rest. You must be patient."

"You know I am not a patient person."

He kissed me on the lips. His mustache was icy and prickly, but his breath was warm. "I know you are not, but now it is up to them."

We held hands through our thick mittens. Ahead of us was the chalet where we were staying, smoke pouring from its narrow chimney. Blue shadow covered the snowy mountains on one side, while the crags on the other were bathed in a golden light, their tops radiant against the blue-black sky.

"It gets dark so early," I murmured, "but it is lovely here."

The wind murmured softly in the boughs of the firs, and we were nearly to the door when I realized there was another sound. I plunged forward, pulling Henry along.

"What is it?"

I stopped before the porch. "*Hush.*"

"But…"

He stopped as he heard it, too, and then the corners of his mouth vanished under his frozen mustache. Something caught in my throat, and a joyful shiver seemed to pass through my entire body, all the way to my toes. A laugh slipped from my lips and flew away as white vapor.

"Oh Violet," I murmured.

The music of Bach, a partita for unaccompanied violin, could be heard faintly, its strange combination of passion, beauty, and intellect echoing dimly across that vast, glacial landscape.

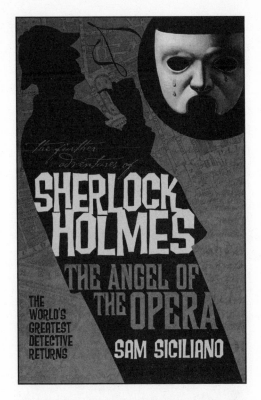

THE FURTHER ADVENTURES
OF SHERLOCK HOLMES

THE ANGEL OF THE OPERA

Sam Siciliano

Paris 1890. Sherlock Holmes is summoned across the English Channel to
the famous Opera House. Once there, he is challenged to discover the true
motivations and secrets of the notorious phantom, who rules its depths with
passion and defiance.

ISBN: 9781848568617

AVAILABLE NOW!

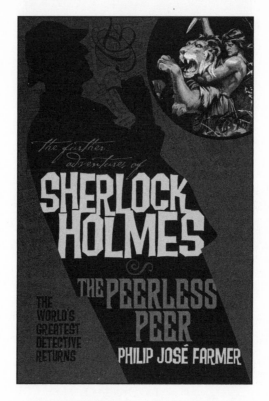

THE FURTHER ADVENTURES
OF SHERLOCK HOLMES
THE PEERLESS PEER

Philip José Farmer

During the Second World War, Mycroft Holmes dispatches his brother, Sherlock, and Dr. Watson to recover a stolen formula. During their perilous journey, they are captured by a German zeppelin. Subsequently forced to abandon ship, the pair parachute into the dark African jungle where they encounter the lord of the jungle himself…

ISBN: 9780857681201

AVAILABLE NOW!

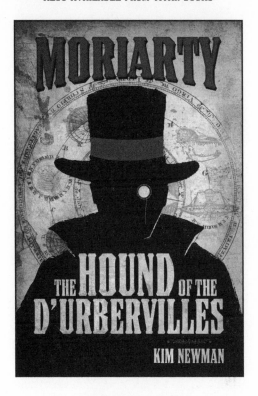

THE FURTHER ADVENTURES
OF SHERLOCK HOLMES

THE BREATH OF GOD

Guy Adams

A body is found crushed to death in the London snow. There are no footprints
anywhere near. It is almost as if the man was killed by the air itself. While pursuing
the case, Holmes and Watson travel to Scotland to meet with the one person they
have been told can help: Aleister Crowley.

ISBN: 9780857682826

AVAILABLE NOW!